C. M. Ward was born and raised in Hanworth, five miles from Heathrow where he began work. Two years later he joined the Royal Navy for almost eight years. He visited various places between Hong Kong, North Borneo, Australia in East to Londonderry in West... he is fairly well-travelled.

After leaving the Royal Navy he moved to Norwich in 1970 where he began writing *Whyte Island*. He has a daughter and loves reading.

Whyte Island

(Part Three)

To Julie Clare Russell, the only young woman to want me mostly for myself rather than for what I possessed.

Acknowledgments

To my wife Margaret for her support, our daughter Helen for teaching me to use a laptop, and the staff at Austin Macauley.

C M Ward

Whyte Island

(Part Three)

AUSTIN MACAULEY
PUBLISHERS LTD.

A CIP catalogue record for this title is available from the British Library.

ISBN 9781849633345

www.austinmacauley.com

First Published (2013)
Austin Macauley Publishers Ltd.
25 Canada Square
Canary Wharf
London
E14 5LB

Printed & Bound in Great Britain

PART 3

Andrew watched her wistfully as she walked down the long quay accompanied by her fellow slave girls; she frequently turned and waved to him, as did her friends, until they and their fellow villa staff members had disappeared from view. Feeling once again at a loss he began to wonder what he was going to do next; without his lover life seemed to lack interest. Then he heard someone behind him say, 'The captain would like to see you on the bridge.'

Wondering exactly what they'd want him for, he followed the man up the adjacent ladder to where a grim-faced officer awaited him. 'What's the meaning of smooching with a girl on my vessel, young man?' he demanded angrily. He was about to reply when the captain's face broke into a grin; he offered his hand. 'I'm only jealous,' he laughed, 'I'm more than half in love with her myself. As a mainlander you ought to be shot for pinching one of our most beautiful girls.' Puzzled, Andrew asked how he knew he was an alien. The fact that he was busily manoeuvring the little ship away from the quayside at the time bothered the captain not at all. 'Apart from its not being done,' he declared, spinning the steering wheel over, 'island males don't show as much affection for their women in public.'

Having straightened the course of the vessel, the captain counteracted the rudders. 'It's the same old story,' he continued, 'if you're unused to something really nice then you appreciate it all the more when you get it; but if it's always available then you tend to get blasé about it. Most females can't get enough attention.' He rang down on the telegraphs. 'That's probably one of the reasons why your little redhead adores you so much. If you wanted to you could doubtless populate much of the island on your own.'

As the ferry gathered way Andrew replied, 'I wouldn't want to, Julie's all I need.'

The captain chuckled. 'That's probably just as well, really, because if you broke too many hearts then one of them might very well break your body.'

'My lover was telling me that, unarmed, she could kill me in a couple of seconds flat; is that correct?'

His companion was deadly serious when he replied, 'Mendacity isn't usually a failing with Whyte Island women; but they're like coral snakes, most of them, beautiful but not to be underestimated and played about with. In a tight corner I think I'd rather have one average island girl by my side than two island males. Many are just as handy with firearms, too.' Before he could react the captain grasped one of Andrew's hands and examined his wrist. 'I see she's been showing you the ropes,' he commented.

Eager to change the subject, the younger man blurted out, 'We received a zigzag invitation this morning and my girlfriend just mentioned it as being some sort of audience participation, but she seemed to make a lot of fuss about it; so what does it involve?'

'If you don't know then I'm not going to tell you,' the officer laughed, 'but like your first time in bed with an experienced island woman, it's an unforgettable experience. But what ship are you off?'

His passenger told him, adding, 'How did you know I was of your tribe?'

'I noticed you walking about, and the easy way you took the companionway,' then he continued, 'You want to get your Julie to take you to see one of our sea battles which take place on this lake; damn great models, authentic miniatures in every way, with sinkings, smoke and gun flashes. No genuine shells, of course, but just as realistic, and naturally no one gets hurt.'

Andrew was somewhat shocked by this information and the enthusiastic way in which it was delivered. 'I'd have thought that in a perfect society you'd want to play down this bestial side of human nature.'

The captain shook his head slowly in sorrow and dismay. 'No, young man, you don't totally suppress mankind's evilness; it's just like trying to preserve a kid's balloon by sticking a pin in it, instead you channel away the air through its opening. The same principle applies to Whyte Line steam ships, of course, with their safety valves and that makes them as harmless as the game you and your beautiful redhead played today, or,' he added, 'zigzagging.'

Andrew was extremely grateful to the elderly captain, for he'd not only helped to while away an hour or so but he'd also endorsed most of what Julie had recently told him, given him some good advice and been responsible for providing him with a mug of tea more than laced, he suspected, with a good measure of rum.

Upon his lover's recommendation he sought out the town hall as soon as he landed, and came away with plenty of leaflets and memories of attention and kindness from the woman who'd supplied them. Noting the nearest post box, he let himself into the flat and was soon composing a letter to Helen, a task which took him far longer than he'd anticipated due to its delicate nature.

Afterwards, for some reason or other, he entered the bedroom where he noticed the forgotten cup of coffee; an inspiration made him take a sip and to his amusement he found it to be a perfect drink, albeit stone cold. It was a labour of love for him to finish off the contents completely, after which he began to consider other labours of love he could concern himself with. Recalling a chance remark of his sweetheart's as he lay tied to the bed he set about taking on the role of housewife, beginning by doing every piece of washing he could discover by hand, for there wasn't enough to make using the washing machine worthwhile.

A woman in one of the downstairs shops directed him to the backyard, and soon the assorted garments were being aired in the sun and the still moderate breeze. His next task wasn't quite so straightforward, being the tidying up of the flat; the difficulty lying in the fact that everything was already neat and spotless. Nevertheless, he cleaned, dusted, polished and vacuumed, after which he prepared some potatoes and other vegetables, and then brought in the washing and ironed it. These were all chores which, as a sailor, he was well used to undertaking and so, unlike his mother, he didn't consider them as being predominantly feminine tasks. Afterwards he couldn't quite decide between books and CDs or a nice walk, but eventually, in view of the pleasant weather, he chose the latter and went for a stroll up to the nearest headland, posting Helen's letter on the way and calling in at a convenient restaurant for a snack during his return.

Julie, when he'd escorted her back to their home, was

delighted at his industry. 'Just for that,' she declared, giving him a special hug and kiss, 'after supper we'll play a nice game.'

Envisaging one as complicated and lengthy as the one they'd played earlier, Andrew protested, 'Oh no, sweetheart, it's late; let's just go to bed.' But she insisted, explaining it wouldn't take long.

After their late meal, which she insisted on cooking, while he washed and wiped up afterward, she went off and found a notebook, biro and a dice. 'Now,' she commanded, 'put the figures one to six down the left side of the page, and then the initial letter of each of the flat's rooms, including the passage.'

'What about number six?' he asked when he'd finished.

'Oh,' she shrugged dismissively, 'just put the bed.' She produced the dice and, holding it in front of him, said, 'Here's a worthwhile game for this little fellow; it'll be a much simplified form of a game much practised by island lovers, it adds variety to the sex act.' She rolled the dice on the kitchen table. 'Number three; that's the lounge. Alright, darling, now your turn, but this time its evens for lying down and odds for standing up.' He threw, and she clapped her hands in excitement. 'Number three again. Right, I'll throw this time. Odds for clothed, evens for naked.......Oh dear, six. Now, you try; what are you going to call?'

Understanding what she was asking, Andrew answered, 'I'll have the opposite.'

'Four, and so that means you'll need to wear protection, we must look after the carpets after all.'

'One last throw, and that's for who's to be the active partner, what do you want?'

He chose evens. 'It's your lucky night, sweetheart!' she cried in delight. 'Come on let's get on with it.'

Sometime later, he leant against the lounge wall, with a naked Julie pressing against him. He couldn't know what she was thinking, but he was savouring the immensely erotic pleasure she'd recently given him. She'd started by selecting a suitable c.d. but kept the main light on; she then stood him against the wall and, after backing away into the centre of the room she began dancing and slowly removing her clothing in as sensual a way as she could manage. Any man who habitually patronised a strip joint would not doubt have given her top marks for her inspired coquettish performance, and gradually she came closer to her lover until she'd completely undressed herself. When she finally reached him she pressed a forefinger against his lips as a sign that he ought to remain silent and then proceeded to seduce him further by oral kissing and touching his face with the tip of her tongue, gently biting his ear lobes and whispering in, and licking out, his ears.

Meanwhile she ran her fingers through his hair and down the sides of his face, and then guided his hands to cup her breasts prior to unzipping him; without stopping she then directed him into her and rotated her hips slowly until they'd both been satisfied.

'How did I do? Did you like it?' she asked while they shared the shower, 'You're very quiet, what did I do wrong?'

'Wrong?' he questioned, 'You did everything right! I'm just trying to recover from your astonishing seduction. I don't know whether you were taught, or it comes natural to you but,' he shook his head in bewilderment, 'I don't know how your previous fellows could ever have let you go!'

She gave him a light slap on his cheek for his indiscretion followed by a passionate kiss for his praise.

As they lay in bed afterwards, half asleep, Andrew murmured, 'What sort of contraceptive are we using, my love?'

The girl stretched luxuriously in his arms and muttered, 'Trust a man to worry about that when it's too late, and don't you mean: what am I using? Anyway, it's a type of I.U.D. and its miles ahead of anything else.' He felt her tongue slide over his cheek. 'Now, go to sleep.'

Julie awoke him early next morning. 'Come on,' she urged, 'don't hang about; we've got lot's to do before I go to work.'

After breakfast she made several telephone calls, and then they sorted through a pile of brochures. His lover was untiring in her efforts to find amusements to occupy him while she was away; and soon she'd come up with an agenda guaranteed to keep him content. 'Put your coat on now,' she said eventually, 'we're going to sort out your evenings.' They were just about to leave the flat when the phone rang; Julie left him by the door and went off to answer it; when she reappeared she rushed at him with a force which almost knocked him over. 'I've managed it, I've managed it,' she cried excitedly, throwing her arms about his neck, 'No red college tours until you've become an islander.'

Andrew, bewildered at her joy, asked, 'So what does that mean?'

'The authorities still won't trust you,' she laughed excitedly, 'therefore, you'll have to tour the colleges with this ugly, decrepit woman to ensure you don't seduce naïve, innocent island girls.'

'Who will she be?' he enquired, still wondering what all the fluster was about.

Repeatedly jumping up against him, she squealed, 'Julie Lucas!' And she pulled his head down against her own and kissed him passionately.

'That's wonderful, my love,' he finally managed to say, sincerely meaning it, 'But will you be able to work and show me round the colleges at the same time?'

Still in his arms Julie frowned and stared up at him. 'You don't understand, do you?' she asked more soberly. 'It all means you're closer to becoming a citizen; the authorities are already planning your future. I'm being given leave of absence from my job to be able to escort you, and all you need to do now is withstand zigzagging and satisfy the powers that be you'd make a good Whyte Islander. Now, show me how pleased you are by kissing me again.'

Upon leaving the flat she took him round the corner, past the public house with the fishing décor, to a building similar to theirs. 'Here's the squalling brat,' she informed the blonde woman, some five years older than Andrew, who opened the door of the first floor flat.

'Come in both of you,' she invited after proper introductions had been made. During the course of their subsequent conversation over cups of tea he gathered that Susan and her husband Trevor, then at work, were more than willing to take him into their care whilst his lover was over in the villa. 'I'll tell you one thing in front of Julie,' she warned, 'even though she can take care of herself physically, don't you dare hurt her mentally because it's obvious she's mad about you, so don't go making passes at me, or at any other woman while I'm around otherwise I'll personally strangle you. You've got an angel there.'

Nodding sagely he replied, 'Don't worry, I'm equally mad about her. She may be an angel, though, but really she's got a mind like a sewer.'

Instantly Susan's face changed; with an expression of anger she immediately stood up. 'I won't have people with filthy minds in my home!' she shouted, pointing toward the door, 'get out both of you.'

Julie looked bewildered and dismayed at her dramatic transformation, and Andrew began to stand up uncertainly. But then, simultaneously, both women burst into howls of laughter; they staggered into each other's arms wracked with mirth, and every time their hilarity threatened to diminish they glanced at him and burst into laughter again. Eventually Susan managed to say, 'You mainlanders are priceless, Andrew. Go on, shock me,' she challenged, laughing once more, 'perhaps you could teach Trevor and me a few tricks.'

At last, when both of them could laugh no more, they sat down again, Julie putting her arms about her sweetheart in a maternal fashion. 'Don't forget,' declared their hostess, 'if you aren't here by seven thirty tonight, Andy, we'll come looking for you.'

Henceforth, Andrew's entertainment was assured for each day was divided up neatly for him. During the morning and some of the afternoon he had his lover's company then, when she'd gone to work, he tidied up the flat and undertook any other household chores which required attention, and afterwards he went off to a pastime of his own choosing where, invariably he met and mixed with people who were happy to make his acquaintance. A particular favourite of his became self defence, an activity which Julie was so anxious to encourage that she not only bought him a new martial arts outfit, but she personally introduced him to the local blue school, and began to practise there with him and the pupils; on a few occasions she even left her lover there and made her own way to work.

Although Andrew, through his sessions onboard Whyte Line vessels, was far from being a novice at self defence Julie and the male instructor soon taught him he still had much to learn. It was at these lessons that love for his sweetheart probably reached its zenith; the instructor was a handsome man and whenever he and Julie had a bout, generally in order to demonstrate defence against a molester to the children, latent jealousy and self doubt were never far away in his mind as he looked on.

Whether or not his lover suspected his feelings he never discovered, but after each contest she always immediately returned to him with a fond smile, a whispered term of endearment and a brief, but warm, embrace as though she was telling him he was the only man in her life. Ironically, when they had bouts with each other they were utterly useless because neither wanted to throw the other down or strike out; and so they were compelled to engage in contests where physical contact was unnecessary. Latterly, his lover, taking on the dual role of instructor/sparring partner, confined her fights to schoolgirls.

As Andrew quickly discovered, his evenings with the Russell family, Susan, Trevor and their four year old son Neil were always entertaining. He never knew whether the couple ever resented his presence, but if they did they must have been masochists for on one occasion, thinking to allow them a night to themselves, he failed to show up; but Susan, as she'd threatened, soon came round to find out what had kept him. Yet when they were aware Julie had nights off they took it for granted they wouldn't be seeing him. Neither they, or his love, would explain just what special relationship or friendship united them, though little Neil always referred to Andrew's sweetheart by her first name, but he only knew the amiable couple seemed concerned only with keeping him amused, an objective which they carried out very well.

A pattern soon developed in their relationship for they would spend one night at home and the next on the town, and the fact they had a young son didn't interfere in the least with their plans, for they simply left him in the care of one of the many willing and able babysitters in the area. Andrew soon experienced almost every haunt in Laketown, the bars, restaurants and cafés, the clubs, theatre and church cum concert hall; and always his companions and mentors were there to keep him entertained. Susan was especially useful in helping him to budget his allowance, for he required practical knowledge of the government's policy of permitting its citizens enough money to enjoy life, though not enough to make it too commonplace and thereby liable to be a corrupting influence.

The nights which they spent in their flat were equally enjoyable; one being that his new friends possessed a piano, of which they were both masters and they had fine voices and a large repertoire of songs and melodies. On several occasions they invited other couples in and had musical evenings or games nights; and once or twice, Andrew left one of their parties to collect Julie, and returned with her. A television orientated society would've had little inkling of the pleasure and amusement which he was able to derive from being in the home of his lover's enjoyable friends.

In such a manner did the days pass until the Saturday of what Andrew had come to think of as his initiation ceremony arrived; Julie, in attempting to prepare him for his ordeal, did her best to lessen its possible impact upon him. 'Zigzagging is just about bearable,' she explained, 'if you remember one or two things. When we arrive don't eat or drink too much, keep your bladder and bowels as empty as possible, and whatever happens don't argue or fight against it otherwise they'll assume you want special treatment. Just behave as I do and you won't go far wrong.' She kissed him gently and then studied his face sympathetically. 'Just remember, my darling, that other men and women, including yours truly will also be undergoing the same ordeal. It might help you to bear in mind that it happened to me not long before we first laid eyes on each other, so I should've been exempt for another four or five years; but I'm doing it again to be with you and because I love you.'

Shortly before they showered and changed preparatory to their engagement his lover took him to bed, telling him ominously, 'This could be our last time; you might not want to know me or the island after experiencing zigzagging.'

Gallantly he whispered in reply, 'Unless it's anything like that fly torture stunt you played on me when I was freshly in your bed, I doubt it very much!'

Although Andrew believed implicitly in what his sweetheart had told him, he found it all difficult to credit at first for everything started off so agreeably. Carrying a suitcase containing Julie's evening dress and his suit, both hired, they set off for the station; their destination was only a few stops down the line and much to his amazement and pleasure he found a large expensive limousine awaiting them as they emerged from the station. Another couple was also obviously en route for the card party, for they, too, had luggage and this the driver promptly stowed in the boot along with Andrew's case They soon got into conversation with their fellow passengers during the ride, but Julie made it clear to them from the first that her companion, being a mainlander, was unaware of what was about to occur. He, on his part, studied the couple carefully; the man was comparatively calm, but his wife chatted nervously and constantly fingered her wedding ring.

A short drive down a country lane and along a leafy driveway brought them to their destination, a small, yet ornate regency-style red brick manor house set on a grassy knoll, and it wasn't far off dusk when they finally entered the main door. Immediately Julie and her lover were escorted upstairs by a trim young blonde maid and shown into a bedroom. 'Are we going to sleep here then?' Andrew asked when they were alone.

His sweetheart smiled and shrugged, 'Who knows? One thing you can be sure of with zigzagging, and that is you can't be certain about anything. We could end up anywhere, but as far as I know this room has just been allocated to us for changing in.'

She'd absolutely refused to allow him to see the dress she'd hired for the occasion; but now, when she'd changed, she looked entrancing: it was a glossy green creation with a square neckline, long sleeves, and almost ankle length. She'd pinned up her hair once more and tied a silver threaded green ribbon, matching her dress, around it and allowing the ends to fall down behind. The only thing which jarred with Andrew was that she wasn't displaying the emerald necklace and earrings he'd given her, instead she wore a set of diamond earrings and matching necklace. 'You're my darling slave girl turned into a princess,' he declared admiringly as she stood before him.

'And you,' she replied, 'Are my handsome.......lover.' She arranged his bow tie and brushed his hair to her satisfaction, and when she'd finished she pressed up against him. 'Hold me tighter and kiss me longer than you've ever done before, please, darling,' she begged. When he eventually released her she pleaded, 'Please, please, please come through this ordeal for me, sweetheart, I think it would kill me to lose you!'

Andrew held her tightly again, and whispered, 'I know it would kill me to lose you!'

He didn't realise how distraught she was until he noticed the tears flowing down her cheeks; pulling out his neatly folded handkerchief he dabbed at her eyes as she cried out, 'Don't say that, Andy; if I died tomorrow I'd want you to go on living. Death might be oblivion, and then the only part of me left alive would be in your memory; but if I die promise me you'll go to Helen, you like her and she loves you; but always remember me!'

Her lover, unable to comprehend this near hysteria, found his attempts to stem her tears utterly inadequate until he said, 'Julie, you're too upset to go through with this, so let's go home.'

Immediately, she pushed his hand away and took the handkerchief from him. 'No!' she asserted, 'tonight is crucial; they won't offer you citizenship otherwise.' Moving back to the dressing table she wiped off her makeup and reapplied a fresh amount; when she'd finished she stood up, gave him a brave smile and announced with determination, 'I'll be alright now. Let's go down; and remember to watch everything I do.' She gave his hand a squeeze. 'I love you!'

A man who, as it turned out, was their host awaited them at the foot of the staircase; he was an agreeable enough person of little more than Andrew's age, and before he led them into the drawing room he presented his male guest with a snakeskin wallet, then he said to him, 'You're a mainlander, aren't you?' Receiving a nod in reply he continued, 'In that case, what is about to happen to you might technically be regarded as an assault.' Putting his hand in his pocket he brought forth a piece of printed paper and a pen. 'Therefore we must have your assurance you won't complain to your government about any of your treatment.'

Andrew took the paper, scanned the writing and then glanced at his lover. 'Will I be treated any differently from the other participants?' he enquired of the man, who subsequently shook his head. 'Well, then,' he said, signing his name, 'I'll put my trust in my sweetheart; if she can take it, then so will I.'

Suddenly smiling, the young man gestured with his arm in an inviting fashion. 'Shall we proceed then?'

The other guests, comprising four couples, were already seated at a large rectangular dining table laid out with silverware and various glasses, and as they entered Andrew vaguely noted that the men all sat with their backs almost against an interior wall whilst their partners had a space of some ten feet between the backs of their chairs and the generously windowed exterior wall. The room, which was similarly rectangular, was decorated in subtle pastel shades and contained an impressive number of portraits of former owners and their families, the men invariably wearing a grim countenance, their consorts displaying cheerful faces and an inordinate expanse of flesh above their bosoms. There were also three great chandeliers, the presence of which made the pair of lit candlesticks on the table entirely unnecessary. Rich red velvety curtains screened each of the five windows and a deep pile carpet of similar hue, for which the young man was soon to be extremely grateful, covered the entire floor; the various items of furniture, including a venerable grandfather clock were all apparently constructed from ebony.

'I'm sure I have no need to introduce our two old friends, Julie and Andrew,' their host exclaimed as the approached the table. Immediately a young woman seated at the far head end, and concealed until then by the glare of the candles, arose and came toward them. 'Of course,' he continued, 'you remember Melanie. We're hoping to be married quite soon.' Andrew was certain that when the two girls shook hands he saw a look of recognition pass across the said Melanie's face. She was a petite attractive thing with jet black hair and innocent brown eyes, but when she took his hand he felt her give it a distinct squeeze.

The young man, who was evidently named Mark, then gallantly handed Julie into the centre chair while her lover made his way round to the vacant seat opposite. As soon as they were seated, Mark addressed them all. 'As usual, I thought you'd like a little refreshment before we repair to the lounge.' He chuckled. 'And then we can look forward to a pleasant and profitable evening, for some of us at least.' His words were greeted with murmurs of approval from his guests.

When the food and wine had been brought in by the neat little maid Andrew, recalling Julie's advice, watched his lover closely and whenever she took a sip of wine or nibbled at a sandwich or piece of cake he followed suit after an appreciable interval. To his slight amusement none of the guests appeared to have much appetite, and the conversation seemed forced and desultory; there was also a great deal of coming and going around the table. In order to pass the time away he began to study his fellow diners, none of whom gave him the least inkling of what might be about to happen. It was difficult for him to observe the men properly, but he judged the man to his left to be, at roughly forty, the eldest person present. However, he was able to examine the bevy of beauties opposite to his heart's content, much to his lover's obvious amusement.

At the end furthest from the door, and seated at a right angle to Melanie, was another beautiful redhead although, unlike his sweetheart's, her more chestnut hair was shorter and fell free; next to her sat the woman who'd shared the limousine with them, she had an attractive face but with hair which might have been described as, unkindly, mouse-coloured. On Julie's right was a raven haired woman of some thirty five with flashing eyes as dark as her locks. But although he hated to think it, the most striking looking female present was an ash blonde seated near Mark. She had straight hair which curled in slightly where it ended at shoulder level; her eyes were made up with brown mascara and highlighted with silver eye-shadow, her lips enhanced with ruby coloured lipstick and her make up had been beautifully emphasised by the red satin dress, pearl necklace and matching earrings she wore; she was an extremely attractive and sophisticated woman. She must have sensed Andrew's prolonged appraisal for she glanced straight at him and gave him a brilliant smile; abashed, he turned his head away and in so doing caught Julie's eye, she also smiled but then motioned meaningfully toward the door with her eyes.

Taking the hint, he stood up and left for the toilet, his sweetheart following his example upon his return; in the event they were only just in time for Julie had scarcely seated herself when the sound of a distant telephone was heard coming from the direction of the hallway. Mark, after apologising, arose and left the room only to reappear a few minutes later; he bent down to whisper in the ash blonde's ear and she, in her turn, got to her feet and, preceded by her host, departed the room. Few of the guests seemed to think anything of the episode until, during a lull in the conversation, the girl's partner was heard to exclaim in surprised outrage, 'I say!'

Everyone glanced round, and a gasp came from a number of throats. The blonde had returned, but in a most unconventional manner, for her ruby lips were now concealed by a large piece of tape and her hands were somewhere behind her back; standing directly behind her was Mark holding a revolver beneath her chin. 'I'm afraid I've had to make a small alteration in the usual procedure,' he told his guests in a pleasant tone; then his voice changed, 'Now, unless you want Anne's brains scattered about the room you'd all be advised to do as I say. Right ladies,' he commanded, 'push your chairs back from the table, about one foot. Alright Melanie, go and get everything.'

He waited until his accomplice had gone and then addressed the men, 'Slowly, and in single file, gentlemen, please be so good as to pass behind Melanie's chair and then lie prone with your feet against your consort's seats.' There was some token resistance to this order, but upon Mark's threat of, 'I mean it,' they all reluctantly obeyed; Andrew, for one, had no wish to receive, in Julie's own words, special treatment. As soon as he lay down he heard Mark say, 'Go on Melanie, dearest, you know what to do, we've rehearsed it often enough.' Raising his voice he warned, 'And I don't want to see any physical or oral protest from anyone.'

Andrew turned his head in the direction of the door to watch Melanie; she knelt by the first man, pulled his hands behind him and tied his wrists together with a stocking taken from a pile alongside her, then she moved down to his feet and bound them also, with a third stocking she attached his feet to a rear leg of Anne's chair, though she allowed some slack. Quickly and efficiently she went to each man in turn carrying out the same task, though when she came to the men on either side of him she made them press the backs of their hands together and then lashed their wrists in place; when she reached Andrew, he'd already crossed his hands behind him upon some advice Julie had previously given him, and that was how she tied him.

He then heard Mark say, 'When each of you gentlemen has been attended to kindly turn over onto your backs.' As soon as she'd finished securing the last man, and he'd rolled over, she cut a length of tape with some scissors and pressed it over his mouth, after which she made her way back down repeating the operation until she'd attended to Anne's partner. Mark was visibly more relaxed when his supposed lover had finished her task, and he released his hold upon his captive and allowed her to return to her seat. As she turned to sit down Andrew noticed the palms of the unfortunate girl's hands were pressed together by a tie which bound her wrists tightly; she looked most uncomfortable, and even more so when her former captor bent down, took hold of the loose ends of the tie and fastened them together around the centre upright of her chair.

'Now for the rest of the ladies, darling,' he informed Melanie during his activity, which then consisted of forcing Anne's ankles together and binding them to one of the front legs of her chair. Afterward, he moved over to one of the recently vacated men's chairs, put his hands behind the back of his neck and seemed prepared to take things easy. Andrew, lying in the middle of the line of his fellow captives had a clear view of Melanie's administrations and, obviously taking advantage of the freedom, as she seemed to think, of choice, began to render her victims helpless in a variety of ways.

'You're not going to truss me up,' the red haired girl declared from her chair.

'Perhaps you'd prefer your brains dispersed instead,' an unperturbed Mark suggested, and this had the desired effect upon her, for she submitted quietly while her female captor tied her up in what, to Andrew, was a most barbaric manner. Melanie pulled her arms behind her forcefully, folding them until they were resting on top of the chair's back and then lashed them in place; she, too, had her mouth taped up, and her feet were bound together and positioned between the back pair of chair legs by another stocking. Julie's lover watched in fascination as the black haired girl swiftly dealt with each woman in turn; he was feeling distinctly uncomfortable by now, for he was beginning to find the whole experience extremely erotic and with the expected consequences. Although Melanie's subsequent female captives weren't being treated as badly as the first, she was definitely showing a sadistic nature for Andrew was certain they could've been bound and gagged more comfortably; for when she came to his sweetheart, who'd already crossed her wrists between her body and the chair back, she pulled her arms over the top and lashed her hands back to back and tied them to the centre upright. She then picked up a further stocking and bound her arms together just above, and on the far side of the chair back causing Julie's upper trunk to lean forward. Melanie, leaning down and astride his body, causing her short skirt to ride up, thus allowed Andrew to learn her underwear matched her hair colour, she forced his lover's ankles together and tied them both to a rear chair leg. She then did something which puzzled him at the time, for she then removed one of his slip on shoes, pulled the relevant sock off and stuffed it into yet another stocking. This, after standing up, she forced into Julie's mouth, bound the nylon's end together at her nape, and moved on to the last untied captive.

This woman she gagged with a tape and tied up in a different position from the others before moving on to Anne who, although already immobilised, had a string of stockings knotted together and bound just above her breasts and arms, and tied to the chair back. Mark got up from his seat as soon as he'd judged his accomplice had completed her task; 'I see you've used your initiative and created some quite elegant forms of bondage, but not, I think, this particular one.'

Andrew had a first rate view of what happened next for Melanie was spun around, forced onto her face on the carpet where her supposed former lover crossed her arms up close to the back of her neck and fastened her wrists together with a stocking, another one served to bind her ankles and he then removed a round length of wood from his pocket, turned her over on her side and forced it sideways between her teeth like a horse's bit. Thin rope dangling from each end served to fasten the simple device to the back of her neck and his last move was to pull a length of obviously prepared rope from his pocket and connect it between her wrists and ankles, the latter of which he'd slightly pulled backwards to prevent her standing upright. All this activity was carried out at lightning speed giving his final victim little time to react. Leaving her helpless on her side he stood upright and stared down at her with undoubted pleasure.

'Unfortunately, my darling,' he smiled as she glared back at him, 'despite your commendable work I've found a much nicer and far less expensive companion for my forthcoming overseas flight, so I'm afraid you'll need to play hostess for the remainder of the weekend. You see I've known about your little affair with Roderick for some time. You can lie there amongst the men where you belong and enjoy being trussed up like the little sow you really are!'

He then left the room, and Andrew distinctly heard him call out, 'Sophie?' During his absence everyone began to struggle madly with their bonds, but all movement ceased upon his reappearance; he was doubtless aware of what had been happening, but if so he said nothing. Instead he went from one man to the next removing the wallets which, presumably he'd presented them with, from their inside pockets, and these he threw into a plastic bucket. He didn't seem to be interested in loose change or watches.

However, he was interested in the women's jewellery; going up to the redhead first he removed her earrings and emerald pendant necklace and held the jewel of the latter to his tongue. 'Very good, Ruth,' he declared, evidently well pleased, 'I do hope all the others are just as genuine.' And he continued systematically removing the rest of their ornamentation; he didn't even neglect Melanie's, apparently being amused by her resultant look of malevolent hatred. 'After all, I did buy them for you,' he chuckled.

In spite of what she'd done to Julie and the other women Andrew couldn't help feeling sorry for the girl, because he realised that for as long as she remained bound in that manner she would be unable to find a comfortable position, so brutally had she been dealt with. As he lay there, staring into her face which was only about a yard from his, he wondered how much of this drama had been rehearsed and how much improvised, for her eyes seemed really angry. They were soon to appear even more irate because Mark suddenly exclaimed, 'Oh there you are Sophie, do come in.' With some difficulty Andrew raised his head and saw the little maid, now clad in a smart blue dress, standing in the doorway. 'Come closer,' he beckoned, 'and say goodbye to your former mistress.' Putting his arm about her shoulders he escorted her up to Melanie where they stood gazing down at her. 'Of course, if you'd treated Sophie less unkindly you wouldn't have driven me into her arms, but you see, I just had to comfort her.

But all is forgiven now because she loves your clothes, especially the lingerie, and as you can see they fit her perfectly. She's far more inventive in bed, anyway.' The erstwhile maid smirked down at the helpless girl but said nothing and Mark then kissed his new lover on the mouth and said, 'Go and wait in the car, darling, and I'll be along soon.'

When she'd gone he began counting the money he'd taken from the wallets and subsequently appeared to be delighted with the total. 'Well,' he declared as all his victims looked on in mute impotence, 'you've each done me proud. We've more than enough here to set us up with a fresh life in a new country. Well, I think I owe you all an explanation; under your circumstances,' he smiled broadly, 'I think it's the least I can do. I'm afraid that due to dear Melanie's love of the high life, my ex-wife's and children's maintenance, my gambling and my debts, I've been compelled to borrow heavily. Unfortunately, I received a rather nasty, but abrupt, letter a few weeks ago. I'm sure I needn't go on, you all know how it is. So I hope you'll understand that the longer you stay under wraps, as it were, the more successful will be our disappearance; to this end I've sent my staff away for the week. Perhaps some of you might be missed by, say noon Monday at the earliest. Please accept my humblest apologies for your enforced sojourn; I'll send you all postcards.'

All heads turned to watch him leave the room, and he gave a little wave before closing the door behind him. To Andrew's surprise, he'd left the light on; with a bit of luck, he thought, entirely forgetting their predicament was only make-believe, this fact together with the drawn curtains might serve to attract attention to their plight at daybreak. As soon as the party of captives found themselves alone everyone began to struggle again; all, that is, except Melanie, as she began to make as much noise as her bit would allow; for a moment all those who could stared at her as, wild eyed, she shook her head repeatedly, but hardly surprisingly they quickly went back to their contortions.

Andrew, after watching his sweetheart's feeble attempts and realising she was tied too securely and intricately to accomplish anything worthwhile, wriggled the few inches to her feet and contrived to tap her with his own. Craning her head round she gazed down at him and, slowly and deliberately, she closed her left eyelid in a long wink; he winked back, full of sympathy and love as he recalled she was enduring all this for his sake; with great effort she then shifted her gaze meaningfully in the direction of Melanie and then turned to face forward once more. He scarcely dared to wonder at the torments which she was probably experiencing, doubtless not improved by the taste of his sock in her mouth; this latter thought encouraged him to ponder on the reason why Melanie had carried out such a pointless gesture. He turned his head to face the girl beside him, she'd long since abandoned trying to communicate with her fellow captives and merely lay with her eyes closed, and with saliva beginning to run down from the side of her mouth.

One by one each of the room's occupants ceased struggling as they came to terms with the futility of their efforts; and as he watched them Andrew gradually understood with growing despair that neither he nor they were going to get out of this predicament without the aid of an outside agency. Surely, he wondered, they weren't expected to remain trussed up until half way through Monday? If only he'd asked Julie how long zigzagging usually lasted for, at least then he'd be able to have some sort of goal to aim at. One feature of their incarceration began to puzzle him; although an attempt to release his lover was out of the question on his part, he was still close enough to Melanie and the men on either side to make an endeavour at mutual release perfectly feasible. Yet neither of the men, or the girl appeared to consider that simple fact; the removal of the sticky tape which muted the former would surely have been simple enough but, as he was after all a mere novice in the game, he certainly wasn't about to make the first move.

Although he was longing to roll over and so ease the weight of his body upon his forearms, hands and wrists he remained as he was for a little longer to study the women. He'd always loved younger women, before life with all its cares and need for strength made them generally less attractive, and so he hated to see them distressed or in any sort of discomfort; it was well known to him, as Julie had also pointed out, that womankind were able to withstand boredom and suffering better than men, but he still wished he could release them all, beginning with his lover followed by Ruth and Anne. But as he studied them he realised his estimation of their character had been quite correct for now they were each seated in perfect fortitude, patiently awaiting the release which must surely come, whilst their men folk were even now beginning to fidget.

And so the time began to pass painfully slowly until, as Andrew glanced at the grandfather clock close by the door, the loud insistent tocking of which was starting to jar on his nerves, he noticed the door opening. It heralded the return of Mark whom, he saw, had now changed into casual wear; but optimism that their ordeal was at an end quickly evaporated when he announced he'd merely come to check no one had loosened their knots. 'Telling Sophie to wait in the car was a perfect little ruse of mine,' he informed them, 'in fact we've been testing some bedsprings. However, this time's for real and if you couldn't free yourselves within forty minutes then you should last out the weekend.' But he still made a protracted and thorough examination of his captives, making adjustments whenever he deemed necessary. When he came to Melanie he appeared to obtain sadistic pleasure out of teasing her for he pinched her cheeks, told her how uncomfortable she looked and, finally, forcing her over onto her face so her feet stuck up in the air.

When, at last, he'd satisfied himself they wouldn't be able to escape he returned to the door and switched off the chandeliers; with the aid of a candlebra he then went to each of the windows and drew back the curtains; lastly he blew out all the candles. From the doorway he wished them all a cheerful goodnight and with a final flourish he threw something heavy into the room, for it landed on the carpet with a dull thud. 'It was only a starting pistol,' he chuckled, 'as I don't believe in violence.' Shortly after he softly closed the door behind him, the hall light was extinguished followed by the slamming of the front door, and then the sound of a car being started and driving away.

No wonder Melanie had made such a fuss, Andrew thought, she'd been trying to warn them that a successful attempt at release would've gone for nought; but now it was her turn to try to get free, because she began to writhe like a stranded whale in the darkness, annoying him on several occasions as she knocked against him; he couldn't help admiring her tenacity, however, for frequently when he awoke from dozing during that endless night he heard, and felt, her struggling. Apart from Melanie everyone else remained relatively motionless.

Although his eyes soon became used to the dark he was unable to see anything in much detail for it was pitch black both inside and out, but his hearing eventually became acute and so, aside from the rustling of the girl next to him, the annoying clock to the tocking of which had been added the hourly heavy chimes, always too long in coming, and expansion and contraction of old timber, the only other noise was the subsequent sound of steady, relaxed breathing and the occasional snore.

Deep sleep in such a predicament might have been easy for some of his fellow prisoners, but for Andrew it proved to be impossible because as far as he was concerned the word ordeal as a description of his situation was an understatement. For presently his body began to experience all sorts of discomforts, both real and imaginary. He had long since rolled onto his stomach but soon he'd found the weight upon his chest unbearable, so with great effort he turned over onto his left side, but before long his left arm began to object; no matter what position took up some part of him began to ache and only when lying on his back did his head feel properly supported and even then only partially so. Then his hands and feet began to get pins and needles, his arms felt cramped, the back of his head began to itch, he longed to lick his lips and his nose felt blocked up.

Eventually, having tried all four positions innumerable times, he jerked back on his feet violently for he wanted to see if he could rest his head on Julie's lap; the stocking which held him to her chair took the weight but wrenched against the one tying his ankles together. The resulting pain was intense though of short duration, but he ignored it and continued in his attempt to sit upright; however, on his second try he hadn't raised enough force for he twisted and then fell back. His right shoulder took most of the impact but much to his surprise his head came into contact with something relatively soft, round and, finally, warm; he had no need to wonder what the mystery object was, for Melanie had obviously managed, by some miracle, to kneel upright, and it was her left thigh upon which his head now rested.

It would have been simple for her to nudge his head away, but although the upper part of her body was continuously moving she made no attempt to rid herself of him, so he shifted his position slightly and let his head fall into her lap. Evidently she experienced as much comfort and gratification from the contact as he did for she allowed his head to remain, and finally she ceased to struggle for a while; the intimate situation was extremely pleasing to Andrew and he didn't mind in the least the new feeling of discomfort which assailed him. Finally he fell into his first brief sleep, hoping, as he did so that no one would come along and switch on the lights thus revealing his situation to his lover.

He was rudely awoken from his slumber by Melanie's jerking as she tried to change her posture without his encumbrance, for the unfortunate girl must've been suffering agony with her hands. Andrew made a mental note to ask Julie to immobilise him in a similar fashion during one of their games just to see what it felt like. But when the girl had finally rid herself of him, he was enchanted when she used his belly as a head rest, and throughout the remainder of that long night they took it in turns to use each other as a pillow, an experience which the young man was to remember for the rest of his relatively short life. Forgotten was the way she'd treated his sweetheart and the other women, so in need was he of her services, as the psychological effect of her presence far outweighed her physical contact; but she rarely ceased trying to free herself for long.

Once, during a particularly long period of sleeplessness, he kept asking himself what all this nonsense was about. It was so childish and pointless, so unlike the attitude of profound common sense which seemed to be a byword within Whyte Island society; he wracked his brains continuously for an answer, but the problem proved too great for him and eventually the effort drove him into the arms of Morpheus once more. When he awoke he felt Melanie's head resting upon his rump and very close to his bound hands; with a little manoeuvring he managed to reach the knot which kept her bit in place and by dint of protracted effort he finally loosened it enough to enable him to pull it out.

Immediately, with some difficulty, she was able to whisper in his left ear, 'Thank you, but you needn't have bothered as I'm part of the act. Still, I'm very moved.' She paused, then continued, 'Look, it's beginning to get light so I'm going to get well away from you; I don't want you to get into trouble with your Julie. I've had a little accident with my dress, so I'll give you a nice reward.' Again she paused. 'I'm going over to the nearest window; when it gets really light feast your eyes.' Then she added, 'Julie's an old acquaintance of mine. I hope you realise how lucky you are.' To his great pleasure she then inserted her tongue into his ear and slowly, seemingly endlessly, explored its every feature; his lover's previous effort almost faded into insignificance beside her performance, and he loved every second of it. 'Thank you again,' she murmured so quietly she was scarcely audible before commencing her laborious and ungainly journey toward the window.

Andrew, more by curiosity than expectation, kept his eye on the light; he dozed again and when he was fully conscious again once more he noted that every feature in the room was vaguely discernible. He rolled over onto his stomach, the only way in which he could look toward the windows with any degree of comfort. Melanie was in a kneeling position facing away from him, and at first he thought she was asleep as her head was resting on the windowsill, but soon she lifted it and stared directly at him, then she glanced about the room as if checking on the other occupants. Apparently satisfied she began to turn her body round until she was facing toward him; Andrew instantly gasped and mentally blasphemed for the girl's dress, appropriately coloured blue, had slipped off her left shoulder. It was fairly obvious to him what had happened; during one of her gyrations across the carpet she must have caught the single large button which held the halves of her somewhat daring neckline together, her subsequent struggles had then caused her left shoulder strap to work its way down her arm. The absence of a brassiere had thereby served to complete the exposure of her small, perfectly rounded, vivid white breast.

Melanie winked at him, licked her lips and then glanced round the room once more to ensure they were not observed, and slowly she continued to turn until she presented her left side toward him. The nipple, as if to compensate for the diminutive breast, was long, and stood well proud of the surrounding pink disc on a peculiar mound and pointed upward at a distinct angle; the effect was to make the entire breast seem most blatant and provocative.

She'd promised him a feast for his eyes and that was exactly what she gave him, for she was in no hurry to conceal herself; had she been a mainland girl he'd have thought her a teasing trollop, but he was sure she was presenting him with a memory he could recall the next time he entered his lover. Eventually she must have realised she was steering them both into danger for, after winking at him again and blowing a kiss, she slid to the floor and faced the wall, almost certainly to hide her breast and uncovered mouth; she remained that way until he released her just over four hours later.

Gradually everyone stirred with the arrival of broad daylight; and as soon as Andrew thought Julie was awake he touched her feet again; he loved her more than ever now as she wearily turned her head to gaze down at him, and once again she exchanged winks with him. However, he felt intense anger rising within him as the morning wore on and there was still no end to their suffering in sight.

But at last, when the grandfather clock, indicated eleven minutes past ten, the door opened and Mark reappeared; quickly he went from one woman to the next, starting with Ruth, and untied their wrists and ankles. Apart from Julie, their first concern upon being freed was to rub life into their hands and feet and any other part of their bodies which they felt needed stimulation, but Andrew's lover instantly stood up and hobbled over to him; she knelt by his side, removed her gag and whispered, 'Do you still love me?' He nodded vigorously; then she asked anxiously, 'Promise you won't make a scene; because if you do you won't become an island citizen and I certainly won't go and live over there. Promise?' she urged. Reluctantly he nodded again, and only then did she elect to release him. When she'd helped him to his feet they embraced and kissed briefly, but then he remembered Melanie; so he went over, scooping the bit from the carpet as he did so and dropping it between her and the wall in the hope that no one had been watching, then he untied her hands. But before he could free her completely Julie intervened and, seating him on her chair, she put his sock and shoe on him.

'How did you like the flavour of my sock?' Andrew asked in the hope that she'd welcome a little cheerfulness from him. 'I can't think why Melanie gagged you with it though.'

'Because she's a sado-masochist, that's why,' she replied

bitterly, but obviously well pleased he'd come through the experience with his sense of humour still extant, 'and I'm very glad your sock was washed quite recently.'

He nearly said, "She told me she knew you", but managed to say instead, 'I didn't know she knew you.'

'Only too well; but anyway we'd better get to our room as we'll need to change and have a bite to eat. I don't know about you darling, but my mouth is as dry as an indoor sandpit.' So they shuffled out of the room like an elderly couple, with their arms about each other. Climbing the stairs was a nightmare, but eventually they reached their room without mishap.

'What was all that about?' Andrew fumed when he'd closed the door behind them, 'I've never known anything so infantile and pointless. I just don't understand. How could they do that to you, and those other lovely creatures?'

His sweetheart put her arms around his neck and fondly stroked his hair. 'Calm down,' she murmured gently, 'I was hoping you'd have understood what it was all intended to convey; but surely you must realise by now, my darling, that everything on Whyte Island has a purpose? We can't discuss it now because we've got to get changed and have some breakfast.' She kissed him forcefully with her mouth half open. 'I'm ravenous, and I'm sure you must be.' While they showered and changed back into their travelling clothes she told him, 'You might've thought that was an ordeal but we got off lightly on at least two counts, we could've been tied up for a maximum of sixteen hours whereas we did only a little over twelve, and also we could've gone for a ride in the special packing cases they have; as I said before, we might've finished up anywhere.'

Andrew was surprised by this information, and it led him to ask, 'But why does the ordeal need to last so long? Wouldn't a couple of hours suffice? And supposing one of us had managed to free themselves, what would have happened then?'

'I said I'd explain it later,' she reminded him, 'but, briefly, you might think of our island as being a paradise, and maybe it is, but paradises are appreciated more if they have to be paid for. Also, that experience was intended to be authentic; in real life if Mark had wanted us to be out of the way for an entire weekend then that's what'd have happened. Lastly the ordeal was meant to teach us an important lesson: the longer it lasted the more likely it was to form an enduring lesson. As for people releasing themselves,' she shook her head dismissively, 'it's virtually impossible, because most of us are pretty good at tying knots. I've only ever heard of one victim getting their hands free, and she was promptly handcuffed before she could get any further, then she and her companion were given two extra hours as punishment.'

'In that case, why did everybody struggle last night? Melanie scarcely stopped.'

Julie smiled at her lover's alertness. 'We love playacting, don't forget it's a valuable part of our education, and there's nothing like a bit of realism; besides, struggling gives some people a pleasant feeling and also helps pass the time.' She raised a hand in warning when she saw another question coming and refused to answer any more on the subject; instead when they were dressed in their casual clothes and had packed away their evening attire, she sat on the edge of the bed and patted the space next to her. Let's have a look at your wrists and ankles,' she invited, and subsequently she rubbed some salve into his wheals.

'I could've murdered that Melanie for what she did to you, as well as to Ruth,' Andrew observed as he tended to his lover's bruising, 'but in the end it was she who got the worst of it. But we were a great comfort to each other.' And rather unwisely he went on to tell her all that had occurred, omitting the details, though, of her unusual kiss and the private sex display.

'Melanie!' Julie exclaimed scornfully, apparently not at all annoyed by his confession, 'She's sex mad and loves discomfort; had she been born a male she'd have been exiled long ago. I was at the red college with her and she, I, and three other girls were primarily responsible for establishing zigzagging; but she actually planted the seed, and no wonder, because it was right up her street!'

Somewhat bemused by this revelation, he asked, 'Is she a beautician then?'

His lover shook her head, 'No, a nurse; but the two professions have quite a lot in common, which is why they're situated in the same college.'

Mention of nursing suddenly reminded him of Jill. 'Oh dear,' he exclaimed, 'I ought to have contacted the girl I had a date with on that glorious day you and I were first united. I promised her I'd introduce you.'

Julie, as kind and thoughtful as ever, answered, 'Perhaps it can be arranged for later today. Now, there's one last thing before we go down.' She withdrew a small plastic carton from her bag and mixed the white powdered contents with water in the tumbler provided. 'Drink this, sweetheart,' she told him, 'because when our stomachs receive some food after all this time they'll probably ache and moan.' And she warned, 'Don't eat and drink too much, either.'

Before they left the room Andrew pulled her to him passionately. 'I hated that, Julie darling, but I'd go through it again and again for just one kiss from you. I really love you, because you're unsurpassable in every way.'

With tears of love and gratitude in her eyes she murmured, 'And please, never stop loving me.'

Again they were the last to arrive in their, now, erstwhile dormitory; with their ordeal now behind them the guests' relief was obvious: for where there had once been taciturnity, now there was cheerful conversation; where there had been lack of appetite, now there was relish. Melanie had evidently taken on the role of hostess once more, and Sophie was wearing her uniform again and attending at table; as soon as the latecomers had seated themselves she came and asked them what they'd like to eat. Andrew solved that problem by replying, 'I'll have the same as Julie, whatever that is, please, Sophie.' And so he received a plate containing a small portion of scrambled egg on toast, followed by bread and marmalade, and a cup of tea. His sweetheart smiled across at him approvingly as he began this repast.

'I understand this is your first experience of zigzagging, Andrew,' one of the men addressed him, 'so what did you think of it?'

Everyone stopped eating to gaze at him expectantly, but it was Julie who replied on his behalf. 'I'm afraid that at the moment my lover feels it was a puerile and unnecessary exercise. Though I think that after I've explained it in detail he'll understand.'

'Wouldn't you like to make any observation, though, Andrew?' asked Ruth's consort.

'Yes, I would.' After his intimate experience with Melanie,

Andrew had a soft spot for her, even though he wouldn't have swapped Julie for a million of her kind, but he wasn't going to let her off lightly despite that fact. 'Why,' he therefore enquired of her, 'did you need to tie up all these lovely ladies so cruelly, especially my sweetheart, and Ruth?' Much to his embarrassment these words were greeted with spontaneous applause from the female guests, though whether because of his description of them, or due to his concern for them, he had no way of knowing.

Melanie returned him the kind of smile which only the participants in a close secret can give, but her reply was overt enough, 'Ruth virtually asked for it, so you must ask her why. As for the other women: well, Mark and I discussed the details thoroughly beforehand and he threatened that if I treated them badly then he'd ensure I'd find myself in a similar situation; in the event, I decided I wanted to be tied up brutally. Anyway, all women can withstand discomfort more than men, so I evened up the odds a little. But if you're also referring to my reason for employing different methods of restraint, Andrew: well, I was simply conveying a few ideas to those present who are into bondage; besides, I think variety is much more interesting than uniformity.' She shrugged dismissively, and glanced at each guest in turn. 'Any complaints?' she enquired. Everyone shook their heads, including, much to his dismay, his lover.

His question, together with its subsequent answer set off a whole train of debate which began with the mouse-haired lady complaining, quite light-heartedly, of the psychological torment of having an ankle bound to one chair leg and the other tied to its diagonal opposite. Eventually that weird gathering began to break up as the guests commenced taking their leave; but just before Julie and Andrew departed the former took her sweetheart by the hand and led him over to where Ruth and her companion were standing.

Immediately, the girls embraced affectionately and then Julie, still with an arm about the other, asked, 'Do you see the resemblance, darling?' He was close enough to the pair to note Ruth's green eyes, but apart from this fact and the obvious darker shading of her hair, the similarity in their appearance was truly remarkable; and when his lover, to emphasise her question, allowed her hair to fall free the girls might have been mistaken for twins. 'She's my maternal cousin, our mums were twins!'

Andrew, recalling her relationship with Jeremy, observed dryly, 'Obviously the maternal side of your family had very strong genes!'

His three companions all laughed and Ruth said, 'You're so right, neither of us looks anything like our poor old dads. But I'm an only child, though.' Her smile, amplified no doubt by his gallant defence of her, was most welcoming as she held out her hand to him, and as he took it she announced, 'Your fame has spread even to the bucolic fastnesses of Whyte Island.'

Her cousin giggled when she noticed Andrew's puzzled frown, 'The old peasant wench is trying to tell you, in the olde worlde tongue they use in the outback, that she's the daughter of a tiller of the soil. Usually she's to be found in dirty jeans and a shirt stinking of sweat and livestock, and,' she winced as the other girl playfully pulled her hair, 'more often than not she's got straw adhering to her back. Isn't that right, Derek?'

The man she addressed, replied, 'I'm not getting into your endless squabbles, but your diagnosis isn't quite correct because she's only a couple of years older than you, and recently we've started replacing the straw with sheets in our bed.'

Ruth let go of her cousin and gave her partner a gentle push, ignoring them both, she said to Andrew, 'Thank you for caring about my discomfort and I'm so glad to have met a real gentleman before I pass on; if Julie ever tires of you, just give me a call.' She turned to her companion, and remarked, 'This, of course, is my boyfriend, but I'm sure he wouldn't mind making way for you.'

During the following conversation Ruth invited them to the farm at their earliest convenience. 'As Julie well knows, Andrew, you'll be made more than welcome, it's a beautiful part of the island and you can stay for as long as you wish.' She smiled and winked. 'Unfortunately there's only one spare bedroom, so I'm afraid you'll have to double up.'

Andrew thanked her profusely and accepted with pleasure, but then asked, 'Exactly why did you object to being bound, Ruth? Surely you were aware of what they'd do to you?'

She nodded. 'Oh yes, I knew what would happen alright. Things had been going too well for me of late, so I decided I needed taking down a peg or two; I wanted to experience the darker side of life and somehow being martyred before other people made it feel much more emphatic.'

'And did it work?'

'I should say so,' she laughed, 'it was bloody painful. But in the long term? Well, in future I believe I'll enlist Derek's aid if ever I need a boost.'

As soon as Julie and Andrew arrived at the adjacent station they parted from their fellow travellers so as to be alone, but their conversation still dwelt upon zigzagging even though she still refused to outline its true purpose to her sweetheart. But she did explain it was far more organised than it appeared. 'To begin with, there's actually a full time unit which plans, coordinates and carries out the practice, and there's also a book of rules available which even covers the little games we've played at home. For instance, when we were all helpless in that room I'll bet you thought we'd all been abandoned?' Andrew nodded. 'In fact,' she continued, 'we were being constantly monitored by highly sensitive audio equipment.

'On one occasion Carol, Jim's girlfriend, made a deliberate scene, so they tied her up in a similar fashion to the way they did Ruth, and she said she soon began wishing she hadn't caused a fuss, when a man in their party began to choke. Within a few seconds the door burst open and he and his partner were released; but unfortunate Carol, much to her chagrin, still had to continue her torment along with the others. A further safeguard is that the room temperature mustn't fall below a certain level or fluctuate too much; neither must a captive suffer any unwarranted mental or physical abuse whatsoever.'

As Julie finished she kissed him tenderly when she saw no one could see them, while her lover, with mounting horror, began to realise that Melanie and he had been taking a terrible risk; and so he wondered if anything regarding their activities had been picked up and, if so, whether it'd be passed on to their respective partners. Fortunately, his thoughts were mercifully interrupted by the shrill scream of an approaching railway locomotive and presently the source of the sound appeared in sight from beyond a curve and shuddered to a halt at the platform.

Andrew found the train a most welcome diversion for his thoughts, as it consisted entirely of apparently ancient clerestory carriages with an equally old fashioned design of steam engine hauling them. He was later to learn that the complete set had been commissioned for a filming session and was on its way back to Harbourtown; but word had got around and, although unscheduled, everyone seemed to want to have a ride. Despite the fact the train was quite full he was loathe to forego the novel experience of railway travel from the distant past, but they found a seat without too much trouble and although Julie had to sit on his lap, which she chose to do in the fashion of a child with her back to him and his hands cupping her waist, neither minded. Ever mischievous, she almost instantly proudly exhibited her sore wrists and announced to the compartment of complete strangers that they'd both just been zigzagged.

The effect of her information was astonishing for, like a tribe of primitive warriors recently returned from a raiding expedition, their fellow passengers began to relate their personal experiences of the ordeal, and the more uncomfortable the event, ironically, the more the narrator seemed to revel in it. One woman began by explaining how she'd spent ten hours tied to a toilet seat in a travelling railway coach whilst her husband sat on the floor with his back against the wall, and how he couldn't move because they were joined together at the ankles. 'Yes,' he added, 'and people kept trying the door and going away. Then we were shunted into a siding when it got dark, and you could've heard a pin drop; when we were released no one would tell us where we were, so we had to find the nearest habitation and stay there.'

'What about us?' interjected a young man, 'we were left on some pews in an ancient church overnight and in a way that neither of us could see the other. It was really creepy.' Everybody laughed when his pretty blonde girlfriend admitted she'd wet herself; but their amusement increased when her companion said, 'So did I!'

Another man, his arms protectively about his wife, told them all about how they'd both been carried like sacks to a well known beauty spot where, on a bank above a frequently used footpath, they'd been seated against birch trees some distance apart, and left tied to them. His wife then explained how a courting couple pretended to stumble across her. 'They stood looking down at me while I tried to tell them to untie me through my gag. But I should have known better because they then had a sham argument; the girl wanted to release me, but her lover insisted my partner must be having a sex game with me, and finally they walked off. I heard the boyfriend tell his sweetheart he'd come back to see if I was still there when it got really dark.'

Her husband took up the story. 'Quite a large group did return much later; we could hear them talking and shouting, and we saw some torches flashing; when they got really close to us we heard the courting couple telling everyone the tree they were standing by was definitely the one my wife had been tied to, and so she'd obviously been freed. So they all went away, and we were alone again. Of course they were all just tormenting us and a couple of hours later someone came back and untied us.'

As Andrew heard each bizarre story he began to realise how, as his lover had indicated, they had both got off lightly compared to other people. 'I personally think the worse torment of all,' stated a woman, 'is having others so close to you and being unable to contact them and, when they've gone, feeling so utterly lonely and helpless even though you know you'll be released sooner or later.' Julie and, especially Andrew, were so enthralled by each account that they allowed themselves to over-run several stops until they'd heard everything the other passengers had to say on the subject.

So when they left the train and had crossed over to the opposite platform to await the next train back, Andrew observed, 'I thought you said the rules disallowed zigzagging outside, due to temperature control and audible problems, at least.'

His lover, as ever, had an explanation ready, 'In the early days they did have outdoor ordeals, but after a few problems and slight mishaps they dropped the idea; but couples, if they feel adventurous enough or want special treatment can still request them.'

Because it was such a beautifully sunny afternoon they decided to walk back from Laketown station to the flat; but at Julie's insistence she took her share in carrying the suitcase. 'Thank you for helping me with my burden,' he told her at one point.

She knew he wasn't referring to their case. 'I was merely showing you how much I adore you,' she replied dismissively, 'but I'm elated you've passed your ordeal; if we work hard on your acceptance exams then island citizenship will be a simple formality now.' Smiling at a sudden thought, she announced, 'We must celebrate tonight, perhaps with Jill and her beau, they're bound to have more stories about zigzagging!' And she giggled over her unintended pun.

When Julie opened the door of their flat she bent down and picked up a letter. 'It's for you,' she observed, handing it to him.

"Dear Andrew," it read, "Sorry for the delay in replying to your kind and considerate letter. But I think it is I who should owe you an apology. I realise now that you were only being nice to me, but I took it the wrong way. It's a dear little brooch and I shall always cherish it. I feel now that I was being very unfair to you and Julie, for when I told you I would wait a year for you it was a mean thing to say. You are ideally suited and therefore you should always be together. So please forget me. Love to you both, Helen."

Without comment he handed the note to his lover, and with an expressionless face she perused the contents, then she frowned thoughtfully. 'Where did you say Jill lives?' she enquired. When he told her it was Harbourtown she said, 'The sooner we phone her the better; have you got the number handy?'

Once again the unknown woman answered the call, but then Andrew heard Jill's voice. 'Oh, Jill,' he said, 'this is Andrew, do you remember? I'm sorry I haven't phoned you before.'

'That's alright, love, but I had been wondering about you. How did you get on that Wednesday night?'

Giving his lover an impish smile, he replied, 'I didn't, I had to wait till Friday and then it was in the usual way. But she came, my little slave girl and I'm living with her now.'

Between the laughter his innuendoes engendered, she replied, 'Gosh, that was quick, what's she like?'

'Very beautiful, very kind, very……… everything! Would you like to speak to her?'

His sweetheart made a face as he handed the receiver over, but once on the phone she came straight to the point. 'Hello, Jill? This is Julie; Andrew has talked so much about you that I'm longing to meet you. Do you think we could have a foursome tonight?' She paused to listen. 'Oh good,' she said, 'Yes, a drink: dine and dance. Your end?' She winked at her lover. 'You will? Good. Eight o'clock at the station, nothing formal. 'Bye then.' Replacing the receiver she squealed, 'It's all arranged,' she hugged him. 'Now, I've got a little proposition for you. I've got the day off tomorrow, so shall we go sailing off Harbourtown and maybe catch a dab or something off the sandbank for tea?' Andrew nodded enthusiastically. 'Well, there's this chap Harry Larke.....' she began to explain.

But he interrupted. 'I know Harry, he's Mr. Maynard's friend; he took me on a tour of the vehicle complex.'

She put up a hand to stop him then, after smiling mischievously, she began to dial. 'Is that Harry? Hello, this is Julie Lucas. Look, do you think I could take the whaler out tomorrow? Oh, great.' She was smirking slyly as she listened. 'Only there's this sexual deviant who keeps pestering me, and I thought I could lure him out.....' She giggled as her lover attempted to wrest the receiver from her, but continued...... 'a sudden tack, and over the side with the help of the boom. He's also a pathological liar, claims he knows you and that he also lived with the Maynards.' Despite his light-hearted endeavours to get at the instrument, she continued, laughing, 'Oh, Arthur, Alan; no, Andrew that's his name.' Only then did she relinquish the receiver and allow her sweetheart the use of it.

'Hello? Mr. Larke? This is Andrew speaking.'

Harry sounded delighted when he heard the young man's voice. 'So you've taken up with our Julie, have you?'

'Until I strangle her for libelling or slandering me; look,' he asked, grinning at his still giggling companion, 'is she safe to go sailing with?'

Harry chuckled. 'I wouldn't trust her in the bath with my least favourite rubber duck.' He paused. 'She's brilliant, Andrew. Congratulations, you've won first prize. Have fun tomorrow.' And he rang off.

After they'd had another mutual shower during which, unaccountably, Julie successfully fought him away from her body, she tossed a coin to see who would wash their underwear and who'd make the soup. He didn't consider he'd lost as, once again, he stood before the wash basin rinsing out their intimate garments, because he enjoyed helping his lover and it seemed to bring them closer together. The task certainly held little sense of eroticism for him but was, he felt, merely a sign of a loving partnership. However, when he went out into the hall on his way to the backyard he surprised Julie with her back toward him, using the telephone; she whipped round startled when she heard him, and immediately replaced the receiver as he passed. 'Just calling a friend,' she mentioned lamely.

Pausing, he turned to her, 'There's no need to explain about anything, my love, I trust you implicitly. Whatever you were doing was, I'm sure, well intentioned.'

Later, with large amounts of thick tomato soup and toast inside them, Julie said, 'Now, I'm going to tell you all there is to know about zigzagging, and your input will be most welcome, and what better place than in bed? Afterward, with a shared glass of brandy and the kind of exercise you seemed to be interested in during our cleansing, we can catch up on some well-deserved sleep. So if you would care to slip between the sheets, my sweet, I will bring you a certain item.'

The article in question, which she removed from her locked drawer, proved to be a small newspaper clipping inside a clear plastic envelope; after handing it to him she moved across to the wardrobe. Before beginning to read, Andrew happened to glance over at his lover and to his horror she was standing there with her dressing gown off her left shoulder, exposing her left breast. Leering across at him, she asked innocently, 'Is Melanie's left tit nicer than mine?' And, in a perfect parody of the brunette, she turned slowly round to exhibit the nipple in profile.

'Goodness, Julie!' he cried out in alarm, 'how did you know about that?'

She laughed, quickly divested herself of her garment, and did a perfect dive onto the bed where, propping up her chin with her palms, she lay gazing up at him in amusement. 'A certain mirror on the wall, my dear boy. I couldn't see you but I could see your playmate. What else did she do for you?'

He bent his head down to the more convenient ear of the two. 'This,' he murmured. Eventually he asked anxiously, 'Did you mind?'

'No.'

'Why not?' Andrew enquired.

'Because it's you.' Pulling herself up beside him she joined him beneath the sheets where she planted a kiss on his mouth, 'I'm only teasing; I enjoyed your prolonged French kiss in my ear tremendously, but I know you were referring to Melanie's show of exhibitionism. I suppose you were,' she emphasised, 'a captive audience. But just consider one thing, sweetheart; if you'd been the one tied to the chair and I and Mark had been performing on the carpet, you wouldn't be here now. You'd have been off like a rocket, wouldn't you? And exactly how did the temptress manage to remove her bit of wood, she could hardly have lapped you out with that contrivance in her mouth.'

After he'd explained, she commented, 'It appears you've got away with it, but you deserve to be refused citizenship; though presumably because you're a novice they've let you off. But you must never interfere again because they can definitely hear a pin drop. Anyway,' she nudged him playfully, 'you didn't answer my question.'

'Which one?' he answered, puzzled. She directed his hand to her appropriate breast. 'Well,' he said, cupping his palm over it, 'this is much larger and so more gropeable, but Melanie's version of this,' fingering her nipple, 'is more interesting because it offers more variety at playtime.'

Julie gave him a slap on the cheek which was slightly over playful and urged, 'Read this,' and she presented him with the plastic covered newspaper article.

The clipping was extremely brief and described how a twenty four year old bank clerk, working late, had been set upon by masked men as she made her way home. They bundled her into a van, bound and gagged her and then drove her around until the early hours of the morning; the bank keys were removed from her handbag and the bank subsequently robbed. The sum of money involved was mentioned in the account. The stolen van was then driven out into the countryside where it, and its hapless occupant, was abandoned, presumably where it wouldn't be easily found. They weren't discovered until late the same afternoon.

'Not much to it, is there, sweetheart?' Julie asked, suddenly serious. 'But let's analyse the article. First of all the poor kid didn't know what was about to happen to her, possibly therefore, her bowels and bladder were quite full, so when she was suddenly attacked she might've lost control of them. If that occurred then her captors, in the hypocritical way of many humans, would doubtless have felt contemptuous toward her and so treated her badly. But let's imagine this didn't happen and the men just neutralised her; but how did they accomplish this? If it was in such a manner that she wouldn't be able to move then it would've meant her being kept in the same position from, say, nine p.m. to four p.m. At least nineteen bloody hours! Perhaps even longer! Because if she'd been allowed some freedom of movement she might've summoned help by banging on the side of the van with her feet; but if she was free to move about was there a mattress, someone to steady her, so she didn't scrape her face, knees, et cetera, her hands especially, as having them tied behind is standard but prevents the arms from becoming adequate buffers for the upper body against large foreign objects, as the van travelled along? If, however, she was secured to something immovable did the weight of her moving body cause her bonds to chafe her skin unbearably, especially when cornering? And how did they silence her? Did they force something into her mouth and keep it in place with a length of cloth covering her lips? If so, it could've been very dangerous as the stuffing might have choked or suffocated her.'

Julie paused and kissed her lover passionately, though gently, 'No, darling,' she chided softly, 'don't touch me there; not yet. I haven't finished my analysis. So what of her captors? Were they perfect gentlemen with her reasonable comfort in mind? Or did they pass the time in taking turns molesting, or even raping her? Judging from the way they apparently abandoned her, there's nothing to suggest they contacted the authorities re her plight after their get away or really cared what happened to her. But whatever occurred, and there isn't any real detail about her welfare during the horrific incident as the newspaper and, presumably, the bank seemed more interested in the amount of cash stolen than in her ordeal, one fact is certain, though: that unfortunate, innocent, unsuspecting girl endured a nightmare which will haunt her to her dying day; and doubtless she'll be permanently terrified of being attacked again. I don't suppose her loved ones will forget or forgive the perpetrators of such an offensive crime too soon, either.'

Andrew's sweetheart sat up and poured a generous measure of brandy into a tumbler and, after taking a sip she handed him the glass and settled down in the bed again.

'So who do you suppose,' she continued, 'would've had any idea of what that poor human being went through, upon reading that little article?' Without waiting for his reply, she went on, 'Well, I and my four college companions would have. You see, darling, I came by that report a few months after we'd become the pioneer zigzaggers. But in our case, although we didn't expect it to occur when it did, we had some idea of what was going to happen to us; we were allowed to visit the toilet before and after the ordeal, and although it was extremely realistic we knew we wouldn't be sexually molested or ill-treated in any way. But we all suffered fear and uncertainty, for none of us knew the final outcome or for how long the experience would continue.'

'Anyway, sweetheart, that's enough for now because we should both be tired. If you'd care to take another gulp of brandy I'll finish the rest, and then set the alarm for five.' Afterward, she raised the tumbler and declared, 'Close your eyes, and if you can guess which way up this has been replaced on the bedside table then you can be top dog.' Much to Andrew's delight, he guessed wrong.

As soon as he heard the alarm sounding off he disentangled himself carefully from his sleeping lover's embrace and, after donning his dressing gown, went off and made some coffee. Back in bed he molested his sweetheart until she opened her eyes, whereupon he presented her with her coffee; but she exclaimed, 'Whoops, I must go to the loo first.' And she leapt from the bed and ran across to the door. He watched her progress, marvelling at her lack of inhibition; she knew she had a faultless body and that he loved to look at it, and so she was perfectly willing to allow him every opportunity to gaze upon her. Had any other man had a more considerate lover? he pondered.

Upon her reappearance she mimicked a ballet dancer, pirouetting, spinning and leaping across the room to rejoin him. 'How was I?' she asked, slipping in beside him, 'do you think I'd make a Prima Donna?'

'More like a Bella Donna,' he murmured dryly, a remark for which she kissed him amorously until his tongue was in her mouth, at which she clamped it between her teeth and wouldn't let go until she'd given him several slaps to the back of the head.

'Anyway,' she said when their mouths finally parted, 'to return to zigzagging. When you were lying trussed up last night and most of this morning you were meant to be imagining it was for real, because in a capitalistic society something like that could occur, or a variation of it, anytime or anywhere. First of all, darling, you should've been considering what you'd have done in an actual similar situation: would you have given in meekly to Mark's demands, thereby endorsing whatever subsequently took place and so risked damaging your pride and, quite possibly, your relationship with your sweetheart? Or would you have fought back and so risked Anne's life, or anyone else's, even your own or perhaps been badly beaten in the process?'

'How would you have felt if, having been bound and gagged, you'd watched me or any of the other women, or even all of us, being systematically fondled by our captors or even worse; or else carried off somewhere? Are you beginning to see now, Andy, why we have something as bizarre as zigzagging in our society?' He nodded, though somewhat uncertainly and Julie, noticing, quickly hugged him.

'Look, sweetheart,' she continued, 'let's make a mental list. By far the most important reason for having the ordeal is because it compels the victims to appreciate the benefits which our combined capitalist/communist society brings, whereby we unite capitalist pleasures with communist ideals: everyone has the same privileges, wealth and opportunity to share in everything our island has to offer without the hypocrisies of pseudo democracy and dictatorship. Therefore, envy and greed, those arch supporters of crime, are unable to flourish. Zigzagging is thus a reminder of what can result if our society is permitted to lapse into a selfish, devil take the hindmost, everything inhumane kind of civilized jungle.

'Perhaps the next prominent purpose is that the ordeal helps to defeat hypocrisy. Do you know what they do in one blue school lesson, darling?' Quite unnecessarily, he shook his head. 'Well,' she went on, 'they play the soundtrack only, of a typical mainland television thriller. It's pretty horrifying, someone shooting or being shot at, people and crowds panicking, vehicles crashing, men being beaten up and women screaming, threats of violence as well as the odd explosion or two, and an occasional building, or whatever, collapsing.

'To the Whyte Islander, enjoying friendship, fellowship, love, pleasure and happiness, as we do; encouraging and presenting such misery and terror is just symptomatic of a sick society. Most of the planet's populace, it seems, are quite content to see others suffering, whether in an actual or a fictional setting, just as long as it doesn't happen to them and theirs. So our authorities, in their wisdom, decided to introduce a little violence into their electorate's life to show them it isn't all that amusing; at first they didn't know what method to employ until Melanie, I and our three companions came along.'

'Are you going to tell me about that, my love?' Andrew interposed.

Julie altered her position in his arms. 'Not today, maybe tomorrow; and I do wish you'd stop doing that, it's extremely disconcerting. Anyway, where was I? Yes, they realised bondage fitted the bill perfectly, especially after receiving the rather mixed accounts from their guinea pigs, or sows, in our case. It was violent, yet in a comparatively mild form, a sort of harmless abuse if organised properly. I mean, they couldn't order people to be beaten up as it was too violent, or of being locked up as that was too mild and would also take too long to be really effective. No, they wanted something reasonably quick acting, uncomfortable and physically and psychologically mildly disturbing. It also had the advantage of allowing the victims plenty of time in which to consider the predicament they were in. This brings me to the third justification for zigzagging. Am I boring you, darling?'

He shook his head, then kissed her. 'Could I find being in bed with a gorgeous, naked redhead boring, sweetheart?' he laughed

His bedmate leered wickedly. 'That depends upon your use of the word "boring", my dear.' Continuing her explanation, she said, 'When I was tied up last night and this morning, unable to communicate, I was in so much torment that I was obliged to think of the other sufferers around me, and what they must have been going through. I thought a great deal about you, Andy, because I wasn't able to forewarn you about what to expect, but I also sympathised with my cousin and Anne especially. I even felt sorry for Melanie. And so you can see what a great relief it was to be able to share discomfort, psychologically, with others as it helps to ease one's own discomfort.

'So that's another good reason for having zigzagging, it teaches people to think of others for a change. Anyway, my sweet, darling, Andy, there are several other logical excuses for employing it, but you witnessed an entirely unexpected side to its validity on the train today, and that was the comradeship and friendly rivalry it engenders. At the time it's quite a trial, but in retrospect it becomes a trophy to be displayed with pride; don't you think it brought us closer, love?'

'Not as close as we are right now, but emotionally? Most certainly!'

Beaming at him with pleasure, she observed, 'I'm not going to say any more about it just now, but I'll wager that when I mention zigzagging this evening, one of them will have some anecdotes to air.'

Andrew whispered in her ear, 'Have we got time for a quickie, my love?'

'What!' she replied in amazement, 'You haven't long done it; if it's for my sake, then go ahead, though I doubt you'll be satisfied. But I don't want you falling asleep during our outing.'

'I'll be alright,' he averred, 'And I don't care about myself, as long as I please a lady like you. Though will you be a damsel I can look up to again? But, kneeling upright this time?'

She smiled and nodded. 'You're a proper sex maniac. But why, especially?'

'Because I like examining the five most beautiful things on Whyte Island.'

'And what are they?' she laughed.

'Well,' he murmured, 'two of them are your face and your hair.' Julie began to giggle helplessly.

'You look fantastic, sweetheart,' Andrew announced admiringly before his lover put her jacket on. She was dressed in a white polo neck sweater and a close fitting green skirt; for jewellery she wore a pair of quite large, green, disc earrings, and a matching brooch was pinned just above her left breast. She'd put her hair in a ponytail and tied it with a green ribbon. 'You like the colour green, don't you, love?'

'Fortunately, I do. Because we redheads should only sport green, brown, white and black, and also yellow, though I don't like that colour personally, but especially when they're next to our hair. You see, any other colour clashes. It amazes me when I see so called models with auburn hair in the mainland fashion magazines, for example, wearing any other hues.' She gazed critically at him. 'Anyway, you look quite sexy with your sports jacket and cravat; I'd almost be proud to see you on my arm. Well, are you coming, sailor?'

On their way to the station Andrew, after admiring her once more, asked, 'Julie, as a beautician and an amateur psychologist, could you tell me why so many of these attractive girls in other countries go in for outrageous hair styles, ridiculous make up and absurd clothes; also, overly obvious tattoos, studs and rings? I mean, you're dressed really simply and yet you're breathtakingly beautiful; and that's typical of Whyte Island women.'

His sweetheart paused and dropped him a curtsey. 'Oh sir,' she lisped, 'you're only saying that so you may have your way with me. But thank you for your compliments, I'm flattered by your faith in my ability to define global fashion trends, so I'll try to explain. I think a lot of the problem is caused by the fashion industry attempting to maintain a constant market; you know, by frequently introducing new styles, and so they need to keep wracking their brains for new designs because they can only improvise so far on something as basic as a woman's dress, for instance. Presumably, therefore, the designers have to keep testing the water, so to speak, to see what they can get away with. But usually, that's all at the top end of the market where fashionable, about town women have a yearning to impress suitors and rival females alike; they'll generally buy anything so long as it's upmarket and different enough.

'The greater number of girls and women, though, aren't particularly interested in outdoing their own sex fashionwise, although many will exhibit as much of their sexual charms as they can to attract, mainly, males. So this group can't in the main be described as outrageous dresswise; they just go with the flow as fashions come and go: just as they always have throughout history.

'So I assume you're describing those, very often lovely, girls who finish up looking like clowns and imbeciles? But you were right to mention psychology, because the human psyche is at the bottom of it. Too many of the more affluent parents think that love toward their children means buying them expensive equipment, toys and games, when what their offspring really need is attention, encouragement and good old parental love, and plenty of it. There isn't much benefit, darling, in buying a child a game, whatever, and leaving it alone to play with it on their own, because they need to interact with their siblings, friends or parents; in fact anyone they know and can trust. And the earlier that begins for the child the better.'

'Lack of these essentials therefore shows itself in various outrageous fashions and self-mutilation among many children of both genders from puberty onwards, hence the passion for weird hairstyles, clothing, tattooing and different types of body piercing; as you mentioned earlier. These kids are subconsciously demanding, "Look at me, I need attention" and at the same time they're also saying, "I don't care what you think of me because I'm an independent individual." It's therefore obvious to anyone with a modicum of social awareness that when youngsters of a similar way of thinking come together, their outrageous behaviour tends to engender the tribal or wolf pack instinct and the larger the grouping grows the more lawlessly and arrogantly they behave, thereby indulging in pointless acts of vandalism and violence. In fact, they can be said to have a combined grudge against society.'

She changed the subject briefly. 'When we reach the station we'll board the first train to come along, shall we? Then tomorrow, as we're going to Harbourtown again, we'll go the opposite way round.' They stopped for a quick embrace and a kiss. Then Julie continued, 'But to be fair to most of the mainland girls, I believe the majority of them will continue to favour sensible clothing: tee shirts, sweaters, skirts, jeans and simple dresses won't be replaced for a long time yet, if ever. But the fashion world, like so many other institutions, is based upon snobbery; and snobbery is just another manifestation of inferiority complex: the constant subconscious urge to be acceptable to one's fellows, as any candid psychologist could explain.'

During the train journey Andrew suddenly observed, 'I've just thought of another very good reason for having zigzagging; when

I was lying helpless I wasn't only wishing I could release you but I wanted to embrace you; at times the desire was so intense it was almost intolerable, but it wasn't merely sexual in origin, it was an amalgam of senses I can't describe. But it was far more intense than when I'm the victim in one of our games; so I've been considering that if other lovers also experience a similar feeling then it must be a means of strengthening the ties between permanent couples.'

Julie smiled in recognition of his experience. 'Yes,' she agreed, 'I felt that way too, and it's a phenomenon well known to island lovers, permanent or otherwise.' And she added dryly, 'It was most fortunate, in your case, that you had Melanie to assuage your suffering.' Then she kissed him in order to show she was only joking.

Jill and her lover, whom she introduced as Michael, were awaiting them outside the station entrance. Andrew's sweetheart had been chatting away quite happily as they emerged from the building, but she suddenly seemed to hesitate when she noticed the couple, and her companion had the unpleasant idea she knew Michael as she took his hand. But she was soon back to her normal self and she and Jill especially, got on extremely well together. There wasn't much opportunity for conversation as they walked along the pavements on the way to their venue, but at one point Jill glanced over her shoulder and informed the two lovers, 'We hope you won't mind but we thought we'd all spend the evening at one place. It's very appropriate, Andy, as it's actually close to the harbour quay and overlooks the straits and mainland coast.'

The public house and combined restaurant that Jill and Mike led them to was yet another example of Whyte Island ingenuity at its best because the building, which was directly connected to the harbour retaining wall, had a rear consisting of three bays, each one of which was a perfect replica of the captain's cabin in an old wooden warship. Even before they'd had time to order their drinks Julie excitedly dragged her lover over to inspect them; nailed to a beam in the left hand one was a brass plaque which read: 32 gun Frigate circa 1810. 'This one's a battleship,' she cried, after taking him on to the centre bay where the plaque stated: 120 gun First Rate c1795. 'And look at this one, darling;

seventy four gun cruiser from seventeen eighty; aren't they beautiful, love?'

They were indeed, and just like authentic pieces of the mainland's former maritime power, each one was as different from the others as was possible within such a limited configuration; the bay representing the largest ship appeared, hardly surprisingly, the most ornate, but the frigate's décor with its light coloured woodwork was no less attractive. The intermediate ship, however, was by comparison almost functional having dark, oaken beams, many fitted cupboards and heavy looking furniture, and a pair of large cannons directed toward the multi paned stern windows. Each bay also contained an oblong table laid out with what Andrew assumed to be typical dining utensils and equipment of the relevant period.

'I wonder which one we'll end up in?' observed Mike, handing them each a drink with the words, 'I hope these are alright, only you didn't stay around long enough to say what you'd like. Now, shall we go and sit on the frigate's window seat? There aren't so many people in that one.' While he went on to explain, in some detail, about how the replica cabins had been derived from authentic drawings and appropriate feature films Andrew, after glancing out of the stern window and being pleasantly surprised by the realistic effect, turned his attention to the visible décor of the remainder of the bar.

Although in no way attempting to imitate the interior of an old ship, its connection with the sea was more than obvious for the walls and black beams were almost entirely concealed by lifebuoys, portlights, cutlasses, flintlocks, bunting, ropes and other kinds of marine memorabilia; but most evident of all were some very large paintings of seascapes and naval battles..

'Come on,' urged Jill when both her lover's information, and their drinks, were finished, 'we've got time for another round, and we can have it outside on the biggest ship's walkway.'

'It's fantastic,' Andrew exclaimed enthusiastically as he leant against the balustrade gazing out toward the sea, 'but it's a pity the tide's out, it spoils the effect a little.'

'Oh, don't be so pedantic, darling,' Julie gently admonished, 'just smell that stranded seaweed; it more than makes up for it. Anyway, I've heard there are plans to enclose this area so these sterns will always have some sea water around them. Though not only because it improves the authenticity you apparently crave,' she smiled, 'but because it'd lessen the possibility of high tides and waves damaging them. This is quite poignant for Andy,' she then told their companions as they all stared out in the direction of the mainland, 'because he's expecting to become an islander soon.'

'I told you so, Andrew!' Jill exclaimed triumphantly, but then added uncertainly, 'though I don't know what you'll think of zigzagging.'

Julie cried out in delight, 'We did it last night to this morning.' And she went on to relate their experience to them.

As she'd predicted, Jill eagerly responded by recounting her and Mike's adventures in that field. 'Our latest summons,' she explained, 'was, by a coincidence, to the hothouse you and I visited, Andy. Some people were bound to trees, others to restaurant chairs outside the canopy, but Mike and I ended up on the catwalk where I was seated on the mesh floor, which was most uncomfortable, and Mike had to stand with his wrists tied to the rails; this was a couple of years ago, and we all expected the nightly tropical downpour which would've been an additional torment, but of course it never came; did it, love?' And they both laughed, while Julie winked at her sweetheart.

Not long afterward, as Jill was telling Julie how downcast Andrew had been, how much he needed a companion of his own at the time and how perfect she obviously was for him, they heard the sound of a whistle being blown. 'The bosun's pipe calls us to our meal,' Mike commented much to Andrew's relief, for he found the subject of the girls' conversation unsettling.

It came as little surprise to him when, after they'd been ushered into the 74-gunned stern compartment and he'd scanned the menu, he noted the choice of main courses consisted entirely of sea food dishes, nor that they were served by waiters dressed as old-time sailors. 'Jill happened to mention you were a doctor,' he said to Mike during their meal, and upon receiving a nod, he asked, 'Would that be a G.P.?'

The other man grinned. 'Yes, and if you've got any ailments then I don't want to know about them.' He glanced at Andrew's partner, then observed, 'Unless they're really unusual, of course, because I have my own specialist subject as well. You know, Andrew,' he quickly went on, 'you're very lucky coming over here to live because the sorry state of the mainland's economy is nowhere more evident than in your health service. I think I'd rather work in a missionary hospital than have a practice over there.'

Apparently feeling he'd said enough he fell silent, but Julie leant forward eagerly and prompted, 'Tell us why, Mike.'

Quite reluctantly, he answered, 'The large numbers of mainland G.Ps. and hospital doctors who take their own lives is a manifestation of how high the pressures are on medical staff. G.Ps., for example, have to deal with many elderly people, hypochondriacs, addicts of various kinds, as well as being pestered by different pharmaceutical companies trying to sell them their products, and all this on top of their customary role; and it's too much for many of them.' He paused long enough for their sweets to be served. 'We Whyte Island doctors have got it easy by comparison, the few old people who persist in coming to see us are simply advised to go and live in one of our mainland nursing homes where they can receive the best of treatment close to hand, or else to take a euthanasia pill as almost all of us will eventually need to do.'

'Hypochondria is merely a subconscious cry for help and attention which, as you two doubtless know,' he smiled at Julie and her sweetheart, 'is rarely to be found wanting over here, while addiction to drugs and alcohol is virtually due to a kind of withdrawal from the pressures and insecurity of a disorganised, inept society; again, not applicable to the island because of our near perfect social order.'

He began eating his sweet in earnest, but Jill reminded him, 'You forgot about the pharmaceutical people, love.'

Mike paused between mouthfuls. 'That's as much your province as mine, darling.'

Taking up his challenge, she explained, 'Such companies don't bother much with Whyte Island now and, when they do, doctors don't receive their literature or samples as it goes to a panel of senior doctors and consultants instead. But after some appalling tragedies in various parts of the world due to improperly tested medicines, our authorities are very wary about introducing new super treatments. So there is a ban of at least ten years on almost every fresh form of medicine; we let other nations thoroughly test these new cures before we'll touch them.'

Julie commented, 'Even in cases where there's a likely cure for an unusual or debilitating illness.' And she added, 'And I don't blame the authorities.'

During coffee the background music, cleverly imitative of the far off sounds emanating from a large sailing ship at sea, gradually abated, and a small dance group began to play alongside an area of cleared floor, encouraging several of the other couples at their table to rise and go off to dance. Julie, who had been quietly humming the catchy tune which had nothing maritime about it, suddenly commented, 'Why don't you ask Jill to dance, Andy? Then Mike can partner me.'

Andrew stared at her in shocked surprise; if there was going to be any dancing within their little group he'd naturally assumed they'd both want to do it with each other, but he gave in gracefully and soon Jill and he were in each other's arms on the dance floor. 'You're right,' she said, 'she's very beautiful. You're very fortunate.'

'Everyone says that,' he replied proudly, 'She's got a heart of gold to match her hair colour, as well as a terrific sense of humour.' He paused and, seeking further confirmation that their relationship was normal by island standards, he asked, 'Jill, I wonder if you'd mind if I asked the sort of question a brother might put to his elder siste?'

She smiled indulgently at him, 'Well, let's see if you can really shock me, so ask away, brother dear.'

'It's difficult but.....you see Julie likes to play these sex games. You know,' he suddenly felt flustered, 'tying up and teasing, things like that.'

'And you want to know if other couples over here do. Perhaps whether Mike and I do?' He nodded uncertainly. 'Relax,' she told him, and then explained, 'Consider a man who consistently patronises a certain restaurant. Now it doesn't matter how efficient the service, or how attractive the décor, although it might help gain his custom in the first place, if, day after day, he receives exactly the same meal then before long he's likely to seek another place in which to dine. In the same way a husband, if he's only offered bedroom press ups, is probably going to look for a fresh playmate.

'Now, from what I understand, your Julie isn't only offering you a very varied menu, she's also liberal with the spice. What you should be doing is ensuring you congratulate the chef at every opportunity, and also cook her a tasty dish or two; but if that's too difficult, onerous or against your principles then patronise another restaurant. No doubt your disappearance would break her heart but she'd soon be open for customers again, and she wouldn't need to wait long, would she?'

They danced again in silence for a while as Andrew digested this advice, until Jill observed, 'The problem with the average mainlander is apparently they've only got a veneer of sexual permissiveness. Deep inside you, Andrew, you're repressed; your moral code has been devised by jealous old fogies who could no longer participate in sex or never had the opportunity to indulge their natural lusts; and they were in their turn repressed.

'Prior to the wholesale arrival of contraception there was some argument about being too permissive, but not anymore; and if relationships among the middle sex are perfectly legal and acceptable worldwide nowadays, then the sky should be the limit where heterosexual affairs are concerned. I know it is with Mike and me, and quite frankly Andy, we can never get enough games to play. Because Julie so obviously loves you she apparently feels the same way. You like playing them, don't you?' He nodded. 'Well then, you're luckier than you know. It's a consensus of opinion over here that the average mainland female in bed is about as enterprising as a rubber doll.'

Smiling at the amusing description, Andrew glanced around the crowded little dance floor for his lover, and was quite put out to see she was evidently engaged in a very serious conversation with Michael, for she was staring up into his face earnestly and emphasising everything she said with her free hand; they almost seemed to be arguing. Something made him ask his partner, 'How long have you and Mike been together?'

'Oh, for much longer than I care to remember, why?'

He shrugged. 'Just curiosity. But what branch of medicine does he specialise in?'

Jill glanced at him in an enquiring manner. 'He's very keen on rare, and often fatal, diseases.'

The next, and most of the following dances were spent in the embrace of his sweetheart, but near the end of one of them Julie, her arms about his neck and her body pressed up against his, whispered in his ear after checking her watch, 'I'm very sorry, darling, but I've got to slip away for half an hour or so. I've arranged to meet someone. I didn't want to tell you before as I thought it would spoil your fun.'

Not unnaturally, Andrew was quite angry at what he considered to be his sweetheart's deceit, but she refused to tell him who she was going to see, nor would she allow him to accompany her. 'Take Jill with you then!' he urged in frustration.

They both glanced over to where their companions were locked together with their eyes closed, oblivious to anything but the sound of the music and their own company and, unconsciously, thereby providing the answer to Andrew's plea. 'Stay here,' she insisted, 'I promise you I'm only going to meet another woman and that it won't affect my love and desire for you, darling; please believe me. I wouldn't deliberately hurt or deceive you.' Still much annoyed, but noticing the beginning of tears in her eyes, he had little choice but to let her go.

To give her credit she was back within twenty five minutes, and nothing else occurred to spoil the remainder of the evening. They both politely refused Jill and Mike's invitation to go back to their flat for some coffee with the excuse that they wished to rise early in the morning to go sailing. Any irritation Andrew felt toward his lover was soon dissipated on the train when Julie fell asleep in his arms; she was still sleepy when they arrived at their station, and so he lovingly carried her in his arms all the way back to their flat, a not inconsiderable feat in view of her weight and the distance involved.

She was still a little groggy before they went to bed, and apart from the compulsory glass of squash each, neither wanted a drink. 'Look,' she suggested, 'we won't get undressed, let's just take our shoes and watches off, and my jewellery, then in the morning we can unwrap our gifts in bed.'

'Sounds like Christmas,' Andrew laughed, 'but it's a great idea.' He was unaware of how tired he really was until, after sliding his hand up her sweater and under her brassiere cup, he instantly fell asleep.

The morning was bright and sunny when the alarm woke them and, later, while they made sandwiches and got their gear together, they listened to the weather forecast. 'Wonderful,' Julie cried, 'I couldn't possibly have ordered better. That front's too far to the north to do us any harm.' After her lover's mild criticism of jeans as feminine attire she'd deigned not to wear them before, but now she sported a pair and these, together with a sloppy brown jumper, a black duffel coat and a brown knitted hat, served to make her appear the perfect mariner.

During their journey to the harbour, made in the direction which Andrew had only travelled once before: via the seaside resort at the end of the island, his lover patted the back of his hand in mild chastisement and observed, 'I was a bit annoyed with you last night for insisting upon paying our way. Mike, and Jill especially, were only trying to show how pleased they were that you've got me, that you'd passed the ordeal of zigzagging, and were expecting island citizenship. Anyway,' she added, holding up a banknote, 'I took your money back with alacrity.'

'Julie!' Andrew exclaimed in shock. But after a moment he suggested, 'Well, when I become an islander we'll have to throw a party for them, and anyone else you think ought to come.'

This plan was well received by his sweetheart, though she advised, 'When you do become one of us you'll need to look upon money in a different light, darling, because it doesn't play a terrifically important part in our lives; and it doesn't really matter who pays for what as long as you don't let yourself get short.'

The whaler, covered from bow to stern in a protective tarpaulin, was tethered alongside a jetty with other small craft, and it didn't take the couple long to step the mast, check the emergency stores and generally prepare the boat for sea; before they cast off and hoisted the sails Julie ensured her sweetheart was fully conversant with the wearing of a life jacket. This last amused him greatly for he was already familiar with them; and she made certain he was also competent in the general running of the vessel. 'So make sure you keep clear of the boom whenever we go about,' she finished by warning him.

Soon they were running free up the wide, deep channel, and then they turned to port when they were well out into the straits;

from almost the beginning Julie left the steering in Andrew's care, giving him instructions as need be while she worked the boat whenever it proved necessary. In this manner they tacked several miles up the island's coast and then ran back on the light, but constant breeze, an evolution which they repeated a number of times on that beautiful day. Eventually, she lowered the sails and they anchored to do a little fishing and have a bite to eat. Like Sandra she was an expert, or else very lucky, angler, for it didn't take her long to catch several dabs and a flounder or two which she dispatched immediately they landed in the boat as, she explained, she didn't like to see dumb creatures suffering, 'Except you, sweetheart, during our games,' she giggled.

Andrew's line, though, merely seemed to be a great attraction for crabs. Every time he pulled up his line one of the little horrors was attached to it; he didn't like them very much and on the first few occasions he let his lover remove them until she showed him how. As she did so she laughed, saying, 'You are a baby, Andy. Didn't you learn anything on your ships?'

Shaking his head, he admitted, 'I was never a great one for being adventurous.'

'That's probably because you're a bit insecure, afraid of making yourself look silly. Still, you can be as silly as you like before me, 'cause I love yer.' She pondered reflectively for a moment. 'Perhaps one of the reasons why I adore you so is because you make me feel a little superior. Love is strange! But I prefer the way you are much better than those people, mercifully no longer found on our island, who pretend to know everything but really know nothing: the result of the mixture of a strong personality with an inferiority complex. Don't worry though, my sweetheart, I'll teach you all sorts of things while we're together like this, and so in time you'll gain confidence and therefore lose your self doubt.'

Once, while they ate their sandwiches, they watched a frigate emerge from the mainland dockyard and make its way between the sails of various yachts to steam off down the channel away from them. 'I wonder how many sailors onboard that ship have embraced their lovers for the last time,' Julie mused.

'Maybe it'll be coming back before tonight.'

'No,' she stated, 'it's bound for foreign parts; you could hear a band playing from the quayside.'

'It's funny,' he confessed, 'but when the "Whyte Hart" berthed I wanted to take a quick look round the island, but then I yearned to get back to sea again. Now, thanks to you, my darling, wild horses would be required. I'd be scared of losing you, just like one of those poor losers onboard that warship.'

Leaning across the tiller she gently kissed him. 'I'd try to get a job onboard as well, but if I couldn't then the strain might cause the knot to part, who knows? But in our society the problem wouldn't arise anyway, so it's only conjuncture.'

Disliking the way in which their conversation was heading, Andrew removed the tiller arm and embraced his lover. 'Tell me,' he urged, 'about how you got zigzagging going.'

'We only planted the germ,' she reminded him modestly, 'and there's not much to tell, but I'll only explain about my experience; you'll need to ask the other girls, if you can trace them, if you want to know what happened to them. Five of us got into a conversation in the college washroom one day; we were only seventeen then, and we merely decided that, although there were many wonderful and interesting things to do around the island, there wasn't anywhere which catered for unexpected excitement; you know, mild danger, because nearly everyone likes to be scared. So together we wrote to the authorities to put forward our viewpoint.

'A few days later we were all summoned to a special Parliamentary session where we were collectively questioned with regard to any suggestions we might have; well, we were all practically tongued tied because not one of us really knew just what we wanted, until Melanie, it had to be Melanie,' Julie emphasised, 'said she and her boyfriend liked immobilising each other, so how about something along those lines? Actually, her concept was the only constructive one proposed, but we were told not to mention the interview to anyone and then dismissed. A couple of weeks later, when we'd all thought the idea had been forgotten and we'd stopped being nasty to Melanie, in a figurative sense, all five of us were asked to report to an old country house to take part in further discussions.'

She removed the vacuum flask from her bag and poured out two more cups of coffee, adding a drop of rum to each. 'I clearly remember,' she continued, 'that we were requested to attend in horse riding gear. In the event,' she laughed, 'only one girl ever saw a horse, and she spent much of that night seated on its back in a field, bound and gagged. Anyway, it was a Saturday afternoon when we were ushered into this room, and one at a time we were called into another room; I was the third or fourth one in, and as soon as the door closed behind me I was immediately set upon by a couple of men who tied a knotted rag in my mouth, secured my wrists behind me and fastened my ankles together.

'Then I was carried off to a garage where my predecessors, in a like predicament, were seated against the walls. Soon all five of us were there, where, at first, all we were able to do was glare at Melanie; time passed by and nothing happened, so we attempted to free each other, but they tied our hands with the knots in the inside between our wrists and our bodies, so it was impossible and we ended up as mixed together as litter of kittens!'

Julie laughed again at the recollection. 'Then the door finally opened and the two men carried one of us away. That was the last each of us saw the others that day, because we were taken away one at a time; when my time came I was thrown over a man's shoulder and carted off to a bathroom with a minute window where I was released and told to go to the toilet and then have a bath. Afterward, without having anything to eat and only a glass of flavoured water to drink, I was tied up like Melanie was during our ordeal, darling, gagged and trussed up inside a special packing case.' Andrew swore, and hugged and kissed her sympathetically at these words, but she continued, 'The case was put on a lorry by the sound and feel of it, thence to a train and eventually to a remote siding where I was removed from the case and tossed onto a cartload of hay and transported to the middle of a wood. I ended up spending the rest of the night on the earth floor of an old barn; it was very eerie, frightening and uncomfortable, but at about five in the morning I was released and, like those people on the train, told to look after myself. I was starving.'

'You poor darling!' her lover exclaimed, holding her closely and smothering her face and hair with kisses.

With some amusement Julie stopped him. 'You've missed the point, love; looking back to the experience I found I rather enjoyed it. Most people like a small amount of fear and uncertainty as I believe I may already have mentioned; that's why they pay to go on those infernal contraptions at so called amusement parks, or see horrific films. The ridiculous thing was when we went back to college and word got about we were treated like heroines, everyone seemed to want to hear our stories and many people, not just at college, admitted to feeling jealous.

'So that was the beginning of zigzagging, sweetheart, for we were eventually recalled to Parliament and asked to say what we thought regarding it; the authorities explained they'd merely been playing a joke on us, and had even asked permission from our nearest and dearest who, apparently, had all thought it a good idea, but no one expected it to have quite the effect it did. We were even responsible for drawing up some of the rules, because our ordeals were to remain unique in several ways.'

She counted off the changes on her fingers. 'We were the youngest ever to have taken part, because most bondage is illegal under the age of eighteen: though no one can, of course, check on what under the limit partners do in private, and also it isn't compulsory over the age of forty. Then again, those involved aren't allowed to be unmonitored including during transportation; this brings me to the third point, which is that never again were parties of one gender only permitted to be zigzagged. In future every person had a partner of the opposite sex sharing the ordeal with them, usually, of course, their spouse or lover but a temporary partner could always be provided.' She smiled, and added, 'Doubtless, for the reason you mentioned on the train yesterday, more than one permanent relationship began under such trying conditions. Anyway, that's all I'm going to say about it; so shall we set sail and travel up the coast again?'

'So there's no more zigzagging outside, either?' Andrew asked optimistically, wishing for confirmation.

'Of course not, as I told you yesterday. It's not much fun having ants in your pants and a myriad of other insects taking bites out of you when you can't fend them off, or else scratch your itches and, naturally the weather can't be relied on. But if you're a hardy soul then there's nothing to prevent your partner and you from volunteering to be zigzagged in the open air; and lovers often arrange such an ordeal in private to share with their partners as an anniversary or birthday treat, as the zigzag team are always on hand to set up a scenario for a sex game, although they're not permitted to actually take part themselves.' Staring down at him, she then said somewhat impatiently, 'Are you ready to take the helm, now? Because I'm about to raise the sail.'

Before they recommenced sailing, though, Julie played another one of her tricks on him; she was leaning over the bows about to pull up the anchor when she shouted, 'Come quickly, sweetheart, I can see a vessel with lots of dead people onboard!'

'Where?' he exclaimed, scrabbling to join her and expecting to see a wreck far below with some bones visible; but when he knelt beside her all he could see was a mass of flotsam consisting of pieces of wood, bits of polystyrene, plastic bottles, globules of tar, a yellow toy duck and a contraceptive with a knot tied in it.

This last item his lover prodded with a forefinger. 'There!' she cried triumphantly.

'Don't be so disgusting, Julie; you really have got a mind like a sewer.'

She faced him, suddenly serious. 'Don't you think the world would be a far happier place if most of the present inhabitants had started and ended in one of those? They might just as well have had, for all the pleasure they've had out of life. Do you know, darling, that if I'd been born anywhere else but Whyte Island I don't think I'd even contemplate reproducing; I wouldn't want to bring a child into this wicked, selfish, cruel world.'

Andrew put an arm about her shoulder, drew her to him and kissed the top of her head. 'If you do decide to procreate one day then I hope you'll permit me to tender a little help.'

Julie was quiet for a moment, then her shoulders began to shake and continued shaking until she suddenly burst into tears. 'Hold me, please, Andy,' she wailed as she sobbed uncontrollably.

Placing a hand under her chin he raised her head up and planted a sympathetic kiss on her mouth; tears, unpreventable, coursed down her cheeks in an unceasing stream, and as he placed his cheek against hers he tasted their saltiness, and so he held her tightly while he waited for her to calm down. For some reason, he couldn't understand why, he was fighting the onset of rising hysteria: something made him want to laugh. Perhaps, he considered, his urge to feel amusement was merely embarrassment. He was, of course, completely unaware of the fact, but for them both the incident was far from amusing; in retrospect he could have wished for a sudden, blinding squall to descend upon them in the midst of which was to be found a super tanker, course set fair for their tiny craft. But there was no hint of a squall in the offing, and the sun glistened on a bright, as yet cloudless, scene.

In time, Julie recovered from her fit of weeping and together they hauled in the anchor and hoisted the sails, Andrew's beautiful lover, always quick to recognise a chance to be humorous, pretended to give orders to an imaginary crew. 'Hoist the main tackle sheets,' she called, hand cupped to mouth and her gaze firmly fixed somewhere near the masthead, 'reverberate the crow's nest and steady on the bulkheads.' And so their recent troubles were soon forgotten as they tacked once more, up the coast; they went further than on their previous runs as she wanted to show him the imposing chalk and granite cliffs at that end of Whyte Island, but it was due to her vigilance that they decided to discontinue their day's sailing. For as they went about off the furthest tip of the island, Julie declared, 'So much for modern weather forecasting,' and she pointed in the direction of a headland far away on the mainland coast above which an anvil cloud was growing. They therefore immediately set course for the harbour, considerably aided by a sudden gust of wind, far stronger than the previous steady breeze which had made their day so pleasurable. Julie came aft and they sat either side of the tiller and steered, her sweetheart's hand resting on hers.

'Tell me what's wrong, darling,' he eventually asked. She looked askance at him. 'Something's bothering you,' he went on. 'Just before we were zigzagged you became tearful and talked about death, then I caught you making a secret phone call, presumably to the mysterious person you went to see last night, and then while we were anchored you cried again simply because I proposed to you.'

Smiling across at him she replied, 'If that was supposed to be a proposal then the answer is a premature "yes" because you aren't a mainlander yet. But there really isn't anything bothering me.' She shrugged and raised a hand in dismissal. 'Even Whyte Island women can be tearful and secretive at times, although I'm trying to keep both feminine characteristics to a minimum with you, my sweet.' So logical did her explanation appear to him that for a long time to come he failed to question his lover's moods; even more fortuitously he completely forgot about Mike's interest in rare and terminal diseases.

Happily the strengthening wind was in the right quarter and this allowed them to steer straight to their berth where, on his lover's insistence, they spent some time in facing the whaler in the direction of the sea as they'd found it. Above them, to the northwest, the clouds threatened menacingly, and they barely had time to stow everything away, tidy the craft and cover it with the tarpaulin before a blast of wind brought a shower of rain to their faces. 'Seeing as how the weather has ruined our entertainment,' his sweetheart shouted as they fled, laughing excitedly down the quay, 'what shall we do now?'

At last, in the reasonable shelter of a group of buildings, they decided to go and see if Harry Larke was at home. 'Perhaps we can interest him in a fish or two?' Andrew suggested, holding up a plastic bag. However, they were to be somewhat disappointed because Harry was at the industrial complex; but his wife insisted they came in for a cup of tea and a chat. Pamela Larke and Julie were old friends, both equally interested in sailing, and before they took their leave he heard many fine and amusing stories about their activities onboard the whaler "Tulyar" as well as Pamela's recollections of the earlier days when she, Harry and the Maynards were constant companions; in the event she refused all offers of a fish with the explanation that they were coming out of their ears as it was. But she took the fish and wrapped them up properly for them.

Their next visit, to Carol and Jim's flat, was less productive for they could get no reply to their repeated ringing. 'Still, you know where they live now,' Julie commented as they came away, 'if you phone them one night when I'm at the villa you could perhaps come over, and give Sue and Trevor a rest.'

'If you know Jim,' Andrew pondered aloud, 'and Linda knows him, does that mean you two girls know each other well?'

'Of course not,' she laughed, 'do you think I'd keep it a secret if we did? I've seen her around and spoken to her a couple of times, but that's all. But she noticed my regard for you when you both came to the villa and she was the prime mover in getting us together, despite your misplaced sense of honour, so we should both be eternally grateful to her. Apart from that I'd seen her a few times down the Station Arms, but she generally stays away. You see, a lot of people think she's nuts about Jim, though if it's true it's all one sided.' A piece of a jigsaw fell into place in his mind; each time Linda and he had been in the presence of Jim she'd become moody and withdrawn afterward. 'I've got just the place for us now,' exclaimed Julie, interrupting his thoughts.

'Where's that? Bed?' he asked eagerly.

Stopping, she draped her arms over his shoulders and rubbed her nose against his. 'Believe it or not, my darling,' she smiled, 'if we went to bed every five minutes you'd soon get bored with me, despite our little diversions, and that I most certainly will not allow. In fact, I'm going to take you to see the massive model railway which can be found in this vicinity. I'm sure you'll find that most intriguing.'

His lover was correct on both counts, it was huge and it was interesting. They gained access to it by way of some steps at the end of a particularly forbidding alley enclosed, upon either side, by high brick walls. As Peter, the railway fan, had already mentioned, the layout was situated in an old engine shed, or rather one half of it, for a great glass partition demonstrated that the other side still housed locomotives, with a big green express engine being much in evidence. It bore the name "GROVE SPRING" on a peculiar "P" shaped vertical sheeting which Julie explained was, with another on the opposite side of the smokebox, designed to lift the boiler exhaust away from the train, 'To give the crew a clear view of the line ahead,' she concluded.

Exactly how long and wide the model railway was Andrew had no way of telling, but it was soon apparent that a miniature engine with its train of twelve coaches seemed insignificant as it emerged from a tunnel at the far end of the shed and wended its way through a mass of points to stop at a station. The actual baseboards were slightly above the height of his waist, and abutted the walls, except where the glass partition was situated and here a false backboard had been erected thereby allowing access to the rear where the actual engine shed and its contents could be viewed.

The wall hugging layout naturally left a large space in the centre and this was mainly filled with an all round stadium featuring several tiers to enable children and short people to survey the railway. For the likes of most of the other visitors, though, only a point blank view of the intricate models and landscape would do, and for much of their time in the shed Andrew and his sweetheart stayed glued to the baseboard perimeter. The great size of the engine shed permitted space to be used liberally so that upon every side a large area between the outermost track and the wall was filled with diminutive landscaping, thereby giving the impression the railway was part of the scenery rather than the other way round.

Just as in the aquarium, the different features in the landscape, in this instance, had been convincingly blended into each other; therefore, on one of the two longest sides, the railway appeared from beneath a mountain and passed through a long cutting with rocky sides, gradually the verges changed to wooded slopes and finally became grassy banks. The tracks then continued through a large area of farmland, onto an embankment which eventually became a viaduct spanning a wide valley containing a river and marsh and thence to an area of heathland followed by dense forest, this last component serving to disguise the generous, though still unrealistic, curve onto the end section nearest the entrance door.

On the opposite side to the longer section the scenery became more urban, the main feature being a large town station which had been introduced midway along the length of the layout by the clever expedient of running four of the six tracks down a gentle incline into the platforms and then up the other side to rejoin the upper pair again; a miniature brick retaining wall behind the platforms added to the impression that the station was actually below ground level. In order to enable visitors to study this particular scene in detail a ramp descended to the same level, and when Julie and he took advantage of this facility Andrew was fascinated by what he saw; the imagination and detail lavished upon the layout in general was beyond criticism but it attained its highest degree within the perimeters of the busy miniature station. And as he examined the model he mused that if the large number of tiny people evident could be made to move then it would be difficult not to believe this was a genuine city railway station.

'It's hardly surprising, darling,' Julie exclaimed when he expressed his feelings, 'because architects, artists, engineers, geologists and other professional people apparently all had a hand in the in the model's construction. Look,' she pointed, 'there's even imaginary rust stains behind the drainpipe and moss at the foot of the wall, and look at all that litter,' she giggled, 'this must be the mainland.' They watched as a local passenger train with its tank engine and five coaches drew to a halt, waited patiently for a minute and then moved off at the raising of a signal arm affixed to the entrance wall of the tunnel sited at that end of the station, and Andrew thought it sad that not one of the tiny figures present took the slightest interest in its arrival and departure.

The designers and builders had resisted the temptation to crowd the layout with lots of factories, docks and other industrial installations, although one large and one small locomotive shed, a marshalling yard and several storage sidings had been included; in fact, as in real life, some parts of the model were almost featureless representing, as it did, a mainly rural aspect; however, there were several stations including a rural terminus served by a single branch line that continuously wove over, under or alongside the main line which, in its turn, never consisted of less than four tracks. 'So what do you think of it?' Andrew's lover finally asked.

'Magnificent!' he replied with great enthusiasm, 'I could stay here all day.'

Smiling, she said, 'Come on, let's go over and see if we can get some information for you.' Leading him by the hand they went across to where the exit/entrance passed beneath the layout, to a far corner where ten people were seated around a table; each one obviously intently involved with something in front of her or him. 'Excuse me,' she addressed a middle aged man, 'but I wonder if you could possibly tell us about the layout?'

As he rose to his feet Andrew noticed the man had been engaged in hand painting what appeared to be a model station building, and after he'd cleaned his brush in white spirit and removed his magnifying glass he was at their service. Even by Whyte Island standards the man proved to be extremely kind, considerate and patient, and as he explained every aspect of the model railway and of his own work it became evident that his enthusiasm bordered on fanaticism.

After informing them that the signals, points, turntables and other moveable fittings were all operated electrically by remote control, he explained the layout could be either managed by hand or else via computer diagramming. 'In the latter case quite complicated manoeuvres can be undertaken, such as shunting, replacement of locomotives or stock and the multiple planning of train routes. So there are no dangers of collisions, or taking curves and points too fast as there could be when using hand operations; our models are too intricate and finely built to risk damaging them so computerisation has been well worth installing as mishaps are unknown now. A very complicated programme can take several hours from start to finish and it pleases both visitors and staff, as the latter can thus watch the trains to their heart's content without worrying about anything. The computer can even simulate the different times of day, from dawn to night, by altering the intensity and inclination of the main lights above the layout; when it's dark the lights from the headlamps and tail lights, cabs, carriages, signals and buildings are quite effective.'

'Do you have miniature owls flying about?' Julie enquired innocently.

Paul, their informant, chuckled, 'Not yet, but we're working on it. But we're experiencing a little difficulty with the scale mice at the moment.' Andrew asked what scale they were working to. 'I presume you mean with regard to the general layout? Well, it's actually 4 millimetres to each foot which would make you near enough 23 millimetres tall and your lovely companion about a millimetre shorter. It's as ideal for us as it is on most mainland layouts, the next usual size up allows greater detailing but takes up too much space, and the smaller sizes permit larger layouts in comparison but at greater cost in detail realism. When it comes to landscaping, though, we juggle around with our scale sizes so as to prevent the foreshortening effect of lack of perspective; therefore, the further an object is away from the railway track the smaller the scale. We found the calculations involved in regard to the size of each given object more than a little complicated, but that was another job for the computer and we believe the result has been quite satisfactory.'

'Do you have many different engines on this layout?' Andrew asked after both his lover and he commented on how realistic the landscaping had looked without actually realising just why it had, at the time.

'Oh, hundreds,' exclaimed Paul. 'All the steam locomotive classes and their variants which ran on the mainland last century are represented, plus some much older designs, even some which were contemplated but never built, and even a number of freelance examples. You see,' he went on passionately, 'even though we've got a real steam railway over here, there just isn't the scope to allow for all the locomotives, different coaches and wagons we'd like to see, nor multiple tracks and massive junctions. We can't have huge long trains or double heading due to economic and track stress considerations, but we can have all these things on our model. We can also, to a certain extent, change our buildings and fittings around to represent the separate mainland railways which all had designs peculiar to them.

'Of course,' he continued more soberly after a pause, 'this layout isn't merely an amusement. It's used by the railway people to train and examine their staff. It also has another, much underrated use which would doubtless cause much hilarity amongst many mainlanders. I've heard that over there they have a lot of amateur builders, men, usually, who are never happy unless they're erecting extensions, garages, sun lounges and such like, often to the annoyance of their neighbours. Really, though, in many cases it's a form of inferiority complex which compels the layman to show off their prowess to others.'

'While I wouldn't disagree with your diagnosis,' Andrew interjected, 'I'm a mainlander and I think you'll find so many professional builders over there are unreliable that those amateurs have little choice, also a lot of them improve their homes so they can sell them on at a far greater price than they paid for them.'

After apologising to him for criticising his homeland, which Andrew waived aside, Paul continued, 'Of course, similar effects of inferiority, in cases where it has been established are almost unknown on our island, but if they were common then the sufferers would be encouraged to construct and paint models instead; you'd be surprised at the intricacy and the skill required to produce a simple miniature building, and the sense of achievement afterward can be quite considerable.'

'It wouldn't hurt our various addicts, either,' Andrew muttered dryly.

Paul went on to explain about how the model railway had brought about an entirely unexpected bonus which had led to the founding of a considerable global export industry. 'The decision to construct a layout encouraged the designers to take a critical look at what was happening in the whole of the model railway industry worldwide, and it immediately became apparent that many areas weren't being covered. For not only were a large number of locomotive classes, carriages and wagons from the mainland railways not being represented, but neither were many different related buildings, nor with regard to other populous and wealthy nations where an interest in model layouts of their home designs might be expected.

'So with concern to the latter market, our authorities decided to test that particular possibility by producing a few lengths of different gauge track, together with matching rolling stock, to see whether they'd prove popular and, naturally, where they found the take up was encouraging they stepped up production. In the event a number of outlets which no previous manufacturers had dreamed about were generated and, with the obvious outcome, our railway modelling industry has now become a world leader.

'Whether or not for mainland, and thus island, markets or for those abroad, our modellers considered many of the designs already available were capable of improvement. Those model buildings available, for instance, were either made from printed coloured cardboard and therefore not particularly realistic, or even if they were constructed of impressed plastic and thus more lifelike, they usually catered for enthusiasts of a particular railway company, or else were freelance. So an entire new range of railway fittings, rolling stock and buildings was subsequently produced for export, and they proved to be a great success. Come and see.'

He led them over to another section of the table where he showed them a length of model station platform with a number of small holes in the upper face. 'This piece can be embossed in one of four ways, either to represent concrete, wood, brick or stonework; the same applies to the station buildings.' Picking up one of the latter to demonstrate, he observed, 'You can see how deeply the individual bricks have been moulded; now look.' He pressed a piece of grey modelling clay into the joints and wiped the excess away, instantly each tiny brick stood out in fine detail. Next, he pushed the building onto the holes in the platform indicating, as he did so, how the structure could be allocated almost anywhere along the platform's length. The remainder of the holes he filled with station fittings such as newsagent's kiosks, gas lamps, toilet blocks, fencing and nameboards; even people, luggage, milk churns and platform trolleys.

'There you are, folks,' Paul declared, putting the completed model down on the table, 'all ready for the next train. In this way,' he continued, gesturing toward the tiny station, 'model railway fans can not only alter their platform layouts, for example, but can also have several different stations which can be changed around as wished. No other model railway manufacturer has got anything to touch it, so we've virtually cornered the market.' He went on to produce many other delightful realistic models explaining, as he did so, that they were constructed in another island town but delivered to the engine shed for detailed painting, the application of transfers and miniature advertisements, and also packaging.

Andrew glancing at the other people round the table observed, 'You must all be worked to death.'

Chuckling, Paul replied, 'Our main factory is over on the other side of the partition, behind the display engines; this little group is just here to show the kinds of finished products we manufacture and to answer any queries regarding railway matters. We regularly rotate around the table so we have turns in dealing with visitors; it helps to break up what can often become a tedious task.'

Finally, having shown them more of the stock, Julie asked in a way which reminded her sweetheart of a mother with an over-indulged son, 'Now, I was wondering if you could show us an illustrated book which has a list of island steam locomotives, and also one with the former classes of the mainland railways?'

Andrew considered this request an extremely tall order, but Paul apparently didn't for he went off without comment and soon returned bearing the relevant books. He looked on bemused as his lover then bought the volumes and handed them to him; he could scarcely contain his impatience as they thanked their considerate guide, but at last he was able to take Julie by the hand and lead her behind the backboard facing the glass partition and the great engine beyond. There he set about thanking her for her gifts in a fashion which no normal mother would countenance from a son but eventually, giggling uncontrollably, she pushed him away. 'I bet you can't identify "Grove Spring" from your mainland book,' she challenged finally, 'but no looking at numbers.'

They sat down on a conveniently sited bench, still with the mainland station name on the backrest, and he began to peruse the pages: a formidable task as there were numerous photos and descriptions within. At first he began to look at each picture in turn but then, after studying the lines of the actual locomotive in some detail, and realising it was one of the more modern styles and an express engine, he also whittled the problem down even more by noting that certain locomotives of a particular railway resembled it in many ways; especially with regard to its eight wheeled, large rectangular coal carrier. 'Here it is,' he exclaimed triumphantly.

'Brilliant!' she answered without irony, 'now see if you can determine which class of engine you like best. No, I've got a much better idea; let's have one more tour of the model railway and then we'll go and have a drink somewhere. That way you'll be able to decide at your leisure.'

In the event they patronised a restaurant where Julie donated their catch, some of which was returned to them in the form of a meal at much reduced cost; afterwards they repaired to the pub of the night before where, as it wasn't a busy time they were able to drink in the first rate's cabin. Over a pint of bitter Andrew studied the photographs of steam engines; eventually he said, 'Do you know, darling, there are some real beauties here, yet in the final analysis I think I prefer the "Grove Spring" type best, especially the version with the double chimney. It's got austere lines, seems strong, and from the point of view of usefulness it's apparently equally at home on express passenger or fast freight trains.'

His lover sat back and gazed at him with an expression of amused tolerance on her face. 'In that case,' she observed, 'perhaps when your birthday comes along I'll buy one for you.'

Glancing down at his book, he remarked, 'According to this they were all named after race horses; so if you did buy me one I'd get a couple of plates made up bearing the legend "Auburn Lover",' Julie actually blushed at this statement, but her companion frowned and said, 'But I haven't got a layout, so I wouldn't be able to see it working.'

She smiled and stretched a hand across to him. 'Yes you have. You've just seen it. People often possess their own models and phone in whenever they want to exercise them. It's a bit complicated though, apparently, so we'll need to get the details later.'

Andrew took her hand and gave it a gentle squeeze. 'Why are you doing this for me, darling? I mean, I'm quite willing to share your hobbies but if I took this one up you might not want to share in it and it could, therefore, cause a rift between us.'

She laughed. 'Running a model locomotive on a miniature railway layout hardly constitutes a hobby. Besides, we can share our pastimes, if you wish to take an active part in railway modelling then I can see no reason why I shouldn't want to as well. Don't worry, my love, there'll need to be a lot of give and take on both sides of our relationship.'

That evening, having returned to their flat, they cooked a simple meal and then Julie introduced her lover to a method of love-making which was to remain a firm favourite with him. After placing the mattress in the exact centre of the bedroom she set the wall lamps in sequence so that each wall lamp would deliver its colour for a period and then change over to the next hue, then they removed their clothing and while Andrew poured out two liberal glasses of wine she selected a classical c.d. featuring the works of various composers. 'Now,' she explained before they coupled, 'every time the music changes we alter position; the trick is that you shouldn't climax before the disc ends. It's a bit like compassing, so you'll really have to keep yourself under control; can you guess what this is called?'

'Rainbowing?' he suggested hopefully.

She giggled and replied, 'Right on target.'

During the half hour or so which followed he found himself in a weird world where endeavouring to control himself wrestled with the influence of the ever-changing room colours and the varied rhythmic and melodious tones of the music; altering their position only made his experience feel even more bizarre. The only way he could refrain from finishing too early, he discovered, was to ensure Julie and he remained locked closely together thereby permitting him only the minimal amount of movement where it mattered. Apart from his sweetheart's murmuring twice each time he'd satisfied her, she remained silent and impassive except when it was time to roll over. Only when she'd finally pleased him did he kiss and thank her profusely for the overwhelming fresh sensation she'd introduced him to.

Over the next weeks the lovers continued to settle down together, getting to know their partners' foibles and mannerisms, and gradually becoming even more enamoured with each other. Andrew could never get enough of his sweetheart's company and he didn't care what they did just as long as they were together. Julie obtained, quite legitimately, written information which would help him to attain statehood and she was tireless in preparing him for their mutual desire by working alongside him, explaining various requirements of him and questioning him to ensure he remembered and understood what was expected of him.

Often she sat with her back against the headboard as he lay across the bed with his head in her lap and she repeatedly questioned him about what he'd learnt, not ceasing until she was sure he'd taken in everything he'd need to know, even though he might previously have answered correctly several days before. Whether or not it had something to do with the pleasing position in which his interrogation took place, he found he could recall much more than what he'd expected of himself, and perhaps that had been his lover's intention.

Despite Sue and Trevor's company and friendship together with the pastimes which kept him occupied in the afternoons, he continued to miss Julie badly. When they were in each other's company once more, whether out shopping, visiting, being entertained, having a meal or in bed, he felt himself to be in paradise; failing to become a Whyte Islander via the exams was an impossibility for him and he longed for the day when he could think of himself as an island citizen so that, for a while at least, they could spend more evenings together.

Of great help to him during this period was, above all else

strangely enough, the book entitled "Living Together" which he'd previously heard about after the blue school sex demonstration. Julie introduced him to it in her typically jocular fashion for, after he'd escorted her to the ferry one afternoon not long after they'd been zig-zagged, she turned and casually said, 'Oh, I've cancelled your appointments up to this evening because I've left you a little present on the bed, I'm sure you'll find that much more interesting.' At the top of the gangway she waved and smiled her goodbye, but in retrospect Andrew was certain that smile had been more of a smirk.

Her gift proved to be a key with a label attached informing him it opened the secret drawer, and on inspection he discovered it contained the book in question; not understanding quite why it should be worth more than his usual pastimes he innocently took it along to the lounge and began to peruse its pages in comfort. He subsequently found it to be fascinating and extremely provocative, and far more so than the books on sex in the bookcase. For apart from passages outlining the more obvious pitfalls of a heterosexual relationship and advice on how to avoid them, there were large tracts concerning bedroom ethics, descriptions of the more sensitive parts of the body, the psychological make up of each gender, various ways of arousing one's partner, different positions for intercourse, and even the safest methods of rendering a person helpless and mute whilst in a variety of postures.

There were articles on the human physique, first aid, cosmetics, contraception and in fact anything considered essential with regard to a pair of lovers in their search for the perfect partnership. Even on their own many of the subjects would've been considered highly erotic, but when they were accompanied by the explicit and finely detailed sketches, diagrams and photographs with which the book abounded, Andrew found them beyond endurance.

He studied the extremely realistic illustrations with mounting excitement until he was eventually compelled to relieve his frustration; on his return he discarded the source of his discomfort, but like an addict he was soon examining the pictures once more. His agitation finally became so great that he went for a very long walk after a cold shower, then at the appointed time he called on the Russell family far too early only to find them still at their evening meal. What they all did on that occasion he never could remember, but he recalled with startling clarity the way he'd snatched Julie away from her slave girl companions upon the arrival of the ferry. His lover always laughed at the event whenever she related how she'd glanced back, as he'd carried her off, to where their friends were staring after them open mouthed.

Just like a mad man with one objective in his mind, he'd borne her swiftly back to their flat, thrown her onto the bed, roughly pulled her dress up and her underwear down and ravished her without recourse to the necessary polite overtures. His lover, after a half hearted attempt at telling him how hungry she was, had treated the experience as most amusing and entirely acceptable and, latterly, had displayed her approval by giggling, kissing, grunting, biting, snorting, licking, laughing, pinching and wrestling with him until his frustrated desire had totally evaporated which was long in coming given his earlier exertion.

'You bitch,' he exclaimed after he'd finished panting, 'you knew that book would've affected me like that!'

Julie said nothing, but left the bed and returned with "Living Together." Turning to the title page she ran a finger nail beneath the words "Designed to inform and excite". 'At least,' she laughed, 'it was far better that your simulated rape. Anyway, I'm starving so on this occasion, only, we'll dine in bed.' And she went off to fetch the meal she'd brought back from the villa.

Henceforth the book was only to be made available when Julie was present. 'Because,' as she'd explained, 'you might not wait for me.' But they spent many a happy hour together examining its contents, and Andrew's sweetheart encouraged him to peruse and memorise every detail so they'd be able to bring their love making to a high degree of sensuality. In this manner he learnt how to become an expert lover, thereby improving their relationship immensely. A device which she allowed him to discover for himself he found inside a pocket in the book's back cover during an early examination, and it was to add even more variety to their sexual activities.

'What's this?' he asked, holding up a plastic disc some three inches in diameter with numerous half round notches cut into its periphery.

'The key to additional sensuality,' she joked, and she put

down the book she was reading and came across to him. Taking "Living Together" from him she turned to the end pages. 'No doubt you've noticed this list of sex games; as you can see, they're individually numbered and there are sixteen altogether. Now, if you look on the disc you'll see an indented line running from the centre hole to each tooth; on one side of each line there's an embossed odd number, with an even one on the opposite side. They also go up to sixteen.' Feeling inside the book's back cover, she withdrew a piece of plastic the size and shape of a short pencil, this she inserted into the disc's centre hole. Placing the resultant spinning top on an adjacent table she gave it a quick flick, and they both watched earnestly as it gyrated about the smooth surface until it slowed imperceptibly and finally toppled over onto its side.

'But which number do I choose?' Andrew exclaimed after examining the two points resting on the table top.

'Do you think it's a nice day for field sports?'

He glanced at the rain soaked window. 'Definitely not.'

'Well then,' Julie smiled, 'you'll want the even number because they're all for inside games. Read it out.' She listened intently to his description then checked the clock. 'I think we can manage to fit it in before I have to go out, and the kitchen is as good a place as any.'

'But who's the aggressor?'

She gave him a malignant smirk. 'The person who spins the top always is, at least in this home. Never mind, darling, it'll be your turn next time.'

By comparison, as Andrew was later to discover, the outdoor versions were far more intricate and time consuming, requiring much more initiative from the assailant who needed to ensure they were conducted where maximum privacy would be guaranteed. And so, very occasionally, they employed the services of the zigzagging team who were only too willing to provide venues and timetables.

In the meantime he awaited with increasing impatience the arrival of his examination summons; despite Mr. Maynard's promise that his lover and he wouldn't be parted he required the assurance which membership of the island's community would bring. Only then could he seriously consider his plan to work on the railway, or contemplate a permanent relationship with the girl he adored. It therefore came as a great pleasure to both when, five days after their sailing expedition, a bulky envelope arrived on their door mat. Julie, overjoyed, handed it to him at the breakfast table, and with much excitement he tore the envelope open and quickly scanned the contents.

Later, they sat down and studied the text in far greater detail; Andrew thought the most interesting section of the documents to be the preamble, for after inviting him to take his examinations for Whyte Island citizenship and informing him in quite complementary terms as to why he had been considered, it warned him about what he'd be getting himself into: "You will be required to renounce citizenship of any other nation," it read, "You must obey without question any orders which might be given you by people in authority, and accept all the legislation, tenets and practices of Whyte Island, and must expect to give your life in her defence if called upon. In return you will be accepted entirely as a true born Whyte Islander with similar privileges and opportunities. Should you prove unworthy of our trust you may expect to be deported, though not necessarily to the country of your choice."

There followed a long list of conditions to his becoming a citizen, each one of which had to be signed, then countersigned by a Whyte Islander who, naturally enough, would be his lover. She even managed to make a game of this by sitting on his lap and kissing him every time she took the pen from him. 'Hang on,' he laughed, when they were half way through, 'we'll never get finished at this rate.' But he wasn't too annoyed when she disregarded him.

'Is that it?' he asked when she finally put down the pen.

Playfully ruffling his hair, she smiled, 'Bless you, no, you've still got your exams which, judging by our mock ones, you should sail through and we've got to face the acceptance board too.'

'We?' he echoed.

'Well, you don't think I'd let you go on your own, do you?' She raised a hand to prevent his comment. 'In matters of state it's my right as an islander to go where I like; even to the toilet with Mr Maynard if need be.'

'Sometimes,' Andrew said, gazing at her lovingly, 'you're

more of a mother and friend to me than a lover.'

'I always thought a lover was supposed to be fully inclusive of everything,' Julie replied innocently. 'As soon as I realised I loved you I naturally thought of all the advantages I could bring you, much more than what you could do for me. Love shouldn't be selfish; because we're not taught to be.' Placing a kiss on his forehead, she added, 'And the sooner we send these papers back, the sooner you become a citizen.'

That afternoon, encouraged by his lover, Andrew phoned Carol and Jim; he liked them both as well as the people they mixed with, but nevertheless he wasn't quite sure why he ought to be contacting them; however, if his sweetheart wished him to then he was perfectly content to do so. Jim answered his call and together they arranged for him to visit Carol and his flat that evening. It was to be the first of many similar visits and later, when his lover was free to accompany him, they became regular callers until eventually a lifelong friendship developed.

The main attraction for him was that, with the confidence which Julie, Carol and Jim together with their acquaintances began to instil in him, he discovered a part of himself he didn't know existed: that of a thinker and debater. He could never tell whether his sweetheart or her friends suspected there was a deeper side to his nature, or merely a wish to accord him hospitality and fraternity, but he was to be eternally grateful to them for allowing him the opportunity to express himself.

To begin with, just like the new children at the debate in the blue school, he was slow and reluctant to voice an opinion in front of others, but in time he began to realise that some of the comments and arguments he heard could have been put, or discussed, better by himself; increasingly he therefore took a greater part in the gatherings until one day, much to his great surprise, he found himself to be one of the foremost debaters in their small group. This was no mean achievement in a society which encouraged its members to be introspective, yet extroverted in their attitude toward life. In one way Andrew had a great advantage over his new companions and that was, as a born mainlander, he could constantly compare Whyte Island's way of life to that of the mainland.

Carol and Jim's flat was the unofficial rendezvous for the

beginning of the group's nightly activities; it was all extremely informal, but it was understood that a phone call by anyone before nine p.m. on a night convenient to the couple would usually find them at the disposal of their caller. Apart from that, one never knew how many people, or whom, would make up the party, or where the group would move off to or what exactly they'd do when they'd got there; the only thing certain was a great deal of enjoyment would be had at the expense of no one.

One day, Andrew, still feeling his way, made a simple observation which was to set off along a lengthy discussion. They were seated around a large table in a local hostelry, some seven couples in all with Andrew, minus his lover, being the odd man out; after listening to the arguments and the banter being passed about, and studying the respective speakers in a detached fashion, he suddenly commented, 'If you lot were in a mainland pub you'd probably be treated with a great deal of suspicion in many areas.' Every individual seated at the table was on the alert for such a statement, for they were the germ of great conversation, so it was scarcely surprising his remark was immediately taken up.

'Why?' asked a girl, quicker than the others.

'From the appearance of most of you,' he replied, 'all beards and beads, and your very relaxed mien. Many people would think, at least, you were drug addicts and ne'er do wells; and at most a subversive element in one way or another.'

'No one, including the authorities, would have anything to fear from us,' laughed a man, 'and that's because we have everything we want and need, we're happy and free.'

But his explanation was objected to by another young man. 'You're wrong there, Joe. We aren't free; in fact we're extremely oppressed. We're not permitted to get married until the junior partner is twenty five, we can't have children when we like and then no more than two, if we're lucky. We can't own cars or motor bikes, televisions or our own homes and we can't negotiate wages. In theory there are many things people on the mainland, for example, can do which we're not allowed to. But we're a superior society to theirs, presumably, otherwise Andrew wouldn't want to live here.'

'My sweetheart's over here,' reminded the object of his last remark, which caused some amusement.

But the young man went on, 'You are right, Joe, in the other respect; we are happy, and we've got everything we need. These are considerations which ought to precede the term "freedom" that revolutionaries are always referring to.'

'Yes,' answered a girl whose name Andrew knew to be Pauline, 'Tony's quite correct, we haven't got freedom, yet paradoxically, we've got the greatest democracy in the modern world. Each one of us has a far greater chance of influencing our government than the average person in any other land has with theirs; the fact that none of us wants to is a reflection on how successful our society is. Take your assumed democracy, Andrew.'

At which several of their companions murmured, 'Please do.'

'All your electorate has is the right to vote for the political party of their choice which,' Pauline continued, 'at the present, is just two plus an outside runner no one seems to take seriously. But after the chosen party has been selected all power is devolved on them, so in reality all the electorate has in the form of democracy is to opt for which dictatorship they prefer. Some terrible decisions have been taken on behalf of the mainland people which have caused them much suffering in one way or another. That just couldn't happen on Whyte Island where we all have the right to question and prevent any decision the authorities might consider, and the latter have to explain in much detail just what benefit it would bring to our nation.'

A golden haired beauty named Jenny observed, 'I think the way our authority takes the trouble to explain and demonstrate to us the reasons for its policies at an early age has a lot to do with our compliance to its wishes. For example, I love kids and ordinarily I might want to give birth to half a dozen and probably at far too young an age.' Her husband pulled a face at these remarks. 'But I've been taught the terrible results which this selfish longing would eventually have on the community; just as my Gordon would love to own a car.'

'The whole point of it all,' observed Tony, 'is that because we're all contented we're not going to cause trouble. Not one of us here would attempt to overthrow the state because none of us could do any better, and in the unlikely event our island produced a revolutionary they wouldn't get very far because they wouldn't find anyone to support them; especially within our circle, because if anyone here heard about such a person they'd shop them. Wouldn't we?'

Everybody murmured their approval, and Jim exclaimed, 'To our eyes, Andy, the paranoia exhibited by the most powerful of the world's leaders toward communityism and other, to them, revolutionary ideals is absolutely ridiculous, really insane; because they shouldn't be sabre rattling and troubling themselves with the social affairs of other nations, instead they should be concerning themselves with their own internal problems, and possibly those of poorer countries where they feel a dangerous situation could arise. As has already been suggested, it's only due to their own incompetence and basic lack of understanding of such factors as economics and the requirements of their own populaces that makes revolution such a threat in the minds of politicians and people of state.

'Take a look at your own land, Andy. Your politicians presumably opted for a nation so grossly overpopulated and without enough employment to go round and, therefore, lots of people unhappy for a myriad of reasons, rather than a small population, as we have, with plenty of work for those who needed it and prosperity for all. And, regarding your country, all without having recourse to the electorate to discover what they really wanted; so, therefore, no one in their right mind could really refer to the mainland as being a truly democratic nation. Anyway, Martin, mugs and glasses are getting low and so it's time for your lovely mistress and you to set 'em up.'

Even after the drinks had been supplied the topic wasn't allowed to drop, for Joe, the first person to reply to Andrew's observation, took up Jim's theme but via Jenny. 'She hit upon a point, but perhaps without realising it. Too many people within a community often results in trouble, especially where more than one religion, or even a sect within that belief, is involved; for it often happens that each denomination vies with the other in size of population for fear of being outnumbered. This is particularly disturbing where a high birth rate is the norm. In that situation the only solution to the problem would be to encourage each side to adopt a low birth rate, otherwise ill feeling progressing to a bloody civil war could develop which might have an unfortunate effect far beyond the boundaries of the country involved. Often the root cause of the trouble is lack of jobs, housing and food, all major effects of overpopulation.'

A middle aged man, a well-respected member of the circle who, along with his wife, had remained a silent observer, suddenly said, 'Actually, you've got a number of different examples of the problems overpopulation brings emanating, at this very moment, from many areas of the world. One particular part was once under developed and almost devoid of human settlement until overseas settlers arrived, and not only did these newcomers farm the land successfully but they also discovered extremely rich and varied mineral deposits which, doubtless, would have remained unexploited without their expertise and drive.

'Now the original inhabitants, who came from far and wide to profit from the discoveries and skill, are threatening to appropriate the land and its wealth to which they've contributed little except to provide labour, simply because they've been far more prolific than the settlers. Many have been living in squalid conditions in cities, towns and shanty towns because the authorities have been so overwhelmed by the numbers concerned that they can't cope with their welfare. So these unfortunate people, not having failed to notice how much better the settlers are fairing than they are, have got it into their heads that if they deposed them, then they would have a similar standard of living.

'But they haven't understood that they, themselves, are living beyond their means by having, on average, the size of family which they can ill afford. It's therefore quite possible that once they've gained control they'll squander the wealth, and degrade or eliminate the people originally responsible for providing them with employment; but whatever happens, the great majority still won't be better off in the long term because overpopulation ultimately engenders poverty.'

'A typical example of killing the goose which laid the golden egg, Pat,' someone suggested.

The middle aged man nodded and sipped his beer. 'Another area,' he continued, adding ominously, 'and one not far from here, was already well developed and adequately populated when settlers were allowed in without the permission of the majority of the inhabitants. The only valid reason for bestowing citizenship upon them as far as the average person could tell seemed to be due to an ability to proliferate, which had caused them to help overpopulate their own countries in the first place; certainly they weren't superior in any way to the original natives but instead appeared to be more volatile and paranoiac by comparison. Now they are apparently reproducing at a faster rate than the original inhabitants while the political leaders of the country in question seem to be intent on concealing this development and have enlisted the media into helping to disguise the problems now being created.'

'Would these prolific people be akin to those in the first example, Pat?' Carol enquired.

'Some of them are.'

The originator of the previous adage mentioned another, 'Sounds like a case of what's yours is ours, and what's ours is our own.'

Pat smiled, then continued, 'Both examples have resulted in ill feeling, death and destruction and can have no foreseeable peaceful solution. But I'll give you one more example; this time, though, where two rival religious groups have fought each other over a tract of land and one side had been driven out. A neighbouring state, religiously sympathetic toward the resultant refugees, has set up temporary camps for their reception; but instead of making do with what they've got, improving their lot and keeping their population size down so they could perhaps merge into their new country, they've increased in numbers until the conditions in their camps have become intolerable, thereby resulting in severe internal pressures. However, rather than blame themselves, they're taking their problems out on the remainder of the world in acts of indiscriminate terrorism.'

Drinking some more beer to allow his information to take effect, Pat continued, 'Now, you've got three instances of the types of problem which overpopulation can cause. In the first example, it should be made clear to the settlers who developed the country that it's in the best interests of everyone to ensure the original inhabitants don't outnumber them unduly. And the latter should realise the settlers ought to be left alone to continue creating wealth for the benefit of both parties, and they should keep their own population in check.'

'In the second case, the original inhabitants should have been made aware that the immigrants were detrimentally beginning to affect the health and wealth of the nation by their proliferation, and it shouldn't have been brushed under the carpet by the politicians who caused the damage in the first place, and the latter ought to be warned that if they threatened the numerical superiority of the natives and continued to cause trouble, then they'd quite likely be oppressed or suppressed at some future date.'

'Finally, in the third example, if the refugees don't put their house in order, lower their population and make do with what they've got, then their global terrorist activities will bring them retribution from any one of numerous quarters.'

There was a brief silence while everyone waited to see if Pat had finished, then Tony commented, 'What seems obvious from what Pat was saying is that throughout the world the public doesn't seem to appreciate overpopulation is basically the prime cause of much of the planet's strife. It's quite possible people might not mind having their homes burgled, their wives raped or their husbands murdered, their daughters kidnapped, their sons mugged. They might not care about having their politicians assassinated, their buildings bombed, their service personnel and police killed and their transport hijacked. But the people really ought be told that overpopulation inevitably leads to despair and envy which engenders violence, crime and acts of terrorism.'

'I despise those who have large families,' stated Jim, 'and then complain because it results in poor living conditions and lack of jobs. They expect others to run around helping them, to give them preference in housing and employment, and act like spoilt brats when they don't get their own way.'

Pauline observed, 'That sort of thing happens on an international scale, vast sums of money have been poured into some overpopulated countries in the form of aid and misguided loans, it's then been entirely swallowed up, and those nations have then asked for more. They accuse wealthy states of being insensitive, and conveniently forget it's due to their own stupidity that they remain poor themselves; it's about time affluent nations stopped giving their wealth away which, in presumed democratic countries, ought rightfully belong to the people, and started to export advice and expertise instead. As far as terrorism is concerned, if the world doesn't recognise the menace of overpopulation soon then one of these days a group of terrorists is going to start playing with nuclear weapons, many of them are fanatical enough to.'

'It's a sobering thought,' commented Hilda, Pat's wife, 'if you'll forgive the unintentional pun, that one day the entire life structure of this planet could be rendered extinct because of a lot of morons who wouldn't, couldn't or weren't permitted to use contraceptives.'

Jim chuckled. 'Take the Christian religion; its namesake could've almost been described as a communist, but he's found favour more with capitalists, and now these pro-capitalist religions are blindly supporting communism by providing the grounds for discontent through overpopulation. They don't appear to realise when people are starving they've nothing to lose by resorting to terrorism and revolution.'

Andrew asked, 'Do you really believe contraception on a worldwide scale would defuse a situation where a full scale war might be inevitable?'

'Well, it would certainly help,' replied Tony, 'at least it would probably stop people from wanting to join a revolutionary group; but as I mentioned before, in our society we go one better than that, for not only are islanders unlikely to support such people but it's doubtful we could even produce a revolutionary for them to follow. You see, Andrew, if you look at the really great men in history, although that adjective doesn't necessarily mean they were particularly humane, you will almost certainly discover that some hidden drive had taken them to the height of greatness. Now, if you are as familiar with psychology as all islanders are you'll generally discover something abnormal in that drive which has almost certainly emanated from some traumatic emotional experience during childhood.'

'Like what?' Andrew enquired when he realised Tony wasn't going to add any more.

The young man took a long, slow drink of his beer. 'Like being ignored, or being badly treated by one or both parents, siblings or schoolmates, and almost inevitably persistent a in nation. This is usually the basis for what is known as an inferiority complex and in certain cases it can be responsible for an intense compulsion to show people, and society in general, that the recipient is someone to be reckoned with.'

Pauline addressed Andrew, 'Are you familiar with our ideas on hereditary instincts and environmental influences?'

'I ought to be,' he replied doubtfully, 'I've had it explained to me enough times.'

'Well,' she continued, 'when a naturally headstrong personality is exposed to continual oppression at an early age the results can be frightening and overwhelming. And this explains how history can throw up dictators who, often from a lowly position have, through fanatical determination, risen to the height of power. Such dictators have rarely known when to stop and have, therefore, often been responsible for horrific wars. Self-made millionaires are another example, and they, too, often continue to make money until the day they die; abnormal obsessions in both cases.'

'So you see, Andrew,' commented Tony, 'because our authorities place so much emphasis on parental responsibilities, on teaching the "Y's" and encouraging people to examine their own minds, hopefully no one is faced with oppression in any form and so there is little danger of a would be subversive or dictator arising, and certainly not of one establishing themself here.'

Andrew was fortunate enough, on that occasion, to have companionship on the ride home, for Jenny and Gordon travelled most of the way back with him; but he was barely in time to reach the quayside before the ferry carrying his lover arrived. 'So what have you been up to today?' she enquired during their embrace. He told her about his visit to Carol and Jim's, and the subsequent debate about anarchy and psychology; but it was the latter subject which caught Julie's interest.

'The human psyche,' she stated as they walked back to the flat, 'is quite easy to understand if you compare it to a vehicle engine, for example; if it's been well built, and then maintained properly, it should give no trouble and so will be simple to comprehend. But if it's been badly constructed, or hasn't been treated properly then an amazing variety of problems may occur which are difficult to diagnose and repair, and that's where the mechanic or psychiatrist, as the case may be, comes into their own; for each one would hate their particular forte to be too well constructed or maintained.'

Julie had brought back another example of Roman culinary art, and as they ate their miniature feast she raised the subject of religious wars. 'It makes me so angry,' she exclaimed, jabbing the air with an unauthentic fork to stress her words, 'because it's so unnecessary; if both communities kept their populations down there wouldn't be any problems. Have you ever considered, darling, that contemporary societies with their reliance upon, and access to, modern appliances and methods have more in common with each other than with their forebears?

'I mean, through the religions which they may follow they're forbidden to eat this or that on such and such a day and have to follow all sorts of peculiar rules and regulations; and yet, at the same time they've been absolutely seduced by modern techniques and customs.' She reached across the table and offered him a morsel on her fork. 'Try this,' she urged, and then continued, 'The ancestors of these various religious groups would doubtless be mortified if they could see what has happened to their various descendants. You could almost imagine a scenario where modern rival sects in uneasy truce undertook a journey together and came across a forgotten valley wherein dwelt their respective forebears, each still antagonistic with regard to each other. Upon the appearance of the combined host of newcomers fear might easily encourage the ancestors to band together as one to fight off the intruders without question, and the modern people to band together in self-defence; so what price different religions, then?

Supposing certain religious mystics of ancient times were possessed of crystal balls and foresaw aircraft, guns, massive ships, computers, televisions, motor vehicles, fridges and all the other paraphernalia of modern living which, if they'd really been special people, they should've been to, and through lack of understanding, forbade their use in their holy books, do you think their direct descendants would've obeyed their instructions to the letter?' She went on without waiting for an answer, 'Of course they wouldn't; when necessity comes along tradition goes out the window. So why don't these religious zealots bow to the inevitable and accept all the other aspects of contemporary civilization, like contraception, when they appear?'

'After all, if it's alright for someone to use a sophisticated guided missile in order to kill people indiscriminately, then surely it ought to be permissible to employ birth control to prevent an unwanted life. Incidentally, sweetheart, we islanders think that when religious differences result in the maiming of innocent people and wholesale destruction of property then it's about time it was abandoned. No religion is worth dying for, and it's only the selfish bigotry of the religious leaders which keeps it alive.'

While they were putting the supper things away Julie asked her lover how he felt. 'A bit tipsy after those pints, and a little tired,' he replied.

'Well, how about a nice little refreshing walk?'

'But, darling,' he protested, 'it's gone midnight.'

She slapped his rump playfully and commanded, 'Go and make up a bundle of a couple of blankets, a pillow and a towel, and don't ask any questions.'

Despite Andrew's continuing dissent they eventually left the flat and set off along the esplanade under a starlit heaven and a full moon, in the direction of the dam.

'Where are we going?' he finally asked.

'For a swim, and perhaps other things.'

'But we haven't brought any gear; and we'll be seen, it's almost like daylight!'

Julie laughed. 'Don't worry, the kiddies and their parents are all abed, and any lovers about won't be interested in us.' And she added, 'There aren't any voyeurs on Whyte Island because everyone's got someone they can spy on, in the form of their partners.'

By the time they'd reached a place which met with her approval her lover had become so accustomed to the idea he was now quite enamoured of it. He watched with interest as she laid one of the blankets out on the sand and then placed the pillow at the end furthest from the water, after which she began removing her clothing. 'Come on my sweet Adonis,' she urged, turning toward him as she unclipped her brassiere, 'divest yourself.'

Finally, completely naked, they waded hand in hand into the pleasantly warm water until it almost reached Julie's chest. 'We mustn't go out too far,' he warned.

But she answered confidently, 'It won't get any deeper because of the barrier protecting us from the main body of the reservoir. Come on,' and suddenly she was swimming away from him. Andrew, after a few second's hesitation, followed after her and together they struck out for the barrier where, as soon as they'd stumbled up the slope gasping and laughing, they sat down and put their arms about each other; the surface hardly touched their bodies, but their legs from the knees down were totally immersed where they rested on the gentle incline descending into the shallow side of the lake.

The promenade lights had been extinguished even before they'd ventured out on their stroll, and so they'd been compelled to use a torch to seek a place devoid of rocks; now, as they gazed shoreward the moonlight shone vaguely on the concrete esplanade and the sandy beach. So both lovers took comfort in the knowledge that, from where they sat, they'd scarcely be visible from the shore; silently they turned to each other, and slowly they bent their heads together until their half open mouths met in an enduring kiss. Andrew felt his sweetheart's right breast gently touching his chest, so he began moving his trunk sideways to caress it. 'I love you so much,' he murmured in her ear.

She made no answer but instead disengaged herself from his arms and lowered her body further into the water until only her face, shining wanly in the ethereal light, appeared above the surface. 'You're a diver,' she informed him, 'see what treasure you can discover.'

Her companion, understanding, turned and slipped out into the water; after taking a deep breath he submerged and came back to where she lay, he felt his way up her body and pressed his mouth against her left breast feeling for the nipple with his tongue. He remained gently biting and sucking at her until he could hold his breath no longer; then he raised his head, took in another lungful of air, and repeated the performance, but on her right breast this time where he also employed his hands to squeeze and manipulate it.

'Well?' she enquired after he'd dived numerous times.

'A couple of very interesting submerged mountains,' he informed her. 'But I wasn't the first to explore them!'

Suddenly serious she asked, 'Oh, and how do you know that?'

'Because someone's built small huts, on the summits.'

'Try diving deeper,' she suggested, her body now trembling with mirth.

'What did you discover?' she asked again when he eventually surfaced.

'A cave,' he panted, 'I explored it thoroughly, though.'

'That's no good,' she replied in mock disgust, 'keep trying.' After many more attempts she finally said, 'That'll do, darling; I highly commend you as a first rate diver: you've got a certain feeling for it.' She gave him a brief kiss. 'Now you stay up here while I have a go: I've had it on good authority there's a sunken city in the vicinity.'

She splashed about in front of Andrew for a few minutes, and then she was gone; almost immediately he felt each of her hands cup his knees and remain anchored there. "Oh, my love," he thought as he stared, glassy eyed, up into the sky at the moon and seemingly countless stars, while the word "heaven" ran incessantly through his mind.

Finally his sweetheart reappeared. 'I think I've found it,' she gasped, 'There's a half collapsed column protruding from some weed. I'm going to see if I can raise it.'

She drew a deep breath and submerged again, and he was certain that, given time, she would succeed in her attempt; she dived repeatedly until he eventually exclaimed, 'Darling, with my discovery of two mountains, a grand gorge and a cave, and yours of an ancient pillar, I think we should unite and produce a paper on the event.'

'That's a very good idea, professor,' she giggled, and promptly lay down with her head above water resting on the barrier slope; and as she carefully drew her lover down onto her she innocently enquired, 'Have you got your pen ready?'

As they lay clasped together on their sides, quite exhausted after labouring diligently at their work until they'd come to a satisfactory conclusion, Andrew asked, 'Supposing we'd rolled the wrong way, my love; would we drown?'

Her lips touched his. 'If we were complete idiots we might, but about a foot below the surface there's a ledge which goes out quite a long way as a warning, but then it drops sheer into the depths. The temperature difference between the ledge and the shallows this side is a good enough reason to dissuade only the most stupid from venturing across the barrier, besides which it's very weedy over there. Years ago, someone was drowned through hypothermia and since then the main lake area has been prohibited to all swimmers, even skin divers.' She paused, then turning to face him she added, 'I do love you, Andrew, and I'll never forget tonight.'

He squeezed her tightly at this remark, unaware of its true significance, then asked, 'What about fishing: would we be able to try that someday?'

Julie was full of enthusiasm. 'Of course we could, my love. There's almost as much variety in fish here as in the straits with the bonus that it's much safer, although you still need to wear a life jacket.' She laughed and added, 'And you won't be plagued by damned crabs.' After a while she observed, 'I don't know about you, love, but I've been in more comfortable spots; I feel grazed all over.' And she stood up whilst Andrew looked on in fascination; Linda's naked form by moonlight had been breathtaking but his lover's was out of this world. 'I'm cold, too,' she stated, 'but there are three ways of keeping warm over on the sands. Besides, my darling, I'm not too happy with that paper we produced and so I think we ought to have another try; it doesn't matter if we don't manage to finish tonight.'

Without another word she stepped down into the water and swam off in the direction of the promenade; he watched her progress until the invisible tie which bound them together pulled, compelling him to swim quickly after her. They emerged from the lake simultaneously and soon found their belongings, aided by the ticking of the luminous clock Julie had thoughtfully left behind to guide them. After mutually drying each other, an activity from which both derived the maximum amount of pleasure, she knelt on the blankets and searched inside her shoulder bag. 'Brandy, this time,' she explained and, after taking a swig and handing the bottle to him, she murmured, 'the first way of getting warm.'

'And the second?' he asked expectantly.

She raised the bottle to her mouth again and fondling part of his anatomy with her free hand as she did so. Without comment, after drinking her fill, she laid the vessel down and placed both hands on the blankets. 'Well?' she enquired impatiently turning her head round to look up at him; taking the hint he coupled with her. Presently she giggled. 'If you're not doing anything with your hands you can remove them from my shoulders and try manipulating the old cow's udders instead!' Afterwards, as they lay side-by-side, Julie wrapped the top blanket tenderly about them. 'Third way,' she whispered sleepily.

They certainly weren't the only ones in the vicinity spending the night out under the stars for in the direction of the dam, above the muffled sound of falling water, they could hear splashing, shouting and laughter, while on their other side a girl called plaintively to, and was answered by, her lover. As Andrew's sweetheart lay in his arms she moved her free hand delicately over his body and gently kissed every feature of his face. 'Never forget this night,' she urged softly; and her companion, as he drifted off into sleep, knew he never would.

The alarm awoke them at 4 a.m., and in the grey light of pre-dawn they dressed casually, Julie stuffing their underwear into her bag; but after consideration, she pulled out her briefs and rinsed them thoroughly at the water's edge. 'Sorry about the flannel,' she said upon her return, and without giving him time to raise any objection, she proceeded to wash her lover's face with the garment, after which she attended to herself in a similar fashion.

'Why apologise?' he laughed when she'd finished, hugging her, 'we're halves of one whole, you know that.'

Andrew carried the bundle as they walked, like a pair of automatons, back to the flat arm-in-arm; on the way they passed more than one heap of clothing marking the resting spot of a sleeping couple less bothered about the onset of daylight than they were. Julie insisted upon their both taking an aspirin and a shower before they retired to bed, although she explained there was little danger of infection from the lake's water. Sleep was strangely slow in coming to them as they lay in embrace and so he remarked, 'Putting aside the fact that you're extremely beautiful, desirable and intelligent, and that I was longing for a girl I could call my own when we met darling, I never expected to fall for someone like you.'

She murmured in sleepy contentment, 'Why, my love?'

He held a lock of her auburn hair between his fingers and studied its hue and texture intricately as he replied, 'I always imagined I'd want a serious, prim wife. What we did during the night I'd have once thought to be highly indelicate and that I couldn't respect any female who'd indulge in such behaviour; but now, because I adore you so, I enjoyed doing it. It's like when I hand wash your underwear, it seems to make us more intimate, cementing our regard for each other, bringing us closer together.'

They'd been lying on their sides facing each other, but now Julie began to insinuate herself beneath him, gradually pulling him over onto her; eventually gazing up into his eyes she stroked his hair and smiled fondly. 'When two people adore each other,' she observed at last, 'there shouldn't be any shyness between them, psychologically or physically.' She paused, and he was certain a flicker of anguish passed across her face as she added, 'Nor secrets. Sex, in all its aspects, becomes ever more satisfying the more genuine love accompanies it; but it's rather pointless when love is absent, for then it's just self-gratification.' She suddenly pulled his head down onto her golden hair, 'That's why I love you so much; I enjoy the act of making love in all its diverse ways and your love makes it, oh, so wonderful; so I want you to experience everything I have to offer.'

Her cheek transferred tears to his face as she continued, 'Besides, what we did this morning was highly recommended in a famous book which took the western world by storm before my parents had even met. Although,' she laughed, 'it didn't specifically suggest doing it under water. Now,' she exclaimed, kissing him on the nose, 'how would you like to try for a hat trick?' And she blindly stretched out an arm and cancelled the alarm.

Several days later, it being Julie's day off, they set out for her parent's home; Andrew had been a frequent visitor with his lover but this was to be the first occasion upon which the weather had been nice enough to justify the hiring of a pair of cycles. But just before they left he received a phone call from Roger Jones at the education centre informing him his companion would be receiving postal instructions with regard to their tours of the red establishments. The principal appeared to know all about his relationship with Julie and just before he rang off she delegated the making of the coffee for their journey to her sweetheart while she had a long and friendly chat with him.

Their cycles, although obviously old, were well maintained and fitted with straight handlebars, five gears, dynamos and saddle bags. 'But they're both ladies,' he'd protested in amusement when he first saw them.

But his lover had giggled, and replied, 'I never thought I'd hear you object to mounting a lady. Anyway, all island bikes are so called "ladies", silly; they're no worse than the "men's" and there's less chance of you ruining our sex life if you met with an accident, is there?'

When they eventually set off he carried a knapsack with groundsheet and waterproofs on his back, sweaters and other extra clothing in his saddlebag, whilst his sweetheart had the picnic gear stowed away behind her. Their journey took them along the esplanade, across the dam and up between the granite cliffs onto the chalk downland; and it was soon apparent to him that she'd been quite correct, for the ride was perfect. They were in no particular hurry and during the course of their ride they frequently paused to admire the view or to examine an item of special interest, for Julie could easily have added natural history to her quota of interests, as she pointed out several species of birds and butterflies along the way. For the second time in his life Andrew understood how delightful it could be to cycle along narrow lanes; to begin with there was scarcely any traffic about: between the dam and the end of the downland they met up with only three motor vehicles, apart from tractors, and two of those were stationary. And the only other people they saw were four cyclists, three people walking along the lane and a man working outside a remote cottage. From the lake the route had taken them up through the steep rocky outcrops, and so by the time they'd attained the top of the downland Andrew felt quite worn out; it therefore came as something of a relief for him to see his lover, who was several yards in front, dismount by a gate allowing access to a track. 'We'll leave our bikes here,' she said as he came up to her, 'only I'd like to show you the highest point on Whyte Island.'

As they strolled up the open trackway she pointed out a large number of alkaline tolerant plants, many of which, she claimed, were now extremely rare in his own country due to unsympathetic land management. A short walk brought them to the inevitable triangulation marker, painted white, around which a wooden bench had been fitted. He'd been half expecting to see the entire island and the mainland coast from the summit, but he was to be disappointed for a ridge behind Laketown, almost as high as the ground they were standing upon, concealed the far horizon; and in all other directions the downland undulated away, punctuated by distant hedges, stone walls, individual bushes and small copses of beech tree. But the view of the lake and its namesake town and the surrounding countryside before them was outstanding; the water, not unnaturally for a sunny Saturday morning, was dotted with steamers and sailing craft, and even from where they sat with their backs against the marker the beach and promenade could easily be seen to contain a fair number of people.

Together they identified the education centre, the Roman Villa so dear to Andrew's heart, the mansion where Helen had cried and the approximate position of their flat. During the course of their stay several trains, smoke issuing from their chimneys, passed along the embankment behind the town, and far away over the mainland huge white cloud billows edged the horizon; a gentle breeze fanned the lovers' faces and hair, and about them skylarks and pipits sang or called.

Julie said nothing as her companion unfastened the top buttons on the back of her blouse, unhooked her brassiere and pushed a hand inside her neckline; she held some sandwiches on her lap, and a cup of coffee stood on the bench beside her. Because both his hands were now occupied she fed the food and drink to both him and herself. 'Don't get too excited,' she advised, apparently unmoved by his activity, 'because that's all you're getting.'

'Isn't this turning you on?' he asked in some perplexity.

'I must admit it's pleasant enough, but as you well know tweaking one of my nipples will furnish the desired result.' She paused, then said threateningly, 'I wasn't dropping hints, I'll throw this coffee in your lap in a minute if you don't stop, and then what'll you look like?'

'There's a lot of gorse over there.'

'Pretty, isn't it?' she teased, and added, 'it's much too early, and we've got too far to go to engage in acts of passion, especially you, so control yourself.'

Changing the subject, slightly, he mused while continuing to fondle her, 'You never venture abroad without a bra, do you darling?'

'That's because I don't want to lose my figure; besides, how do you feel when you see a bra-less woman?'

He answered immediately and with great enthusiasm, 'I think how much I'd love to hold her. I feel really sexed up when I see her breasts wobble, and wow,' he whistled, 'when I see the outline of the nipples!'

She smiled triumphantly. 'You see, sweetheart, there's only one man I want to turn on, and that's you. You've doubtless noticed by now, love, that you won't normally see a braless girl, or woman, over here. If a female sets out to indiscriminately intimidate members of the opposite sex then she must expect to get a reaction, it's only fair.'

The remainder of the ride across the downland to Newtown was quite effortless for the route, although somewhat undulating, tended to descend; at one point, they cycled quite close to a huge brick windmill with a white painted structure, like an upturned dinghy, on top. Julie, noting her lover's interest, stopped her bike and got off. 'It isn't what it seems,' she remarked when he stood beside her, 'because it's actually an observatory, the wooden halves fold back to allow the telescope to function. We'll have to phone for an appointment, though, as it's a great experience.' Forestalling his inevitable question, she went on, 'The authorities considered a more conventional observatory would've been a bit of an eyesore in this area.'

'If we did do a spot of star gazing how would we get up here? It might be pouring with rain or something and we'd have to cancel; and seeing how we've only passed one other building, and that was a holiday cottage, I can't see there being a bus service.'

'See that clump of trees ahead?' she answered. Upon his nodding she continued, 'Well, just beyond there's a crossroads. You wouldn't think it from here, but this bleak downland contains a fair number of valleys some of which are inhabited, so you see, darling, there is a bus route which is centred on Newtown, and can you guess where it terminates?'

He shrugged. 'Laketown?'

'No,' she laughed, remounting her cycle. 'Outside the "Station Arms,"' she called over her shoulder as she rode off. Eventually they saw the sea shimmering into haze in the far distance with a few ships a long way out; somewhere they must have crossed the railway tunnel for after cycling between arable fields at a lower level, past cottages and once through a village, they descended a steep slope and emerged close to Newtown harbour bridge.

Mr. and Mrs. Lucas were in their rear garden enjoying the sunshine: their arrival had been expected and two extra deckchairs were already set out for them; but Julie, instead, went off and fetched a couple of cushions and sat down by her lover's feet where, after drinking a mug of tea and joining in some conversation, she laid her head upon his knees and promptly fell asleep. Jean soon went off to prepare dinner, and so the two men were left to their own devices; they conversed upon various subjects until Andrew eventually enquired, 'Do you mind not owning your own home, John?'

Julie's father smiled. 'If I'd minded I wouldn't have signed the paper accepting the regulation when I opted to become an islander. But no, I don't mind in the least; all Whyte Island householders are in the same situation, and as long as the authorities keep their promise to maintain homes in good repair then it's a wonderful plan.' He lowered the sound of music emanating from the radio a little. 'Let me relate a story,' he said. 'My father would've thoroughly agreed with our island's policy of giving love and attention and attention to one's children, but because of the selfishness and sheer laziness of many mainlanders he was unable to give my sister and I as much care as we really required.

'When my mum and he were married they had, like many other couples, the choice of either renting a property through a landlord, from the local council or else by taking out a mortgage. They rejected the first option because they didn't see why a stranger should profit from their labours, and the second because council run areas were getting a bad reputation and prompt repairs to houses weren't always guaranteed to say the least. So they put a deposit on a cheap house and took out a mortgage; the reason why they got the place so easily was because it was in such a bad state of disrepair; but my dad, who also worked overtime in his job to pay off the loan, set to and eventually turned the house and garden into a palace. However, the cost was great for the worry made him irritable and, as I've said, he rarely had time to spend on my sister, or myself when I came along.'

Andrew was deeply interested in Mr. Lucas' tale, and as he listened he quite unconsciously stroked his sweetheart's hair, just as though he had a cat on his lap. 'Anyway, as I mentioned, he completed the house and both my mum and he began to look forward to many years of relaxation and enjoyment of their house; but unfortunately some new neighbours moved in, and these were so empty headed and self-centred that they soon made my parents' life a nightmare with their continuous, inconsiderate noise and belligerent attitude; so my parents felt compelled to move on to another home.

'On the face of it, it was a good proposition for instead of being a terraced house it was semi-detached with a quite large garden; but here again the previous owners had been half stupid and half lazy, for what little work they'd carried out on the building was worse than useless, and the garden was in a mess as well. So my poor old dad had to start all over again whilst my sister and I were growing up, and silently begging for attention; but on the relatively few occasions we managed to nag him enough to persuade him to play with us or take us out he was obviously under great stress. So it was mostly left to our mum to amuse us in addition to her housework and part-time job.

'But once again my dad got a raw deal, because just as he began to get on top of all the work a right swine moved in next door, and rather than kill the pest he decided we ought to move on again. But it was the same old story, a neglected house which needed a lot of work and money expended upon it; however, this time it wasn't a rotten neighbour who moved him on when he'd finished it, it was a hearse.'

'But why on earth did he keep moving into inferior houses?' Andrew asked incredulously.

John shook his head slowly in surprise at his naivety. 'I don't know what it's like over there now, but buying and selling houses used to be a horrifying business. I can remember seeing innumerable people treading dirt all over our fitted carpets, uncivil, thoughtless, mendacious visitors who used to drive my parents wild with their comments and empty promises, many of whom doubtless had no intention of buying but were either just nosey or merely passing the time away. Eventually our parents would be only too pleased to practically give the vastly improved houses away under such treatment. And at the same time they were trying to sell their home they'd be hunting for some other place to purchase, once again from rude, thoughtless, mendacious people for the most part; legion were the times my parents had promised to buy a reasonably priced house to be told, often at the last moment, that the vendor had taken up an improved offer; finally our parents realised the easiest houses to purchase, were the ones no one else wanted, those, in fact which were in a terrible state.'

He stood up and stretched himself. 'So you can appreciate, I hope, Andrew, why I'm very glad about not having to spend all my spare time in repairing and improving this house, or worrying about selling and buying property. The danger of living next door to terrible neighbours is non-existent, nor of living on a massive housing estate for there aren't any because, if anything, our island is under populated. Instead we can live contentedly in a nice house, doing exactly as we wish without being under any pressures.' He grinned and stared down at his daughter. 'And your love and regard for Julie tells me that we and the authorities haven't gone too far astray in our attempt to raise her successfully. Well,' he added, 'I'll go and see if Jean wants a hand.'

When he'd gone Andrew bent forward and murmured, 'You can stop shamming, darling, I could see you smiling; otherwise....' and he whispered some very descriptive expletives in her ear. The result was sudden and dramatic, for she leapt to her feet and raised a fist in mock threat, but he grabbed her by her waist and she stumbled then fell on top of him, and the deckchair, unable to support their combined weight, collapsed. Neither of them was hurt, though for a long time afterward they could only lie immobile due to their hysterical laughter.

After dinner, a superb salad which Andrew didn't neglect to praise, he insisted they should all go into Newtown for a drink; but in the event they had several in various, yet highly individual, bars each of which featured different forms of entertainment. Jean Lucas wanted them to stay the night upon their return home, a wish which Andrew entirely concurred with, but Julie gave an outrageous reason for their not doing so. 'I promised Andy we'd make love under the stars at the island's highest point.' He gasped audibly at this figment of his sweetheart's imagination but John just winked at him while Jean smiled sympathetically.

As they cycled side by side through the dark and almost deserted Newtown streets, Andrew, slightly annoyed, enquired, 'Why do you tell all these tall stories, Julie? You make me feel quite embarrassed at times.'

She flashed him a smile. 'Well, you shouldn't be; I'm probably subconsciously trying to tell you nobody cares. Besides, if you don't like it you know what you can do.' He was struck dumb by this somewhat callous delivery and, sensing she'd hurt his feelings, she quickly added, 'Anyway, it happens to be true, darling; we are going to dally at the summit if you want to. I merely neglected to mention it.'

Changing the subject, he asked, 'Exactly how much did you hear of your dad's and my conversation this afternoon?'

'Most of it,' she admitted after they'd turned a corner; 'it's a sad story, especially when you consider my paternal grandfather was quite a talented man who, through his misfortunes, was unable to allow his real interests full rein. What dad was trying to explain is the island authorities are so sensible of people's requirements that they're willing to take care of all unwanted work and thereby permit everyone to get on with whatever they really prefer doing. As my dad said, granddad was so frustrated at having to undertake house repair work and gardening that it made him bad tempered against his real inclinations, and this also affected his family in various ways. But you're most unlikely to find any people on Whyte Island going around venting their disappointment on others simply because they're unable to give their talents full scope; nor parents failing to give their offspring all the love and attention they need.'

The lovers were unable to converse for some time after this, for when not toiling uphill, especially upon ascending the steep incline out of Newtown, they were allowing their cycles to freewheel down the slopes; in Andrew's case this usually meant following his sweetheart's rear light. He hadn't cycled at night since he was a youngster and it was an experience he'd long forgotten the joys of; now, under the warm, starry skies, they moved along effortlessly in the thin air, their progress being much easier than during daylight hours.

Julie was as good as her word, so once more they left their bikes by the gate and strolled along the track to the marker where, after throwing the groundsheet down and using their sweaters as pillows; she let him undress her and then they united on their hastily built bed, although not before she'd whispered, 'Ready, steady....start....tweaking.' Soon after she observed, 'I see you know which one to aim for.'

She shook with laughter when he replied, 'Well, it wouldn't be right, now, would it?'

They chose to compass to allow each to have a view of the heavens and so, halfway through their lovemaking, she stopped during repositioning and apologised for being unkind when they were leaving Newtown. 'It just goes to prove, my darling,' she whispered down to him, 'that even in the best of societies people can be hurtful to one another; but at least we do say sorry afterward.'

Later, whilst still naked, she got him to help her to stand on top of the triangulation pillar where she then bent double, thrust her left leg straight out behind her and opened her arms wide in a perfect ballet pose. Andrew, horrified, warned, 'Don't fall!'

She laughed, maintaining her position without the slightest tremor. 'I'd be a poor dancer if I did,' she commented.

'You look really beautiful in this moonlight, sweetheart,' he said in awe, 'but what are you doing it for?'

'So you can remember till your dying day. But also,' she went on quickly, 'so you could study me from all angles.' While he moved slowly round her she explained, 'Besides, I'm the highest nude woman on Whyte Island; and just think, love, of all the teeming millions on this planet I'm undoubtedly the only person doing this right now!'

Having come to the end of his tour of discovery, Andrew said, 'If you care to sit on the edge I'll make you unique in another way.' And he went on to whisper the details in her ear.

'You naughty boy,' she squealed with delight, 'but what a wonderful idea!'

'If only I'd had a good camera with a flash fitting,' he mused after he'd carried her back to the groundsheet, 'I would've taken lots of photos of you posing.'

'I'd have liked that,' she said, kissing him, 'but only if I could've been sure no one else would ever have seen them. However, as I once told you, we don't go in for souvenirs, so it's out of the question.' Something about this last remark puzzled him, but he couldn't quite decide what it was.

Not many days after their cycle ride beneath the stars Andrew's summons to attend a tribunal with regard to his island citizenship came through; and, as she'd promised, Julie accompanied him to the venue which was at the community centre in Harbourtown. No one questioned his lover's right to be with him and she was more than just a companion for she was always ready to interpose on his behalf without request, as well as to give assurances to the panel of three women and three men. 'Now, Andrew,' one of the former said, 'We'd like you to take these papers through to the room over there,' and she glanced in the direction of a side door, 'and answer the questions to the best of your ability, then bring them back to us; meanwhile we'll be having a chat with your lady friend.'

Much to his relief there weren't too many problems to deal with, neither were they too difficult for him and within twenty minutes he was able to return to the main room and hand them back to the panel. After the papers had passed from one examiner to the next for perusal, without comment, the previous speaker addressed him once more, 'Well, Andrew, subject to how you did in your examination, we feel we can already accept you as a member of our community.' She went on to explain that many of the people who were acquainted with him had been interviewed, and all had given encouraging reports regarding him. 'But, I'm afraid,' she continued, 'we're compelled to also go through a list of conditions you'll need to sign, one at a time, to ensure you really understand them and their implications.'

The woman paused and studied the young applicant carefully, 'Before we begin the main part, however, I feel I ought to inform you that sometime ago we took the precaution of advising your government of your probable wishes on the matter and we have only just received a reply, which is favourable toward you.'

'They're obviously only too pleased to be rid of an extra mouth to feed,' commented Julie, but only she and her companion seemed to find the remark amusing.

'Also,' continued the spokeswoman, solemnly, 'we informed your family, though with rather less success.' Which was a statement Andrew found to be less than surprising. 'We're calling a brief break for some tea at this point and I'm sure your Julie will be able to take you to the cafeteria in the meantime; shall we say fifteen minutes?'

The following procedure upon their return might well have been extremely monotonous if it hadn't been for the presence of his sweetheart, with her hand holding his beneath the table and giving squeezes of encouragement as each point was raised and subsequently discussed thoroughly by all those in attendance. Finally the spokeswoman rose, came across to their table and placed two identical certificates before Andrew. 'Would you mind signing these?' she asked, when he'd done so she then offered the pen to Julie. 'Would you like the honour, young lady?' his lover nodded enthusiastically, and appended her signatures; lastly the spokeswoman countersigned and then held out her hand to Andrew. 'For better or worse, you are now a Whyte Islander,' she smiled, 'and we wish you every good fortune for the future.' Upon handing over one of the certificates, she shook hands with Julie and observed, 'I see you've already made yourself at home; congratulations to both of you.'

He felt as though a heavy weight had been lifted from him as, in a complete daze, he went across to the other panel members and shook hands with each of them. Before they left the room the lovers stood with their arms about each other as one of the interviewers asked Andrew what main job he'd like to do. 'I'd prefer to work on the railways,' he began, 'but the only trouble is that I don't fancy the unsocial hours, because Julie here.......'

Unusually for an islander, his sweetheart interposed, 'I've been given permission to accompany him on a tour of the red colleges, and of course he's got to take assault training; so he won't need to worry about a vocation for a while yet.' And she barely gave him time to repeat his thanks and goodbyes before hastening him from the room.

Once outside she threw her arms around his neck and smothered his face with kisses, totally oblivious of who might be in the vicinity. 'My countryman!!' she murmured repeatedly, laughing joyfully; and Andrew hugged her tightly, equally overjoyed and excited. When at last she disengaged herself she held his hands and gazed at him proudly. 'You are a twerp, Andy,' she smiled, 'those people wouldn't have been able to be influential for us in our jobs, they were just being polite. Come on, let's go for a celebratory drink, then we've got to arrange a party.'

On their way to a public house suitable for the occasion Julie led him up the pathway of what seemed to be an ordinary detached house built about the turn of the previous century; in the porch she turned to him and said, 'Now you're an islander, darling, it's time to remind you of the many benefits of your new nationality. It's a reminder, like zigzagging though much less uncomfortable, of how fortunate we all are over here.' She paused, and added, 'I hope you've got a strong stomach.' She pushed at the door and it swung open easily and noiselessly; he was too puzzled to speak as he found himself in a hallway with several doors on either side, and his lover also remained silent as she led the way into the first room on the right.

It was immediately obvious they were inside a diminutive cinema for there was a large screen at one end and some twenty fitted, blue upholstered seats in five rows facing it. 'Find us seats in the middle whilst I turn on the light and draw the curtains,' she announced. Before coming to sit by his side she pressed a button on the wall next the door, and by the time she was seated by him the lights had automatically dimmed and the screen had come to life. 'Stand by,' she warned, and she placed an arm almost protectively about his shoulders.

What followed was an indictment of mankind's stupidity and cruel ignorance, for a complete series of horrifying scenes was projected upon the screen, somehow made even more terrible by lack of sound and by the printing of relevant statistics below each incident. They witnessed a man being beaten up because he was different from his assailants, then a girl being followed, attacked and then raped; a house being burgled, and the misery and despair of its owners upon their discovery of the crime. A child was knocked down by a vehicle and taken to hospital, where it eventually died and the family was shown heartbroken at the funeral. They saw youngsters in the act of vandalising; and riots during a football match, an industrial strike and a political rally.

A thriving factory was closed down and the shop floor and office staff were depicted leaving the premises for the last time, afterward there were shots of the buildings standing derelict and then being razed to the ground; the former employees, in the meantime, were shown without work despairing and gradually becoming more destitute. Large numbers of children were filmed dying of disease and starvation; and people living in terrible conditions with inadequate housing and little food, though still producing big families. A forest was destroyed and transformed into farmland. Warfare was depicted with combatants and civilians alike being killed or maimed, cities, towns and villages demolished, ships sunk and aircraft crashing. Andrew saw many other hideous scenes, but they all had the same theme in common: they were all due to mankind's deliberate efforts.

Eventually the film came to an end, the screen became blank and the lights brightened again. Julie turned to her lover and he saw a tear rolling down her cheek. 'Throw in a little sound and drama,' she sniffled, 'and much of that would pass as entertainment throughout the world.' Raising the armrest separating them she came into his embrace. 'I'm so glad you're safe from all that now, my darling,' she whispered, 'that's why we came here; but we mustn't let it spoil your special day.' But as though in contradiction she then gave herself up entirely to grief.

Her lover tried to comfort her by answering light heartedly, 'It isn't all horror on the mainland and elsewhere, sweetheart.' But she wasn't to be appeased and so he held her until she'd finished crying, marvelling at her sensitivity while he did so and wondering how many mainland girls would be as moved by such cruelty and senselessness waste.

As they left the house he asked what was in the other rooms. 'I suppose you could call it a museum dedicated to propaganda,' she replied. 'After watching the film you can go and look up the question it raises and thereby obtain the relevant details. For example, with regard to all those dying children, it's possible to discover the global annual rate of decease which, I happen to know, is currently around fifteen million; what the solution is and what steps Whyte Island and pitifully few other nations are taking to rectify the problem internally and externally. Every islander obviously knows the answer but that place does serve as a constant reminder; it's a wonderful place to visit if you're feeling a little depressed, ironically, because it soon makes a person glad they're an islander and how terrible the rest of the planet can be.'

Andrew commented somewhat wryly, 'I can't understand why there wasn't anyone else about, not even a caretaker.'

Now completely recovered from her fit of weeping Julie smiled, 'Don't be silly, love, nobody's going to damage the place; and as for our being the only visitors, well it just goes to prove how successful our educational system is. We don't always need to be reminded of how fortunate we are, do we?' She squeezed his hand. 'But the museum, if that's what you'd call it, is always there if needed, and blue school parties in their final term are taken there from all over the island.'

Shortly afterward they crossed the high street to enter a newsagents; she emerged a few minutes later bearing a packet of invitation cards and with a triumphant expression on her face. 'Where are we going to now?' he enquired as they continued down the street in the opposite direction to the station.

'For a drink, of course,' she replied innocently.

But it was to be a memorable one, for she took him to the public house once again where they'd dined with Jill and Mike, and here they were shown to an upstairs room overlooking the mainland. 'It's a citizenship present from the other members of the Lucas family,' she explained as he surveyed the homely décor and the double brass bed, 'I'm here as an extra.' He made to embrace her, but she backed away and sat down on the counterpane. 'Wait a minute,' she urged, putting a finger to her lips. Presently there was a knock on the door and Andrew, upon opening it, had a tray containing two glasses, some biscuits and a bottle of champagne thrust into his hands. 'Let the celebration begin,' Julie smiled when he turned to her.

After an afternoon and evening of comprehensive and passionate love making, interspersed with visits to the en suite toilet and meals brought up to them, they were awakened just before midnight by the alarm clock which his sweetheart had asked for. 'This is my present,' she whispered, handing her bedmate a small, flat package, 'you gave me a unique experience on top of the triangulation marker, so I'm going to give you one here.' And she stole from the bed. Which was why Andrew found himself, as his first full day as a Whyte Islander began, gazing across his lover's right shoulder at the lights of his former homeland, with his lover standing with her back to him holding a glass of champagne while he fondled her feminine attributes, kissed her hair and engaged in an even more intimate activity.

In the morning, after breakfasting in one of the replica captain's cabins, Andrew took his love on a tour of the "Whyte Hart" which was now berthed alongside the quayside, and then they returned to the flat to write out the invitation cards. This was a difficult chore because they knew so many people between them, although Julie managed to make it less onerous by her constant banter. 'How on earth are we going to afford to entertain all these guests?' he exclaimed when a list had been drawn up, 'and where will we find a venue big enough?' But his sweetheart didn't seem to be in the least concerned and merely told him not to worry.

The party, held several days later in Laketown's mock baroque church, was a great success; the only person apparently absent being Charlie Maynard whom, Linda explained to her hostess and host, thought it politic not to attend; even Helen was present accompanied, much to Andrew's unreasonable subconscious envy, by a handsome man of about his own age. A buffet had been laid out, a small dance band provided the music and it was quite a formal occasion because even Carol, Jim and the other people from the Station Arms wore evening dress. Between them Julie and her lover managed to dance with every person of the opposite gender present, and both Maynard girls congratulated him on his citizenship and wished him the best of luck in his life with his flatmate, even though Helen sounded a little wistful; however, if he thought about the inflection in her voice at all he subsequently put it down to the remnants of envy. Later on, presumably emboldened by alcohol, she elected to play a couple of jazz tunes on the piano during the band's rest period, and she was followed by several folk singers including his sweetheart.

Shortly before the party came to an end Jim dragged Julie and her lover onto the stage. 'As a token of our esteem,' he announced to them, 'we've had a little collection for you.' And he handed over a cheque.

Glancing at the amount and with a smile and a wink at her sweetheart, Julie announced, 'What a coincidence, exactly the same as the cost of this party.' She took Andrew by the hand, then told their assembled guests, 'Both my lover and I would like to thank you all for your wonderful gift, and also for attending; though in the light of this surprise,' and she waved the slip of paper in the air, 'it would appear we are now the guests and you the many hosts.' This observation was received with laughter during which she whispered to her lover, 'Say something, darling.' But he was too abashed to consider making anything approaching a speech; noticing his nervous expression she murmured, 'Well, sing one of the songs I taught you instead.'

So, in a moment of urgency, Andrew made his debut as a folk singer; his hastily selected choice wasn't very apt, and the irony of it wasn't lost on his amused audience for it described the burial of a young sailor brought low by a city girl; as soon as the applause had died away Julie turned to him, smiled and commented loudly, 'Thank you very much for the compliment, sweetheart.'

Before having the last waltz with his lover, he danced with her mother during which he told her, 'I'd like to thank you and John for providing me with Julie, Jean; if ever I'd had any doubts about becoming a Whyte Islander your wonderful daughter banished them all away, because I'd endure hell just to be with her.'

Mrs. Lucas gently slapped him on the back. 'I'm sure you're trying to make me cry, young man. But I hope you aren't comparing our island with hell, though.' She smiled, and added, 'Actually, we in our turn couldn't have wished for a better companion for our daughter; we hope you'll always be together and happy.'

Andrew had scarcely recovered from the party when Julie sprang another surprise on him; it began innocently enough when he escorted her down to the ferry on her way to work and, as usual, he continued across the lake with her. Of late the weather had been exceptionally wet but on this afternoon the sun was shining and there was scarcely any wind, making the latter part of the day very warm and humid. To his astonishment, when they reached the far shore she made no attempt to embrace and kiss him goodbye, but instead she held his hand and as soon as the gangway was lowered she led him off the vessel. 'What now?' he wanted to know.

His sweetheart happily turned to him. 'It's my last time today, darling, and because of that and your new status they're having a feast in our honour tonight; but this afternoon we've got the run of the exterior, so we can go boating and swimming,' she winked, 'just as on your previous visit; and we can stroll through the beautiful gardens.'

Overwhelmed by this news he replied, 'You mean we'll be together all day and every day until I'm given a job?' He didn't care who was about when she nodded, for he demonstrated his joy by pulling her into his arms and kissing her wildly while the villa staff passed either side of them, laughing or giggling at their unorthodox stance.

Julie took him straight to the main building and thence to the same beautiful bathroom where she'd previously attended Linda and him; together they removed their clothing, donned swimwear and dressed in what she described as being typically austere Roman day clothing. 'Just for appearance sake,' she added. Before they departed she packed a bottle of wine and two small loaves containing spread butter and cheese into a sheepskin shoulder bag. 'I defy anyone to say we're not genuine ancients going on a picnic,' she joked as they left the room.

They might have been invisible for all the attention anyone paid them and, indeed, beyond the walls of the villa buildings people were notably absent; Andrew felt as though his lover and he were in paradise as they wandered through the lovely grounds, and the fact they were clad in unfamiliar costume merely enhanced the other worldly affect; on innumerable occasions they sat on marble benches, by the sides of pools or fountains, on rocks, or lay together on one of the many grassy slopes in order to survey one or other of the beautiful vistas which that enchanted garden, replica of a bygone age, abounded.

Eventually, having explored every part of the grounds between the stone walls marking the landward perimeter to the main lake's edge, they made their way to the boathouse. Just as on his previous visit with Linda, he chose the punt and purloined a set of paddles, together with some cushions, from the other craft. 'As I've already mentioned, darling,' Julie mused as they headed for the concealing willows on the opposite bank, 'one thing I admired about you was your gallantry toward Linda when she fell in; I'm still feminine enough to appreciate gentlemanly behaviour, although,' she added, 'when we're undergoing assault exercises you'd best not be too considerate otherwise we'll never defeat the imaginary enemy.'

'Do you mean to tell me you'll be sharing all the hardships and dangers of this practice warfare alongside me?'

She laughed as she tied one end of the punt to a bough whilst her lover attended to the other rope. 'Of course,' she answered, 'Don't you remember from your Greek history lessons? Warriors often fought in pairs as friends, and possibly lovers: though in their case, it was usually a man and boy partnership. Just imagine the ferocity with which you'd fight if I was threatened with extinction by your side; I know I'd fight like mad to save you.' She stood up and deftly pulled her woollen dress over her head revealing the two piece swimming costume beneath. 'Anyway, let's not be morbid on such a beautiful day,' she urged as she removed her sandals. Without waiting for him she promptly dived over the side, scattering the panic stricken waterfowl gathered in a motley flotilla about their craft.

For the next half hour or so they played happily together in the water, diving between each other's legs, wrestling and racing like carefree children, safe in the knowledge they'd remain unobserved until, at last, in a state of near exhaustion they helped one another into the punt. 'Are you trying to proposition me?' Andrew asked while they lay in the bottom of the vessel, as his lover insinuated her hand inside his trunks and began fondling him.

She turned her head on the cushion and gazed at him, 'It might be a new experience for you: in a punt: unless, of course, Linda's already shared it with you?'

He shook his head. 'No, she hasn't and it's a great idea, but don't you think we ought to finish off our victuals first? Because, my love, as you very well know, I'm likely to drop off immediately afterward.'

He awoke with a start from his doze, feeling cold where a breeze fanned his naked body; Julie stirred in his arms until he managed to shake her awake. 'What time does the feast begin?'

he enquired as soon as her eyes opened.

Stretching herself she replied with a yawn, 'When it gets near dusk,' glancing about her, she continued, 'quite a long time yet, I should say. Still, as it's a bit chilly now we could get dressed and put the punt away.' She smiled affectionately at him, 'I adore you darling, and you're a wonderful lover.'

In order to fill in the time before they were due to bathe and change for their party, she took him on a tour of the kitchen garden which, she explained, helped to supplement the villa fare besides adding authenticity to the place. Andrew found the herbal section particularly fascinating and they both had great fun rubbing, and then smelling, the various leaves. Afterward they entered the buildings where Julie introduced him to her friends and other workmates and also took her leave of them; it was plain to her lover, from their familiarity and friendliness toward her, that they were going to miss her very much. But he couldn't refrain from pondering, whenever he met one of the more handsome male members of staff, whether they had known a more intimate side to his companion; but if they'd had he'd now come to accept it as being none of his business.

Julie had almost certainly been working to a timetable, for when they returned to the bathroom Andrew found the bath had already been run for them, and there were even a pair of goblets, presumably containing mead, standing on the side; while over on top of the small cupboard a pile of fresh clothing awaited them. 'You don't need a slave this time, darling, do you?' his sweetheart asked as she set about undressing him.

They had as much fun in the bath as he'd had with Linda: and when they toasted each other with mead he asked, 'What do they put in this stuff? Because it's highly potent!'

She giggled, 'Ah, that's a secret, but what did it do to you?'

'It made me feel devil may care and randy.'

Giggling again, she observed, 'In that case we'll need to drink another goblet each before we retire.'

'Are we.......' he began in pleased surprise.

'Sleeping here tonight?' she finished for him, 'Yes, it's customary for staff who are leaving, together with their partners.'

'I'm more pleased you're leaving this job than you probably realise, darling,' Andrew confided as she dried him with a big towel.

She paused and eyed him. 'Why, in particular?'

'Well, I hated the thought of you seeing all those naked men, and having to towel them down as well.'

Julie began laughing uncontrollably, and it was to be some time before she was able to speak again. 'Oh, my poor love,' she exclaimed at last, 'you must have been going through silent hell with your jealous nature, and all for nothing; and our relationship was supposed to be frank and open. I am disappointed.' Recommencing to dry him, she continued, 'Actually, what's supposed to happen,' she emphasised, 'is that the man's companion is expected to dry and dress him while the slave girl is out of the room, or when her back is turned. I can assure you, sweetheart, you're the only naked man I've ever seen here, and the only one I've ever wanted to.'

Andrew sighed audibly in relief. 'But, in your case,' she went on, 'Linda and I arranged things differently, because when I brought over your drinks and displayed as much of my charms as possible to you she was quite aware I was making a pass; her way of telling me you were available was by allowing me to see you in the nude, and even more significantly, by letting me dry you. So you can imagine how we both felt when, after all our intriguing, you refused to take me on!'

He caught hold of her wrists. 'I felt really low afterward; being noble is little consolation when you believe you've lost your chance with a girl as beautiful as you, my love. Anyway, look at me in the same fashion as you did when you were about to dry me before; then I'll show you what I wanted to do to you.'

'Thank goodness we've barred the door,' she giggled with delight when he'd carried out his threat, 'You'd better not go much further, though, otherwise we'll be late and you won't have enough energy left.' Afterward she again dressed him in her own professional way, and as she did so she explained their roles to him. 'It's quite simple, darling; you're still Antonius Aurelius, an officer with the seventh legion, but on your previous visit here you saw me, bought me for obvious reasons and then fell in love with me.'

He grabbed her and gave her a kiss. 'True, true!' he exclaimed.

Laughing, she went on, 'This was bad news for Justinia, because you freed me, divorced her and married me.'

'And who are you?'

'Juliana, of course, silly boy; anyway, by a remarkable coincidence the people who played Marcus Crassus and Livinia before are in the same roles tonight because, as I believe I mentioned before, we swap around a lot; sometimes I end up in the kitchen or laundry, other times I'd be the hostess. But this evening, my lord, I'm your honourable lady wife, so we should have a lot of fun.'

Andrew watched in fascination as Julie dressed herself; her garment was much longer than a slave's, even more so than Linda's had been, the hem almost trailing the floor. She turned her attention to her hair as soon as she'd arranged the gown to her satisfaction; because it was still damp after their swim and bath, she merely brushed it out and then tied it behind with a pale green ribbon, which matched her gown, to form a pony tail. 'How do I look?' she asked anxiously.

Gazing up at the ceiling, he answered, 'I can see Aphrodite growing green with envy, but it's a little too obvious you've broken your rule regarding a foundation garment.'

'As well as briefs, and,' she lifted the hem of his tunic, 'underpants. But we're supposed to look authentic, love; however......' And before he could prevent her she slipped out of her gown, rummaged in her bag and subsequently taped a large piece of sticking plaster over each nipple. 'Does it show?' she wanted to know when she'd dressed again. Loving her, he shook his head.

As they made their way in the direction of the main room he enquired, 'This gathering isn't just for you and me, is it darling?'

'We are the guests of honour, but it's still a case of business as usual.'

'Will you be doing any dancing?'

She gave him a haughty glance though softened with a smile. 'Officer's wives don't perform for all and sundry,' she replied proudly, lifting her chin.

By the time they'd reached the pair of doors to the main room the mead had done its work on Andrew, for he was now full of confidence emphasised by his previous experience of the feast, and so as soon as the doors were opened by two slave girls, one of whom he noted was a redhead, he was fully prepared for the banter about to erupt around them. 'So thou hast lain aside Justinia and art now laying aside of Juliana,' quipped Marcus Crassus after greetings had been exchanged; and the room dissolved into laughter. 'I canst see why your lord should wish to elevate thee from my kitchens and bathrooms to his living rooms and bedroom,' he continued, nodding to Julie, 'for thy beauty, bearing and intelligence are rarely to be met with elsewhere.' She lowered her head slightly in recognition of the compliment.

'Tell us,' shouted a man from one of the couches, 'of thy late fight with the pagan and how thy wounds fare, Antonius.'

Without thinking Andrew answered loudly, 'Should thee refer to my brief skirmish with one or two heathen some time past then my few scratches have long since healed. However,' he went on, somewhat coldly, 'if it is my new wife thou referest to, she is a true worshipper of the best of Rome's deities, but the wounds Eros and she dealt me during our recent battles are still proving somewhat troublesome.' Applause at this rejoinder followed them as they were escorted to their couches by the red haired girl who was almost certainly Julie's replacement.

The remainder of the evening's entertainment was very similar to that enacted on the occasion of Andrew's first visit, except the personnel in the troupe were largely different, as was their routine; far more satisfactory from his point of view was the absence of a teasing, tantalising, dancing slave girl, for she was now lying by his side devotedly feeding him the occasional morsel of food or sip of wine, his own consort. Otherwise, their position as guests of honour was accentuated by the attention paid to them by the other guests, the performers and slaves alike; and by the time they were lighted to their night quarters by a dark haired slave girl Andrew really began to think of his lover and himself as a genuine married couple dwelling in the late Roman era.

The couch upon which they were to pass the night was rather longer than those they'd lain on in the main room, and more than twice the width; it was covered with a pair of sheets, coarse by modern standards, in addition to several layers of animal skins all of which had been invitingly turned back at one corner. The walls were decorated with hand painted murals and the mosaic patterned floor was scattered with rush mats; very few pieces of furniture were evident, but one item, a small cupboard, had two goblets of mead standing on top. 'Is this all authentic, sweetheart?' Andrew asked, gazing about him.

'Well, if it isn't at least it's different,' smiled his beautiful Roman lady.

'Do you think they'd mind if we slept in our costumes?'

Glancing at him in amusement she replied disingenuously, looking down at her garments, 'I thought you'd might like to make love to me, because you wouldn't get far with me in this rig out. But I've got a far better idea; I've left our toothbrushes and paste in my bag in the bathroom, after we've cleaned our teeth you can come back here and wait for me, I won't be long.'

While Andrew awaited the return of his lover he lay, fully clothed though minus his sandals, on the bed watching the flickering shadows projected by a pair of wall lamps and the fire in a bowl set upon a stand. As she'd intimated Julie was soon back, clad in one of the robes they'd each been provided with, and a mixed red and yellow rose in her hair. He sat up on the side of the bed as she entered and observed, 'Linda reckoned the red rose you sent would clash with her wig, so she wore it somewhere else.' Immediately he wished he'd been less indiscreet, but she merely smiled as she undid the knot at the neck of her outer garment.

'What makes you think I've only got one flower?' she asked. 'In actual fact my two roses are symbolic of the areas of my greatest passion for you.' And as she shed the cloak he gasped, for she was naked underneath apart from a red rose covering her lower feminine attribute. 'Now, which one would you like to smell first? They're subtly different.'

'Aren't you jealous? And how did you know?' he queried, perplexed, as he knelt before her.

'Linda told me, how else would I know? And why should I be jealous? I sent her the rose and costume just to make you happy, how she deployed them for your combined amusement was up to her; besides, I'm not bothered about what you did before we became lovers, nothing can wipe away the past, can it? Now why don't you tell me exactly how you made love that night? Then we can do exactly the same.'

During the night the abrupt change in temperature upon Andrew's naked and uncovered body awoke him as the stifling humidity engendered a violent thunderstorm and, after carefully and gently pulling the bedclothes over them both with his free hand, he lay spellbound as the lightning flashes momentarily illuminated the exotic room and its contents. Could anyone, he wondered, experience a similar sublime and sensual event in this modern day and age? Somehow, he mused as he turned to his sweetheart and snuggled up against her, it seemed providential.

It appeared to Andrew as though the authorities were only awaiting his companion's release from her villa employment before he continued his tour of the educational establishments, for when they eventually returned to the flat they found an envelope on the doormat containing their forthcoming itinerary. It seemed as though a fortnight was being allowed for their red college visits and then they'd be joining a group for battle training, followed by an outing to an unspecified but secret place. 'They're certainly going to keep us busy,' he commented after perusing the programme; then he opened the letter which comprised the rest of their mail. It was from his mother and was somewhat defensive and pensive in tone, dwelling upon what, to her, was his abandonment of his family and country though ending on a resigned note. 'What are we going to do about this?' he sighed, handing over the letter to his lover, 'Trust my mum to change her tune when it's too late; I was more or less driven from house and homeland by my family's and government's apathy toward me.'

'I think the best thing to do in the circumstances, darling,' she suggested after reading the letter, 'is for us to go over together so I can meet your people. We should be able to obtain permits by next Saturday, and then you'll have plenty of time in which to prepare your family.'

He wasn't too keen on the idea. 'It'll be too much like taking a linnet to meet a sparrowhawk!' he exclaimed.

But Julie only laughed and patted his head soothingly. 'I'm quite a tough little bird,' she observed.

Now he had his sweetheart's company, the visits to the red establishments were pure delight for Andrew. As both Linda and Roger Jones had mentioned, every trade and profession which could be of possible use to the benefit and welfare of Whyte Island and its inhabitants was represented. The government's strict birth control policy had the effect of limiting the number of young adults entering the colleges and also prevented size fluctuations thereby ensuring the pupil/teacher ratio normally remained the same. The result was the college sizes were comparatively small despite the fact that several, though usually loosely connected, skills were generally taught in each; and the training supplied was always to a very high standard with excellent facilities and equipment readily available.

From the first day Julie organised a routine which they followed religiously; sometime during the previous evening they would read up the pertinent facts appertaining to the establishment they were to visit on the following day from the School Guide Book which Andrew had retained. The alarm clock they took everywhere with them would wake them early the following morning, and this would leave them with plenty of time to make their way to the relevant venue at their own pace. Although their arrival at each college was naturally expected it was all, in true island fashion, very casual for no time limit was ever imposed upon them. Invariably a member of the training staff would have been provided as a guide and a comprehensive, though seemingly offhand, tour would follow, whereupon the lovers would proceed either to the location of the next establishment or, sometimes, they'd book a local bed and breakfast or inn for the night.

Andrew felt very proud when, during a visit to her erstwhile college, Julie was welcomed as a V.I.P. and invited to give a demonstration of her prowess as a beautician. By employing the large array of cosmetics and other beauty aids available she transformed the whole class of females, including the instructor, beyond recognition in a surprisingly short time and with great dexterity. On the occasion of their tour of the establishment devoted to all aspects of engineering which, in consequence, was therefore quite large, Andrew was somewhat taken aback to meet Roger Jones in the cafeteria at dinner break. He came across to their table laden with a tray, and with extreme politeness asked if he might join them. Subsequently, he mentioned he'd had business to attend to at the college but he'd been pleased to see Andrew especially, as he'd been meaning to have a word with him. 'Now you are an islander, Andy,' he began, 'there's a small matter of your future employment. Presumably you wouldn't want to be parted from your beautiful companion for longer than necessary,' he glanced admiringly at Julie, 'so your return to sea would be out of the question; unless, of course, she was willing to accompany you, and if we could find her a berth. A small bird has told me, however, that you're more than a little interested in our railways; is that correct?' Andrew nodded, waiting with scarcely veiled impatience for him to come to the point. 'In that case I'm sure with the contrivance of the authorities we can enrol you here as a student so that you might be accepted as a railway employee at some later date. With your experience of engineering onboard . ship you should find little difficulty in realising your ambition.'

The lovers were profuse in their gratitude, but the Principal of Education hadn't yet finished. 'May I enquire as to what profession you follow, Julie?' She told him, adding her favourite secondary job was caring for the countryside. 'Would you like that as a main alternative employment, Andrew?'

He nodded, 'I think it might be very interesting.'

Roger smiled. 'Well, as Julie is well aware, we always try to arrange for couples to share at least one of their vocations and as you both seem agreeable to an outdoor job I'll see what I can do.' They continued chatting until they'd finished their meals and as soon as Roger Jones had left them Andrew asked if he'd really be able to pull some strings for them; his sweetheart smiled. 'Don't confuse his charm for lack of influence,' she commented, but continued, 'actually as he just explained they do try to employ lovers in at least one compatible job; so there's no real favouritism involved as it's anathema to our way of life, as Roger well knows. But as you're a newcomer and our relationship is still in its infancy he'll probably try extra hard for us.'

Their college tours always ended before five p.m. and usually they returned to their flat but otherwise they went straight to the place they'd booked. Andrew found these interludes most enjoyable; the opportunity to meet, and often dine with, strangers in a totally fresh environment, of sleeping and waking with his lover in an unfamiliar bedroom, were definite aids to companionship and increased sensual pleasure. They frequently took advantage of the area in which they were residing by visiting various places of entertainment, or in taking long walks. Once, in one town, they patronised a Victorian style music hall after being obliged to wear the relevant costumes prior to gaining entry; they joined in the chorus songs, and Julie even went on the stage to sing when volunteers were called for. Afterward they went back to their hotel overlooking a coastal promenade, in high spirits, and spent the remainder of the evening in bed embracing to the sound of waves breaking on the adjacent shingle beach.

On another occasion they experienced the comprehensive delights of a nearby recreation ground. Julie had chatted up a couple in a public house, and all four had subsequently played tennis, bowling, putting and crazy golf, all of which games Andrew would've certainly come off worse in if it hadn't been for his sweetheart's even poorer showing. That night, in the suburban bedroom which was their temporary home, he rewarded her thoroughly for her deliberate ineptitude.

But the best night of all as far as he was concerned was when they stayed at an old coaching inn, virtually the only one on Whyte Island his lover informed him, as the island's small area meant vehicle travellers rarely had to break their journey for a night's rest even prior to motorised transport. After the kind of evening meal which matched the building's style perfectly, they strolled off in the direction of the adjacent downland to watch the setting sun, and then returned homeward in the dusk: a long ramble during the entire length of which Julie had remained uncharacteristically coy. Later, in the oak-beamed bar, she instigated a folk song session; and as the evening wore on and the beer took effect the locals, many of whom had been enticed into the room by the noise of music, began to sing louder and bawdier songs until the night ended in uproar.

Andrew's lover brought her coyness to the bedroom with her, but only to enhance the antiquity of the room with its low beams, four poster bed and furniture leaning at crazy angles on the uneven floor; for she pretended to be a naïve young serving wench of former times alone with the local squire. After she'd nervously allowed him to undress her she stood naked in the moonlight streaming through the latticed windows, trembled visibly and asked pitifully, 'What'll us do, zur, if missus do come 'ome early?' Much later she proved she wasn't really all that bothered, and afterward when Andrew, satiated, began to muse about ghosts she giggled and exclaimed, 'Sod the ghosts, zur; let's do it agen.'

By the end of the first week of red establishment visits they'd received permission to leave Whyte Island for a weekend. Much to their surprise and delight the authorities had even arranged for them to fly over, as an aircraft was making a routine visit to one of the island-owned mainland factories and would drop them off on the way. The appropriate airport wasn't particularly close to Andrew's home, but it would nevertheless save a lot of time and trouble on the journey.

And so at 9 o'clock on a near perfect morning they left the island onboard a small turbo-prop aircraft bound for his former homeland. Knowing his male passenger hadn't flown over the island before, the pilot took the 'plane on a couple of unofficial circuits, thereby allowing Julie and him an excellent view of the landscape below. In addition, as soon as he'd set course for the mainland, he sent the co-pilot back to ask Andrew whether he'd like to sit up in the flight deck for a little while, which was an invitation he was only too pleased to accept after a querying glance at his lover. Upon his return Julie was invited to take his place; and she'd barely had time to rejoin him when the aircraft began to descend to make its final approach on a flight lasting little more than 25 minutes.

The second and third stages of their journey were undertaken with much more difficulty due to Andrew's unfamiliarity with the locality; he was quite willing to follow the advice of one of the personnel at the little airport: that they ought to take a taxi to the railway station a mile away, but Julie insisted they'd prefer to walk, 'It'll only take about twenty minutes,' she declared, 'and I'd like to examine your countryside.'

Their informant flashed her a look of disbelief and warned, 'It's a narrow lane for most of the way.'

At first their route took them alongside a busy main road thereby compelling them to walk the hundred or so yards to their turn off on a grass verge, during which time Andrew's sweetheart was the recipient of three wolf whistles and a shouted observation from passing motorists, much to her amusement and his embarrassment and anger. The view from the beginning of the lane was, in his opinion, quite picturesque, twin hedgerows twisting down the side of a shallow valley toward railway tracks running along a low embankment, with fields on either side of the lane and on the opposite slope. Julie, however, was critical; she'd already drawn his attention to the litter lining both sides of the main road, now she stood and studied the scenery before them.

'Where are all the woodlands?' she exclaimed. 'There aren't even many trees in the hedgerows; in fact there aren't many hedges. Look at that one over there,' she pointed across the valley, 'huge gaps down its length. You can see from here it hasn't been maintained because those bushes have grown up too scraggily; there'll be hardly any nesting sites in there. No doubt they'll be grubbing up that one, like they did with the hedgerow which used to be beyond it.' She glanced at the boundary hedges on either side of the lane. 'They've gone to the opposite extreme with these, they're far too low down and impenetrable; even a wren would find difficulty in getting inside, and come winter they'll become as bare as a colander with absolutely no sustenance and little shelter for the poor creatures.'

She picked up the holdall she insisted on carrying and started down the lane, studying the hedges as she went along with her lover following close behind; after several hundred yards she stopped to face him. 'I've counted 25 tree stumps on this side and 18 on the other, darling. Do you realise why they've cut them down?' Andrew shook his head. 'Probably,' she continued, 'because they're afraid they might get blown down and cause an accident, but mostly because they won't smash up their bloody hedging flail contraptions.' She showed him the shattered twig and branch ends on an adjacent shrub. 'That was only done a couple of weeks ago, right in the middle of the nesting season. I've seen or heard seven small birds in the vicinity of this lane and the road since we started along them, and quite frankly I'm surprised there are so many. If you.......' She didn't finish her sentence because a car, suddenly emerging from round a sharp curve before them and doing about 50m.p.h, narrowly missed her but clipped her holdall, snatching it from her grasp and depositing it some yards up the lane. 'Did she do that on purpose?' Julie asked incredulously after he'd retrieved her bag.

Andrew, relieved that his sweetheart had escaped unharmed,

put an arm about her tenderly and replied, 'She might as well have done, because she seemed to be more interested in her friend than in where she was going.'

'Do you know how many people get killed on the roads over here annually?' she enquired after they'd continued walking.

He shrugged. 'It must be thousands, I think it was 15, 000 one year; I forgot to look at the statistic on that film we saw the day I received my citizenship.' They briefly kissed at the memory. 'I'm overjoyed that cow missed you, but I wished we hadn't chosen to walk.'

Julie laughed sardonically. 'If they lost that many people by any other mode of transport I bet they'd ban it; but they really ought to have a pavement, or at least a verge on narrow lanes like this one.'

'The authorities would doubtless consider it too expensive; besides, pedestrians don't matter over here, the only people who count have their own transport or else live in towns or cities.'

They strolled on in silence for a time until Julie said, 'Anyway, what I was going to say before that lunatic came along was that if your former compatriots don't watch out they'll be covered in insects if they haven't the small birds to consume them. I think the introduction of hedge flails, motorised saws and roadside verge trimmers has made the destruction of the rural ecology far too easy; apart from the fact that if an individual possesses a specialised item of equipment like a power saw or a gun, they're more tempted to use it whether they really need to or not.

'For the latter reason we Whyte Islanders have to make do with hand saws and axes for all but the most arduous tasks; anyway, chainsaws make such a terrible racket. But I've noticed the farmers in this area have already altered the balance in favour of the crow family, members of whom are well known egg and nestling eaters. Still, that's their problem now, isn't it love?'

Shortly before they reached the railway they came to a small humpbacked bridge, and they paused on the brow to admire the stream which they'd assumed it spanned. But to their mutual horror they realised it would shortly be but a memory; already the trees, bushes and other vegetation bordering its length had been removed close to the bridge and, upstream, pipes were lying close to the water's edge, while beyond them only a line of fresh earth marked the route of the now invisible watercourse and its accompanying hedgerows.

'I can quite understand why you should want to abandon your homeland, sweetheart,' Andrew's lover remarked contemptuously as they turned their back on the devastation, 'I expect that attractive little old bridge will go next. Your erstwhile compatriots aren't only philistines, they're bloody idiots. Not only are they deliberately destroying beauty but they're making rods for their own backs in the process. If you don't allow water to drain off the land at its own pace you'll promote floods and raging torrents during periods of extreme rainfall, interspersed with dried up watercourses in times of drought. The effect won't be quite so bad in comparatively flat countryside like this, but when land drainage is undertaken in hilly or mountainous districts the result can be devastating. But I can't understand how the authorities can let it happen; what's the point? Why not leave things as they are?'

Andrew, almost pleased that at last he could solve one of his sweetheart's dilemmas, merely replied, 'Overpopulation simply leads to greater land use requirement: more people need more feeding, more housing leads to loss of farmland, which has to be taken from fresh countryside: mainly through making larger fields.'

Julie smiled with respect for her lover's perception. 'And larger fields mean the destruction of existing boundaries whatever they may be!' she finished triumphantly on his behalf, giving him a quick kiss as a reward.

By some quirk of fate they only had 40 minutes to wait on the tiny, unmanned and nearly derelict station; his lover, however, wasn't impressed by the number of trains which flashed past, and couldn't understand why one of them didn't stop to pick them up. In view of her recent criticisms of the countryside Andrew felt sure their visit would be a failure and that she'd find little worth praising in his former homeland. For even after his comparatively brief stay on Whyte Island the shortcomings of the mainland had become glaringly obvious to him, with the result that he now felt quite embarrassed for both their sakes; he could only hope his parents and brother wouldn't be too rude or offhand with her.

But he needn't have worried, because his lover's beauty and

exuberance were more than enough to overwhelm any hostility which might've been directed toward her. As soon as his mother had opened the door to them Julie's friendliness had disarmed her, as was evident from her flustering attitude as she let them in; and Andrew's father and Billy were immediate victims of her charm, poise and good looks. Much to his amazement, when his mother asked them if they'd like a cup of tea, his sweetheart replied in an untypical display of mendacity, 'On the way here your son and I agreed it would be nice if we all went down to the local for a drink, didn't we darling?' Without waiting for a reply she went on, 'He's told me so much about you all that I couldn't wait to meet you; I'm only sorry your eldest son isn't here as well.'

Before anyone had time in which to think, let alone discuss the suggestion, she'd ushered them all out of the house and, arm-in-arm with his father, was leading them in the direction of the nearest public house. Even when he'd recovered from his shock Andrew felt sure his lover would be unable to carry her design off for he was certain his father would be too proud to accept a drink, and yet would be too sensible of his lack of funds to offer to pay for a round.

But he entirely underestimated his lover's ability to get the best out of people, for neither of his parents, nor his brother, said a word when she sent him off to buy the drinks; he didn't know how she'd managed it, but by the time he'd returned bearing a loaded tray after a long wait at the crowded bar she and his family were talking and laughing like lifelong friends. During his sojourn while awaiting their drinks he'd considered with wonder how she'd somehow even managed to inveigle his mother into the tavern, a thing he'd always thought to be an impossibility.

Now, as he sat at the table with his family and sweetheart, occasionally being drawn into the conversation by the latter, usually to confirm something or other, he obtained an insight into why she was so popular. For she constantly drew his parents and Billy out by taking an interest in them individually, and by listening patiently to all their comments and complaints, adding sympathetic noises at the appropriate moments. She never compared Whyte Island with the mainland; in fact, to Andrew's amusement, she never had the opportunity to, as his family were as typically self centred in their attitude toward her as they were with him, for none of them thought to enquire about any aspect of her life.

Julie easily surmounted the question of who was going to purchase the next round by resorting to a further deceit; for she explained that the island authorities had allowed them a more than adequate grant to cover expenses and that, therefore, it was quite in order for her and Andrew to pay for all refreshments because the island was, in reality, footing the bill. As he observed his sweetheart listening and sometimes talking, admiration for her intelligence attained new peaks in his mind; for she was, after all, a stranger in a completely alien environment, and yet she automatically seemed to know what to do and how to make the best out of each situation. Simply by luring his family down to the public house she was enlisting the aid of alcohol in winning them over, as the more she plied them with drink the more receptive and amiable they became toward her. Clearly Julie was a strong disciple of the old adage regarding first impressions.

Her charm and understanding endured long after they'd left the tavern for she insisted upon helping his mother prepare and cook the main meal as well as offering Andrew's services in laying the table. Although she took on the lion's share of her self-appointed task she was tactful enough to appear unobtrusive, and also subservient to his mother. Half way through the resultant meal Julie turned to her lover and said, 'Your mother has offered us beds for the night, so will we be staying?'

Her facial expression told him she wasn't averse to the opportunity and he therefore agreed, but added, 'What shall we do tonight?'

'We can all go out together somewhere,' she replied cheerfully.

However, Andrew's father, pride and honour belatedly surfacing, objected. 'Oh no,' he said adamantly, 'you've spent too much money on us as it is. After dinner, lad, take your girlfriend down the town, show her round the shops then take her to the pictures.'

'Or that new disco you went to,' put in Billy.

'She wouldn't like it,' Andrew declared.

But his lover waved his protest aside. 'Yes I would; I'd love to go.'

Because of Julie's undoubted attractions, Billy, much to his family's astonishment, actually volunteered to help her with the washing and wiping up when the dinner things had been cleared away. Immediately afterward she disappeared upstairs to change into something more suitable for the evening's entertainment; she'd been allotted her sweetheart's somewhat cramped old bedroom and, after ten minute's grace, its former owner joined her there. 'Will I pass muster?' she asked anxiously. The little green dress she wore, with a white motif, brief vee neck, white collar and lapels, had a knee length hem and short sleeves, and was simple enough to be acceptable in almost any venue, and he told her so; once again she'd pinned her hair up. With a matching necklace and earrings of green plastic beads, and white high heeled shoes to complete, she looked like a work of art.

Prior to leaving the bedroom together he told her to stay where she was, and then disappeared downstairs; he was back in a moment with a little cooking fat adhering to his index finger. 'What are you doing?' she enquired as he attended to the door's inside jamb.

She smiled without comment when he merely replied, 'The hinges squeak,' adding, 'let's hope the bed springs don't.'

The large housing estate of which Andrew's late home was a unit had been one of the first erected in the area and was, in consequence, within easy walking distance of the town centre. Yet in that short stretch their ears were assailed by several wolf whistles and calls as Julie's red hair and provocative figure were rudely appreciated; but fortunately for her companion they were too engrossed in deep conversation to pay much regard to outside interference. Their discourse began almost as soon as they'd closed the gate behind them, for Julie let out a great sigh of relief. 'I see what you mean about people over here,' she declared.

'In what way?' he frowned.

'Well, I don't wish to be unkind to your family, but they're a little one-sided, aren't they? If they're typical of mainlanders and their level of conversation then I'm pleased I've helped save you from a fate worse than death, darling. I'm afraid I couldn't continue trying to take an interest in people over here indefinitely if they didn't attempt to take an interest in me and mine; I'd soon start feeling bitter and resentful, and then I wouldn't want to talk to anyone. I'm glad you aren't like the rest of your family, that you're much more thoughtful, my love.'

He steered the topic round a little. 'I noticed you playing some cards not normally found in the Whyte Island pack.'

She laughed. 'You mean those little white lies and my snivelling?' She stopped and faced him; not bothering to look about to check if anyone was watching she placed her arms about his neck; pressing against him she gazed up into his eyes. 'I love you to distraction,' she told him, 'and to such a degree that I'm perfectly willing to say and do anything to butter up your parents: just for your sake my darling; and I seem to have succeeded, don't I love?'

Andrew had expected to be the guide on their tour of the town of his birth, but his active little lover quickly appeared to take on that role for, as she observed somewhat ominously, 'This might be my only trip to the mainland, let alone to this town, it's all too depressing, but I ought to make the most of it.' So, brimming over with her natural and learnt self-confidence, she led him by the hand into any shop which took her fancy, never purchasing anything but merely to see what it was like inside; this wasn't too difficult when the shop in question was a supermarket, a pharmacist or a department store, but her companion couldn't help feeling embarrassed in shops where personal attention might be expected. However, she was never put out by any such encounters as she had the knack of giving the assistant in question the impression they'd both be returning shortly to buy out the relevant establishment's entire stock.

In between stores they managed to patronise several cafés and coffee bars; and half an hour before closing they finished a meal in the cafeteria of one of the larger stores. 'Well, what do you think of it over here so far?' Andrew prompted as they sipped their strange tasting coffee.

Julie grimaced and looked scornfully at the hustle and bustle of the restaurant customers, the stony faces of the girls who cleared up, and the dirty plates and discarded plastic containers on the tables. 'No change,' she answered, 'Although I adore you, if you hadn't become an islander I'd have had to let you go, because I could never have lived over here. It's a different world.'

The next venue on his lover's agenda was the town's sole

remaining cinema; she seemed amused by the lurid poster advertising the promised entertainment which consisted of a provocatively clad screaming girl, a crashing car and a falling bridge; but despite Andrew's repeated urging she refused to be dissuaded, so determined was she to see the film. 'I've often wondered what they're like, besides how else can we pass the time away until disco time.' She rejected his rather lewd suggestion.

Because they entered in the middle of the programme they were compelled to find themselves seats in a darkness only illuminated by the film, but even though they couldn't see very well they were quite aware that the auditorium was almost empty, and this fact allowed them to choose places right at the back. For Andrew it was a unique experience because he felt as though he were taking a grown up child on its first visit to the pictures. Julie was astonished by the great size of the screen and the activity taking place upon it but, just like an infant, she soon lost interest and thereafter only paid desultory attention to the film, usually whenever there was some interesting scenery.

They hadn't been seated very long when he became aware that his sweetheart was undoing the buttons on her coat after which she took his hand and guided it into the top of her dress. He'd taken a number of girls to the cinema in his time but this was the first occasion a female had shown more interest in him than in the film, because every time he turned to gaze at the screen she'd invariably pull his head down to her face and begin kissing him again.

'God!' she exclaimed as they descended the steps outside the cinema, 'how childish; no wonder the place was practically empty. I don't suppose the high prices helped much either.'

'There are often some very good films to be seen,' he replied defensively, 'anyway, you were too busy teasing me to know what was happening.'

Squeezing his hand, she observed, 'I saw and heard enough to comprehend why rape and other crimes of a sexual nature are such a problem over here; any virile man seeing all that simulated sex would be bound to be aroused and envious if he didn't have a woman of his own to satisfy him; if, though, the makers of the film had shown more nudity instead then our man would have at least obtained some degree of satisfaction. As it was, it was pure intimidation. Now, let's have a drink or two before we go to your disco.'

Andrew had expected her to want to patronise a quiet lounge bar, but much to his disgust she deliberately chose a rowdy public house where they had to listen to bad language and endure being jostled by every other person who passed by, for there were no seats available. But his sweetheart didn't seem to mind, and on the contrary appeared to be enjoying herself immensely. 'You see, darling,' she explained later as they went in search of much less noisy spot, 'it was like being in a zoo for humans; I want to watch mainlanders in all their different types of habitat because I probably won't get the chance again.'

Eventually they came upon a small, almost empty bar in a quiet back street. He'd been contemplating an intimate conversation with his lover in the dimly lit lounge; but she, however, appeared to develop an interest in a dejected looking young man seated alone in one of the far corners. Suddenly she stood up, took her drink and went across to him; for a moment he felt betrayed by her action, then he realised she wasn't deserting him for a new love but instead had felt compassion for the youth in his solitude. By the time he'd joined them she was chatting away quite happily to him.

'Look, sweetheart,' he said on their way to the discotheque, 'I know you meant well, but they don't do that sort of thing over here. That lad must've thought you mad, and me weak to let you do what you did.'

'But he seemed so lonely,' she objected.

'Well he's probably even lonelier now; as I told you before: mainland girls aren't the most thoughtful and communicative of people on first acquaintance, and so if he goes out seeking one after talking to you he's liable to be disappointed and he might not be able to find or afford a prostitute.'

Julie, apparently taken aback by his reversal of her usual role as tutor, replied, 'I don't quite get your point.'

'In short, you've given him a taste of honey in a country where honey is somewhat difficult to obtain except for those with the expertise and temerity to get it.'

Andrew was full of trepidation by the time they entered the

disco because he didn't want to run the risk of meeting up with his lover's namesake or her husband again. But his worse fears were soon realised when, during a dance with his sweetheart, he noticed the girl in question staring across at him from a table she was sharing with a man. It was obvious she bore him no grudge, for as soon as the dance ended she came straight over to them. 'You must leave quickly,' she warned, 'my old man's looking for you, he wants to get even.'

Before he could reply Julie stated, 'If Andrew doesn't knock him down again, Julie, then I shall.'

The other girl looked her up and down in a contemptuous manner and then turned to walk back to her companion. 'He's got some mates who'll help him.'

'Tell me,' she asked, 'is my boyfriend a good lover, do you think?'

The other girl was obviously surprised by this somewhat inept question but then shrugged and answered, 'Better than most, I suppose; but we didn't really get far enough for me to find out.' Having done her duty to the best of her ability she left them and returned to her pick up.

'Well, darling,' Andrew said, 'as you seem to be in charge, what do we do now?'

'Do?' she replied with surprise, 'Why, we stay here and enjoy ourselves of course, until it's time to leave.'

Although he well remembered the ferry skipper's remarks about island women in a scrape, and had often seen his lover's fighting ability, he still couldn't rid himself of a feeling of disquiet and so the remainder of the evening was spoilt for him. He found it quite a strain to keep his true emotions to himself for he daren't let his companion know how he felt; but eventually, though, he noticed the man he'd crossed staring at him, and then he knew they were both in for a lot of trouble.

Despite his anxiety he managed to give his Julie a good enough time; she seemed to enjoy the music both in listening and dancing to it, not minding whether it was slow and fast. 'I take it we have this sort of stuff on the island,' he commented earlier on, having witnessed her skill in a fast rhythm, and also attempting to allay his worries in conversation.

'Oh yes,' she replied as she swayed to the tempo, tapping her feet at the same time, 'and I love it; mind you, I adore nearly all kinds of music; but as you well know, love, I prefer folk and old style jazz above all else.' She glanced at him and obviously noted the expression of concern he was just too late to hide on his face. 'Don't worry, darling,' she whispered in his ear, 'I noticed that fellow glaring at you. Just look upon it as an advanced exercise in battle training; we'll lick 'em because as I mentioned once men are nearly always intimidation. Come on, this is a lovely tune to smooch to.' And she pulled him out onto the floor.

Halfway through their shuffling gait with their bodies locked together in what passed for a dance he heard her quietly giggling to herself. 'I saw that bloke scowling at us again,' she explained when he looked questioningly at her, 'so I made a face and poked my tongue out. He seemed quite shocked.'

Julie's estimation of men in general eventually proved to be far from incorrect. They left the discotheque shortly before closing time without experiencing any problems and began to walk home despite Andrew's wish to phone for a taxi. 'No,' she informed him, 'if trouble wants to come looking for us then we should face it fair and square; our self-respect is far more important than any fight.'

They'd gone about half a mile and he was beginning to think they'd got away with it when his hair seemed to stand on end as he heard the sound of running feet, and then someone began calling to them. 'Look round,' Julie urged as their pursuers drew closer, 'and see what the odds are.'

'Five of them,' he replied, 'including my sparring partner.' For some unknown reason, as the streets were quite empty, their prospective aggressors held back and contented themselves with hurling abuse and threats at the lovers, and this restraint gave Andrew's lover the chance to formulate a plan of action. 'The first thing to do is to try to divide them. Now, when we get close to the next turn on this side with a blind corner I'm going to panic and run off down it. I want you to continue a short distance past the entrance and then turn to take them on. With a bit of luck some of them will come after me, and if so I'll deal with them; if not I'll come back and catch them in the rear.' She stopped and glanced back in the direction of their tormentors. 'Don't forget, darling,' she told him earnestly, 'keep calm, wait for them to come near, then attack. Don't give them, or yourself, time to think; and no soft glove treatment until we've beaten them. But first I've got to get them to charge or give up when we reach the perfect spot, so they'll be out of breath.' She smiled, 'Good luck, and I love you!'

The melee which followed was over so quickly that, in retrospect, it was almost laughable, and Andrew was never entirely able to understand how one apprehensive man and one small, but confident, girl could've managed to defeat five men so easily. Everything went just as Julie had hoped. 'Here goes,' she murmured as they neared the corner of an alleyway; she stopped dead, looked round and called out, 'You aren't going to do anything,' she sneeringly shouted, 'why don't you go home to your mummies? It's way past your bedtimes.' This insult had the desired effect and they began running toward them. But his sweetheart's bravado apparently changed to panic, for she then screamed loudly and cried, 'They're going to rape me!,' then, turning on her heels, she fled down the road and disappeared round the corner; he gazed after her for a second and then followed her, but stopped at the point she'd indicated.

As he turned round he saw the gang rapidly approaching in single file; the first man glanced at him dubiously as he came up, but then ran down the dark narrow alley after Julie, closely followed by the second and third man before her lover could intervene; clearly they thought an apparently defenceless girl easier meat than a man ready to defend himself. However, the fourth man paused on the corner undecided as to what he should do, but Andrew, recalling his sweetheart's advice, didn't give him the opportunity to act for he ran straight up to him and kicked him hard between the legs, at which his knees folded and he collapsed on the ground moaning in agony. The remaining man, Julie's namesake's husband, observing this further demonstration of his adversary's fighting prowess, obviously didn't want to become involved any more for he backed away and then ran off. Andrew stared after him in disgust and couldn't refrain from yelling, 'Keep to toddlers and old ladies in future,' before going to see how his lover was managing. She, though, was coming to see how he was getting on. 'What happened?' he asked as they embraced.

'Nothing much,' she replied modestly, 'the first character came round the corner, I stepped aside, tripped him up and pushed him against the wall; as he fell he scraped his face, I don't know what happened to him then because I was busy tripping the next one up. But as I caught his arm there was a nasty crack; I think his elbow might've broken; anyway, he ran off screaming. The third chap just ran after him.' She bent down to put on her shoes and, noticing her lover's victim crouched against the wall retching, asked with genuine concern, 'What's wrong with him?' Crossing over and placing a hand on his shoulder she enquired kindly, 'Are you alright?'

But the man swore at her. 'Leave me alone,' he muttered with difficulty.

'For goodness sake, Julie,' Andrew whispered, pulling her away, 'let's go before the police arrive, someone might come along at any minute. We mustn't get into any trouble now.'

Reluctantly, but protesting, she allowed herself to be led away; he ensured they put enough distance between themselves and the scene of their conflict before condescending to slow down. 'Well done, darling,' he exclaimed, 'you managed that brilliantly.'

But his sweetheart dismissed his praise. 'It was nothing to be proud of. We hurt three of those people; two of them seriously. What a country!' she sighed, 'All this hatred and violence, when people should be loving and respecting one another instead.' Putting an arm about his waist she added, 'Still, just as long as you're alright, I suppose that's all that matters.'

Brother Billy couldn't stop talking about Julie as they prepared for bed. 'What a girl,' he told Andrew. 'While we were washing up she asked me all about my sex life, and she wanted to know if the birds here were easy to pick up; she gave me some really down to earth advice, too, about sex.'

'I think you ought to know, Billy,' his brother explained calmly, although he was really somewhat annoyed, 'that Whyte Islanders have been brought up to think of sex in the same way as we've been taught about history and maths. So don't read anything into it; she was just interested, that's all. Oh, and by the way,' he added, 'my girlfriend and I are a little past the tiddly-winks stage so don't say anything if I go sleepwalking later tonight.'

Billy leered and winked. 'Don't worry, your secret's safe with me. But are all Whyte Island women like her? Because if they are

I want to go and live over there, too.'

His brother laughed ruefully. 'Well, they're all broadminded and faithful, as far as I know, and attractive as well; but don't forget, though, I've been working for the island for seven years and I've only just been given citizenship, and I only got that because I fitted their very fussy bill. You'd need to apply to join one of their companies, and even then that's no guarantee.'

Andrew lay awake in bed until he was certain his family was asleep and then he slipped noiselessly from his bed and made his way to his lover's room; somehow the stealth required for the operation made the prospect of lovemaking far more exciting than usual, and his heart felt as though it was bursting as he silently opened her door and removed his pyjamas by her bedside. As soon as he'd cuddled up to her, Julie's mouth met his and her hand moved down his body. 'I feel I've got the right man,' she murmured in the darkness. Kissing her again, he began fondling her, but soon she murmured, 'It's the tradesman's entrance tonight, darling, or nothing, because the front door's closed.' Then she added, 'It's up to you.' After groping beneath her pillow she transferred a little packet from her right hand to his. 'A present from the disco,' she told him quietly.

The feeling of disappointment he experienced was of but a moment's duration; there was only one way he could adequately thank his lover for her loyalty and courage earlier, and nothing was going to prevent him from doing so.

Although the weather was dull, but as yet dry, the following morning Julie insisted her darling should take her to the park so she could see where the woman with the child had insulted him; Billy had gone off with his mates, probably to boast about his brother's bird, and neither of his parents fancied a walk and so the lovers were once more quite happily left to their devices. Now, as they sat on the park bench, the scene of his painful experience, she asked, 'Doesn't the mainland government do anything constructive to help the unemployed? Your dad and brother don't appear to have any money to spend, and there doesn't seem much for them to do.'

Andrew chuckled without humour. 'No one in authority wants to accept responsibility for the recession, they won't even explain in detail how it came about apart from the fact that too many members of the public were being permitted to borrow too much money from banks and building societies which, everyone knew except for the politicians, they could never pay back. It merely took one large bank to collapse and the entire economy, almost, came tumbling down like a house of cards. For over 60 years all mainland governments have been encouraging an increase in the population by any means, even though they've overseen a downturn in exports and an increase in imports during that term, and as a result they've watched hundreds of mainland companies closed or sold off to foreigners without doing anything much besides voicing a few platitudes and weeping some crocodile tears.

'To answer your question, my love, when senior mainland politicians can't solve a problem, invariably of their own making, they tend to ignore it and so the unemployed in society's eyes tend not to exist; presumably through parliament's exertions the media prefers to portray the average mainlander as having plenty of money, with expensive houses and cars, all mod cons and going off on exotic holidays abroad. But as you've seen for yourself now, there's plenty of dereliction and poverty by normal standards.

'As I'm sure you can comprehend, darling, when too many people are unemployed they're unable to pay their way in society, they become a drain on funding not a benefit. So in that way the economy loses out and therefore can't even afford to pay people to work, in their eyes, on unnecessary schemes just to keep them busy. It's been tried before and has proved too expensive, so it's far cheaper to leave them to their own devices and give them the lowest allowances. Which is why there is so much desecration and dereliction about us now.' He kissed his lover in her mouth and ran his fingers through her hair. 'Come on,' he urged, standing up, 'let's stroll a little.'

She joined him, and they set off hand in hand. Shaking her head regretfully Julie eventually observed, 'I can only repeat that I'm glad you've been saved, sweetheart. Whyte Islanders are well aware of everything you've just mentioned which was why Charlie Maynard and Harry Larke set up our island society with its unique culture. They, and we: after it had been explained to us, couldn't stomach the notion that those in power could make such gigantic mistakes and still come up smelling of roses while those, who depended on them to have common sense and the health and wealth of the nation at heart, have to suffer for their stupidity. And in a democracy, too! As you more or less pointed out it's due to overpopulation again; it took the mainland eons up until 60 years ago, to reach a total of 50 million and it's 65 million now, what an increase! No wonder the authorities here can't cope against a declining economy.

'Anyway, do you recall the battle of Aradram so long ago when, after defeating the invasion forces, many of our victorious sailors died of starvation, neglect and the effects of their injuries on the streets of the country they saved?' Andrew was aware of the famous battle, but not of the shame associated with it. 'Well,' continued his lover, 'things haven't changed too much over here, they still treat their heroes like dirt!' She stopped, for they were outside some public conveniences. 'I won't be a minute,' she told him.

When she reappeared she pulled a face; glancing about her she declared, 'There's no one about, I want to have a quick look inside the men's side.' Before he could stop her she disappeared into that half of the building. Emerging after a couple of minutes, she exclaimed, 'Just as I expected.'

Shocked and perplexed, he enquired, 'What?'

'Lots of graffiti, but far more in the ladies' section; which appears to indicate a lot of mainland women are mentally and sexually repressed. That doesn't say much for your ex-brethren's ability to make love, does it? But I've no complaints about you,' she laughed, 'especially after last night.'

'Didn't all that graffiti disgust you?' he asked as they resumed their walk.

'Not in the least, but the smell and the state the toilets were in certainly did. Oh, look,' she cried with delight, 'swings and a slide; I must have a go!'

Fortunately, due no doubt to the weather, the park was almost empty so there wasn't anybody in the vicinity of the children's play area; Julie couldn't entice her lover onto the slide but he watched, bemused, as she had three goes. He wasn't averse, however, to having a swing, and as they moved back and forth, side by side she gave him yet another lecture on psychology and sociology. 'Graffiti, just like fashion and humour, for example, is a reliable indicator of how healthy a given society is; although at first sight it seems like mere vandalism it's probably only loosely connected; but it does prove the mainland's educational system is all wrong: the males, it would appear, being only slightly less repressed than the women.

'This obsession with sex, as well as boasting about it, displays a certain inferiority complex toward it, as if it was dirty and something to be ashamed of, to be hidden away. In our society, as you know only too well, darling, although sex is personal it's considered beautiful, clean and natural, not something to be described and drawn about on toilet walls.'

The words came to Andrew's ears as if from a radio with poor reception, sometimes loud and occasionally soft, for although they'd tried to swing in unison at first they quickly found it to be impossible, and Julie was getting far too much pleasure to go at any other pace than her own. 'I can see what you're driving at,' he called back, 'but I think you might be taking it a little too seriously, for most of that graffiti was probably done by children.'

'Even better,' his sweetheart replied, 'the child being the parent of the adult merely proves my point. Being taught the rudiments of sex at school at the earliest possible age by my teachers, not my parents or my friends, ensured I received the full and accurate picture; and we were told we shouldn't experiment with sex until we were mature enough to really enjoy it and, as we respected our teachers, almost all of us obeyed. As you are aware, darling, the permissible age is fifteen and then we're actually encouraged to go out and make love, and given plenty of venues in which to do it. It was all perfectly natural to us: none of this self-conscious giggling and nervous fumbling; always wary of being caught out by parents and teachers. It's ironic that, at an age when the mind ought to be working at full pressure to gain educational ability, so much thought should be diverted to hang ups about the opposite gender. It's far better that each teenager should have their own lover to satisfy their mental and physical needs. If you required proof our system works, darling, then you have only to go into our toilets; you haven't noticed any graffiti there, have you?' He hadn't.

Soon after the mid-day meal they prepared to take their leave of the mainland; much to his secret amusement and slight envy all three family members insisted upon accompanying them to the station, such was his sweetheart's impact upon them; apart from the occasion of his departure for his first voyage onboard a Whyte Line ship none of them had ever considered him worth the effort. There was quite a touching scene on the platform as their train approached, for first his mother, then his father and brother wanted to shake Julie's hand and kiss her goodbye; and when the train moved off Andrew distinctly saw his mother wiping a tear away. Despite their fond farewell he was never to see his family, or set foot on the land of his birth, again; although both his lover and he began to correspond with his parents their replies were always brief and infrequent, and soon they ceased altogether. He could only assume that memory of his sweetheart's charms had faded to be replaced by resentment of his success, and his apparent abandonment of them and his country.

There were plenty of seats on the train for it was practically empty, a fact which surprised Julie; especially, she commented, as it was a summer weekend. 'The people who can afford to travel usually have private transport,' he explained, 'those who can't generally stay at home. Also, just as in the cinema, when customers or passengers stay away the appropriate authority charges the maximum price for the few who do come in an attempt to recuperate losses. As you can see, it doesn't work.

'This is another industry which was formerly owned by the government but due to overpopulation, you'll doubtless agree, they couldn't afford to run it any longer. This route is now owned by one of the nations which, due to the wars they began in the previous century, practically brought the mainland to bankruptcy in the first place.'

'So how, I wonder, can they presumably make it cost affective, when your ex-nation couldn't,' Julie observed, 'it seems more than a little fishy to me. According to what we were taught, your governments were inept in allowing road vehicles to replace a railway network which already served much of the land area; also, when the population was increasing rapidly the authorities should've compelled the house builders to erect homes around the stations on feeder lines.....'

'Branch lines, sweetheart,' Andrew corrected.

'Yes, well, anyway they could've then made those routes more profitable so avoiding closure, and thereby preserving the entire network. After all some workers over here, I've learnt, travel on a round trip of over 120 miles a day to reach their employment!'

'Many, considerably more,' he said under his breath. 'The ridiculous effect of turning to mainly road transport,' he stated more loudly, 'is the increase in air pollution and the traffic jams because of the massive rise in vehicle levels since the rail network began to decline. Perhaps the foreign railway companies foresaw the choking up of mainland roads and realised the prospect of investment in the industry would bring them great profit. Oh, by the way,' he added, putting his arm about her, 'there isn't any prohibition on public lovemaking here.'

'You can cuddle me as much as you like,' she smiled, 'plus a kiss or two; but no groping, or else......'

'I must say,' he interposed, reminded of their fight, 'you were very magnanimous toward our assailants.'

'Andy, darling,' she chided in dismay, 'won't you ever understand? Of course I was, and so should you be. Whyte Island hasn't managed to breed a race of angels, people aren't really all that different basically throughout the planet; we're only as good or bad as our environment makes us. If our attacker's had received an adequate education and everything else they required to make them happy, if they'd been taught the kinds of things I learnt at school, then they wouldn't have bothered with us; we were just an outlet for their anger and frustration.

'As I told you before, in connection with that man: what was his name, Colin? And his wife, they could easily have been you and me. I doubt he likes living off his spouse's immoral earnings, no wonder he's got a belligerent temperament. It's the governing authority, whether secular, based upon religion, or both which is at fault for creating or permitting such terrible conditions to flourish.'

During one of several unscheduled halts in the course of their journey Julie, glancing out of the window at another recently completed housing estate, drew her lover's attention to a certain housewife clad in an apron over her clothes, and a pair of slippers. They watched as she emerged from her end-house garden bearing a large cardboard box, crossed the road and threw the container and contents into a small copse which was already taking on the appearance of a rubbish tip. 'I don't know why your erstwhile government allows or encourages its population to increase,' she remarked in a resigned tone, 'when it apparently can't even control or cope with the one it has at present.'

'Expansionist principles,' he replied, 'additional people creating an eternal market for jobs, that's the theory. It doesn't work, as we both know. Thank goodness the native land of the person I love more than anyone has solved that particular problem.'

Julie took advantage of the liberal ways of his lover's former country to reward him well for his compliment by leading him to the toilets.

They completed their train journey without experiencing any real difficulties; but as there weren't any vehicle transporters running they arranged for one of the island's coastal pleasure boats to put in specifically to pick them up.

'I'm afraid, my darling,' Julie commented on the train conveying them back to Laketown, 'we'll need to tighten our belts for the next week or two because that trip was more expensive than I anticipated; I didn't realise how much our authorities subsidises imports until I saw the original prices, I really don't know how mainland people manage. I was also amazed at the way the cost of any given article fluctuated from one shop to another; one item I kept a particular eye on had five different price tags and varied by 23% across its range. They wouldn't allow that sort of dishonesty over here, every individual item costs the same no matter where you purchase it.'

Despite Julie's economy measures they still managed to pay a visit to the folk, and jazz, clubs that week; but in order to live within their budget they were obliged to spend the remainder of their time in the flat outside of college hours, during which she taught her lover some more folk songs, and on one memorable occasion they spent the entire evening out on the balcony, even to the extent of having a meal there. The only thing which spoilt it was the knowledge that on the following day their battle exercises commenced; but once again his sweetheart proved to be far more than just a lover by going out of her way to explain there was absolutely nothing to worry about and that it could be a lot of fun.

'Tell me, darling,' Andrew said as they set out set out for the training camp, 'has this secret place we'll be visiting afterward got anything to do with the battle exercises?'

She smiled ruefully, 'Only in as much as it tends to make our training rather pointless; I can't tell you where we'll be going beforehand but I believe I can assure you that because you're an islander now, my dearest, it'll be the last official secret to have been kept from you. If our training is as it usually is then we'll be starting off with lectures, the first of which will almost certainly explain how unimportant it really all is.'

'So why've we got to do it?' But Julie only shook her head dismissively.

When the train had departed from the remote station at which the lovers had alighted Andrew noted there were ten other couples standing on the platform; upon briefly surveying them he was somewhat taken aback to see they ranged from teenagers up to a pair who must have been close to retirement age. He was about to comment on this fact to his sweetheart when a woman and a man both dressed in camouflaged combat uniform emerged from the station building and abruptly marshalled them through to the adjacent lane and onto the back of a tarpaulined army lorry.

The following ride into wooded hills was far too bumpy, noisy and impersonal to permit anything more than the briefest exchanges, but when they eventually arrived at an encampment consisting of a number of wooden huts of various sizes Andrew was able to whisper to his lover, 'What are the older people doing here? Surely they aren't expected to rough it as well, although judging by the appearance of this camp it doesn't seem as though it'll be too arduous.'

Julie was unable to answer immediately for it was their turn to alight, but as soon as he'd helped her to the ground she laughed and said, 'Appearances can be deceptive; this is only the base, we've got a lot of rough living ahead of us and that includes the older folk as well, because warfare is no respecter of age or comfort.'

Apart from the youngest people, who hadn't been on battle training before, everybody already had camouflage kit but Andrew's lover went with him to get his, and afterward they found the room which had been allocated to them to get changed.

Their temporary home was situated in one of the larger huts; the interior layout of which was very similar to a railway sleeping coach, for leading off a side corridor were individual little apartments each fitted with a pair of bunks, one above the other, a wash basin and a locker; unisex toilets were situated at either end of the hut. They barely had time to change into their uniforms when a loudspeaker in the passageway outside invited everyone to assemble in the drill hall within five minutes for the first lecture. 'They don't give you much time,' Andrew commented dryly.

Julie smiled and patted him on the back. 'After you've been here a couple of days, soldier, or should I say marine? You'll be glad time isn't wasted.'

There were at least 50 people at the lecture, far more then he'd anticipated; benches were arranged across the width of the hall and set before these were stout desks upon which were provided ballpoint pens and notebooks. Up in front, on a dais, blackboards with maps and diagrams pinned to them had been placed upon either side of a large scale map of the entire island; two people of each gender, though not the couple who'd met them at the station, waited patiently for the hall to fill before beginning.

The first part of the talk, given by the man, was quite straightforward and dwelt mainly upon the various muster points about the island and the action to be undertaken in the event of an invasion; as far as Andrew was concerned there were a good number of eyebrow raisers in the plan because it was virtually a scorched earth policy from the start. The main dam at Laketown and other sources of electricity were to be blown up, as were key points on the railways and roads; locomotives and other vehicles were to be sabotaged, towns destroyed and harbours blocked. On the other hand secret caches of food, and supplies of water in the form of wells had been positioned throughout the island, often with refuges in the vicinity; definite routes had also been designated, not only as a means of retreat or escape but as a way of permitting reasonably safe communication between groups and storage sites. The young man was more than a little disconcerted to learn that the first people to confront the invaders would be the eldest citizens due to a strategy of leaving the fittest and more robust as the final line of defence. Before handing his audience over to his female companion the lecturer doubly ensured the newcomers in the group were thoroughly acquainted with the muster point within the area in which they resided.

'Those of you who've attended these exercises before,' the woman began, 'will be well aware of what I'm about to say; however, the first-timers will no doubt be surprised to learn that the training upon which we're about to embark is utterly pointless. Because once we are attacked, and surely when matters on the mainland and elsewhere throughout the planet reach a critical stage and envy of our contented life becomes widespread, then we will be completely incapable of defending ourselves. But just as a disturbed wasps' nest will cause its inmates to attack the intruder without thought of personal safety and regardless of how small the possibility of success, so shall each of you be expected to fight to the death for every piece of Whyte Island. Too much work, care and love has been invested in this land to allow it to be raped and ravaged in the same manner as the remainder of the so called civilized world has; the authorities would rather see the island destroyed quickly by its citizens than slowly by strangers.'

She paused, then continued with heavy emphasis, 'Now, there are three reasons why our battle training is pointless, two of them should be evident to you all, the third only to those of you who have visited a certain place on the island. The first reason is because of the vast numbers of people available to carry out an attack upon us. On the mainland alone there are more individuals than the governments know what to do with, and they would consider our homeland an ideal site for their expansionist policies and not care about what the future might bring; therefore our small population would quickly be overwhelmed by large numbers in a relatively short time.

'The second reason is due to the fantastic advances made in warfare technology.' Once again she paused, obviously to give maximum effect to her forthcoming words. Andrew glanced at his lover, and she smiled wistfully back and squeezed his hand. 'A lot of nonsense has been bandied about in recent times,' the lecturer continued, 'with regard to what is termed a conventional war. The implication of this adjective is of a conflict which can be kept, and will be kept, within reasonable bounds: usually where weapons in the form of guns, bombs and all the other paraphernalia of relatively modern warfare are employed.' The woman allowed herself a little humour. 'Almost as if these items are nice and proper to use,' she smiled. 'Well, except in the case of minor warfare between neighbouring minor nations, loosely supervised by the leading powers to ensure it doesn't get out of hand, there is now no such thing as a conventional war.

'For not only are there such things as tactical and strategic nuclear weapons, but germ and chemical technology is also available for the waging of war in addition to advances in other weaponry such as guided drones for surveillance and the delivery of all types of weapons, the use of night vision pinpointing and a myriad of other devices. So, all in all, our island wouldn't stand a chance, therefore any given battle might employ any or all of these horrendous inventions indiscriminately dependent upon the whim of the politicians or general staff. You can all imagine, incidentally, how encumbered the forces participating in such battle conditions might be; clad by necessity in protective clothing, one would consider them hardly mobile, and they wouldn't know whether their clothing would be adequate defence against the weapons deployed by the enemy, or even if their opponent hadn't devised a substance capable of dissolving or destroying such protection. It can also be seen that a modern battle might easily and rapidly escalate into a full scale war which, ultimately, could have no bounds.

'All this is by the way, but we're merely illustrating the fact that this is the other reason why we cannot hope to defend our island indefinitely against invaders: because of the large number and variety of intricate weaponry which could be used against us; we would, actually, be fighting back with outmoded hand weapons over a small and scarcely defensible area. But although, like the peace campaigners in many parts of the world, our efforts will have been in vain and wouldn't have affected our collective futures, we'll have all have had the satisfaction that we'd tried.' She stopped and gazed round the hall at her audience. 'Those of you who are here for the first time will be visiting the secret place with your partners which I referred to earlier, after completion of your battlefield training; I'm sure after that experience you'll have been enlightened as to the third reason why our exertions here have been pointless.' She glanced at her watch and declared, 'I see it's dinnertime now; after your meal be so kind as to reassemble here. The loudspeaker will tell you when.'

'She didn't paint a very rosy picture,' Andrew declared as they left the hall.

'There isn't much point in deceiving ourselves,' Julie replied, 'the profiteers on the mainland, and globally, are too greedy to want to emulate our way of life; just as in the case of an oilfield or any other useful mineral discovery which produces wealth, sooner or later Whyte Island will be inundated and exploited by the masses abetted by speculators: and just as in the case of a worked out oilfield they'll all start looking around for somewhere else to ruin when they've finished with us. They'd turn our island into a vast housing estate, a paradise for millionaires or something else that'd do it no good. The power output from our main dam would be lure enough for them.'

After they'd had their meal which, much to Andrew's relief, was a simple yet tasty and filling stew instead of the plain fare he'd been expecting, they lay together on the bottom bunk awaiting the call to reassemble. 'Yes,' his sweetheart mused aloud, returning to the topic of mankind's greed, 'modern society is just like an army of slugs progressing through a plot of seedlings, destroying everything it comes across and leaving behind a mess of slimy devastation; if only those slugs could be turned in upon themselves so they could appreciate the fact that what they're doing is self-deprecating. Slugs haven't the intelligence or means to control their birth rate but humans have.

'It seems strange to us that mankind with all its advantages such as a generally benevolent climate, beautiful scenery, various creatures to aid it and so on, should fail to be content with its lot and should continue to search for goodness knows what in the name of progress; seeking paradise, as it were, in the realms of science and technology, or in other areas when in reality it's to be found in simple pleasures and in its own environment. That time in the bedroom of the Roman villa you told me about, darling, during the thunderstorm when I was asleep, it was obvious from the way you described it that it had a profound effect on you; that's the kind of thing people really need to experience, and it's worth more than all the computer games in existence as well as c.ds, d.v.ds, televisions and other such forms of entertainment.

'Mankind's present attitude regarding religion and the

environment also puzzles us, it worships various deities which, presumably, it holds responsible for all the wonderful things on our planet, yet sets about disrupting and destroying all of those benefits. Don't you think it's rather like a little child who, upon being presented with a delicate and attractive toy, is exceedingly and permanently grateful to the donor but proceeds to leave that gift outside in all weathers until it deteriorates beyond repair? Do you know one of the main aids toward remorseless progress, sweetheart?'

Andrew shook his head, and Julie was about to explain when she was interrupted by the loudspeaker. However, on the way to the drill hall she was able to tell him. 'I was reminded of it when we toured the science and technology college,' she explained, 'but I forgot to point it out at the time. Apparently, before the days of mass education very few youngsters had the opportunity of bettering themselves and so a large percentage of the population was unaware of its true potential; as a consequence there were obviously few openings or facilities for such pupils, students and apprentices et cetera.

'With the arrival of education for all, though, there was an almost immediate influx of ultra-intelligent children and, demand being the parent of supply, a resultant increase in the number of colleges and universities to cater for the new intelligentsia; sadly, when those students graduated they naturally enough expected vocations to suit their special abilities. Of course, at first, when there were fresh fields to discover and develop as in medical science and other subjects beneficial to mankind it was all extremely laudable; but nowadays when really essential projects are becoming evermore scarce there's a lot of unnecessary research being undertaken, which is why vast sums of money are being squandered upon useless and pointless projects, while people a stone's throw away from the laboratories, or whatever, are eating their hearts out for want of a comparatively minimal amount of cash.'

'So you reckon it's all a case of being just jobs for the boys, and girls, to do then?'

Julie nodded. 'Much of the time, yes. A lot of modern technology is concerned with improving ways of killing people, and in conquering outer space in order, so it was recently stated, to help with the plundering of other planet's minerals and elements; or even to populate them if suitable for settlement. In the latter case, they're totally ignoring the fact that separate communities frequently desire to become independent of their parent bodies, and often cause unimaginable strife, wars and rivalry in doing so. Whyte Island's retort is to query the necessity of it: why not lower the world's population drastically and thereby conserve the assets we naturally possess. Star gazing used to be a euphemism for time wasting which, in this day and age seems more apt than ever.'

They paused at the hall door so she could finish explaining. 'As the science and technology college guide mentioned, if you remember, my love, no project or research is undertaken over here unless its value has been painstakingly ascertained and that no other nation, as far as we know, isn't already engaged in it. But more importantly our prospective geniuses are generally diverted toward other goals and interests; our authorities are more than willing to encourage intelligence and self-discovery but not to the extent of allowing science and technology to get out of hand.'

As the last couple entered the drill hall Andrew nodded sagely, grinned, then asked, 'Shall we go and do some more stargazing, darling?'

Smiling in recognition of his wit his sweetheart answered, 'Touché.'

The remaining lectures dealt with the subjects appertaining to self preservation such as what was required of each individual, how to survive in various types of habitat, the way to strip, clean and shoot different firearms, set demolition charges, how to avoid, and ambush, an enemy, and sundry methods of communication, besides a myriad other details which went into producing the near perfect guerrilla. Julie had long since informed her lover that every person attended training once over a three and a quarter year period, the extra three months being added on, she'd mentioned sardonically, to enable all seasons to be experienced; and therefore, over the years, many people became quite expert in the tactics of primitive warfare.

After two days mainly devoted to lecturing came the practical work; at first it was mere routine, involving weapon firing, grenade throwing and other procedures typifying army training;

but later came the field work, which meant irregular hours, discomfort and dirt. Andrew's sweetheart had already prepared him for the ordeal by tying her hair back and, more dramatically, in cutting short her beautifully shaped finger nails. To begin with, the entire complement of the camp, including all the available instructors, was divided into two separate groups and as such commenced field training; but gradually the sections were split into smaller units until eventually, on the penultimate day, Julie and he found themselves alone as an active section creeping and crawling through woodland, undergrowth, water and anything else which came between them and their objective.

At times the conditions during training had been deplorable, especially when out in the field for then the state of the weather, the time of day or night, or whether the individual was female or male, old or young, was a matter of complete indifference to the instructors. Gone was any kindness or courtesy; if an order was given, no matter how difficult or ridiculous, it had to be carried out promptly. Sometimes shelter in the form of a low, inconspicuous tent was provided, occasionally a hot meal was to be had, but on one night they were left to their own devices and the lovers, half starved on their pack rations, lay soaking wet in each other's arms under a single blanket in the middle of a rhododendron bush. 'If I didn't know what love was before,' Andrew whispered with chattering teeth in his partner's ear, 'I know what it is now.'

'Be quiet,' she murmured, tightening her arms about him, 'try to get some rest, because we've only got a few hours if we're going to get there on time. We mustn't get caught.'

'This makes zig-zagging seem about as horrendous as a church fete,' he muttered before falling into an exhausted sleep. Often during the latter half of that week Julie's presence had given him cause to silently thank the authorities for their enlightened views regarding the sexes; all this hardship served to strengthen the bond between the pair, as it must also have done between all the other couples taking part in the exercises. His lover was now more than just a sweetheart and a companion, she was an example to him. If she could endure all this discomfort and misery, then so could he; likewise, if she could retain all the knowledge necessary to the life of a guerrilla, then he could too.

Through all their trials and tribulations he often secretly dwelt upon who had shared her sufferings during previous battle exercises, but he never mentioned this taboo subject to her, it was as pointless as the exercise they were now on. The seriousness with which the entire battle training week was undertaken was evident in the complete lack of entertainment or the provision of any spare time; everybody was either being lectured, undergoing field exercises, eating or sleeping; there weren't even any facilities for bathing. And so on many occasions the lovers barely had the energy to crawl into their bunk, for they only used one at a time, before slipping off into a deep sleep.

On their last full day came the biggest and most authentic exercise of all, for once more the camp's inmates were divided, with the exception of the instructors who acted as monitors, into equally sized armies; each side was then presented with a list of objectives and the times by which they had to be captured. The party to which Julie and Andrew belonged had to run the gauntlet of enemy held territory to invest and overwhelm an outpost; everyone carried guns loaded with blanks, and also firecrackers to act as hand grenades. Unsurprisingly the terrain involved was the roughest and most varied which could be provided, made even more difficult by its having to be crossed, part of the time, in darkness.

Such a venture, often viewed dispassionately by Andrew on the television and in the cinema, looked easy, but when undertaken in real life it was more than a little nerve wracking and hard to accomplish both physically and mentally. But although the exercise had been designed to seem as realistic as possible without having recourse to live ammunition he still thought of it as being only partially serious, even during its more hectic moments; however, when their group eventually breeched the outpost's defences he was to discover a more authentic reason for their efforts.

Unbeknown to him, his temporary comrades deliberately held back in recognition of his becoming an islander, and allowed him to reach the small building which was their ultimate objective, first; and as he burst through the doorway he was confronted with darkness and an urgent sounding, muffled noise. Hastily opening a pair of shutters covering one of the firing apertures he turned and saw three couples clad in mud splattered evening wear seated in a line on the floor with their backs to the wall; one glance was enough to note they were in some distress, so he produced his knife and cut the person nearest him free: a young woman wearing a white satin gown whose hem had been roughly torn off just above knee level. 'Thank goodness!' she exclaimed as he helped her to her feet, 'it's nice to be able to speak and move about again, we've been discommoded since we were abducted last night.' Andrew smiled sympathetically but then turned to help her fellows, but Julie and the remainder of the group had already liberated them.

'So what happened to you?' he asked the woman and her companion, who now stood beside her with a protective arm about her shoulder.

'Andrew!' Julie scolded, 'don't be so nosey, that's their concern.'

But the woman, however, seemed quite amused by his interest and promised that, if he brought them a hot drink each from a canteen urn which had quickly appeared nearby, and gave them time to relax, she'd be only too pleased to relate their adventures to them both. 'I've always wanted to meet a young mainlander,' she added.

'Former,' his sweetheart, all smiles, corrected while she untied her golden hair and allowed it to fall around her shoulders.

'Like most zigzagging,' the erstwhile captive began when all four of them were seated on a bench outside the building, 'it all started innocuously enough; we were attending an intimate cocktail party in one of those old style colonial houses: it was supposed to be a tropical country where the oppressive upper crust are in perpetual conflict with the peasantry, and we were enjoying ourselves on some kind of plantation. Anyway, we'd all just finished a small repast and had taken our drinks out onto the verandah when suddenly there were guerrillas everywhere.' She placed a palm against her upper chest and faced her husband. 'God, Paul, they frightened the life out of me; they seemed to come from nowhere. Well,' she went on, addressing Andrew, 'they quickly rendered us all helpless, and after ransacking the house they marched us off into the woods.

It was all very realistic; after that cloudburst the other day it was stiflingly humid despite the cloudless sky, and of course we poor captives couldn't breathe properly due to the rags stuffed in our mouths; the organisers had already rigged up recordings of monkeys, frogs, cicadas and other typical jungle sounds in the trees, and when it got dark and the moon appeared you'd have sworn it really was the tropics. Originally there were five of us couples; however, two pairs were plants and they were disposed of in order to lend authenticity to our experience. The first couple went because the leader of the terrorists assumed a passion for the girl who was very attractive, and this resulted in an argument between him and his mistress during our first rest period; they really went at it hammer and tongs in a language which they must have thought up, and after a lot of pointing and gesturing at the hapless couple they were manhandled off into the pseudo jungle by the by the leader and his woman.'

'That was a real heart stopper,' Paul, emphasising, declared.

'Yes,' his wife agreed, 'we could hear the girl screaming and her companion pleading until they got too far away to be audible and eventually the two guerrillas came back alone.

'The other pair refused to go any further after we'd been marched through the trees for several hours with only two breaks in between, they'd been our host and hostess and were in reality the Representative for Law and her husband. The memory of looking back after we'd moved off, and seeing them kneeling on the track in the moonlight with a terrorist pointing a rifle at each of their heads while they remained passively awaiting their fate will stay forever in my mind; later, we heard a couple of shots.

'Anyway, we were kept walking until after midnight, I think; then our captors made camp, lit a fire and we were then hand fed one at a time so we couldn't communicate with each other, Afterward they put down ground sheets for each couple, tied our already bound feet to those of our partners' and then threw blankets over us; I don't know about the other four but we couldn't get to sleep, could we, love? It was so stuffy that I think it was even worse than walking. Before dawn we were on the move again after being given a mug of coffee each, but this time instead of marching us about aimlessly we were brought here and incarcerated in the way you found us; the bangs and firing during your attack were quite awe inspiring, I can tell you!' She shrugged. 'That's about it.'

'At least,' Julie commented, pointing to the woman's feet, 'they supplied you with boots; by rights you should've been barefoot.'

She laughed. 'They also took us to relieve ourselves if we made the right grunting noises, thank goodness.'

'It must've been terrifying,' observed Andrew.

'It certainly proved its point,' she smiled in reply. 'Only a complete fool would endorse a class system composed of the extremely rich and the very poor after undergoing such an ordeal; but as a lesson in sensuality it was unbeatable. Actually, it was Paul's birthday present to me, and can you guess what we're going to do now?'

He shook his head, but it was the woman's husband who supplied the answer, 'We've borrowed a guerrilla outfit each, and we've hired the colonial house; after we've had a proper meal, a shower and a sleep we'll get dressed in our uniforms and continue the fantasy on to a more satisfactory conclusion.'

After Julie and her lover had wished the woman happy returns they all stood up and the latter patted Andrew affectionately on the shoulder, 'I hope you'll forgive us for not asking you about yourselves but we're rather drained of vitality at the moment. Perhaps we'll meet again sometime.'

During the lorry ride back to camp Andrew confided to his lover, 'I've met the Representative for Law and I'm sure she was past zigzagging age; she's got a full grown daughter.'

'Trust you to know that,' Julie laughed, 'but no doubt you'll be shocked to learn that Charlie Maynard often takes part in zigzagging, so members of the government also feel they ought to as well. It's more or less traditional now.' He found the mental image which this image created quite awesome.

Before leaving the camp the lovers, along with others who hadn't yet visited the secret place, together with their partners where applicable, were seen by the head instructor who merely wished to know if they knew how to reach the place in question; she also enquired if they'd learnt from their battle training, to which the answer was a unanimous and unequivocal affirmative.

There were several letters awaiting them when they returned to the flat, the most important of which, from Andrew's point of view, informed him he would be required to commence training and studies at the engineering college on Monday week; full details with regard to the establishment and the course were enclosed. Julie received a letter which formally advised her that one of her secondary jobs, in the countryside, was due to commence, the date of which exactly coincided with that of her lover's. She smiled when he drew her attention to this fact. 'It merely proves how excellent the coordination is between various authority departments' she declared. 'Our two sets of personal details have been clipped together, and from now on officialdom will take into account any decision affecting either one of us with regard to its possible effect upon the other. Actually, darling, we've both been given a week's holiday apart from our visit to the secret site on Monday, which won't take long.

Julie gazed thoughtfully at him for a moment, then said, 'Look, why don't I phone up Ruth's and ask them if they could put us up till next weekend? We could go straight there after our visit.' He thought the idea of spending five days and nights on a farm marvellous and agreed wholeheartedly; so she left the room to make the call and returned shortly after, beaming, to tell him it was all arranged. 'But don't you dare make any passes at my cousin,' she warned playfully.

'You needn't worry,' Andrew replied, recognising her remark as a cue, 'no one could replace you in my heart.'

'That's all I wanted to hear,' she smiled gratefully. 'Now, why don't we take that well needed shower at the same time as a little romping, then get dressed casually, go out for a meal, come back to bed and have some more fun.'

The following day was a Sunday and was also one of the dates upon which the sea battle spectacular was due to take place. Although Andrew wasn't too bothered about whether he saw it or not, his sweetheart's enthusiasm on his behalf was so intense that he allowed himself to be taken along just to avoid disappointing her. As is so often the case, when one is reluctant to experience an event, Julie's lover soon discovered it was a display which was definitely not to be missed. They were too late to obtain seats onboard one of the pleasure steamers, the best position from which to observe the show, and so they were compelled to join the large number of spectators waiting on the esplanade for the performance to begin; on the way Andrew bought a detailed programme along with a couple of ice creams from a vendor.

Walking along the lakeside on what was a warm, still, but cloudy day, he read aloud the details to Julie regarding the battles in miniature due to take place. 'An armed merchant ship, undergunned and vulnerable, takes on a heavy cruiser so as to allow the merchant ships she is escorting to escape; the gallant defender is eventually sunk whereupon the cruiser chases after the scattered merchant vessels. However, she, in turn is attacked by a pair of destroyers, one of which is also sunk; finally a battleship appears on the scene and engages the heavy cruiser in a long distance gunnery duel which results in the destruction of the latter.'

Included in the programme were pictures of many of the models taking part in the proceedings, some of which had the builders alongside to demonstrate the large size of the miniature vessels; just as the ferry captain had indicated, the little ships were perfect in every detail. Alongside the pictures were various dimensions, historical notes and facts about the models and their prototypes, as well as further information about the battles. 'From my calculations,' Julie declared when they reached a certain point along the esplanade, 'this is a good enough spot from which to view the action. Besides,' she laughed, 'it's the first gap in the crowd.'

When, at last, they were leaning against the rail gazing out over the lake, he expressed doubt as to how much they'd be able to see despite the large scale of the models. 'You'll be surprised,' his sweetheart commented, 'they show up quite well, especially when they're trailing a lot of smoke. Anyway, it makes them appear far more authentic as they look much larger than real ships would in an actual battle because, apparently, in fairly recent sea warfare opposing ships rarely came much nearer than five miles to each other. So given the law of perspective with regard to the distance shortening aspect of modelling, in full size an actual destroyer would fill everyone's vision close to, yet seem quite small five miles away near the opposite shore, while employing the same ratio scale on the models we'll be seeing shortly, there won't be too much difference between the vessels closest to and furthest off!'

Julie's somewhat complicated and tortuous explanation proved quite correct as the battle scenes began. But first Andrew's lover cried out, 'Look!' nudging him. He followed her pointing finger; coming diagonally toward the spectators from across the lake was a miniature four masted sailing barque, as yet too far away to be seen in much detail but obviously lately launched from one of the pleasure craft lying offshore. Close to them, children began to yell and cheer when they saw the little vessel, and gradually their appreciation began to spread along the line of onlookers until all the children on the promenade seemed to be pleased to see the model.

'Well,' he declared, 'that isn't on the programme.'

'It's just a curtain raiser to occupy the kids,' Julie replied unemotionally, 'like the overture at an opera, very nice but not worthy of special attention.' Nevertheless he watched in fascination as the model drew nearer until it was running parallel to the breakwater and heading toward the dam; as it passed by he was easily able to see it represented a china tea clipper, with three rows of black or white bands with the latter representing a gun deck with its black squares depicting imaginary gun ports. Andrew estimated it to be at least nine feet from the tip of its bowsprit to the end of the shorter one at the stern.

His lover, who had seen it on several previous occasions, told him it was a genuine miniature sailing ship, but its sails and yards were electrically operated so it could tack and be otherwise manoeuvred by remote control. It had scarcely arrived at its destination where people were preparing to hoist it from the water, when Julie nudged him again to tell him the real display was beginning; she then handed him a pair of binoculars which, in her usual thoughtful way, she'd brought along.

The next few hours were thoroughly enjoyable for Andrew, as it was the nearest he, or presumably any other person present, had come to a real sea battle and was especially lifelike when viewed through the glasses. The little ships wheeled and raced over the section of lake reserved for them, smoke occasionally pouring from their funnels, guns flashing and shells splashing in the water around them; he couldn't begin to understand how it was all accomplished. Especially realistic was the way hits were registered on the vessels, and the actual sinkings were painful to watch; the destroyer went down very quickly but the armed merchant ship, which was obviously supposed to represent a former liner, and the heavy cruiser were both battered into destruction. The first ship disappeared in a pall of smoke while the latter was eventually consumed by a mighty explosion.

'You might be surprised to learn,' Julie observed as they walked away after the show, 'that none of those models was the least bit damaged in spite of all the smoke and noise; even the sunken ships are recoverable.'

'Knowing island ingenuity and love of economy, I'm not in the least surprised; but I'm not so sure it was good education for those children, because I could tell from all their gleeful shouting and cheering that they enjoyed every minute of it.'

Glancing sideways at him as they headed back in the direction of town, his lover said, 'Don't worry, darling, if their parents don't explain the less glamorous aspects of it all to them, as mine did, then their teachers will. It wasn't really obvious but it was a lesson to all of us; it didn't really seem so but it was far more of a war memorial than those static and silent cenotaphs still frequently found in cities, towns and villages on the mainland, remembered and noticed by very few people on just one day each year.'

They had a drink in a hotel lounge overlooking the waterside before returning to the flat, where they subsequently spent the remainder of the day in packing for their holiday, listening to music and, at Julie's suggestion, to recordings of Andrew's folk song practice, for she was anxious he should gain confidence and develop a style and repertoire of his own. Later they went to bed early to further catch up on the love making lost during their hectic week of battle training.

As soon as he saw the length of the train which drew into Laketown station and the number onboard Andrew had a good idea of where the secret place was sited. 'But why wouldn't you tell me it was in the region of the factory complex and railway centre?' he asked as soon as they'd seated themselves, 'You had no need to be so secretive,' he chided, ' after all, I am an islander now.'

Grasping his hand placatingly Julie replied, 'There didn't seem much point in revealing where it was beforehand; anyway, because it's a high security risk area the less who know about it the better; you're only being allowed to see it now because it's your right as an islander. The authorities, apparently, would prefer to keep it under wraps though.'

After alighting at the factory complex station they found a convenient place in which to leave their suitcases and, as soon as the remainder of the passengers had dispersed, Andrew's sweetheart led him in the direction of the railway centre. 'Will anyone be expecting us?' he asked shortly before they reached the main building.

Laughing, she answered, 'It wouldn't be a very secure place if visitors turned up unannounced at any old time, now would it? Of course they are, but remind me to get them to arrange some seats for us on one of the departing freight trains as soon as we get there, as it's the only way out of here if we don't want to wait for the day's work to end.'

The interior of the centre displayed much more activity than on his previous visit and he'd have liked to stay and watch for a while, but Julie urged him on saying they'd only get in the way and, besides, they were expected to arrive at their venue on time. So she led him by the hand straight down the hall with its several sets of tracks and a number of locomotives and other rolling stock; when the railway and crane lines ended, the hall extended a little further but was then replaced by an almost featureless tunnel some six feet in diameter with large electrical cables running along the left side.

Finally, after a seemingly endless walk, the lovers arrived at a set of steel doors, on the right of which was a heavy metal cabinet with a single drawer and two rows of numbered buttons just above. 'Put all your metallic belongings in here, darling,' Julie said as she pulled the drawer open; placing their watches, money, keys and other appropriate items inside she then closed the drawer. 'It's so we can't smuggle in any weapons,' she explained, 'the metal detector won't let us in otherwise; try it now.' He pulled hard at the drawer, but it wouldn't budge.

'I hope it's more cooperative when we return,' he joked. She smiled and then pressed a button set in the wall. 'It's like something out of a science fiction film,' he added, but his companion put a finger to her lips in warning.

'Names and numbers, please,' a voice immediately boomed out; Julie answered with their names, but pressed out their numbers on the buttons.

A long pause ensued during which she told him their details were being checked against their photographs. 'All the way down the tunnel we were under surveillance by hidden cameras,' she explained.

'Supposing we weren't who we're supposed to be, or there was some sort of mistake?'

'It wouldn't matter,' she shrugged, 'they just wouldn't let us in; but there'd be a reception committee awaiting us at the tunnel entrance when we emerged.'

Eventually the hidden voice declared, 'You may enter.'

Julie stepped back and motioned toward the doors. 'Be my guest,' she invited. Placing a hand a hand on one of the handles, the door swung open easily; inside was a foyer devoid of any feature apart from a lift with its doors open invitingly. As soon as his lover closed the main door behind them they stood in the lift and were instantly conveyed to the floor below.

Facing them when the door slid back was a smiling young woman clad in a pale blue coverall who greeted them as though they were old friends. 'Hello, Julie and Andrew, welcome to our little nest; though I'm afraid there isn't too much to see.' She stood back to allow them to enter the room. 'What we generally do first,' she went on, 'is to show visitors the monster, then discuss the details and answer any questions over a cup of tea afterward; so if you'd like to come this way?'

He just had time for a quick glance round the room before following his lover and their guide; he was therefore only aware of an area similar in size to the lounge in the average suburban house. Against one wall stood a console fitted with several illuminated lights and labelled buttons, and with another, though somewhat older, woman seated before it; there was a polished dining room table in the centre of the room with matching chairs arranged around it, a couple of armchairs, and a sofa upon which was seated an even older woman reading a magazine. She glanced up during his perusal and smiled.

Their guide, meanwhile, had reached the opposite wall and was pulling open a door; from the outside it appeared quite innocuous, just the plain domestic connecting variety, but as he passed through he noted it was extremely thick and merely faced with wood; it was, he realised, made from some kind of metal and was obviously very heavy. The young woman waited for him to pass by before closing the door behind them. 'My name's Barbara,' she told them as she turned round. 'This is all new to you I take it?' she asked, addressing Andrew and giving him an appraising look. Upon his nodding, she continued, 'You're obviously a stranger to our island because people usually come here when they're much younger, don't they Julie? Anyway, this annexe helps to keep the temperature stable and also acts as a double blast wall, but as you can see we like to have even this section comfortable and homely.'

She was right, for the walls were papered and decorated with landscapes and similarly restful prints, and the floor was covered with a pale pink carpet. On the opposite side from that through which they'd entered was another door of the same design, Andrew noted as Barbara opened it, as the previous one. 'Well,' she exclaimed as soon as she'd ushered the lovers through and had closed the door behind her, 'here it is!'

The object in question was a white painted cylinder about eight feet tall and some three feet in diameter resting upon a shock absorbing cradle, the entire assembly enclosed in a glass case; half a dozen wires protruded from it along with several clock gauges. As if in deference to the device the room was quite austere, the walls and ceiling being painted white and there was a plain grey carpet on the floor. The whole area was hardly bigger than the glass case, but there was plenty of space within which to walk around it; upon one side a sofa had been provided, though apart from another door, which Barbara said was a cupboard, the room was featureless.

'Well, what do you think of it?' she asked as soon as they were seated.

Andrew was silent for a moment, then enquired slowly, 'Is it what I think it is?'

He was only half aware of the girls smiling at each other; then Julie spoke for the first time since leaving the lift. 'If you think it's a nuclear device, then you're correct; it's a sort of welcoming present for unwelcome visitors.'

He couldn't help asking light heartedly, 'What time does it go off?' A remark which made both his companions laugh politely, but then he added, 'Isn't it a bit drastic, though?'

'Not if it means the island is going to be left alone for as long as possible,' Barbara replied. 'I take it you've now completed your battle training?' When he nodded she went on, 'Well, should we be attacked then, as you're now aware, we'd demonstrate our displeasure by fighting back with guns whatever, but in reality this would only be to justify detonating the bomb as a last resort. So this little chappy,' she motioned in the direction of the device, 'is our insurance against molestation.'

'Is it very powerful?'

She laughed without humour. 'After it had been thrust up to ground level by air pressure and then detonated, there wouldn't be much left of Whyte Island and even less of us occupants; and the fall out, blast and tidal wave would cause widespread destruction over a huge area elsewhere. But the political repercussions would be enormous. You know, Andrew, apologists for nuclear weapons bless them by stating that they give rise to a checkmate situation between world powers, which is really our basis for having a device of our own.'

'Do other nations know of its existence?' he enquired.

'I believe it's an open secret among many global leaders, but neither they nor we want to shout about it from the roof tops; the device was constructed in secret though, and only when this place was completed was its existence leaked.' She paused to add defensively, 'After all, if it's alright for other nations, some of them unstable, to possess nuclear weapons then I don't see why our island shouldn't.'

Julie rose to her feet. 'Did you say something about a cup of coffee?' she asked.

'That's Helen over at the console,' Barbara said when they'd returned to the main room, 'and this is Janet.' She nodded in the direction of the woman on the sofa. 'I'll just go and make the drinks; I'm sure Janet will answer any further questions.'

'You've certainly got it very comfortable here,' Andrew observed when his lover and he had seated themselves in the armchairs at the older woman's invitation.

Laying aside her magazine Janet replied, 'Yes, it's like a home from home, isn't it? It's been designed like this on purpose; as you can imagine, playing nursemaid to the monstrosity you've just seen can be a little nerve wracking, so everything has been arranged to make our stay as relaxing as possible.'

'Are there many other people here?' he asked.

'Just the three of us.'

He raised his eyebrows. 'What, no men?'

Shaking her head, she smiled, 'No reflection on your gender, but it's thought that males are unsuitable for this responsibility. Or let me put it another way; the authorities believe women are generally more stable; despite this place being homely, it can become frustrating and tedious, and women seem much more able to cope with such problems. We're less argumentative, less likely to dwell upon thoughts of sex or anything else which might take our minds off the job.'

She stopped for a moment while Barbara served the coffee, then continued, 'Perhaps one of the best reasons why women are employed down here as guardians of the device is because we're all mothers, and therefore less likely to suddenly go berserk and do something stupid, maternal instinct being what it is.'

Andrew looked surprised, but she sipped her coffee and then went on, 'There isn't really much to do, just one person could look after this place and still be under employed; however, it would be a lonely task so the authorities considered using two people, but they then realised that when just two people are alone together it can quite easily result in incompatibility and so they decided three would have to be the absolute minimum. They also realised, for obvious reasons, that the guardians would all need to be of the same gender. Actually, it worked out quite well, because after it was decided to employ women someone came up with the idea of using mothers, for not only are there lots of us but we could also be spared from our chores without causing too much disruption to our lives or those of our husband's.'

From the corner of his eye Andrew noticed Barbara glance at the wall clock; then standing up she went across to the console where she took Helen's place, and the latter girl came over and joined Janet on the sofa. 'You see,' continued the older woman, 'this is such a serious business that it's considered imperative each individual shouldn't be overexposed to the routine, so there are several hundred of us mothers involved and we only serve six hours at a time, and even those overlap with the hours being worked by our companions.'

'By two hours, isn't it?' enquired Julie.

It was Helen who replied, 'Yes, that's right. A couple of hours after I started this shift one of the girls who was already down here was relieved by Barbara, and another two hours after that Janet took over from Elaine. I'll be going home in just a little over an hour's time.'

'What will you do about transport?' Andrew wished to know.

'Pretty much the same as you, I suppose,' she smiled, 'but after 10 p.m. comfortable bedrooms are supplied within the industrial complex. I miss my old man, of course, as he likewise misses me.' She shrugged. 'Though as each one of us women is only here once in a blue moon, it doesn't matter too much.'

Janet said, 'I'm sure you'd like to know something about the communication structure and the facilities here?' He nodded. 'Briefly,' she began, 'we operate in conjunction with the island's main computer and normally we're in continuous contact with each other; however, in the event of an invasion or anything else which might be thought to presage belligerent activity the outside authorities would take control through the computer, and so they could detonate the device without our aid. On the other hand, if we lost contact with the authorities, an event so unlikely it would suggest a real emergency, then we would be expected to take direct action. Likewise, if the authorities were unable to contact us they would fear the worst, and so detonate.' He must've looked worried because Janet gave him a reassuring smile. 'There are half a dozen different methods by which we and the authorities can communicate; there wouldn't be any mistake.'

'You wouldn't think it,' Helen hastily informed him, 'but we're completely independent of the outside world. We can produce our own air and electricity; and we have our toilet facilities, as well as a food and water store in case of emergencies. So we're absolutely immune from outside attacks.'

Julie and Andrew stayed chatting to the three women until shortly before Helen was due to be relieved, but although it had been arranged they would travel on the same train as her it was against the rules for visitors to be present when the changeover took place. Before they took their leave Barbara handed them a piece of paper with a six digit number printed upon it; Julie didn't tell her sweetheart what it was for at the time but when they were in the tunnel again, and the steel doors had closed behind them, she tapped the number out on the cabinet's buttons. 'It's clever isn't it?' she remarked, pulling the drawer open, 'The women select any number they wish, wait for us to leave, then send the information up to the cabinet after the top door has closed behind us; this allows us to collect our effects only after we can't get back down to the bomb.'

They met Helen's relief, a blonde girl who flashed them a smile as she passed, when they were half way down the passage. As it was a warm, sunny day they stood outside in the yard while they awaited Helen, watching a locomotive being prepared for its next duty. 'Just think, Andy, it might be you working on that engine; it's named after a famous poet so you should remember it.'

But her lover, his mind still dwelling on the fearful nuclear device so close to them, was only half listening. 'It's terrible,' he commented finally, 'to contemplate all that death and destruction within such a short distance of us, it makes everything else so unreal and impermanent somehow.'

'That's a worry everyone on this planet has to come to terms with nowadays, darling,' she observed sympathetically, 'But I know one thing, if it ever came to a conflict concerning Whyte Island I hope I'd be standing as close to a bomb when it went off suddenly. I'd rather be blown to pieces in an instant than endure the agonies which others might have to suffer.'

However, when they were at last on the train with Helen nuclear warfare was the last thing on their minds, for like all the islanders Andrew had come into contact with, their companion was an excellent conversationalist, and by the time the three of them had exchanged their life stories Julie and he were due to alight. Most of the freight trains leaving the factory complex were bound for Harbourtown, while the farm toward which the lovers were making was on the opposite side of the island, so necessitating a change of trains at the first station on the main line.

'This isn't too far from the school summer camp I visited,'

Andrew stated when they stood on the platform at their destination, 'but how do we get to the farm from here?'

'Easy,' she replied, 'we phone for someone to come and pick us up.' Noting his surprised expression, she explained, 'We're not totally paranoid about using other forms of transport, you know. If we were going to a village away from the railway then we'd need to wait for a loribus, but Ruth's farm is quite isolated so they're permitted to use their runabout truck; just as long as they go no further in it.' She smiled and added, 'Otherwise it might set a precedent for other people wanting to own motor vehicles.' Andrew waited in the forecourt as his lover phoned. 'There isn't any rush,' she told him as she put the mobile away, 'I mentioned we'd be in the pub.'

They were roughly halfway through their very welcome drinks in the local which, like the remainder of the village buildings, was constructed from honey coloured stone, and looked as if it had been built in the seventeenth century, when they were joined by Ruth and her father. The latter, a tall, thin person named Alastair, was a jolly, carefree man who, like his daughter, was in no hurry to leave for when Andrew offered to stand them drinks he accepted with alacrity. During their subsequent conversation the reason for their lack of haste became apparent when Alastair remarked, 'Unlike your farmers.......'

He was immediately corrected by his niece, 'Andy is an islander now, uncle.'

'Sorry, Andy. Unlike mainland farmers, or ought I to say "many of them", we've got more than enough labour to help us out. This system of each person holding down several jobs means that at harvest time, and other busy periods, we can obtain extra hands, and so there's no great panic to get things done usually or any real need to work long hours; while at other more normal times,' he grinned, 'if you could ever describe any farm work as being normal, there are more than enough regulars to hand to take care of anything which might crop up.' He drained his pint mug then glanced wistfully toward the bar.

Ruth laughed and stood up. 'Alright, dad,' she exclaimed, 'seeing it's a hot day, I'll drive. You'll have the same again, Andy.' It was a command. 'Come on, Julie,' she said turning to her cousin, 'give me a hand.'

As soon as the girls were out of earshot Alastair confided, 'Ruth's one of my workers; she's a good girl and she loves animals, she's well on the way to becoming a vet. You've met Derek?' Andrew nodded. 'Well, he's another one of my hands; he's almost certain to become a full farmer one of these days, he never needs to be told what has to be done.' He paused, then said reflectively, 'There are at least three things we island farmers have to be thankful for. You've heard what one of them is; one of the others is, strangely enough, birth control. I regularly listen to the mainland's farming programme, and an old chestnut which often crops up is the excuse for removing hedgerows and buying up farms to make great agricultural complexes, which is that farmland has to become more economical so larger amounts of food can be produced more cheaply,' He stopped while Ruth placed a pint of beer each before them.

'Julie and I are going to sit outside,' she declared; then glancing at Andrew she winked, 'When dad gets on his hobbyhorse there's no stopping him,' and she added irreverently, 'I've heard it too many times before.'

When they'd gone Andrew observed, 'Your daughter doesn't pull any punches, does she?'

The farmer chuckled. 'That's just her way: inherited characteristic I believe they call it? She's just like her mother, her aunt and, as you've doubtless noticed, her cousin; there's no harm in any of them, they know exactly how far to go and they've all got hearts as golden as their hair. Short of beating the living daylights out of them regularly, Andrew, you'll never overcome their self confidence; but who wants a shrinking violet? I certainly don't. Anyway, as I was saying, mainland farmers claim they've got to produce more to cater for a rising population, yet their radio admits there's too much food as it is. Personally I think it's merely a way for wealthy farmers to get richer. But that's beside the point; however, we island farmers don't have the incentive to overproduce to such an extent; because we've got a stable population we know exactly how much farm produce we need to grow, or rear, as the case may be.'

'I heard you export any surplus.'

'We do, but only by chance, and only if there is a surplus and there's a market for whatever it is. You see, Andy, we can't foretell what the weather, for example, is going to be like; so collectively we overproduce, but nothing gets wasted as we can nearly always export our meat products abroad, and vegetables can easily be ploughed back into the soil. But, because our population has been set at a certain limit there is more than enough farmland for the nation's needs, and so not only is there little worry about constantly increasing production demands but life is also much simpler: we practise crop rotation instead of artificial fertilizers so the guts don't get taken out of the soil, we can get by with smaller fields than on the mainland, and we can afford to retain items of interest like woods, heaths, streams, ponds and lakes. I think if you spent a week on the average mainland farm, Andrew, and then came to our farm you'd think ours was something out of toy town; life on an island farm is interesting because it's picturesque and varied, and we think nothing of letting a meadow grow semi-wild for several years so we can give it a rest, finally to plough its goodness back in.' Gulping back the rest of his pint, he rose and announced, 'We'd better go and see what those girls are doing; I wouldn't put it past Ruth to take the pickup back without us.'

When Andrew returned from taking their glasses back to the counter he asked Alastair what the third benefit to being a Whyte Island farmer was. 'Well,' he replied as they made their way to the door, 'as you're no doubt aware by now, I'm dedicated to agriculture, yet I'm pleased when the time comes for me to take up one of my other jobs because it's nice to have a break from the responsibility of farming and to mix with new people for a while; and when we return to it I'm refreshed and raring to go once more. I couldn't imagine spending an entire life on the land without a break or two, because it can be a hard taskmaster.'

He wasn't able to say any more on the subject because the cousins were actually sitting in the vehicle waiting to set off; he insisted Andrew ought to join the girls in the cab whilst he rode in the back, 'It's a bit of a squeeze with four inside,' he explained, 'anyway, you wouldn't want to get your clothes dirty out here.'

'What sort of farm have you got?' Andrew enquired of Ruth as she drove them down the metalled land leading directly to the farm buildings.

'Mostly arable, though we've got a reasonably large flock of sheep. As you can see, this area is quite flat but there's a fair bit of downland which is ideal for grazing sheep on, especially where it's too steep to be cultivated properly. Of course, we're extremely fortunate on this island in having so much chalky soil, it's just the thing for growing most vegetables and cereals. We bring the sheep down in winter and turn them out on the fields where we can keep an eye on them, and where they can fertilize the soil naturally.'

Julie was silent as they rode along, doubtless being content just to enjoy the beauty of the narrow lane with its wide verges, tall hedgerows and frequent trees. Her lover asked, 'Haven't you got any chickens or ducks, then?'

'Oh yes,' laughed Ruth, 'but they're so common no one includes them; nearly all farms have got poultry in one form or another.' She slowed down for a hump back bridge spanning a sparkling little stream. 'Nearly there,' she commented.

Eventually, after driving some two miles from the public house, they arrived outside the farmhouse or, to be more exact, farmhouses for there were two imposing buildings set at right angles to each other and facing an island lawn with shrubs in the centre; a third side comprised a row of outbuildings and a small stable block, the roof of which was surmounted by a white painted, wooden cupola. The entire scene looked extremely neat and peaceful completed, as it was, by the flowers in front of the houses, several small trees and the small flock of white fantail doves which flew up onto the roof of the stables upon the pickup's arrival only to return to the circular lawn almost immediately. 'I see you've still got your birds,' Julie observed as they drew up.

'Sort of,' her cousin replied dispassionately, 'but we have to keep replacing them due to the gossies, sparrowhawks and the other avian visitors.'

'Which building do you think is the original one?' Andrew's sweetheart asked as soon as they'd alighted from the vehicle.

Before replying, he took the suitcases which Alastair handed down to him, then studied the two homes. The honey coloured stone structure on the left was similar in material and design to the public house and seemed really old, but the building in the centre with its well-worn red bricks and matching pantiles appeared even older; besides which it also resembled the outbuildings. 'I think I'll go for the brick built house,' he said finally, enjoying the game, 'because I don't think the authorities would take the trouble to build a home with matching stables at the same time, it would seem too obvious.'

'You'd be wrong,' the farmer, who'd jumped down beside them, exclaimed, 'our house and the stables are comparatively new. Now,' he added briskly, 'I expect you'll both want to have a wash, and to change into something far more casual; then when you've had a bite to eat I'll take you on a guided tour. Unless you'd like that honour to go to Julie, Andrew?'

His lover, however, demurred. 'But I'll come along with you,' she said.

Ruth's mother seemed younger than her sister but very similar in appearance otherwise with, as her husband had indicated, the same auburn hair; she was also just as friendly. 'You're in the usual room, Julie,' she pointed out, 'and there'll be a snack waiting for you in about half an hour.'

'I think you're going to enjoy it here, darling.' Julie stated as she dressed herself in jeans and sweater in their bedroom, 'nothing to do but have fun, and we can come and go as we please. My aunt and uncle are easy going even by island standards. But if you can survive Alastair's tour with its endless explanation first, which is why I'm coming along for moral support, then we'll have a trouble free holiday.'

Andrew, who had been seated on the bed watching her change, an occupation he never ceased to tire of, stood up and walked over to the open window. Their room was at the back of the house and overlooked the major part of the farm with its yard, motley collection of outhouses, paddocks and an orchard; beyond were hedgerow lined fields and woods. The land rose gradually behind the farm until it met the foot of the downland; here the fields were much larger and edged with stonewalling and, apart from the occasional bush along their length, areas of woodland, and clumps of trees in the centres of some of the fields, they appeared almost barren by comparison. Julie came and stood behind him and placed her arms about his neck. 'I think I will like it here,' he confirmed, 'it's almost as enticing as you, my love.' Pausing, a thought came to him and he asked, 'Do your aunt and uncle live here when they aren't farming?'

'Sometimes; it depends upon how they feel. Uncle often works in the main factory, where we were this morning, and you saw how far that was; so usually they like to move nearer to whatever his current job is. But you'll soon realise this farm takes a lot of leaving.'

'Presumably the other farmer resides in the stone building; so who lives here when your aunt and uncle are away?'

Much to his consternation she'd begun to nibble at his ear, but she stopped long enough to reply, 'Ruth and Derek are only too willing to take their place; they don't mind travelling to work.' Then she returned to her teasing.

'I wish you'd tried arousing me when you were in your underwear,' he remarked, 'but for goodness sake stop doing it now as it's very frustrating and instead of me going up we've got to be going down.'

Julie giggled at his pun and replied, 'In that case we'll both need to wait a little longer, won't we?' On the stairs she turned and glanced up at him. 'Do you like boiled haddock with an egg on top?' she enquired, 'only for some unknown reason Aunt Mary always dishes it up as my first meal when I arrive.'

Her lover's visit was no exception, but he thoroughly enjoyed the snack, especially as it was followed by a great mug of tea accompanying a home made crusty bread slice liberally covered with butter and blackcurrant jam; while they ate they were entertained with leisurely, but interesting conversation from both Mary and Alastair; of Ruth and Derek there was now no sign. Directly afterward they were taken on the intimidating tour of the farm; as soon as the back door closed behind them they were confronted by a boisterous brown and white sheep dog. 'Does it bite?' Andrew asked, tentatively stretching out a hand to pat its head.

Both his companions laughed. 'No,' exclaimed Julie, stroking the dog's back, 'Ben wouldn't hurt a fly; would you, love?'

'He'd soon be put down if he did,' Alastair observed, adding, 'he's just looking forward to our stroll, that's all.' Whereupon he resumed the topic he'd been compelled to finish outside the public house. 'As I was saying,' he began, as though he'd only just left off, 'agricultural work can be a little too demanding if it's a permanent job. No matter how many people you've got helping you it can be a lonely existence and not a little worrying, especially as so much depends upon the weather. So it's hardly surprising we island farmers consider many of our mainland counterparts to have dour, introspective personalities; I'm sure economic pressures compel many of them to dispense with more workers than they ought to with the consequence that they're permanently shorthanded, and therefore have to take too much work upon themselves; this fact, together with the isolation and the unvaried toil from year to year, must have a profound effect on their attitude regarding the land and other people.'

'I've heard a lot of mainland farmers being referred to as bloody minded,' Andrew agreed. 'They're supposed to be suspicious of ramblers, careless with their environment and offhand with their livestock.'

Alastair chuckled. 'Well, there may be some truth in that, though I doubt all farmers are like it, but I think you'll find things a little different over here.'

The younger man looked about him with interest as they crossed the back yard. The entire area was unbelievably neat and tidy for it had been laid with concrete, and so there was little sign of the mud and filth usually associated with farmyards; the various outbuildings comprised, he ultimately discovered, a large garage housing the farm machinery, barns, stores and silos had been built from traditional materials where possible, and formed a compound, a tall brick wall filling any gaps between them. As far as he could see everything was in good repair there being no sign of broken tiles, warped roofs, defective walls or missing gutters; all the woodwork appeared sound and had been creosoted. 'It's more like a prison yard or fortification in here with that high wall and those closed double gates,' Andrew, with a smile, commented at length.

'Ah,' exclaimed the farmer, 'there's a very good reason for that. The idea is to prevent such creatures as foxes, members of the weasel tribe, rodents, whatever, from getting into farm buildings, and not through waging a war of attrition against them; the predators, especially, are encouraged to live off their natural prey like rabbits, rats and mice instead of our chickens and ducks. And we keep our farms neat and tidy, as you can possibly see, specifically to deter rodents.'

The truth of what Alastair had pointed out became more apparent as their tour progressed; the farm buildings, although they looked antiquated from the outside, were very different when viewed from within; the storage units, especially, were aluminium lined and contained shelves which ensured everything edible was kept off the floor; this enabled the floor to be kept clean, and free of hiding places for animals which managed to sneak inside.

The largest building within the compound housed all the farm's machinery and accessories. 'Our attitude with regard to agricultural machines is probably quite unique,' Alastair explained whilst he showed them an immaculate tractor, several types of trailer, a combine harvester and other mechanical units, 'we don't, for example, leave our farm implements out in all kinds of weather and in all seasons only to discard them once they're ruined; when these machines aren't being used they stay in here. Another innovation is that purpose built implements for seasonal work are, due to economic considerations, shared between two or three adjoining farms.

'The onus for maintenance and repair work doesn't rest with the farmer or his staff either; instead the authorities supply able mechanics who service the machinery regularly and are immediately available in the event of a breakdown. We even have builders on hand responsible for the fabric of our houses and outbuildings, fences and gates et cetera; and we also receive frequent visits from the agricultural inspectorate whose members have a very wide knowledge of all aspects of farming, mainly because they're usually retired farmers. No one connected with agriculture lasts long if they fall foul of those experts.'

The area directly beyond the left hand side of the compound gates was entirely enveloped in fine wire mesh; from the outside it was reminiscent of the huge glasshouse in Harbourtown as it contained numerous bushes and small trees, but as soon as they entered Andrew saw the cage had been primarily designed to protect waterfowl. However, a quick glance round the interior instantly convinced him that none of the birds would have considered their environment anything but a home from home; near the centre was a very large pond and there were plenty of huts available for nesting and shelter, 'The wire extends well below ground level,' Alastair remarked as they seated themselves on a bench at the water's edge, 'so the birds are completely free from disturbance. Mary and I enjoy sitting in here when we've got some time to spare hence the decorative plants and the rocks around the pond. Mind you, a lot of these shrubs are fruit trees which is why they've been especially protected; every so often we rake up this soil and transfer it to the vegetable gardens: as you can imagine, it's extremely rich in nitrates.'

'You think of everything,' Andrew observed as he absentmindedly watched the ducks and geese swimming, or wandering unconcernedly about them.

'Waste not, want not,' Julie, who held his hand in hers, commented.

'There's a similar enclosure for chickens abutting this one,' her uncle stated, ignoring the turn in the conversation. 'I must admit I like birds, but especially wild ones. I've got a theory that many of them are a tremendous help to us; it's a point of view, thank goodness, which our government fully endorses because we're encouraged to provide nesting sites. So space is left under the eaves for swifts to crawl into and for house martins to build their mud nests, access above the doors of certain buildings with fitted ledges inside for the use of swallows; and the martins can obtain mud from the margins of shallow ponds especially made for them; those are our insecticides. We also provide nesting and roosting sites for birds of prey and owls, and spaces suitable for bats.'

'I remember reading somewhere,' Julie said thoughtfully, 'about the number of insects the average swift caught in a day; I forget what the actual figure was, but I know it was tremendous. I don't suppose the mainland authorities compel their people to provide special sites on buildings for aerial feeders, do they, Andy?'

'I doubt it,' her sweetheart dryly replied, 'they probably couldn't care less.' As they rose to leave the enclosure he enquired if all island farmyard fowls were free ranging.

'Oh yes,' declared Alastair, 'what is commonly referred to, I believe, as factory farming is entirely unknown on Whyte Island. We think it cruel, and it's a side to overpopulation which is often ignored; we can easily provide our inhabitants with eggs, meat, milk and so on without having to resort to such methods. That's just another aspect of our agricultural policy which is different from most of the rest of the globe's; we don't, for example, go in for artificial fertilizers or for crop spraying with herbicides, insecticides, or any other "cides", to such an extent. In an idyllic world we'd have been able to dispense with such aids but unfortunately we can only reduce their use, and we're constantly striving to strike the happy medium.'

'Yes, there's quite a lot of international concern about overuse of chemicals in agriculture and industry,' Julie observed, 'and the side effects from certain chemicals entering the soil and water and being passed onto humans by way of the food chain can have far reaching consequences. So our policy appears to be quite wise.'

'Have you told Andrew about our two experiments with regard to forestry?' Alastair enquired.

She shook her head. 'The first,' she turned to her lover, 'is to see whether woodland soil can be directly transferred to farmland to enrich the content sufficiently without recourse to artificial fertilizer. In this experiment the idea is to harvest the autumn leaf fall each year, and in order to compensate the trees for their natural humus, fertilizer is applied to the woodland annually. Providing the amount of humus taken from the woodland is sufficient to make it all worthwhile, and the trees are happy with the arrangement, then it could mean the end to the problem of undernourished and heavy soils. The other experiment is similar in concept though much more long term. 'It's widely known as the travelling wood plan; an area of flat downland has been planted with a mixture of deciduous and coniferous trees.......'

'Rather like the forest above Newtown?' her sweetheart interposed as he held the farmyard gate open ahead of her. She smiled and nodded, but fetched his hand a stinging slap as she passed him. 'What was that for?' he winced.

'Well brought up islanders don't interrupt, and you're an islander now!' she scolded as Alastair looked on grinning.

'I told you none of our women will put up with what they don't like,' he laughed.

'Anyway,' Julie continued as if nothing had happened, 'the idea is that when the trees reach maturity a certain acreage width will be felled, the wood utilised in various ways and the stumps and upper roots grubbed up, the area would then subsequently be utilized as farmland, meanwhile a similar acreage of downland on the opposite side of the forest will have been planted with mixed alkaline tolerant saplings. It's been estimated this process of felling and planting will occur at regular intervals of over fifty years; and as you can see, darling, the forest really will travel over that period. The reasoning behind this procedure is that our part of the world owes the high quality of much of its soil to the forest which used to cover it in ancient times.'

Andrew chuckled. 'When you described it as long term I reckon you were making an all time understatement.'

'That's very true,' Julie's uncle agreed, 'but we don't believe in allowing the future to take care of itself; just because we'll never see our great, great grandchildren it doesn't mean we're not bothered about them. The experiment my niece has just described could bring untold benefits to both us and them.'

From the gate they'd made their way along the farm track to its junction with the lane where it replaced the latter and turned left toward the fields devoted to various crops, pastureland and the downland beyond. In the first of the former on the right, containing brassicas, they came across Ruth and Derek who, together with several other workers, were busily hoeing out weeds and stacking them into heaps. 'That's one way of cutting out a degree of artificial fertilizer,' Alastair exclaimed, 'we compost the weeds and then put them back into the soil; it's time consuming and not very economical but it certainly doesn't do any harm.' They didn't stop because the toilers were apparently occupied with the popular music emerging from a transistor radio, but everyone exchanged waves as they passed by.

'These hedges look very attractive,' Andrew observed as they neared the next field.

'That's due to the islander's love of beauty and variety,' grinned Alastair, 'it isn't enough just to have hedgerows, they've got to be special; not only is there a remarkable number of plant species in each one, but some of them are quite rare. We also plant evergreens alongside the deciduous shrubs to provide year long shelter.'

Julie, who, through one of her secondary jobs, was thoroughly conversant with hedgerow culture prompted, 'Presumably each plant is there to do a different task besides allowing shelter.'

'Oh yes,' her uncle replied, 'some have flowers much beloved of various butterflies and other insects, others have leaves which certain caterpillars prefer to feed upon which, in their turn, supply food for fledgling birds, while other shrubs bear berries which attract winter, and resident, birds alike. Because we also have plenty of conifer shrubs mixed in, birds, especially, who favour them such as siskins, coal tits and goldcrests are more frequently seen than otherwise. Of course, a lot of the shrubs are especially ideal for providing nesting sites. You know, Andrew, I wonder how many farmers realise, when they eliminate hedgerows, they're doing harmful insects a great favour?' He didn't wait for a reply but continued, 'Because, you see, insects can breed under leaves, stones, in grass and the soil, virtually anywhere, whereas birds need quite a large area of cover in which to raise their young, all of whom, incidentally, are fed upon live food, especially insect larvae. So when you destroy bushes and trees you're balancing nature in favour of insects.'

'But surely,' objected Andrew, 'spiders and predatory insects also feed upon harmful insects, and as birds can't tell the good from the bad they'll tend to nullify any good they do?'

'No,' his lover replied, 'as with all creatures there are always more prey life forms than predatory ones; so for every spider a bird might eat it could take thirty insects, for instance; also, remember spiders don't normally prey upon caterpillars, especially larger ones.' By now they were approaching the downland; on either side of the track was a ditch, the right hand of which carried the stream they'd crossed in the pickup truck earlier. The afternoon had become quite hot and so, apart from the occasional swallow or some other small bird flying along the hedgerows, or crossing from one side to the other, there was little movement or sound other than from the myriad of insects which seemed to swarm everywhere.'

'Do you remember how I criticised the mainland hedgerows, darling?' Julie asked, gesturing toward the sides of the track, 'Well, as you can see, even though these hedgerows are tall they aren't straggly, and that's because when they're flailed it's only to keep them looking trim and then not too much is taken off. But when the coniferous side of the hedge is done then the cutting is much more drastic as those shrubs normally grow much faster; the work, incidentally, is only carried out at the end of the nesting season.'

'I must say,' her lover observed, 'You're both very knowledgeable about all aspects of natural history.'

'Not quite about everything,' Andrew chuckled, 'but Whyte Island farmers need to be pretty bright when it comes to their environment. Our authorities are so concerned about the dreadful changes which the agricultural policies on the mainland have created that, to prevent the damage happening over here, all farm workers are required to declare a love of nature even before they're permitted to set foot on the land. To be able to progress up the land management ladder we have to sit examinations at regular intervals, and these include questions on natural history to ensure we really are interested and that we know what we're doing.

'You see, Andy, a farmer is similar to a ship's captain in that he can be a law unto himself; despite the frequent visits by the inspectorate I could still wreak havoc here in the course of a few days; I'd be able to cut down a dozen eighty year old trees within a week without anyone in officialdom being aware of it until it was too late. But because I love this farm and everything on it, and because I more or less know what I'm doing, the chance of any permanent changes being made without authorisation is minimal.'

'What are these inspectors like, will they listen and agree if you'd like a tree removed or this and that done?'

'As I said before,' Alastair smiled, 'they're experts and so they'll examine what I think needs doing, have a little chat on the spot in my presence and, depending on the result of their opinion, they'll decide on the spot. If they approve and I can go ahead they'll sign a form giving permission and as a receipt for me. There won't be any time wasting delays that way and no masses of paperwork, either.'

'Tell Andy about those before and after photos, to prove what can happen without proper regulations, uncle,' Julie urged.

'Alright; though it's much better told when we've got them in front of us as comparisons; but I'll show them to you later, Andy, so you'll be able to compare them properly. What my lovely niece is referring to is a photo which a pilot friend of my grandfather's took while he was flying over his local mainland village, and this included much of my grandsire's farm. The old man died a year or so after the picture was taken and the farm was consequently sold, due to too many of his children wanting a finger in the financial pie; about five years ago, which was roughly 30 years after we lost the farm my dad heard that the whole area had been modernised. So, as a matter of interest, he went along to the island airfield and persuaded one of the pilots to take another aerial photo; he even gave the pilot the original snap so he could get it exactly right. Well, as you will see, the man did a perfect job, he must've been in virtually the same position, but the changes which had been wrought were terrible.

'Both pictures featured the village in the foreground with grandfather's farm just beyond, as well as a considerable amount of landscape behind, almost to the horizon in fact. The main difference between the two photos was in the number of trees and hedgerows; most of the trees adjacent to the church were still in place, but to the left a small wood had disappeared having been replaced by bungalows - one of two sites occupied by these buildings; the railway station and its track had gone, and there was now a motorway in the middle distance. But the greatest loss was evident in the farm where the large number of relatively small meadows had been turned into just two huge fields. Although some of the boundaries retained vestiges of their hedgerows, the division between the fields comprised a ditch with only one or two trees and no bushes along its entire length.'

He ceased talking as they came to where the stream widened, or had been widened, into a large pond; here a grassy bank sloped down to the water's edge, and beneath the shade of an ash tree a wooden park bench awaited them. 'Time for a rest,' Alastair announced, and as soon as they were seated he went on, 'When he saw the later photo my old dad had a terrible shock because, naturally, he used to play on the farm during his childhood, you see, and went to the village school, sang in the church choir and knew many of the locals only slightly less than their kids. He reckoned the whole area had been turned into an interest free, sterile desert; the woods, orchards, barns, outhouses and ponds had all been swept away.' Pausing, he added thoughtfully as he stroked his dog, 'I shouldn't be surprised if I'd been conceived on that farm because my parents spent their honeymoon there; frankly, I couldn't imagine anyone wanting to spend a honeymoon there now because neither the farm or the village seems particularly picturesque today, as you'll doubtless agree after you've seen the pictures, Andrew.'

Not too unexpectedly, Julie removed some liquid refreshment from her shoulder bag although, for a change, it was non-alcoholic and after they'd each taken a swig they continued their tour, the farmer diligently describing the various agricultural processes and crops as they went along. Where the downland began in earnest all three leant over a five barred gate whilst Alastair pointed out items of interest and explained the rudiments of shepherding to Andrew; when he'd finished he commented, 'You two can go on alone now because I've got to go and see what needs to be done.' Winking conspiratorially he added, 'There are some fantastic views from the top, aren't there Julie? Especially under the shade of that beech wood; and I happen to know that no one will be working in this area today. See you later, then.'

'I've rarely seen such an abrupt difference in landscapes,' observed Andrew when their late companion and Ben had departed, 'it's like being on another farm.' He pointed toward one of the curious circular woods growing in most of the centres of the large stonewall enclosed fields. 'Are they purely decorative, or have they a useful function?'

She laughed wearily. 'I'd have thought you'd have had enough lecturing on the techniques of farming by now; why didn't you ask my uncle if you really wanted to know?' She sighed impatiently. 'They've been there for eons, or some of them have; but they're used as compounds now after a number of trees had been removed from the middle; farmers find them useful as sheep pens to inoculate their flocks, mark them and check how many ewes are pregnant, and the sheep, which are usually more intelligent than most laypeople give them credit for, often shelter in them during foul unseasonable weather.' Julie then gave him a lingering kiss to make up, he presumed, for their lack of any real passion for quite some time. 'And now,' she chided, 'if you don't mind, I've had quite enough of agriculture for today, even if you haven't. So, enough!'

Soon after they'd continued their walk hand-in-hand up the gradually rising chalky track, she stopped and began removing her sweater with the words, 'It's too hot for clothing.' Horrified she was about to strip down to her brassiere or worse, he began to remonstrate but when she revealed that undergarment she explained, 'It looks just as much like a swimsuit top as a bra; like my knickers.' And she immediately removed her jeans. 'Well, don't just stand there like a dummy,' she coaxed, 'take your shirt off and give the sun a chance, and then we'll skin lotion each other.'

Upon continuing their stroll Julie explained that the scenery about them was as much as for the benefit of wildlife as for the farmers and their livestock. 'Quite a few bird species prefer this type of habitat in addition to the more usual larks and less common kinds of falcons, for instance; also many kinds of wildflowers and of all the fairly numerous varieties of blue butterflies found in our region only two aren't normally found on chalk downland.'

'Like you pointed out during our first cycle ride together, my living statue,' he commented, slapping her rump hard. For all its arid and apparent bleakness there were plenty of beautiful things to admire; at the foot of the stone walls on either side of the track numerous alkaline loving plants, many of them pale and mid blue, flourished, and as the lovers, now arm-in-arm strolled past, many different butterflies rose up and flittered before them, blue, white and speckled brown ones predominating.

As the track steepened Andrew, especially, began to get short of breath, and so they stopped frequently; but Julie insisted he shouldn't look back, 'I want you to see the view from the top in all its glory,' she declared.

Shortly before reaching the ridge's summit their walk took them through a cutting, the sides of which were almost hidden by flowering brambles, briars, gorse and broom in a mixture of reds, pinks, white and yellows which was almost too dazzling to behold. Amongst the blooms butterflies and bees in large numbers flew or rested, the former making no noise as they visited each flower in turn. 'This place is well known to naturalists,' Julie explained as they wandered through the extended defile, 'because it's so near the coast it's occasionally visited by uncommon, or even rare butterflies and other insects as well as birds, especially insectivores.'

'So where are the crowds today?'

'In my experience,' she glanced at him with a smile, 'Whyte Island nature lovers prefer to combine bird and insect spotting, and on a hot day like this most birds prefer to rest up, and there are comparatively few species of butterfly to be found on these shores whether accidental or resident, so most naturalists will have already seen them. Things can get quite hectic around here during the spring and autumn migration periods though, I understand.'

Soon after, where the ground had levelled out at the summit, they passed through a gateway on the right and, leaning against an adjacent wall, they gazed back in the direction of the farm where, far beyond the buildings, the sea lay; unlike on the occasion of their visit to the island's highest point there wasn't a cloud to be seen or a breath of wind to be felt, everything shimmered in the haze of a hot summer's day. Obviously disappointed at the lack of a splendid view which she'd promised, Andrew's sweetheart presently urged, 'Come on, it's too warm to hang about here, let's go to the beech wood my uncle referred to, then I'll give you something nice.'

'Like what?' he grinned.

'Like another drink,' she giggled.

'There isn't likely to be anyone about,' she hinted upon their quenching their thirst. They had seated themselves on a mossy bank amid the giant silver trunked trees overlooking a small area of grassland upon which a small flock of sheep grazed.

'I'm sure I don't know what you're talking about,' he jokingly replied, but then took her into his arms in an ardent embrace. Later, they arranged their outer clothing into a reasonably adequate ground covering and pillow and, after mounting him while still wearing her brassiere, for safety's sake she observed, they made love. She then changed her underwear around, lay down beside him and permitted him to fondle her until he fell asleep.

It was almost dusk when the coolness of evening and the pangs of hunger united to awaken him; his sweetheart, too, had surrendered herself to the sultry warmth of the afternoon, and he stared down at her affectionately before gently shaking her awake. Strolling down the track with their arms about each other Julie suddenly said, 'You remember what Uncle Alastair mentioned about how he didn't think anyone would want to spend their honeymoon at his grandfather's old farm because the area had been ruined?' Andrew nodded. 'Well,' she went on, 'I wonder if the thought had occurred to the owners of hotels and boarding houses in rural districts? If I'd been one of them I'd have been tempted to take any progressive farmer to court because I'm sure I'd have had a valid case.'

Tightening his hand upon her shoulder, he pulled her against him briefly. 'It isn't quite as simple as that, my love,' he told her. 'In theory you'd have every reason to sue, but mainland law is a gamble at the best of times and you could theoretically lose a lot of money, especially if your legal representative was incompetent; besides which you'd probably find yourself up against a very powerful body in the form of the agricultural association which certainly wouldn't allow a precedent to be set.'

'You mean because everyone would then be putting in a claim? Well, I think they should; it's a shame many innocent people have to lose out so a relatively few farmers can become wealthy.'

He shrugged. 'Too many mainlanders argue that farmland is for growing food on and not specifically for the enjoyment of the naturalist and tourist. Most modern people look upon the countryside as being merely the gap between one favoured destination and another, unworthy of interest; the authorities claim national parks have been set aside for sightseeing, exercise and nature lovers.'

His companion made a scornful noise. 'No doubt those so called national parks usually consist of mountains and moorland which look very beautiful and wild, but are also too difficult and sterile to be farmed successfully and profitably. Possibly, too, those parks are adequate if you can afford to run your own car or if public transport is available; but if you're unemployed, like your dad, they might just as well be on the moon. I'm sorry to keep knocking your birthplace, darling, but its government really should start using its collective brains and realise everyone needs to be able to walk where there are few habitations and people, and shouldn't have to be wealthy to do so. If I lived on one of those big housing estates over there I'd go insane if I couldn't get away from it occasionally.'

Andrew, sensing how emotional his lover was becoming, sought to change the subject. 'Sweetheart,' he began, 'so far all the people I've met on the island and, if my memory serves me right, onboard company ships have been great thinkers; you know, with really intelligent personalities. Having seen our educational at work I realise it seeks to bring out the best in its pupils; I also understand really brainless people aren't permitted to attain maturity; however, surely not everyone can be turned into an intellectual, no matter how beneficial or thorough the teaching methods?'

His subterfuge worked; one thing he was beginning to understand about his lover was that she was easily diverted from a subject. 'I was wondering when you were going to ask that,' she exclaimed. 'Seeing we're on a farm it's extra appropriate for me to state you can't always make a silk purse out of a sow's ear, even though schools are designed to improve each pupil's intelligence and personality. The thing is, darling, it's extremely difficult to judge each person on Whyte Island from a casual acquaintanceship because we're all of a certain high educational standard; it's only when you get to know a given person thoroughly that it's possible to know what their actual intellectual level is.'

She squeezed his waist in physical emphasis of what she was attempting to explain. 'When I first talked to you at the Station Arms you weren't aware of the fact, but I immediately began testing you to see if you were intellectually compatible with me; I decided you probably were, but by getting you to come and live with me I made certain. The fact I'd marry you tomorrow if I could, demonstrates I'm aware we're on the same intellectual plane; the same factor applies to our friends and the circle of acquaintances within which we socialise: all islanders have been encouraged to automatically identify the level of society which best suits them. Therefore, my sweetheart, the reason why you think everyone's extra intelligent is because you've either only had a casual acquaintanceship with them, or else they're a member of our particular grouping.'

'But I haven't seen any sign of different societies,' he objected, suddenly bewildered, 'it all sounds a bit snobbish to me, and I didn't think snobbery existed here.' It was now almost dark, but they'd reached the metalled lane, and the moon, nearly full and already high in the heavens, was beginning to shed adequate light.

'There aren't any different social classes, silly,' answered Julie in amusement, 'It's complicated, I know, and perhaps I haven't explained lucidly enough, but there aren't any psychological or physical barriers; it's just that everyone discovers the group they're happiest in and uses it as a kind of base to set their personal contentment on. Look,' she announced with an air of finality, 'we'll forget it for now, but during our stay here we'll go and visit the nearest holiday resort; it's only a couple of stations away, and that should demonstrate what I've been attempting to explain. I don't know about you, darling, but I'm getting cold as well as starving, so I'm going to do something about it!' And she immediately disengaged herself from him and ran off down the lane. In spite of the twice weekly jogging sessions his lover had insisted they undertake Andrew was unable to catch up with her, and by the time he reached the farmhouse, tired and breathless, there was no sign of her.

After they'd had their customary post jogging shower, Julie told him that despite the late hour Mary had arranged a supper party in their honour. 'Just a family affair,' she said in answer to his questioning expression, 'but candlelight, silver, the works. So,' she continued, going across to the wardrobe, 'you'll need your suit, while I wear one of the dresses Ruth has so kindly lent me.'

The little gathering comprised of Mary, Alastair, Ruth, Derek, Julie and Andrew; mother and daughter bustled about to begin with, placing the food already in containers on the table and pouring out the wine, refusing all offers of aid until everything was in place; then it was a case of helping one's self to chicken soup followed by the main course of sliced duck with salad, and a sweet of mixed fruit and cream. Apart from an occasional request to pass over a dish or a condiment the meal was largely consumed in silence, it seeming impious to spoil the repast with mere conversation. Andrew was therefore able to indulge in what he considered to be one of his favourite pastimes: gazing at attractive women; Julie, seated directly opposite him, was wearing a black gown, she was flanked on one side by her aunt in green, and her cousin in white on the other; candlelight, the room's only other form of illumination during the meal, highlighted the three auburn haired women's tresses, eyes and jewellery perfectly.

'That was wonderful,' he announced after laying down his spoon and taking a sip of wine.

As Mary smiled in acknowledgement her husband replied, 'And everything came from the farm, including the herbs and the wine.'

'Except for the salt and pepper,' Derek chimed in.

'There you go again, splitting hairs,' exclaimed Ruth, thereby starting a mild argument between the pair of them.

'Well,' announced her mother, rising, 'as it's so late and we've gone to the trouble of getting dressed up I don't intend bothering about clearing this lot away tonight.'

'Don't worry, Auntie,' Julie interposed, 'Andy and I will see to it in the morning.'

'In that case,' Mary continued, 'if everyone's finished we'll adjourn for drinks.'

At the opposite end of the lounge/diner more than enough seats were available to cater for them all, but as soon as Andrew sat down in an armchair his sweetheart arranged herself on his lap; at the same time a generous glass of whisky was thrust into his hand by Alastair and, without asking him whether he smoked or not, Derek made him the recipient of a large cigar. After lighting it for him Ruth went over and joined her lover in another armchair whilst her parents sat arm-in-arm on the sofa.

In such a relaxed atmosphere conversation came easily, much of it directed toward hearing about Andrew's feelings with regard to his former homeland and Whyte Island but soon, much to Mary's obvious annoyance, the talk drifted round to farming. 'I promise we won't mention agriculture again while Julie and Andrew are here,' Alastair vowed placatingly, 'but Andy is obviously interested.' An audible groan came from Ruth but her father took no notice, his cigar glowing in the half light shed by a table lamp as he drew upon it before continuing, 'No, we don't have farms of varying sizes over here; that would cause too many complications, some farmers would think they had too much or too little acreage and there would also be the problem of how many farm workers to allot per area of land.

'So as soon as the island was established farmland was parcelled off into just three different acreages: which didn't go down too well with some of the original farmers. One of the reasons for this decision was to prevent the kind of thing which tends to occur in your old country, Andrew, where small farms become unprofitable due to economic considerations and are then abandoned or fall to large combines, people who are making piles of money out of prairie farming at the expense of smallholders. You also raised the subject of inheritance I believe, Andy?'

'Dad,' pleaded Ruth.

'In a minute, dear,' he insisted. 'Well, when I reach retirement age that'll be Mary and I finished with the land, but that doesn't mean Ruth, or Derek for that matter, will necessarily share the management of this farm with the other people. I could propose either of them, of course, but their confirmed ability to run a farm through rigorous examinations would be what really counted; even then they might be judged suitable to manage a small farm, not a large or a medium sized one like this.'

'That'll do for now, Alec,' his wife said wearily, 'Ruth, go and get your guitar or something.'

The remainder of the evening was entirely devoted to amusement and everyone, without reservation, did a turn; Alastair sang some poems set to music in a fine bass voice and his wife recited and sang some love songs, both Ruth and Derek were more than proficient on a variety of instruments and performed several duets together; a particularly fine one involved an instrument called a hammer dulcimer, accompanied by a harmonica. 'That sort of music more or less comes under the broad description of country and western,' Derek replied to a query from Andrew as the applause died away.

'There's a club meeting Thursday evening, you'll have to come along,' Ruth urged, 'Derek will lend you the right gear, Andy; a broad rimmed hat and a checked shirt will make you look the part.' Julie accepted for them both.

He never knew exactly when the party broke up; frequent

refills of his glass made his surroundings appear ever more hazy, and he didn't know when the last song was sung or by whom. He was vaguely aware, on one occasion, of Mary's voice admonishing gently, 'If you're going to arouse your lover, Ruth, do it in the proper place.' And then he knew no more.

When Andrew awoke, Julie's assertion that her aunt and uncle were easy going was amply demonstrated by the position which he found himself in; grey light filtering through the curtained windows revealed himself with his head resting on his sweetheart's half uncovered cleavage whilst a hand clasped one of her legs beneath her dress. They were still seated in the lounge armchair though the room was now empty. 'Come on, darling,' he whispered, gently waking her, 'let's go to bed.'

In the middle of clearing away the supper things, a task which involved, at Julie's insistence washing up, wiping and putting everything away, Mary asked them what they'd planned for that day. Andrew by way of answer clutched his head in a theatrical gesture. 'To do as little as possible,' he groaned.

'For a hangover,' she laughed in reply, 'I'd recommend a suitable pill, a round walk of ten miles and a good, long swim in the sea. As soon as you've finished here go and sort out some swimming gear, in the meantime I'll have packed you both a picnic lunch and then off you'll go.'

Andrew was cursing inwardly as they set off, but in the event he thoroughly enjoyed the outing. Large white clouds, each one an island, drifted across the sky and did nothing to spoil the heat of the day but helped to cool the couple by shading the sun every time it threatened to scorch them. Not that they had any particular need of shelter from the sunlight, for the footpath to the coast seemed to have been designed to provide as much shade as possible, there being plenty of trees together with tall hedges along the route. The path rarely continued straight for long, but instead skirted round fields; it had been well kept with no encroaching plants and was never blocked by barriers, crops or farm animals; stiles or kissing gates were the only obstructions. Quite often other paths diverged, converged or crossed with theirs causing Julie to comment it was possible to visit it every part of the island without having to walk along a metalled road for long. 'Although,' she added, 'it wouldn't be very direct.'

Eventually, not long after the path had passed beneath a railway, they came to the place where they intended to bathe. Flights of wooden steps descended a near vertical cliff and allowed access to a tiny cove, so enclosed that only a small vista of the actual sea could be seen from the beach. The water in the bay was calm and so extraordinarily translucent that stones and sand on the bottom were clearly visible even though some distance from the shore. Andrew, glancing about at the foot of the stairway, was taken aback by the cove's beauty; the cliffs were an unusual mixture of chalk overlying a dark brown granite with a narrow seam of sandstone separating the two. 'No wonder they call this place Christmas Cake Cove,' he murmured to himself as he followed his lover.

'I wish there weren't so many people about,' he exclaimed as he removed his clothes, 'then we could dispense with swimwear.' Lying down on the sand with his back resting against a convenient smooth rock he awaited with agreeable anticipation for his sweetheart to undress; this she presently did, and as slowly and provocatively as possible to finally reveal a green one piece costume finally.

'I'd hardly call thirty or so people "many,"' she belatedly answered. 'Most of them are women and children anyway; still, I doubt if your nudity would go down very well.' She joined him on the sand and thrust her face close to his. 'Besides,' she added, staring into his eyes, 'your body is for my own personal gratification, and I don't intend sharing it, darling.' Rummaging in her bag she eventually brought forth two sets of underwater goggles and a swimming cap. 'The speciality of this cove,' she explained, 'is diving down to the rocks and the base of the cliffs to inspect the sea life; come on.'

While she led him along a stone pier which extended some distance into the bay he asked anxiously, 'What about our gear? Will it be safe?'

'Don't be silly, love, it'll be alright,' she chided, 'this isn't the mainland.'

When they reached the end he stood looking down at the water and wondered aloud how cold it might be, while entirely forgetting his companion's wilful sense of humour; she stood beside him adjusting her bathing cap as he uttered the fateful words. 'Why not find out?' she remarked giving him a nudge with her elbow. Although temporarily put off balance, he would've recovered if she hadn't deliberately placed her foot where he was certain to trip over it. He experienced a brief shock of horror at the rapidly approaching water before becoming totally immersed; his fears with regard to its temperature were all too well founded as he struggled in its cold grasp. 'You bitch,' he shouted at her as he surfaced, 'it's freezing.'

Julie knelt at the pier's edge and smirked back at him. 'That's the trouble with deep water in a sheltered bay,' she laughed, 'it can be somewhat cool.' Before he could decide what he ought to do next she stood up and launched herself in his direction. 'You're quite right,' she agreed, blowing alongside him, 'it is bloody freezing. Still,' she puffed, handing him a pair of goggles, 'we'll get used to it.'

Andrew knew very well his body would fail to adjust to the low temperature as they swam and dived in the distinctly cool sea, but he had enough pride and strength of character not to let that fact defeat him whilst his lover and the other swimmers were managing to endure the cold. It was only too obvious the cove was a popular site for both amateur and more serious divers, for he'd noticed amongst the several couples exploring the bottom of the cliffs in their vicinity and further out, swimmers in wet suits with oxygen bottles strapped to their backs. 'It's an ideal spot for novices to practice in,' Julie told him after he'd mentioned his observation to her.

'Have you tried it?'

'Only when I was at school,' she replied, 'but I didn't like it much; this is good enough for me.'

Andrew lost count of the number of times he followed his sweetheart down into the depths, but much to his delight each of the areas they explored displayed different characteristics from the previous sites, not only in topography but in the position, colours and variety of its marine life, and so their diving wasn't as tedious as he might've expected.

Eventually, Julie advised him to take an extra deep breath and to follow her carefully; then she disappeared below the surface with her lover close on her heels. Several feet below they came to the mouth of a cave into which, without hesitating, she disappeared; following, he found himself in a natural tunnel which gradually inclined upward. He began to experience fear in the gloomy, claustrophobic environment, but almost immediately his head broke surface. The sight which met his astonished eyes, however, was more than enough to banish apprehension from his mind; they'd arrived inside a small cavern illuminated by a shaft of sunlight streaming through a narrow cleft in the roof. Kneeling on a stretch of sand with the light shining on her as though she were an actress in a theatre drama was a topless girl who, as soon as she saw Andrew, immediately covered her breasts with her hands. Laying beside her a naked man also attempted to conceal himself.

Julie, treading water beside her lover, promptly called out, 'Sorry for intruding,' then disappeared beneath the surface once more. Left alone and still in a state of surprise, her companion briefly gazed at the pair of lovers and then followed after her; unfortunately, in his haste to escape an embarrassing situation, he neglected to inhale an adequate amount of air with the result that his lungs were almost bursting by the time he saw daylight again. 'Oh well,' Julie remarked as he fought for breath beside her, 'it was worth a try; it's obviously less of a secret than I realised. We'll just have to wait until we get back to the farm.'

'If we caught those people out,' he managed to gasp, 'someone could've done it to us.'

'We'd have gone further in, there's a short passageway with a smaller cave at the end.' She began to swim toward the beach. 'Let's dine, then sunbathe,' she called over her shoulder.

Lying in the sand, enjoying the heat from the sun on his back and the well fed sensation in his stomach, Andrew turned his head to face his beloved who was stretched out alongside him. 'Darling,' he announced, 'seeing I'm so jealous of you, don't take me to any of your secret love nests again, will you?'

'Sorry, love,' she smiled, 'my mistake; perhaps I was subconsciously attempting to prove to a former boyfriend that the present one has replaced him in my affections; anyway, I thought you might like some loving in a romantic setting.'

Suddenly angry at her mention of an erstwhile rival, Andrew rolled over and sat up. 'It can wait!' he declared impatiently.

'I don't know what you've got to be annoyed about,' Julie

replied, also sitting up, 'because I'm not jealous of your former sweethearts, or of your old love nests.' She paused, then added more soberly, 'You know, darling, you take a lot of understanding at times. Everyone has had previous lovers, and frankly you don't seem to realise how lucky you are; I daresay if this was the mainland one of my ex-boyfriends might well approach you to cause trouble, or else secretly pester me to take him back. You might hear deliberately dropped hints referring to my promiscuity, real or imaginary. But nothing like that ever happens over here, so please take life as it comes.' Placing a hand on each of his shoulders, she firmly pressed him down on the sand. 'I love you madly,' she averred, gazing down at him, 'but if you're intending to continue being jealous of ghosts then perhaps we'd better go our separate ways!'

Realising how boorish he was becoming, and that he was acting more like a mainlander than an islander, he shook his head in refusal and quickly changed the subject, 'This is the tidiest beach I believe I've ever seen,' he commented, saying the first thing which came to mind. 'Besides, your tits were much better than that mermaid's in the cave.'

Julie giggled at his whimsical comment, but added, 'What did you expect? Of course the beach is tidy. Sometimes, sweetheart, I think you'll never forget your origins.' She pushed his hands away as he tried to pull her down on top of him. 'Further proof,' she declared. 'This is a public place. Go on, have a nap instead.'

Before he took her advice and rolled, once more, onto his stomach, he said, 'I was merely remembering the number of times I've seen places on the mainland, even beauty spots, spoilt by litter strewn about.'

He was awoken from his doze by a sharp blow to the side of his face; however, his shocked anger quickly turned to amusement when he saw his assailant was nothing more than a beach ball accidentally kicked in his direction. Julie, who was obviously already awake, immediately jumped up and threw the ball back to its owner, a child of about five; the next hour or so was spent in playing a number of ball games with three children and, to Andrew's delight, their mothers, a pair of attractive young women each clad in two piece swimming wear.

'I wouldn't have thought this minor cove important enough to possess toilet facilities, let alone a café,' he mused. His lover, occupied in watching the three youngsters scampering away with the ice lollies she'd just bought them, hadn't heard him, so he repeated his comment. They'd seated themselves at a metal table beneath a colourful sunshade drinking coffee in the late afternoon sunlight; Julie, before replying, absentmindedly poured some rum into his cup.

'They're simply here because they provide a necessary amenity,' she shrugged. 'As you're now aware, love, our society, unlike most others, isn't motivated by profit but by requirement; capitalism might encourage enterprise in some areas where the income might be perceived to be beneficial to the purveyor in question; but it often results in hardship for those residing in a place which is thought to be unprofitable. Some villages on the mainland, for example, have been eroded away by the loss of public transport, shops, businesses, taverns, et cetera due to their perceived lack of profitability, regardless of the detrimental effect upon the community.

'That sort of thing just doesn't occur on Whyte Island because our authorities put the people, as an entirety, first; what does it matter if a shop, or whatever, fails to pay its way? As long as it's needed then it'll be subsidised out of the central fund which, as you know, darling, is maintained by the profits from the more successful operations. Anyway, amenities like this one are also essential in providing secondary jobs.

'But the average islander looks upon free enterprise as being uneconomical both in cost and labour; take a bus route, for instance: we hold that it's far better to run one bus with a full complement of passengers than to run two only half full so, with our stable population, we have buses exactly suited to the passenger numbers expected and run at a time most convenient to those people. It's the same with shops: you won't normally find, let's say, two bakeries within walking distance of each other unless they're both well patronised. Free enterprise to us is as absurd as attempting to fight a battle with an army, navy or air force in which each unit commander is a law unto theirself; you need to have an overall controller wholly responsible for conducting the groups available if victory is to be assured.

'Consider our farming policy as an example; when our island

was founded there were areas comprising rich soil and others which were exactly the reverse, just as there are in other countries, but our authorities weren't going to allow some farmers to have an easy life whilst others struggled. So, extra nutrient and labour was allocated to those farms having poor or unworkable soil; in some rare cases, I believe, earth was actually transferred from one area to another in bulk. The result, darling, is we've now got an extremely efficient and productive agricultural system: and you couldn't get that by employing free enterprise.'

She drained her cup of coffee, stood up and gathered together her clothes. 'I'm off to take a shower and get dressed; I'll see you back here, love, don't forget to return the cups.'

Even after they'd both changed they made no attempt to leave the cove but instead sat on a rock whilst afternoon became evening; all the family groups had gradually departed until only a few couples remained. Julie had pulled her hair behind her head and fashioned it into a ponytail; and as he idly fondled it Andrew suddenly recalled she'd once told him she liked horse riding. 'Why, would you like to try?' she enthusiastically asked after he'd mentioned the pastime. She frowned when he nodded. 'We've left it a little late because we need to book up well in advance; but we might be lucky enough to get a ride during this holiday.'

'Doesn't your uncle keep any horses in the stable then?'

'No,' she laughed, 'he's got enough on his plate without worrying about horses. They keep the pickup in there along with its roof attachment as it's more convenient. No, we'll need to contact a local riding school.'

Before they set off back to the farm Julie made a couple of phone calls. 'Well, that's settled then. Thursday, and it isn't far away.' Giggling, she added, 'You'll have to wear Derek's hat and after riding's finished we can mosey down to the old country and western club like a coupla real cowpokes,' she drawled. Their return walk was taken at a far more leisurely pace with several stop overs for dallying and enjoying the peace and beauty of an early summer's dusk and twilight, they sat on the bench by the pool for a while and soon bats appeared, often to drop down almost to the water's surface to pick up some invisible insect. 'Oh, by the way,' Julie whispered, 'I also phoned up aunty and explained we'd be an hour or so yet. We've got to go to the other farmhouse because they'll all be round there; apparently uncle's opposite number would like to meet you and celebrate your arrival in our midst.' Andrew groaned, but she continued, 'We'll try not to stay long, I'll give the excuse that we're going to one of the coastal resorts tomorrow and we'd already booked a sea trip,' she glanced sideways at him, 'if you fancy it?'

He smiled back. 'I don't care where I go, my love, as long as it's with you; but,' he went on with mock indignation, 'imagine you telling a falsehood!'

'Goodness,' Andrew exclaimed when he'd settled himself comfortably on the train, 'I'm whacked out. I can't take many more nights like that.'

'Which part?' Julie asked, smirking.

'Both parts,' he answered, 'but can't we take things easy today?'

'Hardly. We're going to the seaside to enjoy ourselves. But why not have a little sleep? My shoulder's available and sleeping against someone in public is quite acceptable.' He was only too pleased to avail himself of his lover's offer, and awoke much refreshed as the train arrived in the resort's station.

'There's one thing about Whyte Island I never can fathom,' he declared as they strolled along the promenade.

'Yes?' Julie answered expectantly.

'All these people. Look at them, on the beach, coming toward us, on the pier, in the cafes and amusement arcades. Where do they all come from?'

'You mean you still don't know the facts of life?' she joked.

'No,' he replied scornfully, 'Alright, so it's a beautiful summer's day. But the island can't be described as huge and we're supposed to have a small population relative to the land area. I mean, darling,' he protested, 'every town we've been to, for example, has been quite full of people.'

'I didn't come here just to answer questions,' she replied mock seriously, 'but if you must be a bore then be one as we're paddling along in the surf.' And she pulled him in the direction of the nearest set of beach steps.

'The answer to your query is very simple,' she began as the sea caressed and cooled their feet, 'the centres of our towns are quite compact but generally appear to be bigger than they actually are; each one is usually surrounded by a large residential area which, because of the great number of trees and other greenery in the vicinity, doesn't seem to be as extensive as it actually is. So therefore you've got a bigger population than you might expect adjacent to a relatively small area. In addition, transport is easily available and inexpensive thereby encouraging people to travel in from outlying districts; and if you take into account the fact that we islanders are fun loving, sociable souls by and large, and that entertainment is also cheap and available to all, then you should understand where all the crowds come from. Incidentally, I noticed that even on the mainland, despite their recession and items like television and all those other stay at home entertainments, there were still plenty of people about. Now, no more questions, sweetheart!'

Andrew, realising how thoughtless he was in allowing any other consideration than pleasure to interfere with the day, agreed. 'This is a perfect place for a sea resort,' he exclaimed brightly, attempting to prove he had, indeed, decided to enjoy himself at the expense of everything else. His observation had been prompted by the size of the breakers which, though imposing when further out, became mere ripples by the time they reached the shore; this, he subconsciously knew, was due to the way the beach gently shelved. Children would therefore need to go a long way out before putting themselves in any real danger, and the shallow water bestowed the bonus of being much warmer than normal due to maximum contact with the sun's rays. Although the day was slightly hazy, the sun shone out of a cloud free sky, and he was able to see the coastline of his former homeland receding away into the distance.

'The last one to reach the end of the groyne has to do what the winner tells them,' Julie suddenly cried out, letting go of his hand.

'It's alright for you,' he replied, grasping her arm and so holding her back, 'you've got your skirt tucked into your knickers.'

'Swimwear,' she corrected.

'While my trousers,' he went on, ignoring her remark, 'are only rolled up to my knees.' Her answer was to kick water over him until he released her, and then she was off, laughing, to win their unequal race.

'Now, what shall the forfeit be?' she pondered as she leant against a wooden groyne support alternately laughing and panting. Her gaze eventually alighted upon a dejected seeming donkey tethered to one of the pier piles. 'The very thing,' she declared.

'Did you enjoy your ride?' Julie enquired as her lover climbed down from the animal. 'I must say, you looked perfect: two asses together.' Kissing him lightly on the cheek after fussing over the donkey and putting her arm through his possessively, she added, 'Still, it'll have been good practice for tomorrow.' As the emerged from beneath the far side of the pier she exclaimed excitedly, 'Look, darling, let's have a ride on the pleasure boat.'

After their trip out to view the seals basking on the sandbanks, the semi-sunken wreck and to stare at several ocean going vessels from close to, during which his sweetheart pretended to be sea-sick, they decided to visit the pier. Immediately they'd passed through the turnstile she went across to a kiosk directly before them and shortly returned to her companion with her hands cupped together. 'Help yourself,' she invited, offering her hands up to him. Much to Andrew's surprise he realised she was holding a pile of obsolete brass coins together with a few silver ones. 'An object lesson in the futility of gambling,' she observed to his puzzled frown, 'see how quickly this lot goes.' And she headed toward the adjacent amusement arcade. The answer, some fifteen minutes later, was very quickly; no profit at all was made from any of the machines, most of which offered tantalising proof of the money or wares which could be won by an apparent minimum of effort or skill.

'Even those "what the butler saw" contraptions were a con,' Andrew complained light-heartedly while they sat on a bench sharing a portion of fish and chips, and gazed out to sea, 'the demonstrations at the blue school were a billion times better, and free.'

His lover tossed a chip high into the air and then laughed with delight as a gull seemed to appear from nowhere to deftly snatch it away. 'I wonder, in that case,' she mused aloud, 'where my efforts at seduction on your behalf come in your estimation?' She abruptly stood up, flicked the used wrappings in a convenient bin, and asked, 'Where to now?'

At the seaward end of the pier was a little tower and, once

inside, the lovers joined other holidaymakers in staring into the white bowl of a camera obscura; as they came away afterward Andrew declared, bemused, 'This place is just like a holiday resort of half a century or more ago.'

'And here's another piece of living history,' Julie answered pointing to a fortune teller's kiosk, 'I must have a go.'

She emerged five minutes later looking a bit depressed. 'What did they say?' he enquired taking her hand again.

'I'm going to have a long life, lots of children; the usual stuff.'

'But why look so miserable? You know we won't be able to have more than a couple of kids.'

'That's true,' she agreed, smiling wistfully.

Distinctly not old fashioned was the vision of a pair of approaching lovers clad in swimming gear; Andrew eyed the girl's two piece clothed figure appreciatively whilst the other man did the same to Julie. As soon as they'd passed, he glanced down at his sweetheart's bare legs, and observed, 'Isn't it about time you untucked your skirt?'

'Jealous!' she accused, but pulled out the cotton material and vainly tried to straighten out the creases. 'That girl had a lovely set of boobs,' she added, eying him sideways, 'and much better than the ones we saw yesterday.'

'I wouldn't know,' he answered tactfully, 'both pairs were covered up. Anyway, I've seen plenty so far today, but I don't suppose any of them compete with yours.' They both knew it was utter nonsense but his sweetheart, ever gratified by a compliment, squeezed his hand in pleasure and beamed happily: restored to good humour once more. As the pier also contained a theatre they checked up on the commencement of the next hour long matinee as they passed by. The interior, when they were at last seated on the hard wooden fold up chairs, was conspicuously seedy, compelling Andrew to realise the authorities had deliberately put authenticity before comfort. Although the subsequent concert was varied and well performed, an undefined corniness permeated the whole show; but his companion seemed to enjoy watching the acrobats, conjurer, ventriloquist, comedian and singers, while he wasn't averse to the high stepping chorus girls, who made up the entertainment.

'Do you realise we haven't imbibed today?' she stated as they left the theatre. 'I think we've experienced most of what the pier has to offer, don't you?'

The tavern they chose had been sited between the promenade and the beach and was therefore long and narrow to allow patrons the choice of overlooking the beach and sea, or else viewing the passing activity on the promenade, through plate glass windows. 'Nectar,' Andrew declared as the slightly chilled beer cooled him. 'That poor old comedian didn't go down very well, did he?' he mused after a pause.

Julie, eyes intent upon what was happening on the strand, drew him out skilfully, 'I thought he got a lot of applause.'

'Yes, but it was more polite than enthusiastic.'

She turned to face him. 'Real professional comics would have a difficult time over here, darling. Our sense of humour has altered since our society became established; what amuses people in one era often becomes pointless in the next, as may be seen from jokes in old books and magazines; but our idea of what's amusing has changed as drastically as our society.' After taking a sip of her lager she continued, 'Sexual innuendo of the nudge, nudge, wink, wink kind is out, for instance, because sex is an open book to us; it'd be like making jokes about eating one's dinner. Then there are jokes regarding people's stupidity; as you know, Andy, our educational system seeks to obtain the best from everyone, so where a person is stupid in one area they're often brilliant in another.

'As a matter of interest, the reason why most people laugh at another's ignorance is because they subconsciously feel themselves to be inferior to others and are therefore relieved when someone else is shown to be more foolish than themselves. Likewise, if someone has a physical accident, like falling off a ladder, islanders would either pretend not to have noticed or else provide physical help if serious, rather than smirk or laugh as most other peoples would. Attacks on a person's traits and character would also be a non-starter because we've been taught it's hypocritical and cruel to say really bad things about others behind their backs. I could go on forever as there are so many different types of humour, but I didn't want to get into a serious discussion.'

She finished off her drink and, despite her lover's protests, went off to buy another round. While she was away he thought hard about her explanations and soon found a flaw in her assertions. 'You're not above playing various tricks on me,' he accused as she placed a fresh pint of beer before him, 'some of which would fall within the categories you previously mentioned.'

She smiled as she sat down. 'That's because we're intimates,' she immediately answered, 'My pranks aren't intended to harm you in any way, but rather to provoke you into retaliation; though I'd enjoy making up to you if I really scored a bull's eye on your emotions. My tricks are just a means of strengthening our pair-bond, an assurance of my possession in that I can approach you in a way no other person can.' With a fingertip she thoughtfully traced a pattern in the condensation on her glass. 'It's interesting that Whyte Islanders have devised their own form of humour to fill the vacuum,' she eventually observed, and at his querying glance, continued, 'You know, darling: slandering one's friends and relations to their faces in a mock serious fashion, sometimes in order to goad them; and teasing one's sweetheart.'

Their next visit was to the fun fair for, as Julie termed it, a bout of self-inflicted masochism; and so they were twisted and twirled, bounced, taken to various heights at great and lesser speeds, and made to feel thoroughly sick and terrified on the type of contraptions which no serious amusement park should be without. In between rides they consumed toffee apples, candy floss and popcorn in quantity. Their hectic diversion came to an abrupt end when Julie emerged from a ladies toilet with watery eyes and a red nose to admit, in an undertone, that she had been "not pretending to be sick." By this time it was late afternoon and so, to recover from their ordeal, they went down to the beach for a swim before the sea became too cold.

Later, as they lay stretched out on the sand in their swimming gear someone suddenly sat down heavily beside them. 'Hello Mr Larke,' Andrew exclaimed in surprise after sitting up and preparing to remonstrate with the unknown intruder.

'Hello, Harry,' echoed Julie.

'I thought it was you two,' their visitor replied. 'Did you enjoy your sailing trip?'

Instead of the suit and tie which Andrew always associated with the factory manager Harry wore a pair of old blue overalls and matching cap. 'We would have,' replied Julie, apparently not in the least surprised by the newcomer's apparel, 'except for a sudden squall, but we escaped it just in time. You're a long way from home, aren't you?' she added.

'On a day like this some of us get drafted to a holiday resorts to help out; the litter bins soon get topped up and so need to be emptied frequently.'

Andrew, who'd forgotten about Harry's other jobs, asked, 'Don't you really mind being a waste disposal person?'

From the direction of the promenade a voice shouted, 'Come on, Harry, you lazy dog.' The manager ignored it. 'Not likely. It's wonderful not having to think too much for a change; unlike many another factory boss I'm not prone to stomach ulcers or heart disease.' Then he glanced shrewdly at Andrew's lover who, by now, was kneeling by his side. 'However, I'm afraid I'll be giving my old ticker a pounding tonight,' he predicted solemnly. Diving headlong into the trap, the younger man asked why. 'Because every time I see Julie I can't leave my wife alone,' he laughed.

She gazed at Harry in fascination for a moment, then her jaw dropped slowly until she suddenly threw herself onto her sweetheart knocking him backward onto the sand, where she buried her face into his left armpit and giggled hysterically. Harry, in the meantime, rose to his feet, winked down at Andrew then walked off without a backward glance.

'How much do they charge you for this stuff?' he wanted to know as his lover presented him with some more old coins. After her almost interminable laughing fit they'd returned to the promenade and were now patronising another amusement arcade.

'Nothing,' she replied as she fed some of the money into a machine which, via a film and a dummy gun, allowed her to take pot shots at imaginary aircraft attacking her equally bogus bomber. She moved on to a fruit machine.

'Why not?' he persisted.

Her reply was another echo of the ferry captain's on the occasion of Andrew's first trip across the reservoir lake with his sweetheart. 'Gambling is a strong instinct in many people; too strong to be safely suppressed.' As she explained, she went from one machine to the next, rarely facing him but talking sideways as she concentrated upon what she was doing; any money she won went straight back into the machines. 'This is a harmless way of venting off the compulsion; the authorities won't allow the public to gamble with genuine money because it would threaten our one class system by making some people richer than others. There are other precautions against that occurring, of course, but they feel it's better to be safe than sorry.' She rolled a coin via a ramp onto a bed of more coins in the hope of dislodging some, but without success. 'This money is worthless throughout the island except for one or two other seaside resorts, and then it's only of use in places like this. If it wasn't for the expense of altering the mechanisms or making fresh machines these coins would've probably been replaced by plastic discs.'

Andrew, disturbed at the way his lover devoted all her attention to the machines and fearful she was becoming addicted to them, finally exclaimed, 'I hate this place.' He stared round the arcade in disgust, at the lurid lighting, the all too brash plastic veneer together with the loud pop music and the sickly sweet smell of burning sugar. Everywhere people with expressionless faces fed coins into machines in silent concentration whilst he just longed for the unsophisticated world so essential to him.

Julie turned and stared at him with an expression almost approaching adoration. Pulling down his head she whispered, 'So do I.' And, taking his unused coins, she added her own and pressed them into the hands of the nearest person, then, facing her lover, she said, 'Coming?'

At the far end of the promenade it was much more peaceful; here, large hotels faced the sea; most were grand buildings with pinnacled, high, narrow windowed turrets standing proud of their walls. Into one of the finest of these edifices Andrew's sweetheart disappeared without a word leaving him waiting at the foot of the long flight of stone entrance steps. 'More surprises?' he commented as he playfully lifted her off the lowest step and held her aloft.

'Don't show me up in front of others,' she hissed down at him through clenched teeth. 'Now,' she said as soon as he'd lowered her to the pavement, 'it's time to unwind, so let's go and see what's at the back of the town.' They went no further than a secluded little park where they sat on a bench, and the only sounds came from chirping birds and an invisible game of tennis.

Julie rested her head on her lover's shoulder and they silently contemplated their own private thoughts; having asked her once and not received an answer Andrew knew his companion well enough not to enquire about her business in the hotel; though he hoped it was what he thought it might be. Eventually, as the light began to fade, they drifted across to a backstreet public house where the jukebox music and general conversation were both subdued.

'You were really dropping in my esteem in that arcade,' he commented, breaking the silence at last.

He felt her hands clutch his under the table and the fingernails dig into his chest; she beamed at him. 'I was wondering when and whether you were going to break, love. Listen, thanks to you I've had a gorgeous time today, but if I came here again within a year it'd be too soon. This just isn't my scene; it's far too gaudy and false.' Raising his hand she kissed it. But most islanders, I should think, come to this type of resort regularly, which proves the point I wanted to make recently. Those people prefer this kind of town for their entertainment, and I don't feel contempt for them, but I'd exchange all this amusement for a sunset on a hill with you!'

Before they left the tavern Julie visited the toilet; when she reappeared she'd transformed herself, for now she wore the black dress from the farm party, set off with a pearl necklace and earrings; the effect, together with her loosely brushed hair, was to make her appearance simple yet extremely elegant. 'You look beautiful,' Andrew declared, amazed, 'but what about me?'

She smiled triumphantly as she produced a pair of neatly pressed trousers from her bag, and exclaimed, 'This is the first time I've worn a swimsuit with nylons beneath a dress.'

'I don't suppose you've brought me a pair of shoes as well?' he asked, glancing down at her shiny black ones. When she shook her head he pushed open the men's room door muttering to himself that anyway her shoulder bag must be bottomless.

'That's it,' she cried in delight upon his re-emergence, and after adjusting his tie and combing his hair to her satisfaction, added, 'your shoes will pass for suede, and our coats are passable.' And so they departed for their last port of call in the seaside town.

'I informed them that, as you were an ex-mainlander, you'd

prefer a view of the distant coastline,' Julie explained, her eyes sparkling in the candle light. They were seated inside one of the turrets of the hotel she'd entered earlier, which contained a small dining table and a pair of chairs but, due to its small size, little else. The view from the windows was magnificent, a whole coastal panorama from the strings of coloured lights adorning the resort's pier and esplanade to where the red sun was about to touch the horizon beyond one of the largest seaports on the mainland. On the other side of the golden/red flecked channel a myriad of twinkling lights picked out the opposite shore line; out to sea a lighthouse, guarding a reef well-known to Andrew, regularly flashed, and ships steamed by, oceanic Christmas trees.

As soon as the door had closed behind the waiter after he'd shown them into the turret, Julie began playing one of her embarrassing games, for she immediately leapt from her chair, sat down upon her sweetheart's lap and began nibbling at his ears, kissing his head and thrusting her tongue in his mouth in a frenzy of passion. But by the time the waiter had returned she was seated demurely back in her chair, the picture of innocence once more. The entire operation was repeated after the soup course, and Andrew had no doubts it would be re-enacted after the main and sweet courses as well; in the event he wasn't far wrong, but by the time the brandy and coffee had been served the game had been played out. She sat quietly in his lap sharing his cigar whilst they stared out at the last vestiges of dusk together by the light of a single candle. 'How do we pay for this little lot, darling?' he murmured. Throughout the day it had been her hand that had dipped into the bag whenever a reckoning was due.

She blew some cigar smoke at him. 'With our private fund,' she merely said.

'Are we sleeping here, then?' he asked enthusiastically. She shook her head. 'In that case I'm not looking forward to the walk from the station to the farm.'

'Don't worry,' she soothed, her half open mouth caressing his hair, 'it's all been arranged.' At the end of some ten minute's silence she pondered dreamily, 'Don't you think it's wonderful, sweetheart, that anyone can sit up here, can afford to?'

He nodded over in the direction of the lights of the land of his birth. 'A prospect of hell from heaven,' he whispered.

She giggled. 'Yet we're the heathens!'

'Quick,' said Julie, pulling her lover along as the sound of the departing train muffled their running footsteps; waiting outside the station was a darkened vehicle and, with a warning finger to her lips, she then grasped the door handle. After listening carefully for a moment she quickly pulled the door open wide and simultaneously shouted, 'Hello.'

There was immediate confusion inside the pickup as the courtesy light automatically came on and the two reclining figures struggled to sit up. 'Ouch,' a male voice exclaimed preceded by a dull thud.

'You cow!' squealed Ruth, adjusting her clothes.

But her cousin just laughed as she urged Andrew into the cab. 'Show us something we haven't already seen,' she suggested, climbing in after him.

'Are we already, then?' Derek enquired after rubbing the top of his head. 'Don't forget girls,' he added before switching on the engine, 'the gear stick is on your right hand side only.'

Both girls giggled, but it was to be some time before Andrew saw the joke. 'No innuendoes about sex,' he muttered disdainfully, nudging his lover in the side.

'It doesn't hurt too badly, does it?' Julie enquired in genuine concern, gently feeling his right shoulder as the loribus pulled away from outside the riding school.

'Well, they reckon there aren't any broken bones,' Andrew joked ruefully. 'But I would have to land on the same shoulder twice.'

'Both the instructor and I warned you to keep your knees tightly together, but,' she laughed, 'in time you'll get a feel for your mount and then you'll know exactly when to tense your muscles and when to relax.'

Apart from his two falls Andrew had thoroughly enjoyed himself, despite his only being of novice status. One factor which had aided him was his sweetheart's inherent humanity; even though he knew her to be an accomplished horsewoman she'd remained silent when the instructor assumed neither of them had much experience of horse riding. But when he'd shot his lover a puzzled frown during a lecture on horse anatomy she'd merely shaken her head warningly back at him. Eventually, following a lesson on riding equipment, they were taken out to what were probably the two smallest and most docile horses in the stables, with which they promptly made friends by patting and talking softly to, and by the offer of an apple each. After being loaned a specially hardened helmet each the lovers were allowed to mount up.

Bernard, their middle aged instructor, must've realised soon after the trio had walked their mounts out of the stable yard that his female pupil was no stranger to riding, but he made no comment and instead confined all his subsequent advice to her companion. Andrew, however, after the first few sensations of disquiet so often experienced by the novice with regard to anything new, settled down surprisingly quickly to his position astride his grey mare.

The riding school was situated in a locality similar to that of Alastair's farm, but instead of there being a metalled lane and then a farm track allowing access to the chalk downland, a wide sandy bridleway, well churned up by horse's hoofs, served a similar purpose. Along this track they repeatedly ambled until Bernard had satisfied himself his pupil was reasonably confident in his handling of his horse. 'We're going to try some trotting now,' he said, reining in alongside Andrew, 'now forget all that wild west stuff, and bounce up and down in the saddle to the rhythm of the horse. Like this.'

'It looks bloody daft,' he confided to his lover as they watched their instructor riding away.

'Yes,' she agreed, 'but when you're fully fledged you needn't bother with it; if it's good enough for cowboys...........'

Bernard checked his watch. 'Well, you've mastered that part alright, Andrew; now, soon there'll be a group of more experienced riders coming past on their way up to the downs, and we'll tag along behind them. However, on no account should you attempt to follow them if they should break into a canter from a trot; you've learnt enough for one day.'

Failure to follow this excellent advice resulted in Andrew's first fall whereby he simply capsized out of his saddle; the vision of his sweetheart smiling down at him in stark contradiction of what she'd told him the previous day, as she sat confidently upon her horse whilst Bernard helped him, was to remain in his memory for the rest of his life. During their return to the stables he unwisely rode slightly too fast and too close to a low hurdle especially sited near the bridleway; at the last moment the mare, misunderstanding, increased speed, veered and took the obstacle whilst her rider carried on in a more horizontal fashion. On this occasion he was gratified by Julie's concern for she immediately leapt from her saddle and rushed to his side. 'You haven't been put off horse riding, have you?' she asked anxiously after ensuring he wasn't badly hurt. Still in a daze, he shook his head vigorously.

When he'd first boarded the loribus Andrew had been surprised at the small size of the passenger saloon; he'd considered there couldn't have been room for much more than twenty passengers. 'While we were visiting your family,' Julie replied to his comment during their journey back to the station, 'I noticed those massive buses often conveying only half a dozen people. Such wastefulness wouldn't be tolerated here.'

'Yes,' he replied defensively, 'but they were specially designed to cope with rush hours too.'

'That's another area where the island transport system differs so radically from the mainland's. This loribus has been specifically designed for this particular route; apart from isolated farmhouses, it travels to every habitation and village in the immediate area, all of which are arranged in a direct line; when it reaches the furthermost building it returns to the railway station carrying, as you know, darling, freight, mail and people in both directions. So everyone has the opportunity of travelling whenever they wish.' She paused to draw his attention to a white painted, wooden water mill close to the road. 'We'll have to see if we can stay there one day,' she remarked, then continued, 'But where the cunning bit comes in is in the liaison between the population on a given route and their bus service: instead of everyone jumping on the bus whenever they feel like it, each individual more or less knows when they ought to travel; so therefore no self-respecting mother would normally set out for the coast or town at a time when others were on their way to work or school, for instance.'

She ceased explaining as the bus drew into the station yard but resumed as they sat awaiting their train, 'Of course it's all been simplified by the fact that the number of people and habitations on each route remains constant, but although the passenger capacity on that loribus was limited, there were still enough seats left over for casual travellers like us, and this allows for a little flexibility for the residents on the route. If the bus operator found they'd underestimated their carrying capacity requirement they'd either get the authorities to replace or modify the vehicle or else they'd simply increase the number of round trips, because a loribus driver's job is far from hectic.'

On the train Andrew enquired, 'When you mentioned that all the buildings on the loribus route were in a direct line what on earth did you mean? That road went all over the place, darling.'

His lover laughed. 'I must admit the route was picturesque, but you couldn't see the metaphorical woods for the trees. The island authorities can be very ruthless with their means to an end: apart from necessary farm buildings like uncle's, and a number of cottages which were converted into holiday homes, every isolated habitation was abandoned, often to be dismantled and then reconstructed in a more suitable site adjacent to a bus route. So some of those beautiful cottages set in old world gardens we passed on the bus were often only decades old. At first the original inhabitants of the condemned houses must have cursed the likes of Charlie Maynard and Harry Larke for forcing them to live close to roads, but as you saw for yourself, sweetheart, the lanes were almost empty of vehicles.'

'I noticed that fact during our first cycle ride,' he agreed, adding, 'so if I saw a building in the distance it would either belong to a farm, be a holiday home, or on a regular bus route?'

'You've got it,' Julie answered, squeezing his hand, 'This island's transport problem is virtually non-existent. You could say we're laughing all the way to the bank.'

'Would you like me to do you afterwards?' Andrew enquired hopefully.

'That won't be necessary,' his sweetheart replied as she rubbed soothing balm onto the inside of his thighs while he lay trouserless on the bed, 'I put some on before we went out.'

'You might've warned me,' he complained.

'What, and forego this pleasure? Anyway, a lesson learnt in pain is a lesson well remembered.'

'Hey!' he exclaimed shortly, 'that area isn't sore.'

'Not yet it isn't,' she giggled, adding defensively, 'besides, I'm merely maintaining my equipment.'

'Well you'd better make certain it's still in working order now.'

'I intend to,' she answered, getting off the bed and going across to the door to lock it, 'and afterward we'll take another look at your shoulder.'

'I feel a bit wet!' Andrew suddenly exclaimed.

'You dirty devil!' Derek immediately replied with heavy emphasis, making both girls break into peals of laughter. The insinuation was only too obvious, for once more Andrew found himself squeezed inside the cab of the pickup truck sandwiched between two vivacious auburn haired girls whose uninhibited contact and perfume were distinctly disturbing.

'I meant,' he blustered, 'that I feel stupid dressed in cowboy gear. "Wet" means ridiculous in naval slang,' he added lamely; which only created more mirth.

Ignoring his explanation Ruth eventually answered, 'You won't feel "wet" when we get there because you can't get in if you don't look the part.'

'What would happen if you drove straight there?' he asked as they pulled up outside the station.

'My farming career would be over,' Derek said, 'Ruth's too, probably, maybe even her dad's if they didn't report me.'

Had it occurred on the mainland, the train ride would almost certainly have got out of hand because it was only too apparent, as the train approached their platform, that one particular coach was full of country and western fans; and as it rolled past them, the numerous heads poking from the windows called out, 'In here, Ruth, Come on, Derek.'

Once onboard Andrew was introduced to as motley a crew of women and men, girls and boys as could ever have graced an unsettled subcontinent; no one had actually gone to the length of posing as a native Indian but there were at least several representative half breeds present. 'You haven't seen anything yet,' Ruth murmured when he voiced his amazement, 'you won't

216

be able to move inside the special bar they had to erect for all these seedy individuals.'

Even Julie, after staring in some awe at the authentic looking characters around them, whispered to her lover, 'Imagine being zig-zagged by some of these, darling!' The subsequent journey to their destination, though, was accomplished with an unusual amount of decorum under the circumstances, but Derek averred that the return ride would probably be slightly more lively. This statement compelling Andrew to observe dryly that, in that case, he hoped the various firearms evident weren't loaded.

From the outside the public house appeared attractive, though not particularly unusual; but the interior, though, was a mixture of all the western saloon film sets in creation. The place was enormous, which was an essential requirement because of all the individual round tables, and chairs, arranged throughout the floor space. Derek was extremely fortunate in being able to procure a table for the four of them, as the saloon wasn't quite full. 'What'll it be, boys?' demanded an authentic voiced and clad waiter who'd appeared as if from nowhere, and who now flicked dispassionately at their table with a soiled cloth.

'Beers for us, sherry wine for the ladies,' Derek told him casually. As soon as the man had gone he then produced a pack of cards. 'They're just to set the flavour,' he explained, 'Partner whist, not very original I guess but somewhat more apt than snakes and ladders.'

His ploy was very effective because, as Andrew began to realise during the course of play, it had the ability to make them all a living part of some true life drama of the old wild west, and soon he heard himself drawling and otherwise aping those well known characters of modern visual entertainment. Even when the stage curtains had been drawn back and the main lights in the auditorium lowered they continued to play their game, an activity which, in similar circumstances, Andrew would've considered callus were it not for the fact that others at adjacent tables were doing exactly the same. Nor did matters change when the first turn came on: an attractive girl clad in buckskins playing a violin accompanied by a banjo strumming man similarly adorned.

By this time the place was filled almost to overflowing: all the tables were taken, the bar counters couldn't be seen for customers, and even the minstrel gallery running round three sides of the hall held people standing shoulder to shoulder against the safety rails. The constant stream of musicians, singers and dancers who occupied the stage had a real fight to make themselves heard above the din, but it was obvious their efforts weren't entirely in vain because frequent cheers, yells, cat calls, wolf whistles and applause rent the air.

All types of musical instruments put in an appearance but guitars were by far the most prominent; most of the singers, both female and male, presented prairie type songs in the appropriate style whilst clad in authentic costumes; but once, a girl wearing a long Victorian style dress and with a choker about her neck sang several mildly suggestive numbers which, she claimed, were all the latest from back east, while bending low over the footlights in a pretence at being confidential but in reality to display her charms. And soon afterwards a line of chorus girls danced provocatively, a vision received with even more avid enthusiasm by the male portion of the audience. Andrew, watching with fascination as Ruth adeptly shuffled the deck of cards with unbecoming professionalism, loudly declared, 'Those poor people on the stage ought to have a bit more quiet.'

She smiled across at him, then began to deal. 'Most of these people about us,' she explained flicking the cards to each of them with great rapidity, 'take it in turns to entertain, including Derek and I; so who's going to object? Your call, Julie.'

'When will you be going up, then?' Andrew asked, throwing down a card.

'With this crowd here,' Derek laughed, trumping it, 'in about five week's time, I reckon.'

As the evening wore on and more drinks were consumed the audience became ever more boisterous, and Andrew could imagine that any sober person entering the saloon at that time would have been half frightened to death, be they woman or man. But the uproar was good humoured, and he noticed no verbal or physical fighting or acts of vandalism, either in the public house or onboard their train during the subsequent ride home. This was almost certainly due, as Julie later pointed out, to the calming presence of each man's female partner and to Whyte Island's other wise policies.

As their train sped ever nearer their destination Andrew began to grow increasingly concerned about how they were going to reach the farm, for no one in the party was fit to drive. However, he was glad he'd kept his uneasiness to himself when he saw Mary behind the steering wheel. 'Right,' she said when they were gathered unsteadily round the cab, 'tails in the back. Call, Andrew.' She tossed the coin and showed him the result then, handing him out a blanket, she warned, 'Watch out for the bike, and knock on the roof as soon as you're ready.'

Julie said, 'I'd better go with him; he's bound to break something.' It was only after they'd started off that he remembered his apparent multitude of bruises, and even his lover's body couldn't cushion the resultant shocks completely, although their mutual embrace prevented them from moving overmuch.

'What shall we do today, darling?' Andrew asked as he sat on the edge of the bed gazing down at his sweetheart.

'What would you suggest?' she replied lazily before hastily pulling the bedspread over her breasts upon seeing the look in his eyes.

'Let's stay on the farm and see whether your aunt and uncle would like us to help them out.'

Julie smiled knowingly back at him. 'Go on,' she challenged, 'ask them.'

Mary was most indignant when he put the suggestion to her. 'Certainly not,' she exclaimed, 'I shouldn't even have let you help on your first morning here; and don't go pestering Alec or the farm workers, they've all got their own jobs which they can manage quite well thank you. If you want to help, make yourself some sandwiches and keep out of the way.' Then she promptly smiled and gave him a broad wink. 'I happen to be aware no one's going near the pear orchard; you can borrow a radio. Take things easy on your last full day,' she urged.

If Andrew had thought his lover had worn a dress which buttoned down the front on purpose he was soon to discover his mistake, because she just lay smiling dreamily beneath the shade of the pear tree until he reached her waist, then she began to button herself up faster than he could undo her. 'Why not?' he pleaded when he realised she wasn't teasing.

'Give me a cuddle and I'll tell you,' she replied, and explained as soon as he held her comfortably in his arms, 'You know what you're like when you've had a drink or two. I had a wow of a time last night, but it took you almost half hour nonstop.' She giggled at the recollection. 'I timed you. I thought you were going to drop dead with exhaustion. So we're just going to lie here and chat, listen to the radio, and maybe have a little sleep later.' As she finished speaking, the sound of chamber music which had subtly filled the air, came to an end and the announcer introduced the next programme: a session of heavy rock music. 'We don't fancy that do we?' she enquired, reaching over to find another station. 'Let's try the mainland's national service, they can be quite good sometimes; when they're not repeats, that is.'

'.......we hope she enjoys her holiday in sunnier climes,' a well-spoken female voice was saying. 'And now for "Save it", the programme especially for those of you who wish to invest your money wisely.'

Andrew's bruised shoulder was badly wrenched as his sweetheart suddenly sat up, then jumped to her feet; startled, he gazed up at her and was shocked at the mixture of hatred and disgust imprinted upon her face. After switching the radio off in a fury she began to stamp round the tree, swearing and blaspheming in a shocking manner. 'The thoughtless, selfish, ignorant bastards,' were her better selected words, 'that always happens sooner or later,' she continued, 'on that side.' He sat up and leant against the trunk of the fruit tree, too astonished and bewildered at the reaction of the girl he loved to do anything else.

Eventually she calmed down enough to sit next to her lover, where she immediately embraced him. 'Hold me tightly,' she murmured, 'until I cool off.' He knew she was close to tears, but he also knew her too well to attempt to make a comment at this stage. At last she observed irritably, 'How many millions are there out of work over on the mainland? During the day they and their spouses have only got radio and other forms of home entertainment, probably all they can afford. So what do they get? Their poverty rammed down their throats by thoughtless fools, idiots who can't realise the unemployed need a holiday to break up the monotony of their existence, that they'd like savings so they could have the luxury of investing in their future....'

Knowing from the tone in her voice and the tenseness of her body she was about to blow up again Andrew stopped her mouth with his. At first he could sense he reluctance, but gradually she gave in until he was able to insinuate his tongue between her lips and then she began to respond. He was longing to cup one of her breasts in his hand but he instinctively understood it was solace she needed, not sex. But his hope that she'd forgotten about her complaint was shattered when their lips eventually parted.

'I don't know what's wrong with those mainland broadcasters,' she began immediately, then answering her own enigma she exclaimed, 'Yes I do!' Staring at her sweetheart as if seeing him for the first time she said decisively, 'They've got no imagination; just like everyone else. Those top media people receive damn good salaries, which allows them to have all the good things in life that money brings. They obviously don't understand what it's like to sit at home bored stiff, worrying about the mortgage or rent and how they'll afford food, clothing and service charges as well as other items; they're more stupid than deliberately callous, I suppose. No wonder the unions are able to get their members out on strike when places of employment are threatened with closure, the poor devils must be petrified of losing their jobs; especially when one of their main forms of entertainment,' she concluded, pointing at the radio, 'is that trash.' Disengaging herself from his arms she patted her lap. 'Lay your head here, love, I want to stroke your hair.'

As soon as Andrew had made himself comfortable she began to speak again, 'I suppose you've been told all the advantages of having a main, and several other different, jobs?' he nodded, and he sweetheart continued, 'Well I think by far the best justification for the practice is that it does allow the individual to understand, and empathise with, what it's like to experience circumstances normally outside their province. A person can be told, or read, about a given situation repeatedly and it would be like water off a duck's back: as I stated before, no imagination; but compel them to endure that situation, then,' she emphasised, 'you'll get a response. So Harry Larke understands how a refuse collector feels, and Uncle Alastair, a factory worker. I could guarantee if those radio and other media announcers had to spend half their time on the dole they wouldn't be so thoughtless toward the poor when they broadcast again.'

'I doubt it's quite as straight forward as you suggest, darling,' he commented, 'I don't suppose the announcers and broadcasters in general have much choice. I think you'll find that to some degree or another the party in power over on the mainland has a certain control over what gets broadcast or doesn't. The government would almost certainly prefer to paint a rosier side to current affairs than otherwise, and many employees of the media, if they value their job, would be more than happy to submit to that notion. I also believe that many former announcers and actors are well aware of what life is like on the dole, because the turnover in the entertainment profession is enormous with perfectly accomplished artistes having a very brief career. So if they don't toe the line, they're out!'

Julie nodded in acquiescence, 'No doubt you're right. I had noticed the sudden departure of various well known voices on the mainland radio without warning.' She switched the set on once more and eventually tuned in to a programme of fairground music: this must have reminded her of their trip to the seaside for she enquired, 'Did you notice how little evidence there was of women being portrayed as sex objects at the holiday resort, darling, such as beauty contests, pictures of girls in revealing swimwear, girlie magazines, things like that?' She went on when he nodded, 'That's to stop you men from thinking of us as anything other than real people; men, in their desire for us, often can't see any further than our faces, figures and the promise of all things naughty and nice; they forget we're as individualistic as they are. Many women, for instance, have minds more in tune with men's than with their own gender.'

She frowned as he interrupted her line of thought. 'You're forgetting those "what the butler saw" machines. They were most certainly sexually biased.'

'They were there merely to make the pier seem more authentic,' she said dismissively, 'besides, as you mentioned, there was nothing to them.'

Andrew sat up, this was much more his idea of a topic. 'That schoolboy looking through the keyhole at the maid stripping off....' he began enthusiastically, but his lover uncharacteristically stopped him.

'Perversion!' she exclaimed, 'What an ideal subject, but let's have our picnic first.' Noting the lack of irony in her voice Andrew mentally rubbed his hands; this was much better, he thought.

When they'd finished their meal Julie settled her head in his lap; and as she talked about her erotic topic he teased and fondled her golden red locks wondering, as he did so, at how a creature as gorgeous as she was could know so much about, and come to terms with, such a debasing subject. It was hardly the sort of thing for an environment as beautiful and peaceful as an orchard, either.

'Your mention of the maid and the schoolboy was particularly apt, Andy,' she began, 'because it gives rise to a classical example of perversion. But first I'd like to put in a plea on behalf of the pervert because, as you might well agree from the examples I'll be giving you, he's the real victim: and I use the masculine gender because it's predominantly a male characteristic; and he only becomes really dangerous when he's inherently a forceful person.

'Now, let's set the scenario: imagine the sort of old time household where they're wealthy enough to have servants, darling; one of the boys from the family is home from boarding school and he's just reached the age of puberty, say about twelve to fourteen. So he's at a sexually impressionable age, especially as he's probably recently been attending a male only establishment. We'll study a particular servant now: imagine a pretty girl of, say, eighteen; which shouldn't be too difficult for you; she's been employed in the house for four years, the work is hard, repetitive and allows her little time off within which to enable her to mix with the opposite sex. Possibly, one might say probably, she's already been seduced and abandoned by one of the boy's older brothers.

'So when she observes this fresh faced kid on the verge of manhood a variety of emotions might overcome her; to begin with, sweetheart, here's a chance to ease her sexual repression, then there's a way in which she can dominate someone who is superior to her by way of his gender and status; lastly, but not least, she can revenge herself on the lad's strict mother by seducing her son. Which she proceeds to do, slowly at first by verbal hints and tantalising glimpses of her body until at last the day arrives when she is able to get him alone in an appropriate place; as his mother keeps her staff on their toes there's little time for finesse, so it's a case of off underwear, down on the floor or bed, legs apart and away we go!'

Andrew couldn't refrain from sniggering at her description, but his sweetheart merely smiled up at him. 'We'll have to re-enact it one day, darling,' she stated, 'but it isn't really very funny, Andy, because the chances are that the boy, when he becomes mature, could have a fixation about women dressed as maids displaying white thighs, black stockings and suspenders. Which isn't a problem in itself when there's a ready supply of such ladies, but could become extremely dangerous when there isn't; of course, the child could have found the experience so frightening or disturbing that it might make him impotent or put him off females for life, with the possibility of all kinds of unfortunate results dependant on his hereditary nature.'

He was about to make a comment when Julie raised her head, placed her arms about his neck and gave him a lingering kiss. 'Wait a minute,' she urged, referring to his attempt at intervention, 'examples first, discussion afterward. Here's another case which is quite common, but rather more perverse and I'll describe it in an extreme form.' She considered for a moment. 'Yes,' she decided, 'we can use the same characters in the following example as well; it'll make it simpler, and we'll have it occurring in a more modern setting this time.

'First we have a boy, a bit younger on this occasion, not quite sexually aware. Then we have the girl who lives next door, we'll make her fifteen and she's very advanced for her age, highly sexed and on more than intimate terms with the boy's older brother. Both sets of parents go out a lot; and on this particular day we'll have the older brother away from home, perhaps it's a case of familiarity breeding contempt and he's trying to keep out of his young lover's way. So when she goes next door for her regular servicing all she finds is the immature younger brother; of course she's annoyed but, to condense the story, she attempts to arouse him but with utter lack of success and to make things worse he's even too shy to touch her where it counts.'

'Ouch,' Andrew suddenly cried out, holding the back of his right hand, 'that hurt.'

'So it should,' his lover laughed, 'I wasn't dropping any hints.

Anyway, the girl is so angry and frustrated that she berates the boy verbally and then physically. That's one situation; another on the same theme, and probably less common in this more enlightened age, and I'm not referring to Whyte Island, love, is where a mother or elder sister catches a boy abusing himself, and reacts by scolding or actually beating him. You can therefore assume the boy might consider himself to be inferior to, and reviled by, the opposite sex and so by the time he attained manhood it could mean he'd enjoy being beaten and abused by females.'

Julie paused while she and Andrew, in silent and mutual agreement, altered position; when she lay comfortably in his arms with their bodies lying laterally she continued, 'To return to our imaginary trio: as I indicated, the older brother may have been growing tired of his demanding and sensual girlfriend, so he seeks to rid himself of her by mistreating and humiliating her.'

'Sort of by dropping hints?'

'Or by more practical methods; if a person is being constantly harassed by a clingy individual then it might amuse them to see how much they'll put up with; so let's assume that one day the younger brother, not unnaturally curious, follows the couple upstairs and peeps through the keyhole, perhaps to discover what the girl had expected of him. Instead he witnesses one of the methods employed by his brother: binding and gagging his girlfriend and then teasing her in various ways. For the immature voyeur this could mean problems enough in the future, but supposing he accidentally made a noise and his brother dragged him in to watch his antics? Let's say he trusses him up also and leaves him on the bed alongside the girl, or actually has intercourse with her whilst the impressionable youngster looks on in helpless fascination. Elder brothers can be extremely cruel at times.'

At these last words a chill seemed to ascend her lover's spine. 'Is that what happened to you?' he demanded angrily, beginning to sit up. 'Is that why you like bondage?'

Instantly Julie disengaged herself from his embrace and rolled over on top of him. 'Of course not, silly,' she laughed, gazing down at him with tears of mirth filling her eyes. 'Jeremy might have been a pest at times but he'd never have done anything like that, I wouldn't have let him, anyway; island children have been taught not to. No, the first time I was trussed up was during the pioneer zig-zagging.'

'Then why do it if it can encourage perversion, why tie people up?'

His sweetheart, still laughing, replied, 'I thought I'd explained one very good reason the day you pretended to rape me for the first time, but I'll tell you about some other motives another day; really, though, it's just a means to an end.' She lay down alongside him again as soon as she realised he'd regained his composure. 'We haven't finished with our unfortunate perverts yet,' she chided. 'All the cases I mentioned, though quite terrible, can be reasonably harmless when practised by the sufferer if, as I hinted previously, he can find a female such as a wife, girlfriend or prostitute with enough understanding or motivation to help him.'

'By substituting for the maid, et cetera?'

She squeezed him in affirmation. 'But sadly, due to their lack of empathy because they haven't been taught the origins of perversions, and owing to the average pervert's reluctance to reveal his deviation, especially to his loved one, such women and girls are probably fairly rare. Now, the examples I've described, darling, come under the influence of environmental characteristics: in other words they were forced into the recipient's personality without his sanction. How he handles his problem, if he can't find a partner to help him out with it depends upon his hereditary characteristics; if by nature the man is shy and retiring he is quite likely to be satisfied by pictures or written descriptions of his particular deviation, but it's doubtful if he'll be permanently and entirely contented even if he's got an unsuspecting female partner, because he'd still be sexually repressed and so might be difficult to live with or understand. But the deviant who is strong-willed and ruthless can be a very dangerous person.'

Julie paused to consider exactly how she was going to give an example when Andrew, clutching at her in jest, called out, 'Get the ropes, someone!'

'That's it!' she exclaimed, 'A bondage man. If he had a girlfriend or wife totally subservient to him he might be contented enough with occasionally restraining her forcibly without explanation; but it's quite likely he might be compelled to search out genuinely innocent victims in order to gain full satisfaction. If, for instance, he broke into a house just to tie a woman up he might decide to add rape and possibly burglary to his crime, perhaps even torment or murder her.'

Presuming to understand, her lover observed, 'I've heard much of this before from my blue school visit, and also from your sweet self, my darling, although you've gone into it in even greater detail now. What you're leading up to is that all this information has been taught to Whyte Island children so that if they meet up with a pervert during adulthood they'll be able to understand them, perhaps even help them with their particular problem should they feel so inclined.'

'Well,' Julie smiled, 'that's partly it; though I believe you've missed the point in that there are most unlikely to be any deviants on our island. Look, Jeremy and I, being twins, were taught in the same classes and therefore received exactly the same education until red school age; so when we played together neither of us thought of being deviant with regard to the other as we both realised it could damage us psychologically and, thereby, also innocent people. That means, therefore, I've grown up relatively unsullied but knowledgeable because I've also been schooled with regard to various deviations. So eventually I've arrived upon your doorstep where we subsequently begin to practice what most mainlanders might describe as kinky activities, but what are actual ways of ensuring our love life covers even greater areas of sensuality.'

Andrew, recollecting Jill's information and advice in the Ship Inn, added, 'Also to bring variety and interest into our relationship, and to ensure our love endures.'

'Once again you've got it partly right; but the original reason was because we females were expected to please our chosen partners in any way they wished so their physical and psychological requirements wouldn't be inflicted upon innocent victims; in the event, that is, that some deviants might emerge into our society. I know that sounds as if it's a terrible burden upon us poor females, but in fact it's entirely voluntary and many women do manage to restrict themselves in their sexual activities with their lover. The whole point to our free love policy is everyone ends up with the partner who suits them best, and if you don't agree with the way your lover practises sex then you've no right to be cohabiting with her or him as you might be depriving them of their dream lover. But I, and many of my sisters, believe you don't know what you like until you've tried it; however, darling, as I've mentioned many times before, although I love us to take it in turns to be the helpless victim, if ever you treated me with brutality or to prolonged pain whilst I was within your power I'd have nothing more to do with you.'

She then kissed him passionately, thereby silently informing him that his treatment of her was entirely to her satisfaction. 'Many mainland women and children who've been sexually assaulted often complain about the unnecessary violence used against them; it's the type of passion which sometimes ends in death. This is often the result of the assailant's suppressed love for, and attraction toward, women, and his hatred of them because they don't return his affection adequately enough; he also has contempt for himself for abusing his innocent victims, and loathing of them for being second rate substitutes. The proof of this is to be found in the fact that the mildest of sexually deprived men often admit to having fantasies involving the torture and degradation of women.

'Whyte Island females, by offering themselves up in affection, if not in love, help to prevent such horror stories occurring over here; with a little additional aid from their knowledge of martial arts, of course. Oh, by the way, I've overlooked the reason why many shy men are fascinated by the idea of trussed up and muted women: if your prospective sexual partner is your helpless victim then you've no need to go through with the rigmarole of chatting them up, have you? Which, if you feel inadequate, the root cause of the majority of violent and sexual attacks, is a great advantage.'

Andrew stirred in his sweetheart's arms. 'That was all very interesting my love,' he announced, attempting to sound sheepish, 'but the only trouble is I happen to be perverted.'

'Oh!' she exclaimed, taken aback; then she asked uncertainly, 'Well, what can I for your problem, darling?'

He laughed out loud. 'I must be perverted, lying in a beauty spot with an even more beautiful girl and not even attempting to ravish her.'

Julie smiled gratefully. 'Thanks for the compliment, my sweet, but sex is out of the question, anyway, because we're being watched.'

'Who by?' he asked in some alarm, sitting up and glancing about.

'By Ruth and Derek: trying to get their own back for the other night, no doubt.' Staring in the direction of their hidden audience she suddenly shouted out, 'You won't see anything. Andrew's indifferent to sex; I've been trying to bed him ever since we met!'

Well used to her humorous slandering of him by now he merely grinned when, after hearing Derek's ribald laughter, Ruth's voice called back, 'What are you doing with him then?'

'How on earth did they find us?' he whispered.

Completely unconcerned, Julie lay flat on her back and stared up at the foliage. 'We were both so preoccupied with our topic that we forgot about the radio, I suppose they just followed the sound like a pair of hyenas; anyway, I'll switch it off now. Come on, sweet, put your head where you usually put something else and we'll have a nap; forget about those two idlers.' Relishing the thought of using his lover's body as a pillow, and the smell of her laundered dress Andrew willingly obeyed.

As they made their way back to the farmhouse refreshed, but still a little groggy after their hour long slumber, he asked, 'I know when Whyte Island first started there were some difficult problems to overcome, love, but even so, how did the authorities manage to persuade parents to allow their offspring to be taught the required way? Surely they weren't told their children would be given lessons in sexual deviations just so they could keep the occasional pervert off the streets?'

Julie, after kissing the side of his neck to soothe him, didn't deny that was what had happened. 'But,' she added enigmatically, 'the bitter pill was sweetened by the sugar of knowledge. Actually, people can come to terms with practically anything if they're forced or trained to do so. At school we were told a story which is a brilliant example of this fact. You understand what occurs inside a woman's womb when she has more than one embryo during a given pregnancy, Andy?' He shook his head uncertainly, wondering what this had to do with education methods. She flashed him a rather pitying look. 'Well, if two eggs are produced they become fertilised by different male sperms, which is what happened in Jeremy's and my case, thereby forming unalike twins. But occasionally only one egg is produced which, after fertilisation, subsequently splits; this is how identical twins, triplets, and so on come about.

'So, for the sake of our story we have three girls, each a mirror image of the others both in intellect and physical appearance. They're reasonably attractive and intelligent, have received a faultless education and had a happy home life; no real problems at all. But at the age of eighteen they split up and make their own way in life. One girl obtains an office job and remains with her parents. The next becomes a nurse and lives in hospital accommodation, the last trains as a policewoman and also resides away from home.

'During the following seven years the triplets experience their chosen ways of life to the full and never come into contact with one another; but on their twenty fifth birthday they plan a reunion. On the way to their venue, however, a screaming woman dashes out of a house pursued by her enraged husband bearing a knife; and before the girls' eyes the man catches and then stabs his wife repeatedly, afterward he starts to run off. The girl who has spent her life at home up to that moment reacts as most of us would and is emotionally and physically sick at the dreadful scene; the nurse is terrified by the violence and man but is unmoved by all the blood and gore, yet she immediately sets about aiding the injured woman. But the policewoman is not only unaffected by the bloody sight but catches, overpowers, disarms and arrests the husband.

'Now, doubtless, all sorts of interpretations can be placed upon that story, darling, but the one our teacher was trying to make was that what was virtually one individual person will react differently to a given situation dependent upon what they're used to, either due to necessity or through some sort of training.' Pausing, Julie asked, 'Do you see that, Andy? Because it explains a lot; what Whyte Island's authorities were saying to parents was that their children would be unlikely to experience any emotional problems through being taught about sexual deviations because they would've been trained to think them perfectly normal even though not necessarily particularly attractive. In actual fact, love, such emotional stress is only caused when people are made to feel sex in all its numerous forms is disgusting. Sadly, various religions resorted to brainwashing their children at an early age, thus ensuring sectarianism which, throughout the centuries, has led to horrendous acts of cruelty within different societies. Our society generally thinks there's nothing wrong with indoctrination if it's employed for the good rather than the bad.'

'But how can you reckon what's one or the other?'

'By a sense of what is right, open debate and having recourse to the electorate,' replied Julie casually.

By the time they'd reached the farmhouse it was close on six o'clock. 'Thank goodness,' Mary exclaimed when she saw them, 'I was just going to send someone down for you. As it looks like being a lovely evening we've decided to dine down by the pond, and two couples who work on the farm are also coming; I've almost loaded the truck, so when you've had a wash could you both give me a hand?'

Distributing food and drink to ten people seated upon the ground proved to be somewhat difficult, but despite this minor problem the picnic was very enjoyable and, for Andrew, quite unique in that he'd never before eaten with so many in such an informal fashion. By comparison the meal he'd had with Sandra at the Summer Camp had been more like an outdoor dinner taken, as it was, seated before a table. Of the four strangers at the picnic, one amusing, talkative man with his confiding wife were in their forties, whilst the other couple were some ten years younger and somewhat more reserved but still very friendly. The party spirit really became evident after the meal had been consumed and the dirty crockery and utensils stacked away, for then several flagons of cider were produced upon which Alastair declared that no one was to depart until the last drop had been drained. 'God help us,' Julie, who was in her lover's arms, murmured.

With so many agricultural personnel present, and tongues being loosened by the effect of the potent, home-brewed beverage, it was scarcely surprising the conversation should quickly turn to farming subjects until Mary, becoming increasingly impatient, asked Andrew if he'd enjoyed himself in the orchard. The enquiry was really intended as a means of breaking the monopoly of farm talk, but it almost made the recipient's hair stand on end for he subconsciously knew what would be coming next. 'Actually,' his sweetheart blithely replied for him, 'we spent much of the time discussing various sexual perversions.'

In the ensuing silence he felt his face flush; but Mary scarcely faltered for a moment, she'd achieved the result she'd wanted and wasn't going to lose the initiative. 'How interesting,' she observed, 'I remember just before Alastair and I were married we......'

Andrew listened in embarrassed fascination as she bluntly recounted, in intimate detail, a game she and her husband had once played. Then it was the turn of the man in his forties, and soon descriptions of various forms of sexual antics were passing back and forth like recipes at a women's social gathering, or dirty jokes at a stag party. Fortunately for his peace of mind his lover didn't add their experiences or, even worse, her previous encounters to the conversation, mostly because she was too busy giggling. 'You minx,' he whispered in her ear, 'you planned this on purpose.'

She paused long enough to reply, 'I hope you're taking mental notes,' then returned to her mirth.

The picnic seemed as if it was going to end in a bacchanal as the night wore on and the liquid level in the flagons gradually dropped, for the stories grew ever more risqué and the laughter louder and less inhibited. Before it became too dark and they got too drunk Julie suggested to her lover that they neatly stow everything bar the cider and blankets into the pickup, which they did, and afterward he turned the vehicle round to face the party and switched the dipped headlights on.

At one stage Andrew asked the company, during the briefest pause in the anecdotes, 'you wouldn't call yourselves perverts would you?'

'No, of course not,' several individually laughed back.

'Well, how would you define perversion?'

It was Ruth who answered whilst waving her half filled glass unsteadily in the air. 'If you were out walking along a cliff top and chanced upon Derek and I disporting ourselves a la naturale on the beach and stopped to watch, then that'd be normal masculine curiosity.' She gulped unsteadily at her drink. 'But if, ever after, you returned to the same spot hoping for a repeat performance...'

'An obsession,' someone, probably Katherine the older of the two farm women, interrupted.

'Or forced someone against their will,' came another voice. But soon they were back to descriptions of games which they, or someone else, had played mixed with accounts of zigzagging experiences.

Andrew was somewhat surprised when, much later, he glanced across to where the younger pair of farm workers had been seated only to see, instead, a blanket covered mound, and immediately he realised they'd retired. Gradually all conversation waned as one after the other each couple, even Mary and Alastair, lay down beneath their blankets. 'Oh well,' sighed his sweetheart, 'party over.' And she rose to her feet and went across to the pickup to turn its lights off. 'Come on, my darling,' she murmured upon her return, 'let's go and stand in the pond. It's quite safe, hardly any weed, and cattle never use it.'

He knew he was drunk as they made their way down to the water, and yet his mind seemed surprisingly clear, only the environment appeared hazy; there were no stars visible for the sky was overcast but, paradoxically, the night was far from dark being more like the heavy grey of early morning, even though dawn was far off. So he was able to stand at the pond's edge and easily watch in admiration as his companion removed her sweater, skirt and underwear to reveal her distinctly pallid body to his appreciative, though stupefied, gaze. She glanced at him expectantly and, taking the hint, he hastily removed his clothes; then, naked and holding hands, they waded down the gentle slope until Julie was up to her neck in the slightly cool water. She turned and faced him, pressed her body against his and placed her arms about his back. 'I love, love, love you,' she crooned in his ear.

Before kissing her wildly in return he whispered, 'No more than I love you, sweetheart.' It didn't occur to him to wonder why she wanted them to stand together in the nude, drunk, in the middle of the night almost totally immersed in pond water. Doing strange, apparently pointless things occasionally, seemed to appeal to her; but he was perfectly content to remain silent in static embrace for as long as she wished which, in the event, was for a remarkably long time.

'Let's go back to our blankets now, love,' she eventually murmured, 'we're too tipsy for any water sports.'

He soon discovered that his lover had dispensed with her underwear when they lay together beneath their blankets whilst their heads rested upon her folded up skirt and sweater; she, meanwhile, was busy with his jeans. 'And now,' she intoned solemnly, though quietly, in a deep masculine voice, 'Andrew will be making an all out attempt upon his previous endurance record of twenty five minutes.'

Andrew felt himself being nudged awake; his lover was kneeling by his side fully clothed. 'Let's take the pickup back to the farmhouse,' she urged, 'then we'll have a nap in bed and afterward wash up the crockery. If, by then, the survivors of the massacre haven't shown up we'll start breakfast.' With difficulty he sat up and looked wearily about him, he was confused by the sudden stream of information directed at him and was suffering from an overwhelming hangover; it was still very early with the grey sky merely altered to a lighter shade but tinged with a faint blush from the approaching dawn.

He was more than a little surprised, when Julie climbed into the driving seat and started the engine with the confidence of one who does it every day of their life, because he had no idea she could drive but he made no comment and instead declared, 'I assumed this was a well-run farm. Alastair must be mad for allowing a simple picnic to turn into a near orgy.'

His sweetheart laughed as she slipped the vehicle into gear. 'My uncle knows full well his cider's got a kick like an angry dinosaur's and so he'll have made provision for others to look after the farm. Letting your hair down once in a while and saying to hell with everything is as vital in farming as it is in any other profession. What about all those stories?' she giggled, slapping his knee in emphasis, 'I can't wait to try some of them!'

Much refreshed after a shower, a headache pill and a brief but deep sleep, Andrew helped his lover with the picnic gear. 'I must say,' he exclaimed, sounding pompous but not meaning to, 'I thought it a little disconcerting your aunt should describe the sex games which she and Alastair practised while she was still nursing Ruth, especially in the presence of her daughter.'

'Oh dear, Andy,' she replied sadly, 'you seem to have forgotten the lesson of the triplets already. My cousin wouldn't have been embarrassed by her mother's descriptions because she's used to that kind of talk. As for the other point: auntie was probably being very wise, as many heterosexual partnerships receive a mortal blow after a child is born; my aunt was ensuring uncle didn't feel the baby was replacing him in her affections.'

The way she began over-zealously polishing a plate told him she was in deep thought. 'There's a theory beginning to take root among some anthropologists,' she eventually stated, 'which argues that permanent pair bonding between Homo Sapien couples might be abnormal. They say post natal depression, plus the frequent transference of love and attention by a mother from her partner to her new offspring, and the infamous roving eye exhibited by many husbands and some wives, is proof that our genes are meant to be more widely sown than at present.' Picking up another plate she thoroughly dried it. 'Apparently we were intended, according to these scientists, to gather within a tribe and are all expected to work for the common good, gathering food, making tools, cooking and so on; but when it comes to sex you just lie down with the nearest appropriate person; so when a female becomes noticeably pregnant she's left alone while other women and girls do the satisfying.'

'I wouldn't fancy that,' Andrew declared.

'Neither would I,' agreed his sweetheart, 'but it'd have its advantages: no sexually frustrated men running about, for example. I suppose such a society would collapse when some bully boy saw a woman more attractive than the others; or a female noted a big, strong male who might provide her with children of a similar physique and who could obtain larger chunks of meat for her and their offspring, and so decided it would be worth while reserving him for future use.' She shrugged. 'But it's all only a theory.'

'Right, love,' she said, hanging up the tea towel, and giving him a quick hug, 'let's change the subject along with our chore.' They began laying places for ten on the long table in the centre of the kitchen. 'Did you notice how nearly all the games mentioned last night involved immobilising their partners?' Andrew glanced up and nodded. 'Well, you asked for an explanation and I told you bondage was merely a means to an end; it's like a carpenter enjoying the actual driving in of nails, but it's the end product which really matters. Just as with the card game "strip poker", instead of being bound by stockings,' she paused, 'as in our case, you're bound by rules. So you see, darling, I'm not perverted because I don't mind being trussed up.' She went over to a cupboard and returned with an armful of condiments. 'Now,' she observed after they'd arranged them on the table, 'it isn't worth starting the actual cooking, let's see if we can rouse them.'

As they walked across the farmyard Julie delved even deeper into the subject she'd been outlining in the kitchen. 'When you've tied me up and left me to sweat out my fate I often pass the time away by examining my emotions; there is, for instance, a lot of hypocrisy in the average woman's soul: she often says "no" when she really means "yes" and vice versa. So when I'm helplessly awaiting your attentions I think to myself "I don't want him to ravish me but I can't do anything about it, so I might as well enjoy it". In other words, sweetheart, you've become my conscience, and I find that very sensual. Another pleasure I experience is the fact it can become an ego trip; I contemplate, 'He's left me here just so he can enjoy my body, not anyone else's: he could go off and find another girl and I wouldn't be able to stop him, but he'll be coming back just to possess me. Of course, if I was feeling masochistic I could assume you wouldn't be returning; then I'd have the sense of outrage a person naturally feels when they're confined against their will, and also the thrill of wondering just when you're going to reappear and exactly what you'll be doing to me. Also, because I love you so much, I'm pleased you're going to obtain pleasure from me only, and I like proving to you that I've complete faith in you.'

She put her arm around him possessively as they stepped out into the lane. 'Last but not least is the usually subconscious wish in most women to be dominated.' She thought for a moment. 'Do you remember how, at the country and western club, the simple action of playing a game of cards instead of merely gawking at the stage made us an actual part of what was happening? We really were in the wild west of so many years ago.'

She stopped and kissed him. 'Well sometimes, my precious, when you've left me alone bound and gagged, I pretend I really am a kidnapped or burglary victim. I think "what will my husband say" or "I'm only fifteen, I don't know about sex and I'm frightened of what's going to happen to me" and so I try to free myself and writhe and struggle, attempting to shout and scream. I get into a proper frenzy, so that by the time you come to me I really am a helpless captive completely hyped up, which makes whatever follows even better. Some people claim rape doesn't exist, that it's actually enjoyable for women. I don't believe it for a minute because few women like to be forced against their will, but I can understand how the legend arose, love, because deep down inside many of us females are very primitive.'

There was an early morning mist but the sun was already beginning to rise above it; although the lovers walked a considerable distance along the lane there was still no sign of their erstwhile fellow revellers, and so far they'd only seen a family of three out for an early stroll. 'I like tying you up almost as much,' Julie confessed after they'd overtaken them, 'When I see you helpless I think, "shall I use him as a whipping boy for the sake of oppressed womanhood down the ages?" But then, my sweet, all my adoration for you surfaces and so I play around with you until you're at the peak of sensuality, and then I give you everything my imagination and body has to offer.'

Andrew had listened enthralled at this baring of his sweetheart's soul, but now he grabbed her and kissed her passionately. 'You know what we ought to do?' he suggested when they'd resumed their walk, 'we should get that book 'Living Together' and go across to the mainland, and like the evangelists of old we'd go preaching the gospel of bondage.'

She was entirely serious when she replied, 'If it helped to save marriages and family life then it would be well worth it.'

'The only trouble is, a lot of spouses would welcome the opportunity of settling old scores.'

'Yes,' she agreed, 'you'd need to have exactly the same environment as we've got over here, and you wouldn't achieve that in under twenty years or so. After all, darling, you'd hardly expect a battered wife to allow her husband to immobilise and silence her. If I didn't have complete faith in you I wouldn't let you do it to me!'

Changing the subject he asked, 'Where do all your uncle's workers live? I haven't noticed any other houses or cottages on the farm.'

'Actually, my love, farms are considered to be no different from any other form of employment: therefore uncle's helpers reside where they please; however, I think you'll find that several live in the village, but anyway the local bus will conveys them to and from work. Derek, of course, lives with Ruth in the farmhouse so they're both on hand should any emergency arise, and if my uncle needs extra help at any time he'll send the pick up down to the village.' She stopped walking, and turned to face her lover. 'Anyway, darling, did you enjoy your stay here?'

He squeezed her hand in affirmation. 'It was perfect, even the weather's been magnificent, and the hospitality displayed by your kinsfolk has been beyond criticism.' Frowning in perplexity, he added, 'But do farmers always have so many parties within such a short period?'

His sweetheart smiled and shook her head vigorously, 'Usually only when they've got a special visitor.'

No one had stirred by the time they'd reached the pond area, so Julie went over and shook her aunt awake; when she'd learnt what the lovers had done Mary was embarrassingly grateful, took both their hands in hers and told them what good children they were. 'Now,' she exclaimed, 'it's gone eight o'clock and high time we got this show on the road.'

'I think they liked you,' Julie observed dryly as soon as they'd returned to their seats.

Andrew grinned. 'That would explain why your uncle invited us to stay whenever we liked and, of course, why we had a good send off; but I felt bad about not giving your aunt, at least, a present.'

Rain trickled down the window pane as their train gathered speed. 'If you mean something to pay for our keep, then I gave her some money, darling; but you know we rarely bother about keepsakes. Mainland houses must be full of unwanted and useless gifts; besides, Whyte Island allowances would need to increase if the public began buying gifts for every occasion. Talking about money, love,' she added, 'we really must begin to economise again soon; however, because our tenancy of the flat is almost expired, together with the end of our holiday and the imminent arrival of our new jobs I think we ought to splash out on one last outdoor romp.'

Andrew attempted to object, but his sweetheart was adamant. 'I know we've just had a nice holiday but if we don't do it this weekend we might not get another opportunity: after all, darling, you'll be starting on your course Monday, and from then on we'll both be studying to help you become more than proficient in your chosen main career. Anyway, apart from this drop of rain the weather's supposed to continue fine, but it might not last!'

'Alright,' he chuckled, realising he couldn't deny her anything within reason, 'but I was hoping for a little relaxation before I began training.'

When they arrived at the flat they found the official notice to quit awaiting them, but this was a mere formality as Julie had long since made arrangements for them to move in with her parents at short notice. 'As you know, love,' she said to Andrew, 'dad's something of a handyman and he's making some officially approved alterations to our room, but we're not supposed to know about it.'

'Probably constructing some stocks to keep you in,' he laughed, at which she slapped him.

After they'd had a short rest and a reviving cup of tea they went out and bought some groceries; and, apart from a brief visit to Sue and Trevor, they spent the remainder of the day quietly preparing themselves for their forthcoming move and also for their respective occupations. Later, they played some tapes while making plans for the following day's adventure. 'Oh, by the way,' she announced, 'you'll need to lift your ban on sexual antics when we're living with my parents because I'm not going to play games outside in inclement weather, and it would be hypocritical to practice them in friends' homes.'

By the time they'd gone through the smallest detail of their project, which was intended to last for much of the afternoon, it was quite late and so Julie went and made them a cup of cocoa each; after compelling her lover to take a temporary vow of celibacy they then retired.

The entirely unexpected sound of the alarm clock ringing

close to his ear shocked Andrew awake; after automatically cancelling the noise he sat up and looked about him in bewilderment. Not only did he feel slightly groggy and nauseous, as though he'd been drugged, but his rude awakening and the absence of his lover from their bed confused him. As far as he was aware they were supposed to be having a lie in and the alarm would thus have been unnecessary. It was only after he'd dragged himself from between the sheets that he noticed the piece of paper tucked beneath the clock. "Sorry about the nightcap", the message read, "but look under the door mat if you want to find me". The note was the first in a chain of eight which finally led him, via many hiding places throughout the flat, to the pocket of one of his jackets hanging in the wardrobe. The enclosed message advised him to make haste, after he'd breakfasted, to the public house in a certain village on a far side of the island where he would obtain further news of his lover.

In the train taking him to his destination Andrew's brain was filled with mixed emotions, although he'd been amused by his sweetheart's little paper chase he was more than annoyed at her deceitful handling of him the previous evening, and he'd also become so used to her near constant companionship that he felt distinctly lost and lonely without her comforting presence. Upon his arrival at the hostelry indicated in the note, the publican insisted he should partake of a pint of beer before answering any questions. 'The young lady you're looking for,' he grinned at last, 'did leave a letter for you, but said you mustn't have it before noon.'

Despite becoming involved in a game of darts which, due to his urge to continue his search for his loved one, he played embarrassingly badly, the following three quarters of an hour passed far too slowly for Andrew, but upon receipt of the long awaited letter he was soon walking along a farm track bound for the promised rendezvous with his sweetheart on the local common. However, when he reached the location there was no sign of her anywhere amongst the hawthorn bushes and brambles comprising the area of wasteland, and his repeated calling elicited no response.

Wandering further along the track, becoming increasingly annoyed and concerned in equal measure, he came to another, lengthy, patch of hawthorns beyond which the smell of wood smoke emanated and, after much diligent searching he happened upon a scene more in keeping with fantasy than with modern real life. Latterly guided by a vertical, thin column of smoke which rose from behind a thicket into the still, sunny air he discovered a gaudily painted gypsy caravan with a couple of tethered piebald ponies busily cropping the grass nearby, beyond were gorse bushes draped with articles of clothing drying in the sunshine. But the prime object of his attention was seated upon a log stirring the contents of an iron pot slung over a blazing fire, for she was the typical story book example of young Romany womanhood. Seated on the ground by her bare feet was a rough haired fawn lurcher which pricked up its ears and wagged its ears at the young man's appearance.

As soon as he saw the girl Andrew's feelings of frustrated anger immediately evaporated; assuming this was the heavily disguised figure of his loved one he went straight over to her and stared down at her in amusement. She gazed up at him for a moment then, after mouthing a jumble of unintelligible noises to indicate she was dumb, she motioned him to sit by her side. Instantly deciding to go along with her little game he did as she bade, whereupon she produced a small earthenware flagon and took a long swig of the contents before passing it onto her visitor. What the liquid was remained a mystery to him, he only knew it combined the ferocity of neat spirits with the mellowness and flavour of the finest wine, but its ultimate property was to take a little longer before making its presence felt. After he'd handed back the flagon she presented him with a clay bowl into which she began to ladle the contents of the cauldron.

He studied her carefully as she did so, he'd already noted her grimy ankle length green dress with its brass buttoned bodice which would've been indecently provocative but for the green silk scarf about her neck, its ends tucked into the neckline. It was the type of top, he realised, which had been devised specifically for the easy nursing of babies. Now he examined her face for the familiar features of his sweetheart, but it was a difficult task as her skin was excessively bronzed and grubby and she was entirely devoid of make up. The red bandana tied low about her forehead almost completely covered her black wiry hair making identification even more impossible, as did the only adornment she wore: large, golden ear rings.

After filling his bowl the girl rose, went over to the caravan and disappeared inside; upon her return she handed him a wooden spoon and unbuttered portions of oval shaped bread. Much to her guest's astonished delight she'd removed the neck scarf to reveal pale flesh oddly at variance with her sun bronzed face; she was only too well aware of his fascination for the freshly exposed area of her bosom, for as she sat down she leered at him displaying, as she did so, a row of stained and apparently rotten teeth. At any other time the sight of such ill-kempt dentistry might well have cooled his rapidly rising ardour; but Andrew was beginning to feel distinctly strange, for a warm, self satisfied sensation which had started in his stomach upon receipt of the liquor, had begun to permeate his brain making him feel disembodied, relaxed and extremely passionate. It was an experience akin to those at the Roman Villa and the evening after the picnic by the pond a few days previously.

With his eyes firmly fixed upon the gypsy girl's cleavage he began, in increasing stupor, to sample the stew she'd given him: he dipped his bread into the bowl and then bit at the crust. The flavour was just as unique as the liquor's had been, it was rich, meaty and heavily spiced. His companion, in the meantime, had begun to ladle the stew into the bowl which she held on her lap; then she, too, began to eat, alternately spooning the food into her mouth and tearing at the bread with her teeth; she never ceased gazing at him in an intimidating manner, and every time she took a mouthful of food she undid one of the buttons on her bodice.

Transfixed, Andrew watched as the bulging flesh above the young woman's neckline gradually disappeared as her breasts sought to burst from the ever widening gap between the halves of her bodice. Tentatively he reached out to touch the exposed area of skin, but the gypsy laughed and slapped his hand away; pointing at their bowls of stew and at the flagon by her side thereby indicating the contents of each needed to be consumed first. It was a gesture not lost on him and so he quickly demolished his meal and then took great swigs from the vessel whilst the girl looked on in amused satisfaction. Whether or not she really was Julie was beyond his comprehension, he only knew he had to possess her as soon as possible and so it was with rising impatience that he waited while she finished her stew.

At last she slowly placed her bowl on the log between them and with a laugh took the flagon from him; together they drank the vessel dry, although whenever he received it, it seemed to contain the same amount of liquid as before. Finally, after patting the lurcher and commanding it, with gestures, to remain where it was, the woman stood up and then helped Andrew, who was feeling really groggy by this time, to his feet whereupon she grasped him firmly by the arm and lead him unsteadily to the caravan. She experienced some difficulty in getting him up the steps, for although his mind was clear and he could see with remarkable clarity, the part of his brain controlling physical activity had been rendered almost totally useless.

Once inside, she bore down heavily upon his shoulders, forcing him to lie in the floor space between the twin bunks: after positioning a pillow beneath his head she closed both halves of the entrance door, lit a paraffin lamp suspended from the ceiling and then pulled the window shutters to. Standing astride Andrew's recumbent form she fumbled at the back of her neck, then, with a few rapid movements she slipped her shoulders out of her bodice and her dress the latter of which subsequently fell in a heap about her ankles. Staring up at her in a state of near paralysis he vaguely wondered why his Julie should have gone to the trouble of increasing and darkening the area of her body hair and enlarged the perimeter of, and brown tinted, her nipples. This was to be his last rational thought for some time because the gypsy girl immediately fell upon her knees and began to kiss and fondle him in a fury of passion.

What followed lay beyond the wildest fantasies of an opium addict, for time merged into a perpetual dream of sensual pleasure which overwhelmed and stifled him utterly; eventually he lapsed into exhausted oblivion with his satisfied intimate's sweat soaked body sprawled on top of him, her air-gasping head against his cheek and the musty smell of her exertions heavy in his nostrils.

When he awoke, surprisingly clearheaded and refreshed, he found himself gazing up at the leaves and tangled twigs and branches of a hawthorn bush; he sensed from the angle of the shadows it was late afternoon. Glancing at his wrist to check the actual time he saw his watch had gone; in a panic he leapt to his feet, narrowly avoiding the thorny twigs close to his head, and searched his pockets; everything, except a crumpled piece of paper, had disappeared. Still disorientated by his late bizarre experience he quickly scanned the crudely hand printed message: "If you want your woman, follow the track to the outcrop. She's among them".

Before setting off on yet another search for his sweetheart Andrew hastily located the site of his amorous adventure, but caravan, horses, dog, fire, clothing and Romany girl had all vanished; even the log had gone, only a pile of wet ashes remaining to bear witness to the genuineness of his weird experience. His thoughts as he continued on his way up toward the downland with its prominent granite crags were in a turmoil; he'd naturally assumed the young woman who'd so recently seduced him had been his own lover despite her crude treatment of him. But if so, why had she gone to the trouble of robbing him, and why was she continuing to tease him, surely she had nothing left to gain?

If it hadn't been Julie, then who had it been and what part had she played in the affair? Of course, he didn't believe she'd actually been kidnapped because such things never happened on Whyte Island, as she was so fond of telling him, but on the other hand he couldn't credit the fact that she'd deliberately permit another female to have her way with him......would she? He frowned; whatever the solution to this enigma might be, his best course was to find his sweetheart as quickly as possible for she might have got herself into something she mightn't get out of in a hurry; one thing he was aware of, though: whatever pleasure he'd derived from the mystery girl's attentions had gone for nought due to the worry he was now undergoing.

When Andrew reached the rocky outcrop he found a veritable labyrinth of clefts, crevices and ravines awaiting him; fortunately most of the latter were easily accessible having packed earth floors which made his task much simpler to accomplish. But in spite of calling out Julie's name at the top of his voice and exploring each of the natural passageways in turn it was to be some time before he eventually discovered her. She was kneeling against a rock wall at the end of particularly long defile with her head resting upon her bosom; at first he thought she was asleep but suddenly coming across her made him stumble causing her to raise her head wearily and fix him with a baleful stare. He was upon her in an instance, tearing the rag from her mouth and kissing her lips, face, head and hair ecstatically in overwhelming proof of his joy and relief at having found her.

'I didn't think that was very funny, Andrew,' she exclaimed bitterly when circumstances eventually allowed her to speak, 'that was supposed to be my game, not yours. And if you would kindly untie my wrists and ankles you can explain yourself and also why you took so bloody long to arrive.'

'I don't know what you're talking about,' he stated as he fumbled with her knots. 'I thought you were playing with me!'

Freed at last she winced as she straightened her legs. 'I'm beginning to realise how Melanie felt, now,' she observed in a slightly more amicable tone.

Her lover removed his jacket and tenderly helped her to sit down upon it, then he sat by her side, placed an arm about her shoulder and gently pulled her against him. 'I've been so worried about you,' he whispered in her hair. 'We'd better wait here until you feel up to walking; besides, we've got some mutual explaining to do.' He kissed her once more, adding, 'Ladies first, darling. But I can assure you I'm entirely innocent of all charges.'

'Alright,' she agreed, 'I'll tell you exactly what occurred if you really don't know. When we made those plans last night I thought I'd liven them up a little by changing round the time and venue, so I phoned up the landlord of the pub at the bottom of the hill and arranged a little drama for you: I've booked a room there for this evening by the way. Then I slipped a couple of sleeping pills into your cocoa, and while you were asleep arranged the paper chase.

'I was waiting on the common at shortly before midday anticipating your imminent arrival when a young couple came along, I thought it a bit strange because the landlord had promised to keep the track clear of people during that stage in our game. Anyway, the couple told me the publican had divulged my plan to you and that you'd devised one of your own; so they asked me to come along with them.'

'What did the girl look like?' Andrew interposed, 'What

colour were her eyes and hair?'

'Well, she was about my build and she had coarse, black hair,' she gave a dry laugh, 'as for the colour of her eyes – I may be a beautician but I don't always notice such features when I'm not working; however, as she had a Latin complexion, I should imagine they'd have been brown. No, wait a minute! They were definitely green; yes, green.' He grimaced to himself but said nothing as Julie continued, 'When we arrived at the rocks the girl brought me down here and then persuaded me to allow her to immobilise me. I know it was stupid and illegal but we islanders have grown up to be trusting of others, and why should I expect trouble when our country is entirely crime free? Besides, she said that's what you wanted. As she was leaving she told me you'd be along inside half an hour: but after what seemed several hours without a sign of you, Andy, you can imagine how infuriated I was getting, and finally I vowed I wouldn't have anything more to do with you.' She lifted her head from his shoulder and looked into his eyes. 'So you'd better have a good alibi; but I trust you really, darling,' she smiled, 'and I know you wouldn't deliberately do such a thing to me.'

'You're so right,' he exclaimed indignantly, believing every word of her account, 'and when I get hold of the people who did that to you I'll tear them apart. Are you sure they didn't harm you in any way, or steal anything?' From what he subsequently learnt Andrew later realised the intensity of his anger and concern at that time must've thoroughly alarmed his lover, but she merely shook her head. 'Well,' he continued through clenched teeth, 'if they were the same people they also stole everything I had.' He then went on to tell her all that had befallen him including the events inside the caravan, and ended his narrative by averring, 'I genuinely thought it was you, my sweet darling, and by the time that liquor had taken effect I was too paralytic to object, anyway. Do you believe me?'

She appeared to take the revelation of his infidelity with surprising calmness for she merely smiled sympathetically and nodded, she then stood up with some difficulty. 'I presume you'll be too worn out from lovemaking to want to compare my sensual abilities with those of your erstwhile lover? Was she any good by the way? Honestly,' she demanded.

'She was very good,' he admitted grudgingly, 'but nowhere near as accomplished as you, if she really wasn't you, that is!'

'Sorry, but I think I'm too stiff now to allow you to make a proper comparison, though I should've recovered by bedtime if you'd like to compare us? But before we rush off in search of the villains I need some spiritual guidance.' She bent down and removed a bottle of gin from her shoulder bag. 'You can't imagine how tormenting it was to be aware sustenance was so near to hand yet impossible to reach,' she commented after they'd taken several swigs each.

'I hope that particular beverage doesn't mean the onset of you know what.'

'I'm afraid so, darling, mother nature is approaching. Never mind though,' she added cheerfully, 'we might just have time!'

On the way back to the village Andrew could talk of nothing else but of his loved one's ordeal, his hoped for revenge and how he was going to report the incident to the authorities immediately they reached the inn. Without warning, Julie suddenly burst into tears. 'I'm sorry, sweetheart,' he whispered soothingly, drawing her against him, 'it must've been very frightening.'

'It isn't that,' she sobbed, 'you've shown me how much you love and care for me, and instead I've been proved unworthy of you. I didn't think you'd take it all so seriously, that you'd realise there wasn't any seducer, thieves or abductors over here.' She raised her tearstained face to gaze at him. 'It was all just a game, darling, that's all. We made it up to entertain you, but I went too far, I should've been by your side when you woke up, but I thought you'd understand and so when you found me helpless you'd either pretend I was your captive, or else I was your kidnapped lover just so we could have a passionate reunion. But when you went all naïve on me I couldn't resist stringing you along.'

Andrew listened to this explanation in silent horror. When Julie had finished he pushed her away contemptuously, then, in sudden rage he gripped hold of her shoulders with the intention of shaking her violently, but at the last moment he relaxed and pulled her into his embrace once more. 'I know you didn't mean to,' he sighed as he buried his face into her hair, 'but you put me through hell. I was worried sick about you; I know there aren't any criminals on Whyte Island, but I couldn't think of any other explanation. I also didn't like the idea I'd had another woman: you're more than capable of doing what she did to me – and making more of a success of it, besides I love only you, I don't want some painted trollop.' He paused, remembering she had, in truth, admitted she was the gypsy girl. 'Alright,' he said, annoyed again, 'if you were my seducer describe what you were wearing.'

Without hesitation Julie described not only every detail of the Romany's apparel, but the colour of the dog and ponies, and what had happened inside the caravan; finally she rummaged in her bag again, and presented him with a plastic bag containing his personal effects. 'I believe you,' he said, partly appeased, 'but what about the swines who trussed you up?'

'Those swines,' she murmured, 'are officially allowed to do what they did. It was the girl who did the binding and gagging, her companion wasn't permitted to; men aren't. Are we still friends, Andy?' she pleaded.

He grinned and began to wipe away her tears with his handkerchief. 'You know bloody well I'd forgive you anything, but you might as well tell me the true story this time.'

While they completed the remainder of their walk she further enlightened him, 'I planned it as a surprise quite a while ago, long before your job notice came along, the zigzag people set it up, and then removed all the props when you were asleep, but the general idea was mine; the worse part about it was the hanging around waiting for you to wake up because I had no idea how long you'd be under for. As soon as you stirred a secret observer phoned our mobile and Erica and I went down the ravine where she incapacitated me.' She giggled. 'Oh, by the way, when I took swigs from that flagon I stuck my tongue in the neck; so you drank it all yourself.'

Andrew had to be content with his lover's explanation, but there were one or two flaws in the details which he couldn't fathom out: although he was practically comatose by the time the naked gypsy had straddled him he sensed she didn't look, or feel, familiar; also, he was certain she'd had brown, not green or blue, eyes.

Upon their arrival at the inn the lovers sat down to a splendid meal comprising of local fare washed down with one of the many island brews then adjoined to their own private room where, in the light of the early evening sun, Julie demanded her sweetheart should undergo that which she'd recently experienced. Seated in one of the bedroom's armchairs she watched, in great amusement, his vain attempts to free himself; eventually, after about half an hour, she grew tired of his struggling and senseless mumbling, for she'd taped his mouth up, and began to taunt, tease and torment him both verbally and physically in her own incomparable fashion. Finally, when she was sure he'd reached his peak of infuriation and frustration, she condescended to satisfy him in the same position as she or the unknown woman in the caravan had. Later, after a brief nap, they patronised the bar where they drank, played darts and enjoyed listening to some old county songs accompanied by the playing of a melodeon while they waited for the bus to start for the station. They were in bed back home at the flat by ten p.m. 'All ready,' as Julie declared, cuddling up to her erstwhile victim, 'for tomorrow's big events.' And so Andrew ended an enigmatic and exciting day not knowing whether he'd been seduced by each of two women once, or one woman twice.

The almost coincidental circumstances of Andrew commencing his first job on Whyte Island and the lovers' departure from their flat to Julie's old home marked the beginning of the final stage in their brief but glorious relationship, and at its close the young man rarely visited Laketown due to its cruel remembrance of the girl he'd always love so dearly.

Becoming a railway worker was relatively easy for Andrew after the initial strangeness of the new environment had worn off, for both the training and the work experience were very similar to the procedure on Whyte Line ships. He'd already become reasonably proficient in engineering workshop practice and skills, and in the course of his marine service he'd become acquainted with most other vocations on a trial basis. Therefore the various tasks which subsequently followed, from platelayer to ticket collector, footplate man to signalman, et cetera were more interesting than difficult, while the railway staff and his fellow trainees were little different from the sailors in their general kindness, thoughtfulness and encouragement, and, especially in the case of the former, their patience and knowledge. Andrew with his passion for steam locomotives, had his sights set on becoming a fireman; hopefully, one day, even a driver, but he would be required to sit an examination on all aspects of railway work before a decision could be taken on which vocation best suited him.

In the meantime he kept to the island's normal working hours which were from nine a.m. to five thirty p.m. exclusive of travelling time with a bias of half an hour either way to help ease transport congestion. Julie and he were happy in the knowledge that, even when he began shift work, the railway rarely operated between one a.m. and six thirty a.m.: and even then the actual time worked averaged less than during the normal working period in recognition of the unsocial hours involved. When, however, the occasions eventually arose when he would be required to work in the early mornings or late evenings his sweetheart would have the benefit of being in the bosom of her family and so wouldn't lack companionship.

With his new home and, as he increasingly felt, his new parents Andrew could find no fault; certainly Mr. and Mrs. Lucas treated him as a direct replacement for Jeremy, and were it not for the fact that he called them by their first names and slept with their daughter, he might well have considered himself their natural son. He quickly discovered that John, underneath his reticence, was really a very shy person but one who was more than intelligent and quite communicative once his trust had been obtained; he and Andrew soon became firm friends.

In another time and place John might well have suffered badly at the hands of his wife for, as Alastair had intimated, Jean could be somewhat overbearing at times; if she wanted something done then one was advised to do it and, as he was to discover on one memorable occasion, she never made idle threats. But she was no trouble if one kept a step ahead of her, and he was fortunate in the fact she doted on him, however, between Julie's parents it wasn't too difficult for him to deduce where his sweetheart's character originated.

The surprise which awaited the lovers when they moved into Julie's former bedroom was greatly appreciated by them, for John had fitted a double bed in the wall as a replacement for the more usual item of furniture. Being unable to excavate an alcove for the bed's reception he'd solved the problem by fitting deep shelves on the right hand side of the wall, and these helped to disguise the protrusion when the bed was in the stowed position. The bed's underside had been strengthened with polished wood panelling and fitted with a great landscape painting of a wide river edged with trees and a cottage, and high mountains as a backdrop and the result, when in the upright position, was that the viewer saw a wall, not a bed. To the left was a large window to which no alteration could be made, but Mr. Lucas had attached a curtain rail above it which stood well proud of the pane so that, in the evenings, with the bed stowed and the curtains drawn, the entire wall gave the impression of being perfectly solid. Fitted furniture in the form of a large wardrobe, dressing table and drinks bar/ tea making area were added to a new suite of furniture comprising a pair of armchairs and a settee capable of seating six, of a hue matching the curtains, completed the room's modifications.

'So there you are,' Julie's mother exclaimed, showing them the room, 'you'll have the run of the house, naturally, but whenever you want to be alone, or are entertaining personal friends, you can come up here. Of course,' she went on, indicating the three piece suite, 'if you don't like the colour or design they can go back as they're only on approval. You can also redecorate as, or whenever, you wish.' But the lovers were highly delighted with everything as it was, and said so.

None of the items of furniture in the Laketown flat had belonged to Julie and, as they'd taken the opportunity of sorting through her collection of books and c.ds. for unwanted items and to return others to their respective libraries, they'd brought surprisingly little with them and so they were soon comfortable in their new home. The domestic arrangements were easily settled, full accommodation being provided in exchange for the cost of their board, a little help about the house and garden when required, and that they should both be tidy and clean in their ways. Once Julie confided in her lover, 'When my mum first met you she liked you immediately but realised she didn't really know you, so she reserved her judgement. Which was why she was a bit worried at your coming to live here, because you were formerly a mainlander: she thought you might lapse into scruffiness.'

Perplexed, Andrew had pointed out, 'But your parents were also mainlanders.'

'Yes,' she'd answered, 'but they were specially selected.'

'Well, so was I.'

His sweetheart laughed. 'You don't really count because you were a hasty replacement; but, anyway, now she sees how you behave yourself she doesn't like you anymore,' and added, as she'd pushed him down on the settee, 'she loves you!'

As time passed Andrew became aware that his adopted parents were more than a little pleased their daughter and her lover were living with them; their house must've been lonely at times when they were on their own, despite their many acquaintances, and so he was never averse to including them in any plans Julie and he had arranged for their own amusement. The four of them were thus frequently to be seen together on visits to the theatre and other places of entertainment, or out on walks in the countryside. Jean and John were also able to venture out on their own more often, safe in the knowledge that the children, as they referred to them, would have a hot drink or, occasionally, a hot meal awaiting them upon their return home, in addition to a warm welcome.

Meanwhile Julie and Andrew kept in touch with their large circle of friends whom they often went out with, or visited, and by whom they were frequently visited in their turn. Susan and Trevor, for instance, had also moved from their place in Laketown and now occupied a house in a village not too far from Newtown; and the lovers often called on them, Julie, her sweetheart suspected, being especially attracted to their little son whom she apparently adored. When not engaged in visiting friends they continued to sample the many pastimes and interesting places which Whyte Island had to offer.

Once, after a pleasure flight above the island, they decided to experience some gliding, and although they both enjoyed the subsequent sensation of almost silently drifting high above the clouds and countryside, the fact they were unable to share the diversion simultaneously, for there weren't any three seaters available, meant they quickly lost interest in further flying. On another occasion they took a ride on the special train which, on summer Sundays, toured the island; composed of specifically designed stock it contained bars, a dancing area, a band, restaurant and observation cars, and combined sightseeing along with frequent halts in remote sidings for the purpose of merrymaking. Similarly, the lovers had taken several trips on the steamers providing a similar service on the reservoir lake.

As the summer came to an end and autumn, with its strong winds and sudden, unexpected rain storms set in they dropped sailing, and fishing in exposed places, from their selection of pastimes and concentrated more on horse riding, in addition to swimming and other indoor activities. An especially favoured hobby of theirs, which they continued into the autumn and, occasionally, the winter, involved exploring the lanes, tracks and villages in various parts of the island. Usually they chose an afternoon just prior to a full, free day and travelled to a spot some ten to fifteen miles from their intended destination whereupon they would continue on foot. At the end of their stroll they were always guaranteed a train, a bus or a bed, and much preferred the latter because they loved to sleep together in an unfamiliar room.

One particularly wet afternoon, while Andrew was perusing a full map of the island in their room in Newtown, he suddenly thought up a way by which they could make their exploration even more interesting. If, he reasoned, a frame, the inside edge of which matched the coastal margin of a detailed map of Whyte Island were constructed, they could use the spinning top from "Living Together" to select the location of their next ramble. More often than not the point marked a position some distance from a path or village and so they would plan the nearest most suitable route to it. When Julie mentioned his innovation to some of their friends they were most enthusiastic, and much to his bemused astonishment the idea caught on to the extent of his finding his sweetheart's and his photograph together with an article in the island's news sheet one day.

With the onset of winter the lovers confined their activities almost entirely to indoor pursuits; it was about this time that Andrew began to take a practical interest in railway modelling, enthusiastically abetted by Julie; and under her expert tuition and much practice on his part he also eventually became more than adept at the martial arts, folk singing and horse riding. The latter exercise he enjoyed immensely; it was a simple matter to obtain horses if they were booked early enough for it was a popular hobby and so there were plenty of stables about. As long as Julie was with him he didn't care if they were simply jogging along an icy lowland track, or galloping over the turf of a downland hill during a thawing gale off the sea, the wind lashing their faces and only the scudding clouds, the vast sky and the featureless landscape to keep them company.

Whyte Island winters were feared more by repute than from actual fact, snow and ice were rarely severe or persistent, but when bad weather arrived the authorities' policy of spending money in the present in order to prepare for the future paid dividends. The Lucas' house was standard with its insulated roof and exterior walls, double glazed aluminium windows and doors and with central heating; so the government not only kept its public comfortable, contented and free from the chills and related illnesses which might result in loss of labour, disruption and increased health charges, but it also saved on energy costs. This latter consideration was passed onto the consumer in the form of inexpensive fuel, and therefore there was no excuse for any person to experience the effects of severe cold whilst inside their own home or place of employment.

Andrew's new home additionally had an open fireplace fitted in the lounge: however, its use was restricted due to Newtown's unusual situation of being sited in a basin surrounded by chalk cliffs. Normally the close proximity of the sea, with its bracing winds, helped keep the atmosphere in the town clean and fresh, but occasionally, when the air was still there was a danger of thick fogs arising which made the use of a coal fire undesirable. But when solid fuel fires were permitted then the entire family liked nothing better than to sit before a blazing fire piled with logs or coal with the main lights turned off and the firelight flickering on the walls. At such times even Julie and Jeremy ceased bickering on those occasions when he was visiting with his latest girlfriend.

Travelling about in winter posed few problems, even in the worst of weather; sheltered bus stops were commonplace, the bus services intensive, especially in residential areas, the individual vehicles rarely entirely full and with heating systems more than adequate. When there was ice and snow about Andrew noticed the special fitments on the bus tyres, and also the way gangs of people seemed to appear as if from nowhere, particularly in urban districts, to disperse the snow.

At such times he was more than pleased with the island's public transport service, for he remembered how worried his actual father became whenever the mainland roads had been treacherously icy and he'd had to go to work using his current mode of transport, whether car, motorbike or cycle. There had been several steep hills between their house and his workplace and there was no guarantee they would've been sanded, and Andrew was aware his father had narrowly missed being involved in several bad accidents as a result. By comparison, even cycles were frowned upon as a means of commuting on Whyte Island.

If he'd had any fears with regard to the winter then it was largely on his sweetheart's behalf; he'd assumed she and the others engaged upon the task of husbanding the countryside would be out in all weathers, but when he eventually made his apprehension known to her she smiled. 'Most winter days are quite mild, darling,' she explained, 'but when the weather's bad we work inside; there's always plenty to do in the greenhouses, for instance: collecting, sorting out and sowing seeds, tending plants, cleaning and maintaining tools, attending lectures......'

'Alright,' he laughed, 'you've convinced me, but even so I'll be much happier when we're working together.'

Throwing her arms about his neck she kissed him, whispering, 'So shall I, love.'

Andrew's concern, though, was tinged with more than a little jealousy; he continuously experienced a recurring mental image of his lover being wooed by one or other of her workmates until, eventually, his fear became an obsession and he began to observe her closely to see if her attitude toward him had changed in any way. One night, just before they retired, all his secret worries suddenly surfaced. He lay on the sofa with his head cradled in Julie's lap whilst she gently and rhythmically stroked his hair; from the c.d. player the soft strains of a symphony helped them to relax; but despite his lover's attentions and the peaceful music he couldn't prevent his basic feeling of insecurity from marring the intimate atmosphere. 'Darling,' he murmured, 'you haven't found anyone else, have you?'

The rhythm of her hand didn't falter. 'Has someone told you I have, then?' she enquired softly, and his heart seemed to miss a beat. When he shook his head she went on, 'Well they won't.

Because I've only got, and only want, one lover, and that's you.' His eyes watered at these words, but she continued, 'People who know me, including those who work with me, are honour bound to inform my partner, you, if they've good reason to believe I'm being unfaithful to you. But they wouldn't have the chance, because in the most unlikely event I'd seek someone else then I'd tell you myself immediately; anyway, why should you think I'd got another love?'

'Well, our relationship appears to have changed,' he replied. She went on stroking his hair as she waited for him to explain further. 'You seem to be leaving much more of the decision making to me, and when we go out you spend a lot of time talking to other people, when before you used to just want me.'

'I'd hardly call those grounds for jealousy,' she muttered, 'But what about our lovemaking, any complaints in that department?'

'Well,' he considered uncertainly, 'it doesn't seem to be quite so frequent, varied or passionate.'

'I've told you I love only you,' she insisted, 'You love me in return, don't you?' Andrew nodded, and Julie stopped stroking his hair. 'Get up,' she ordered abruptly.

He studied her anxiously as she rose to her feet, wondering whether he'd pushed her too far this time; but to his relief she only went over to the drinks cabinet to return, shortly, bearing two glasses of wine. 'Take this,' she offered, handing him one. 'Now,' she exclaimed, touching her glass to his, 'a toast to our wonderful and happy union, and may it last until one of us goes before. You've just recognised a reef upon which many a loving relationship has foundered.' And she added, after they'd swallowed their drinks, 'Let's go to bed; according to you, darling, we've got a quota to make up.'

Andrew stirred contentedly as he lay with his arms locked about his sweetheart; often, after they'd made love, he'd fall into a profound sleep, but sometimes he'd wake up again and find it impossible to drop off again. On this occasion he lay awake revelling in his lover's warm presence and cursing himself, not for the first time, for doubting her. Suddenly though, she turned on the table lamp. 'I'm pleased you're awake,' she announced, 'because it's time for our chat. You were quite right, our relationship has changed, but only because we're entering a new phase, darling. Love and friendship are vital cornerstones in a heterosexual union, and what we're doing now is shifting the emphasis from the former onto the latter. You also say I'm forcing you to take more decisions; well, I think you should because I want you to be dominant so I can look up to you.' She laughed. 'In this very room you told me you were going to be more assertive once you'd learnt to understand our society; well, I'm helping you to that end. You were also right when you claimed I talk to other people a lot more than I used to, and so do you I'm glad to say; but I've been doing it deliberately.'

She gently placed a hand over his mouth when she saw he was about to comment. 'No, love,' she averred, 'I wasn't trying to hurt you but merely ensuring our future happiness. You see, if our relationship had continued as intensely, as passionately as it formerly did then there'd have been a real danger of its burning out; instead we've got to keep it simmering quietly away. It'll therefore do us both a deal of good if we share our minds and presence with others occasionally, but our bodies and secrets belong only to each other.

'By the way, you remember when we visited that seaside resort and I kept you inside those amusement arcades? Well,' she continued when he nodded, 'I've been doing exactly the same thing to you as I did then: provoking you into making a response. And that's why my lovemaking hasn't been quite as perfect lately as it formerly was, so you were also entirely correct on that score. As I've tried to explain on several previous occasions, darling, lovers should always make their fears and wishes known to their partners: your particular problem was growing inside you like a canker, and if you hadn't revealed it to me when you did it could've eventually ruined our relationship. I hate to say it, sweetheart, but the day could come when I'll no longer be by your side; and your next partner might not be quite so open minded or understanding, so that you'll need to compensate for those faults.'

Obviously realising these last words appeared too gloomy Julie promptly encouraged Andrew to make love to her once more, but afterward they still couldn't sleep. 'Darling,' she eventually said, 'you're jealous because you're basically insecure, and so you don't know why I should be loving you; but I'm not above feeling worried I might lose you. You've no idea how I felt when Ruth was about while we were on the farm, because I was afraid you might find her more attractive than me.'

As she spoke these words her lover thought he'd like to sleep with all the suitable women on Whyte Island, including Ruth, but only the girl beside him would have his genuine love and devotion. What she said next, however, made him start and wonder if she could actually read his mind. 'I see and meet lots of attractive men, my sweet, but I don't want to go with them because they're only faces and forms as far as I'm concerned; but I know you, and your personality, and I love and like them both. No man could possibly do more for me than you; with the additional bonus of this,' she giggled and grasped hold of him, 'and that just couldn't be improved upon.

'But if you need even more proof of my adoration for you, darling, then listen to this: there's a lot selfishness in each individual's love for another person. I could tell you right now, for example, that our affair was over; but I'm not about to because it'd hurt me just as much as it would you. In other words, I'm tremendously happy when I'm with you. If, though, you require the ultimate test with regard to my genuine affection for you, love, then you should bear in mind this isn't the mainland: I'm not as dependent upon you as a girl in a similar situation over there might be, and there are lots of reasons why I wouldn't suffer overmuch if we parted, and you can identify them all while you're nodding off, it'll make a change from counting sheep. So there aren't any constraints upon me to stay with you; again, I'm with you because I love your companionship, and unless you change dramatically I'll remain with you until death parts us.'

Looking back that wonderful time, the pinnacle of Andrew's relationship with Julie, two incidents stood out above all others in his mind; neither was particularly amusing at the time, one being a product of his lover's wilful sense of humour, the other, completely unexpectedly, due to her mother's equally perverse love of fun. The first occurrence began when the lovers received an official invitation card bearing a straight border requesting their attendance at a costume ball. 'Oh, good,' exclaimed Julie after glancing at it, 'it's the empire period, one of my favourite styles of fashion. And what will you go as, my darling,' she asked, turning to her sweetheart, 'an officer or a gentleman?'

'The latter,' he replied immediately, and subsequently refused to change his mind despite her arguments in favour of a uniform.

'Oh, well,' she sighed eventually, not bothering to conceal her disappointment, 'we'd better go and visit the outfitters and see what they've got to offer, then they can send our costumes off to the venue.'

Upon their arrival at the costumiers they separated, each going off with a personal attendant; and this arrangement meant Andrew wouldn't know exactly what his sweetheart would be wearing until she'd she changed at the place where the ball was to be held. He'd neglected to ask her exactly what the empire style looked like and so was relieved when his adviser brought forth various coats, shirts and trousers for him to try on. Eventually they chose a costume between them consisting of a dark green coat, which the assistant mentioned he'd selected because it went with Andrew's consort's hair, a ruffed shirt with a high, stiff collar, a pair of slipper-like shoes, a black top hat, and a pair of white trousers which seemed, Andrew thought, indecently tight. Before they left the changing room the attendant enquired, 'You have, of course, the appropriate underwear?'

Taken aback by this peculiar remark and so not understanding what he'd meant, he could only blurt out in reply, 'Yes, thank you.'

Upon leaving the shop Julie gave her lover an appraising look. 'I think we ought to get some advice on your hair, darling, don't you? You're due for a trim, but if we allow it to grow for a few more weeks it'll save you from having to wear a wig; I think you'll need to have some false sideburns attached though.' Her surmise was correct, and by the evening of the ball they'd both received expert attention to their hair; Andrew now looked like a poet of the early romantic period, but his lover concealed her coiffure beneath a turban because she wanted to keep it as a surprise.

As was usual at such an event, everything had been arranged to make the experience seem as authentic as possible; and so they were not only met at the nearest station by a horse drawn carriage of the appropriate style but they were thence driven to an imposing gatehouse where they were presented with their costumes, shown a room each and allowed to change. This arrangement enabled them to arrive at their final destination in a fresh coach, already dressed for the part.

The ball's venue was a massive greystone Georgian mansion, well known to every islander due to its being the home of the main computer; not only was it the largest non-industrial building on Whyte Island but it was also renowned for its beautifully landscaped and extensive grounds, always an attraction to large numbers of visitors on fine days whenever they were they were open to the public. Because the authorities were loath to allow a building of such size to be underutilised, many of its numerous rooms were employed in one way or another; in the process a fair number had been stripped of their original ornate decorations but enough, however, had been left unaltered to permit the mansion an air of grandeur. The portion which remained in its original state was available for a period of one month in each yearly season to any Whyte Islander who cared to make a booking, but as the accommodation was necessarily limited there was consequently a long waiting list. Julie and Andrew, though, like most of their compatriots, were quite willing to be patient for they, too, wanted to pretend they were of the nobility for a day or two.

As soon as they'd entered the mansion's ante-room Julie's hooded cloak together with her lover's overcoat and hat were taken from them, but before the latter was able to turn and observe his partner's appearance the pair of ballroom doors were thrown open and their assumed names announced. There then followed a few minutes of confusion for Andrew whilst they were ushered into the room and everyone turned to stare at them; Julie and he had visited the mansion on at least two previous occasions, so he was well acquainted with the beautiful ballroom with its lavishly decorated lofty ceiling, its large number of huge allegorical paintings and the elegant white marble pillars supporting an overhead gallery, and this was the reason why his lover was able to claim his full attention.

He couldn't refrain from gasping with admiration and wonder as his gaze fell upon her. His sweetheart's hairdresser had done her work well for she'd piled Julie's hair up on top of her head and arranged several kiss curls along either side, finally she'd set off her creation with an emerald studded diadem positioned just above her forehead. Her high waisted, white gown was trimmed with gold threaded green braid, and she also sported white arm length gloves and white slippers; the emerald necklace and earrings Andrew had given her completed her costume. When he congratulated her on her beauty she lifted a white feathered fan to her face and pretended coyness, gazing at him over its top edge with eyes which appeared to convey embarrassment and coquettishness simultaneously; playing along with her he offered his arm in an exaggerated manner, and together they moved further into the ballroom.

Although a small string orchestra was playing a lively tune at the far end of the room, the large area of dance floor was entirely devoid of people; instead everyone seemed to prefer the margins where they chatted to each other or else stared about the room in a way which appeared to suggest they were waiting for something in particular to occur. After Julie and he had been accosted by one of several servants carrying trays of drinks, they took up a position about half way along one side and, while they also waited, he passed the time in studying their fellow guests.

The brilliant light cast by three enormous chandeliers glinted most attractively on the women's jewellery, and the gold braid and other decorations on those men dressed as army or naval officers. All the ladies wore gowns similar in style to that of his own consort's with their high busted waists and shapeless, full length skirts, but they all varied in their, mainly, pastel hues and in the design of their sleeves and necklines; some of the latter, Andrew was quick to notice, almost venturing on the immodest. Just as varied were the hair styles, all of which reminded him of old pictures and statues of Greco-Roman goddesses. About half the men present represented military personnel thereby allowing even greater scope in the variety of styles and colours on show; many of the uniforms being, as a result, quite flamboyant. Some of the men who, like him, were dressed as civilians were rather dandified, but most were soberly clad thereby providing a foil for the more exotic gowns and uniforms. As he surveyed the scene he thought he'd rarely witnessed such an attractive and interesting sight.

With well over a hundred people in the room it was scarcely surprising that the lovers should recognise a few faces; once Julie nudged him and exclaimed, 'That man over there, darling, I've seen delivering milk on our way to work; he must be an admiral at least, with that order, all those medals on his chest and that mass of gold braid.' Another familiar face belonged to a girl in a pink gown with ash blonde hair piled up on her head in a similar fashion to his sweetheart's; Andrew could hardly take his eyes of her for she was extremely striking and, besides, he disliked being unable to place people.

Eventually, almost as if at an unseen signal, couples began to take to the floor in a graceful waltz; he lost count of the number of dances he had with his lover in his arms, but he never tired of whirling her about the great room, intermingling with the other couples and comparing her with different women as they came into view. He noted some beautiful faces and figures, but none could compare with Julie in his eyes; with her white dress and innocent face she looked so virginal that he could scarcely believe this was the girl who'd played so many sex games with him, and who could be so embarrassing at times.

The waltzes were the only dances open to all the guests but, to add an air of authenticity to the ball, special dancers gave displays more in keeping with the pertinent period; many of these dances were quite complicated and often performed with an abandon which entirely belied the fragile appearance of most of the women taking part. Another diversion especially arranged to add realism was a harpsichord recital given during the interval, when a buffet was opened to provide authentic snacks in addition to the wines already freely available.

Julie, who'd had plenty of previous experience of other similar social gatherings, guided her lover around the periphery of the dance floor between waltzes, and whenever she saw a likely couple she introduced Andrew and herself in the manner of old friends and acquaintances. There would then follow a completely fictional conversation regarding topics and people of the period, a fiction which the recipients invariably entered into with the greatest enthusiasm; at first Andrew found himself quite tongue-tied but with practice he eventually invented some fairly elaborate stories to fit each occasion. He'd assumed this imaginary form of socialising had been his sweetheart's personal idea until another couple approached them and began a fabricated dialogue of their own devising. This compelled him to look about and he was somewhat surprised to see many people engaged in deep conversation where, previously, they'd all acted as complete strangers.

It was toward the end of a waltz in the latter part of the evening that Julie played her prank on him; they'd both imbibed more than enough wine, and Andrew, though far from intoxicated, was feeling more amorous than usual due to its effects and the presence of his alluring lover. The longer he gazed at her the more beautiful and desirable she became until, finally, he couldn't refrain from telling her, 'You look so demure and virtuous, darling, that it would seem impossible for a crude thought or word to have ever crossed your mind.' She gave him an innocent smile in reply and fluttered her eyelashes, then, raising her lips to his ear, she began to whisper.

The words she murmured were extremely provocative, coarse and very descriptive of what she'd like to do to him if they were alone together, and what she'd love him to do to her in return. Even after the dance had ended she continued to intimidate him until, with mounting horror, he suddenly realised what she was attempting to do for he sensed, rather than felt, one of her knees pressing between his legs. Presumably as soon as she thought she'd achieved the desired effect she relinquished her hold on him and skipped lightly though quickly away in the direction of the toilets. In confusion he followed her progress with his eyes, but she deigned only to shoot him a laughing glance over her shoulder before the crowd parted to engulf her.

It was only when he looked about him that Andrew realised the terrible position Julie had left him in; although his coat had long tails behind, it was cut square to waist level at the front thereby exposing the entire forepart of his trousers; she'd deliberately aroused him and had then deserted him so his discomfiture would be obvious to all those who cared to notice. As far as he was concerned this meant a large number of people, for he was now standing alone on the ballroom floor at least twenty feet from the nearest person.

Such was his temporary deformity that walking with anything approaching dignity was entirely out of the question; fortunately for him however, help was at hand though from a completely unexpected quarter. As he stood, embarrassed and indecisive, the young woman with the grey hair and pink gown suddenly emerged from the crowd and came directly toward him; as she approached she smiled, a gesture more akin to sympathy than amusement. 'Hello,' she exclaimed brightly, 'do you remember me? My name's Anne; I'm afraid I've forgotten yours, but we were at the same zigzagging together.'

Andrew could've hugged her for she was obviously trying to alleviate his dilemma by shielding him with her body and also by distracting him from his problem through engaging him in conversation. But much to his astonishment she was to go even further, as she was about to transfer some of the attention he was receiving onto her own shoulders. 'I couldn't help noticing your predicament,' she went on, 'but I wouldn't worry too much if I were you, men only display the outline of their gender when they're aroused, but we poor women are generally always self-evident.' And she cupped a hand beneath each breast in emphasis until they threatened to pop out of her neckline; he was aware the gesture was intended more for any onlookers than to intimidate himself, so was suitably grateful.

Anne remained chatting to him in a completely unselfish manner until the orchestra struck up another waltz tune; and as the dancers began to fill the floor she enquired, 'Do you feel easier, now?'

He shook his head. 'I'm afraid your presence has done nothing to ease my problem; you're far too beautiful and, well, sensual.'

Smiling broadly at this compliment, she suggested, 'I think, in that case, it'd be best if we danced once round the room and then stopped off near the toilets; that way you'll have saved face.' He thought this an excellent idea, but as he put his arm about her she remarked, 'I owe a lot to your companion, Andrew, because she gave me a great deal of advice on beauty care. You told me I was attractive, but actually I'm rather plain beneath this make up, and my hair is quite colourless really.'

He was pleased at the gratitude shown toward Julie, but shocked by Anne's frank confession. 'I don't believe you,' he answered gallantly as they danced, 'and even if it were true it wouldn't matter, because your heart is made of pure gold; I've been overwhelmed by your kindness and unexpected loyalty to me.'

She was visibly moved by this observation, and before they finally parted she said, 'If I were in your place I'd treat your sweetheart's trick as a silent request for special treatment the next time you play a sex game.'

With the aid of some fish paste and a friendly neighbourhood cat Andrew took Anne's advice, and his own revenge, a few days later.

His discovery of Mrs. Lucas' latent sense of humour arose from a chance remark he made to his lover as they lay in bed one Sunday morning: at that time he hadn't yet learnt that offhand comments could often mature in her mind into memorable action, and so he had no qualms about voicing his thoughts. 'You know, darling,' he mused, 'we've been tied up together in public, and done it to each other, but wouldn't it be nice to be left alone together just once?'

Julie's appetite for anything even vaguely sensual involving them both was boundless; even the incident with the cat, although it must've been excruciating, wasn't without its appeal to her. However, fortunately for them both, she'd taken it as ample reprisal for what she'd done to him at the ball, so avoiding the possible escalation of their games into depravity. She therefore reflected, 'Presumably on a bed without any clothes on?' Improving upon the scenario in her mind's eye still further, she added, 'I wonder if a couple could make love like that?' But enthusiasm quickly died. 'It would be impossible,' she declared in a tone of finality, 'For a start it's illegal to leave people alone in such a situation unsupervised, and whoever did the tying up would need to see one of us naked, which would also be legally unacceptable.' Sighing in disappointment, she added, 'There are lots of other reasons against it, but the authorities are mostly worried that kind of thing could encourage orgies for instance. If we were caught, sweetheart, you might well be exiled because, despite my protests to the contrary, they'd probably blame you for tempting poor little innocent me.' On this last note the idea was abandoned for good, or so Andrew thought.

A week or so later they had a free day off work which fitted in nicely with the weekend; Julie went straight across to the window as soon as they'd woken up. 'What a beautiful morning for a walk, love,' she cried joyfully. 'Let's go up the forest and kick some leaves about. Then we'll come back here and play a wonderful new game I've devised.'

'Who's going to be the victim?' Andrew asked dubiously.

'You are,' she giggled, turning round to face him, 'who else?'

Before they left the house they removed the mattress from their bed, placed it on the floor against one wall, and stripped off the sheets and blankets. Somehow the thought of what might be about to happen to him gave added zest to their autumnal stroll, and both lovers returned home greatly refreshed though not without a little apprehension upon his part.

After breakfast, and back up in their room his sweetheart said, as she handed him three stockings, 'You know what to do, but if I were you I'd soak the knot in water before putting it in your mouth because it could be a couple of hours before you're released. Tie your ankles together on the mattress after you've removed your clothes then lie face down; I'll see to your hands then.'

Rather puzzled, he followed her instructions; this was an entirely new departure for Julie because normally she attended to every little detail herself. He watched her as soon as he'd undressed and incapacitated himself, intrigued as to what she might do, but she merely tied her hair up on top of her head with a ribbon. She glanced over to him when she'd finished and seeing he was ready came over and knelt by his side, meticulously binding his hands behind him and testing the knots afterward. In Andrew's opinion this last act was entirely unnecessary for he'd never managed to free himself before, and he didn't expect to now; apparently satisfied with her work she then placed a hard pillow beneath his head and left a similar one beside it. Her next move was strange indeed for she arranged a hand towel over his naked buttocks. 'And don't move,' she commanded, gesticulating at him with a finger in emphasis.

It was only after his lover, seated once more in front of the dressing table, began to make a large knot in the middle of a stocking that Andrew had an inkling of what was about to occur. After soaking the knot in the little wash basin she placed one of the dining chairs beside the mattress and then left the room; but she was soon back, and there then followed a flurry of activity which her captive watched in helpless fascination. First she removed all her clothes then, after picking up the knotted stocking and adding two more to it, she came and sat sideways on the chair to face toward her sweetheart. She draped one stocking about her neck and used the other to bind her ankles together; before tying the knotted nylon in her mouth she gazed down at him, smiled, and said, 'Your suggestion has borne fruit, darling, but mother is not happy. Enjoy yourself!'

The girl's appraisal of her parent's mood was only too apparent when, after some five minutes, the door burst open and Jean stormed in; Julie glanced round wildly upon her mother's appearance, hastily threw down the magazine she'd only just begun to read and quickly positioned her hands behind her. Mrs. Lucas positively snatched the stocking from her daughter's neck and, whilst she knelt at her back she blazed away in an undertone at them, disregarding Julie's outraged mumblings as she attempted to communicate with her mother, 'What you're doing is illegal and dangerous,' she raged, 'and if it wasn't for her constant nagging I'd have nothing to do with it. I blame you for this, Andrew, you give in to her far too easily. It would serve you both right if you choked to death or suffocated.'

Jean's bad temper only added extra eroticism to their predicament as far as he was concerned. Observing an attractive woman tie up her beautiful naked daughter in readiness for what would once have been termed a fate worse than death was uniquely intimidating enough, but to be berated whilst bound and naked oneself was almost beyond endurance. Having finished her task Mrs. Lucas stood up and released her daughter's hair which she began to brush out in a displacement activity whilst continuing to scold them; Julie, meanwhile, having given up her attempts to gain her mother's attention as futile, raised her eyes to the ceiling in a gesture of patient resignation. 'This business is between the three of us; I don't want your father to hear about it. The prize for him doing so, or for untying yourselves will be making your own breakfasts for a fortnight.' This was very bad news, indeed, and virtually changed the nylons binding them into shackles, for not only was Jean a marvellous cook but her insistence upon regularly making the morning meal allowed the lovers extra time in bed.

But worse was to follow because after picking up the magazine and placing it, together with the hairbrush, on the dressing table and snatching the hand towel off Andrew's rump with the words, 'You won't be needing this,' she went over to the door. Upon opening it she turned to face them. 'I'm doing this for you just this once,' she told them in a more sober manner, 'and I'm going to ensure you make the most of it. You see,' she continued, obviously savouring each word, 'you neglected to tell me when I ought to release you.' Both lovers stared back at her in helpless stupefaction, but as soon as her mother finished speaking Julie began, once more, to attempt to communicate with her, but her words emerged as an incoherent jumble of noises. Jean listened patiently for a while with a self satisfied smile on her lips, but then left the room while she was in full flow and closed the door firmly behind her.

Cut off in mid-sentence Andrew's lover continued to stare at the door for some minutes before transferring her eyes to her sweetheart who, as soon as the door closed, had managed to turn onto his side to face into the room; then she began to address him, trying to tell him something, but she again soon gave up when she realised how ridiculous she sounded. He would've liked her to stay where she was while he feasted his eyes upon her, for her naked beauty and obvious helplessness made her unbelievably attractive and desirable; but instead she wriggled to the edge of the chair and, after shrugging her shoulders in recognition of defeat, she permitted herself to join him on the mattress.

If, after two or possibly three hours, Mrs Lucas had reappeared to release them then Andrew might have rated the subsequent experience one of the sexiest he'd ever enjoyed, but tedium and discomfort latterly marred the event even though it was sugared by a little light relief. As soon as Julie had arrived on their austere bed she'd dragged and manoeuvred herself alongside him; at least, he'd considered when she'd pressed her lips against his, we can kiss after a fashion. There then followed a difference of opinion occasioned by their inability to converse, for his lover apparently wished to be aroused whilst he wanted to know whether coition was feasible in view of their obvious handicap.

Fortunately she allowed him to have his way, and while her eyes twinkled in amusement they tried innumerable contortions before success was finally assured; but as they attempted to finalise their union he thought ruefully that dipping a brush into a paint pot doesn't automatically guarantee an ability to paint, and so more evolutions were essential before satisfaction was achieved.

Having expended so much time, trouble and effort into filling the breach Andrew felt loath to retire, and so they lay facing each other whilst he regretted the weight he was imposing upon his lowermost arm; he began to regret other things as well. Although they were at the peak of physical contact he felt unfulfilled; Julie now had her back against the wall and he was pressed up against her as much as he could manage without hurting her hands and arms, but he didn't feel as one with her. He began to wish his hands were free so he could put his arms about her and pull her tightly to him, he wanted to fondle her breasts and stroke her hair; he wished her legs were locked about his. He longed to remove the stockings from their mouths so he could kiss her, to entwine his tongue with hers, to whisper words of love and encouragement. But instead they lay like a pair of beached whales, staring into each other's eyes.

As usual it was his sweetheart who ended the impasse to demonstrate the possibilities of their plight by showing him how to make the best out of a bad situation. She began in a small way by twisting her head and kissing him, next she nuzzled her face against his, nipping at his nose and ears with her lips, then humming a medley of tunes. When she'd finished she started to push him away with her hips, he took the hint and withdrew from her whereupon, with a tremendous amount of effort and patience, she managed to raise herself into a kneeling posture; turning her back on him she then began to fondle and caress those parts of his face and body which came within easy reach of her questing fingers. This wasn't a simple task, as Andrew immediately realised the instant he saw her wrists, for her mother, instead of crossing them behind his sweetheart as his were, had fastened them so her palms were facing each other; a position which simultaneously ensured her elbows became virtually useless and seriously impeded the movement of her hands. No wonder she began making a fuss as soon as Jean began binding her wrists.

It was while Andrew was occupied in repaying her attentions

in kind that several of the questions preying upon his mind were answered in the worse possible way, By their clock they'd now been trussed up for almost four hours, and he was beginning to wish he could visit the toilet, he was also wondering exactly how he would be able to conceal his nudity from Julie's mother. Once, when he'd first started to learn about steam railway locomotives, he'd described their components to his lover; when he'd come to the terms "coupling, and connecting, rods" she'd burst into uncontrollable laughter and, henceforth, had referred to what she claimed as her most cherished possession by the same names. Now, this part of his anatomy was in full view as he knelt upon the mattress, for he'd been in a state of continuous arousal since she'd bound his wrists, and his hands were now groping blindly at her breasts as she lay behind him, while he faced directly into the room.

At this precise moment Jean reappeared, opening the door without warning to stand gazing at her daughter's reclining form and her lover's more upright stance. 'Well, well, well,' she exclaimed in wonder and admiration as her eyes immediately dropped to the region of his waist, 'the reason for Julie's infatuation has been revealed at last.' She laughed. 'Your parents certainly did you proud, dear, that's for sure.' After this observation she became brisk and business-like. 'John's having an after dinner nap, so put your feet where I can reach them; it's time for a wee break.' As she untied his ankles she called over her shoulder, 'And I want you ready, my girl, by the time we return.'

Andrew felt himself to be all kinds of fool as he followed his sweetheart's mother out of the bedroom; the contrast between the domesticity of the neatly dressed woman, her plush, tidy house and his bound, naked body was too extreme for comfort. But when she awaited him by the open door to the bathroom she again stared blatantly at the prime source of his embarrassment and remarked, 'Don't look so put out, love; we didn't find Julie and Jerry under a gooseberry bush. But,' she added reflectively, 'I don't know how you're going to manage like that. You'll need to use the shower if it's only a bladder job, so I'll turn it on for you. But flush the loo if you use that.'

Left to his own devices after Jean had gone Andrew was compelled to follow her suggestion; he couldn't help admiring her broadmindedness, but that didn't prevent him from wondering when Julie and he were going to cease being her prisoners, and when they were going to have something to eat. When she came back she washed his face and helped him to sip half a glass of water; it had long been evident she was no longer angry with them; now it seemed as though she'd discovered the possibilities of having further fun at their expense for she began treating him like a little boy, talking down to him and telling him in the finest detail of the wonderful meal which she and John had so recently consumed. He couldn't help wondering what he'd do if she began treating him more like a man; however, fortunately for his peace of mind, the only time she laid hands on him unnecessarily was when he left the bathroom, for then she gave him a mighty slap on the rump.

Julie was seated on the edge of the mattress upon their return, so her mother untied the nylon which bound her ankles and transferred it to Andrew's, after which she escorted her daughter out of the room while he, having no option, lay down on the mattress to await their return. It wasn't too long before his lover was lying face down beside him while Jean untied her hands and rebound them in a more comfortable and convenient position before attending to her ankles. They were then forced to listen while she explained why it was too risky to allow them any sheets or blankets, that the heating had been switched on though it was essential for the window to be slightly ajar for safety's sake. 'You'll have to put up with any draughts,' she added, but was then interrupted by her husband's voice calling from below.

'Are they back, dear?'

Mrs. Lucas smirked maliciously as she cast a sideways look at her prisoners. 'Yes, love,' she shouted in reply. 'Apparently the show was captivating; they're absolutely speechless.'

'Well, aren't they coming down?'

'No, dear,' she answered, 'they've already eaten and they're having an early night; they're bound to be tired.' Immediately after this brief exchange, during which she hadn't taken her eyes off the lovers, she moved to the door and blew them a kiss while they stared impotently back; after the door had closed behind her Andrew distinctly heard a key turn in the lock.

Julie groaned and snuggled up to him; all the life appeared to have gone out of her as she just lay pressed up against him; probably she'd hoped, as he had, that her mother was going to release them. Now, he assumed, she'd lost heart and only wanted an end to their ordeal. Soon the light began to fade and so he was deprived of even the simple pleasure of gazing at her beautiful face and body. Later, though, in complete darkness he rolled over on his side and began to press his mouth against her adjacent cheek, responding she turned over to face him and with her aid they eventually managed to make love again, an endeavour which he considered to be a major achievement.

This time they remained locked together until the early hours of the morning when Jean roused them for a second trip to the bathroom; she had no words or pity for Andrew on this occasion, or presumably even for her own daughter, because they were quickly back on the mattress just as helpless as before. Up till then he'd managed to sleep quite well, but now he began to suffer badly from pins and needles as well as from cramp, he was also experiencing extreme hunger and thirst, and he was unable to escape an irritating draught on his back and buttocks. He tried not to move about too much for fear of disturbing his unseen slumbering sweetheart, and the result was he couldn't find a comfortable position. He must've dozed off on numerous occasions but he seemed to spend most of the time lying awake in torment; more than once he heard the door open to be blinded by a torch flashing in his face, and about the room. So Mrs. Lucas was obviously concerned about them.

Their ordeal finally came to an end when Andrew awoke from a nap in the grey dawn light to find his hands unaccountably free; with much difficulty he managed to undo the knots at his neck and feet, and then turned to examine his lover's bonds. She, however, was sleeping peacefully with her back to him, so he left her alone, dressed, and made his way down to the kitchen. His intention was to awaken her as soon as he'd a hot drink and a snack to hand; but much to his delight a flask and sandwich box stood upon the table together with a note. "Dear children", it read, "hope you enjoyed yourself, and that you've learnt your lesson. No retaliation please, or else, love, Mum".

Returning to their room with the refreshments he immediately freed his sweetheart, a task requiring the use of scissors for her wrists, and together they consumed the snack whilst seated on the mattress. Remembering his companion's advice about going easy on one's food after they'd been zig-zagged, he was more than a little amused to note the way she wolfed down the sandwiches and took great gulps of her coffee.

It was only after they'd cuddled up to each other between sheets beneath a mountain of blankets that they began to speak about their experience. 'I had no idea your mother would leave us like that for so long,' Andrew observed.

Julie sniggered. 'That's what I was so upset about when she told us we'd have to make the most of being tied up together. My mum never does things by halves and she won't repent of a threat; that, and the way she tied my wrists: she deliberately wanted to make things difficult for me, which meant she was really peeved; thinking about it, though, we've got off pretty lightly in the circumstances. But I wonder if Carol and Jim called to see why we stood them up and, if so, what excuse mum gave. Were you embarrassed when she took you to the toilet, by the way?'

'Of course I was!' he exclaimed, 'and I couldn't help wondering what I'd have done if she'd taken advantage of me, but all she did was to smack my behind.'

The notion, combined with his brief chastisement, was too much for his sweetheart and so she had a giggling fit, but afterward she said, 'If it had all been a story in a pornographic magazine the possibilities would've been endless; but in real life, on Whyte Island at any rate, couples are trained to cater for all their partners sensual requirements as you, darling, will concede. Therefore, my dad supplies all mum's physical and psychological needs. Mind you,' she added, biting his ear lobe, 'I bet the thought of putting you through your paces did at least occur to her.'

Andrew had assumed that because he'd thought it an ordeal then his lover would be of a similar opinion, but she claimed for the most part it had been great fun and highly erotic. 'But if it hadn't been for your gallantly shielding me with your body, my sweet darling, I'd have probably suffered just as much from the draughts, but thanks to you I was able to sleep for much of the time. You've got to admit though, sweetheart, it was doubtless more entertaining than seeing a sexy film, and far less degenerate than watching a violent one.' Laughing suddenly, she added,

'Could be the island's answer to video nasties: is that what they call them?'

During breakfast Julie's father commented, 'Your mother's told me about your visit to the theatre yesterday afternoon.' He frowned and glanced from one to the other of the lovers. 'So where would that be? Only I didn't know there were any matinee performances on weekdays.'

Julie took on an expression of puzzled innocence, and her sweetheart began to choke on his tea as she replied, 'I don't understand. We didn't leave our room after we'd returned from our walk because we were otherwise occupied. Mother made us some sandwiches.'

This slight distortion of the truth appealed to Andrew's sense of humour, but his scarcely concealed mirth quickly changed to dismay when Jean promptly turned the tables on them. 'Oh dear,' she exclaimed, also looking puzzled, 'I was obviously mistaken.' She then banged the table with her palms. 'What a pair of lovely children we've got, John,' she declared brightly, 'they've volunteered to get up early to make breakfast over the next fortnight.' Beneath the table the tip of Andrew's slipper connected none too gently with Julie's ankle.

BOOK TWO

When Andrew opened his eyes for what seemed the hundredth time and saw the almost horizontal shaft of sunlight shining through the windows he was more than a little pleased. He lowered his eyes to the young woman who half knelt, half lay with her head resting in his lap: Whyte Island's first lady, if the title had existed, he mused, trussed up like a chicken. No wonder it had taken her so long to crawl to him, he thought as he gazed at the length of rope which bound her wrists to her ankles with very little slack to it. He'd only seen her tied up once before and that was when he'd raped her; she'd nursed, comforted and consoled him, and instead of being grateful he'd physically abused her in the vilest fashion. Had she cared to use the term she could in theory, at that time, have rightfully called herself the first lady, but his punishment for ravishing her so brutally hadn't been imprisonment or exile, but instead they'd married and he'd subsequently fathered their child.

He moved his fingers and toes to keep the blood circulating; he would've liked to alter the position of his legs, the only major part of his body really free, but he didn't want to risk waking his wife. If she could sleep through zigzagging so much the better, the rules said nothing about staying awake to experience the ordeal. He stared about the shed, seeing it clearly for the first time and marvelling once more at the distance she'd dragged herself along the earthen floor, homing in on him in the pitch darkness, presumably by the sound of his breath, from her starting point just inside the door. She was no Julie, but he loved her for her loyalty and devotion toward him, above all for loving him intensely in return; there had formerly been a time when he'd thought himself incapable of ever being able to love again, but she'd shown him in innumerable ways that his heart was capable of such emotion.

The shed was almost empty, a few boxes and crates, some

gardening tools stowed safely away; he couldn't see what was behind or beside him because the scarf in his mouth was tied, like his wrists, to a post, stanchion or something at his rear. How to pass the unknown number of hours before their release he pondered. He thought back to the arrival of their invitation card with its sinister edging, so innocent seeming with its request to attend a dance at a popular country tavern, the dress to be casual, circa 1965.

Several years previously an option to the practice of zigzagging had been proposed in a referendum, the alternative was to be a week's authentic labour in the replica industrial town which had been completed a few years after Andrew had become a Whyte Islander. However, apart from the fact that either ordeal would need to have been undertaken in one's own time, and that the week long option would have involved long hours, hard work, poor food and accommodation with an element of danger, a difficulty concerning younger mothers immediately emerged. Because as it was undesirable for such women to be away from their offspring for any great length of time this meant they would either have no option but to undergo zigzagging, or else they'd be exempted from both ordeals which would, therefore, mean their husbands' non participation.

So almost the entire population decided, for one reason or the other, that this alternative was unfair and so it was voted against; significantly, no one questioned the validity of continuing zigzagging. It was to be Andrew's second experience of the ordeal and his wife's third: Helen had been quite excited at the prospect, it held as little menace for her as it had for Julie and consequently she'd merrily gone about selecting an appropriate dress to wear, learning the correct jargon of the period and making arrangements for the care of their three year old daughter Clare. This latter task was easily accomplished, for Jean Lucas would have considered herself insulted if she hadn't been chosen to look after her, as both Helen and Andrew regarded her as being their real mother as well as grandmother to their child; which, in a way, she was!

Of course, their experience differed from everyone else's; the only thing to be relied upon with regard to zigzagging was its uniqueness on each occasion. They'd arrived at the public house by the stated time and had joined a good sized crowd in jiving and twisting to rhythm and blues, and soul music; they drank a little and had a few things to eat, and danced some more. Then, just after they'd finished smooching to a slow number, Helen went off to the ladies room and had failed to return It didn't take long for Andrew to realise she'd been intercepted, and he was therefore not particularly surprised when an anxious young woman soon came up to him and informed him his wife had been taken a little faint and was resting in an upstairs room. Upon his arrival at the relevant door his knocking was answered by a couple of men who, after a token struggle, overpowered him, bound him hand and foot, taped some sticking tape over his mouth and dumped him unceremoniously on the bed alongside his similarly treated wife; their task completed the men left them in the care of a middle aged woman.

During the course of the next four hours wife and husband were guarded by a relay of adults of all ages and both genders, never more than one person at a time and always, as Andrew noticed from a bedside clock, for a period of twenty minutes each. He didn't mind too much if their custodian was a male but felt distinctly uncomfortable when their captor wasn't; on one occasion they were in the care of a fragile looking old lady who, apart from gazing down and soothing them by stating she hoped their ordeal wouldn't be too uncomfortable, sat quietly knitting in an armchair.

An hour later a beautiful girl took over from a man and promptly came over to their bed, lifted Andrew's legs over toward his companion's and then silently pushed the remainder of his body against her; this manoeuvre accomplished she lay down in the vacant space and read a book. Although this stage in their captivity could hardly be said to have been horrible in any way he found it extremely tedious with only mutely gazing into Helen's eyes and contemplation of their ultimate fate to relieve the monotony.

Eventually the pair of men who'd inconvenienced them returned, and after they'd told Andrew some nonsense about doing exactly as he was ordered because they still held his wife, he was released, escorted through the still crowded dancehall and taken to the men's room where he was made to change into a pair of overalls; finally, he was walked to the back garden shed and left in the position in which he now found himself. Not long afterward the door reopened and Helen was deposited, already helpless, on the floor: fortunately, as he discovered later, she too was clad in overalls.

He closed his eyes and tried to sleep; he was weary from sitting there, the weight of his wife's head resting on his thighs gave him cramp and he was bored. He detested having nothing to do for it made him think of Julie, and that remembrance frequently brought tears even after all this time. But he couldn't sleep, and very much against his will his mind slowly and persistently returned to their last days together.

His eyes moistened as he thought of that New Year's Eve at the Lucas' home; he'd thoroughly enjoyed the three day's break which culminated in the first day of the year, the only official national holiday recognised on Whyte Island when almost everything came to a stop for the enjoyment of all. Julie and he had visited most of their friends and attended several parties in the process, but now, on the last night of the old year Mr. and Mrs. Lucas had thrown the house open to all their acquaintances. He could recall only a few details of that hectic evening; once, he remembered gazing down at his loved one's face as the clocks chimed midnight and seeing the tears of happiness, as he'd assumed, in her eyes as they'd toasted the new year in.

Then, in the early hours of the morning, they'd gone up to their room to gain a little privacy and found it full of couples in various stages of intimacy, so they'd immediately turned the light off again and lain down on the floor where they'd noted an empty spot. Too intoxicated to care about respectability he'd begun to make love to her, but she'd giggled helplessly when he couldn't finish and he fell asleep while she was attempting to help him.

Andrew couldn't really say just when Julie's illness had become apparent to him; he supposed it had been about the beginning of February that she started to look tired and drawn, but even at that date it was something which could've passed off as a temporary ailment. She was so skilful with cosmetics she must've been able to disguise the more physical symptoms of her disease long before he began to notice anything was wrong. The deterioration in her condition was finally brought forcefully home to him near the end of March whilst they were attending a dance:

the brown satin dress she wore on that occasion exposed a large area of upper chest from her shoulder tips to just above her bust, and so it came as a shock when, upon returning to her with drinks, he noticed how the outline of her uppermost ribs was quite evident from some distance away.

On many women, he was aware, this feature wasn't unusual but he hadn't noticed it on his sweetheart before, and at first he attributed it to the way the light shone on her. But during the course of the dance he studied her face with extra care and soon detected signs of debilitation: her eyes seemed slightly shrunken and dark about the rims which even dextrous make up had failed to disguise adequately, and her skin appeared to be pallid and lacking in freshness.

Andrew said nothing at the time, not wishing to spoil her evening, but a few days later he voiced his disquiet at an opportune moment and finished by hoping she'd seek medical advice. Much to his surprise Julie accepted his suggestion enthusiastically, and subsequently she informed him the doctor had diagnosed mild anaemia and had put her on a course of iron and vitamin tablets. But throughout the following weeks he could recognise no real improvement in his lover, and the silly arguments which had first begun in the early part of the new year became more frequent and heated until they culminated in the terrible rows on what was to mark their last full day together.

On that fateful day they'd taken a bus ride to an adjacent coastal village, and had then set out to walk back to Newtown along the cliff top exploring the several picturesque coves which traversed their route on the way. Although it was a typically blustery, late April day it was warm and dry, and they'd often undertaken the walk before in both directions within a day and in far worse conditions. They reached the third little bay, had a paddle and then they picnicked in the shelter of a rock; so far nothing unusual had occurred and in fact Julie was more like her old self than she'd been for a long time. Andrew was quietly overjoyed because he thought the vitamins flowing through her veins might be helping to restore their relationship to its former glory and, upon studying the blush in her skin, the sparkle in her eyes and the expression of exhilaration on her face he could well believe it: that is until they set off on the remainder of their walk.

They had the choice of two routes out of their cove; one was a wide metalled lane running alongside a rivulet in a gentle ascent up the valley and leading directly to the town. The other way surmounted the cliff and was therefore much steeper though not particularly dangerous; Julie had frequently climbed it with the agility of a mountain goat, and had been known to mock her lover for wishing to take the more level road. It had the attraction of being the more scenic of the routes with the bonus of leading to the headland overlooking Newtown harbour with its breathtaking views out to sea and along the coastline. At this point the cliff top path connected up to the road which continued down into the town.

Not unnaturally Andrew therefore began to direct his steps in the direction of the path, but his sweetheart held back. 'I'm not going up there,' she declared, 'it's too dangerous.' When he replied to the effect that she'd been known to take it in her stride even through the worse weather conditions, the comparison with her former self seemed to make her furious. 'I said it was too dangerous,' she screamed. 'You can go,' she shouted, pushing at him, 'but I'm going up the roadway.'

He hesitated uncertainly: from a girl who'd once been so pliable with regard to his wishes and so companionable she'd apparently suddenly changed into a stubborn virago. He was more than aware of the several people in their immediate vicinity who'd stopped to stare, they were obviously as shocked as he was at his lover's display of rudeness, such unseemly behaviour being virtually unknown to the island, especially in public; it was doubly ironic in coming from one who'd done so much to ensure his own comprehension of Whyte Island etiquette.

He attempted to take hold of her hand in a conciliatory gesture but she shook him off and, after giving him a glance of hatred and contempt, she turned abruptly and stamped off up the lane toward Newtown. But Andrew, although dismayed, loved her too dearly to allow her to go on alone and, after catching up with her he took one of her hands forcibly in his; she didn't resist but continued to march on proudly without acknowledging his presence. But he wasn't going to permit this state of affairs to continue indefinitely so, when they drew close to a seated refuge, he dragged her into it. 'As soon as we reach home, Julie,' he began firmly, standing over her when he'd pushed her down on the bench, 'I'm going to move out; then you can consider whether you really want me. I can't......' He stopped in mid-sentence because there was something strange about the way she silently held her face away from him; gently placing a hand beneath her chin and carefully easing her head round he saw tears flowing down her cheeks, and the sight promptly compelled him to embrace and then kiss her.

Her response was immediate, she threw her arms about his neck and returned his kiss with a passion which astounded him; even as their lips bruised each other's she began to empty out her emotions in a flood of tears. Refusing to remove her hands or her mouth she surrendered herself totally to the sobs which wracked her very soul; Andrew was well aware that his sweetheart was prone to such fits of despair but he hadn't previously experienced one as severe as this. She'd cried badly when they'd been out sailing together that first time, and on that occasion he'd unaccountably felt like laughing, but now he was overcome by an overwhelming sense of foreboding. This feeling wasn't allayed by two strange remarks she made when her bout of weeping began to ease. 'If only you understood,' she wailed. And shortly afterward she sobbed, 'I can't say goodbye.' He couldn't understand why she should want to say farewell, but comforted himself with the assumption that at least she wasn't going to leave him now. These latter words, placed by retrospect into their right context, were to haunt him to the day of his death; but now he made a desperate effort to clarify the situation.

She shook her head vigorously when he asked her if he had a rival, but when he attempted further questions she removed her arms and rose to her feet. 'Come on,' she exclaimed pulling him from the shelter with one hand whilst roughly wiping her tearstained face with the back of the other, 'take me home, I want you to make love to me as you've never done before, and I want to be your victim in all the sex games we've ever played.' Allowing himself to be manipulated Andrew said nothing to these requests but he thought that although he wasn't averse to the sensual aspect he certainly wouldn't subject her to any sex games until she was well enough to properly enjoy them.

During the walk home he tried one more query. 'You're not going to leave me, then?'

She replied straight away, but not with regard to his question. 'I'll never stop loving you,' she murmured.

Julie immediately went up to their room when they reached the house after informing her lover she required nothing to eat because, she'd continued, he was all she needed. Andrew, however, called in on her parents before joining her; he described as best he could the events of the day and how their daughter had asked to be excused from not seeing them for the remainder of the afternoon and the evening. Jean and John were, as usual, more than understanding but they didn't seem to be as cheerful as they normally were, and on at least two occasions they glanced sadly at each other upon some comments he made.

If he'd hoped his sweetheart and he had finished arguing for that day he was to be sorely disappointed, for when he tried to explain he thought her in no state to play sex games she shrieked back he considered her to be a weakling and he didn't love her anymore, in addition to accusing him of a host of other ridiculous things. The climax of her tantrum came when she produced some stockings and threw them at him, but he remained unmoved being heartily thankful for the house's installed soundproofing and double glazing.

When at last her temper dissolved into tears of frustration he carefully removed her clothing and put her to bed where, after also undressing, he joined her; their subsequent lovemaking began gently enough but soon accelerated into unbridled passion as Julie forced him onto even greater exertion until their union bordered on the violent. When, as was inevitable, Andrew, through over demand had nothing left to give to his lover she continued to require satisfaction, and so to the best of his ability he tried to please her. But she proved to be insatiable and when he was too exhausted to continue she reversed roles and smothered his face and body with kisses and caresses.

Throughout that evening and much of the night they made love in a variety of ways, his sweetheart telling him she loved him and repeatedly begging assurance she was loved in return: she insisted they perform with the lights on and whenever they faced one another she stared at him with an intensity he found to be most disconcerting. Such was the extent of her passion and the strangeness of her behaviour that he could never comprehend, later, how he had failed to realise what she was about to do. Eventually, however, the physical and mental effect of their continuous exertions proved too much for both of them and they fell asleep, held fast in each other's arms.

When the alarm clock woke them in the morning Julie told her lover she'd set it half an hour early because she wanted them to make love again; this wasn't an entirely unknown device on her part but rather strange, he thought, after their more than hectic night, and especially as they were supposed to be going to work afterward. Even stranger was her decision to take the day off, giving as her excuse her tiredness and forthcoming period. Before leaving the house Andrew brought her some breakfast, and so he took his leave of her, most aptly, as she lay in bed.

Such is human nature that by the time he'd reached his place of work much of his uneasiness with regard to his sweetheart had evaporated in the early spring air; somehow worry didn't seem to mix with the warm sunshine, and whenever he thought of Julie that morning he felt optimistic at their continuing relationship.

His progress on the railway had been almost phenomenal, and for the past three working days he'd been entrusted with a signal box of his own, a responsibility not quite as great as it sounded for his duties merely consisted of accepting and offering trains on both sets of line, as well as controlling two pairs of points at each side of the station of which his box was a part. It was just child's play as everything was automatic, and it would've required a work of sheer genius to cause even a minor accident. At just after 12.30 he offered the noon train bound for Harbourtown on to the next station and, having received the acceptance, he gave the driver the road. With a mixture of smugness and fascination he watched the locomotive begin to move its train; the word "schools" came idly and unwarranted into his mind as the engine steamed past him, but his reverie was interrupted by the arrival of a uniformed stranger in his cabin. 'If you're Andrew,' he announced, displaying his relief ticket, 'I've come to take over from you temporarily.' As he raised his eyebrows at this information the newcomer added, 'I think someone's been taken ill at Newtown Station and they've asked for you as a replacement.'

Andrew stood at the far end of the down platform awaiting the arrival of the next train with nervous anticipation, he still wore his overalls but he'd be able to wash and change onboard the train should he be frustrated in what he'd planned. As he waited he thought about his being relieved from his job, it was the first time such a thing had happened to him and, while not being unusual in railway work, it was strange when added to the events over the last 24 hours. Eventually the dot and minute plume of smoke and steam in the far distance resolved itself into a train hauled by the square shaped giant with the peculiar patterned wheels. 'Any chance of a ride?' he pleaded as the green locomotive shuddered to a halt alongside him.

The driver gazed down at him and at the footplate pass he held. 'Can you swing a banjo?' he enquired with a grin.

Laughing, Andrew replied, 'If it's got a "g" string on it I can.'

'Alright, you'll do,' the driver answered also laughing; he gestured to the young man who'd appeared at his side. 'I could do with a real man; I've never met anyone called Andrew who was any good.'

'But that's my name,' he stated with mock indignation.

'It's also mine,' the driver replied with a wry smile before stepping back to allow him access to the cab.

His subsequent trip on the footplate, although of only comparatively short duration, was pure joy for Andrew; whilst he and the official fireman took turns in feeding coal to the firebox the driver told the life story of the unusual engine. And all three of them made the most out of the coincidence of having three men with the same name together in one small place. Julie's lover was still laughing when the train rolled into Newtown Station, but it was a joke which was going to have to last him a long time.

The first thing he was required to do, after he'd climbed down from the engine and bade farewell to his erstwhile companions, was to report his arrival at the station foreman's office, but as he turned to carry out this task he suddenly became aware of someone standing close to him. Much to his surprise it was Helen Maynard; she looked different from when he'd last seen her at his citizenship party, for her dark hair was now as long as Julie's. 'Hello, Helen,' he greeted her cheerfully, but instead of replying she grabbed hold of his hand and began pulling him along the platform. He was so astonished at her behaviour that he was only half conscious of the passengers who were staring at them with puzzled amusement, and of the derisive calls emanating from the engine crew behind him.

But when he attempted to resist she glanced back at him and exclaimed, 'It's Julie, she wants you immediately!' This mention of his lover disarmed him completely and made him compliant with everything Helen wished him to do, but this didn't prevent him from feeling dumbfounded when she dragged him straight into the gentleman's toilet. More than one man turned his head in amazement from what he was doing at the vision of a most attractive young woman dressed in running gear hauling a boiler suited man across the floor of that substantial convenience. But Helen didn't waver or hesitate until she'd forced Andrew into a cubicle where she proceeded, quickly and roughly, to strip the overalls from him. Taking charge of the bundle she pushed him out again and propelled him toward the wash basins where she made him clean his hands and face; all the time he tried to question her but she adamantly refused to reply.

Outside the toilet she began to run, and he, with his hand tightly held by hers, had no option but to follow suit; down the subway she led him, out of the station and along the roads leading to the Lucas' home, never stopping and entirely oblivious to any shouts or impediments to their progress. Straight down the garden path they went, through the open front door and up the stairs, only halting when they were at last in Julie's and his room. Immediately Helen pushed him back onto the bed where, after she'd locked the door and hurled the key out of the window, he was horrified to see her pull her top over her head and then tear off her brassiere.

Under any other circumstances Andrew would've been most impressed by this sudden appearance of her imposing round breasts, but instead anger welled up within him at what was, to him, blatant disrespect for the only woman he really loved. He began to protest vehemently, struggling for breath and beginning to get off the bed, but Helen with hands on hips and magnificent bosom heaving, prevented him with coercion. 'If you don't do everything I want you to do,' she threatened, 'I shall try to bind you hand and foot, and even if I don't succeed it'll delay me from telling you something important about Julie. Incidentally, she approves of everything I'm doing, and going to do.'

This further mention of his sweetheart finally ended all his resistance and he could, henceforth, only do as she indicated. Helen came and lay down next to him on the bed and, with the judicious aid of a few pillows, she arranged his head comfortably upon her right breast. 'What I'm about to tell you now won't be very nice, Andrew,' she began, 'and it will break your heart; but I'm here to help you and so if you want to cry or make love or even hit me I don't care. You see, I love you and I also loved Julie.' She paused, letting her reference to his sweetheart in the past tense sink slowly into his mind.

Hardly trusting himself to speak he murmured in disbelief, 'Julie's.........'

Helen finished the fearful sentence for him. 'Dead,' she announced solemnly, 'her mother found her in this bed some time after you'd gone.'

'Where is she?' he asked, raising his head to stare at her, trying to keep the awful realisation of his terrible loss at bay.

'At the hospital,' she answered, pressing his head to her breast again and beginning to stroke his hair, 'they've got to carry out, well, certain tests.'

The suggestion of defilement to his sweetheart's body was the final barrier against the onslaught of Andrew's grief, and as it came crashing down he gave a groan and turned his face to the soft cushion of Helen's flesh; as he did so his misery erupted in a flood of tears which soaked her large flattish nipple in wet salt and saliva.

If Jean, John and Helen had ever required proof of Andrew's profound love and devotion to Julie then the following four days were to provide more than enough demonstration; for, apart from a period of a few hours when he'd attended his lover's cremation, that was the length of time in which he was in a state of deep shock. Even Jean's natural mother's love was surpassed by this supreme evidence of his sense of loss. United in a common aim, these three people, his dearest friends, elected to nurse him in his time of need; Helen willingly took on the lion's share of this work, leaving his side only for personal sanitary reasons; she washed and dressed him, fed him, took him to the toilet and slept with him.

But even though she did everything she could he remained in an insensible condition, perfectly pliable yet unable to act on his own account. For Helen, especially, it was a race against time: if, at the end of seven days, he hadn't recovered then he was liable to exile or death. Her greatest wish was that he should become her father's son-in-law; however, distinction between different individuals was utterly alien to Whyte Island culture and so if the law said he was to be disposed of then that was what would be arranged.

As far as Andrew was concerned the onset of his grief in Helen's arms marked the beginning of a twilight world of disjointed scenes: of vague awareness of being fed with a spoon, of lying in the arms of an unknown person and being led along a carpeted passageway. But he recalled with vivid clarity his being left alone with Julie's body after her mother had told him gently and slowly that he had the right to be the last person ever to see her. From his pocket he'd brought out the emerald necklace and earrings he'd given her on the first day they'd made love and carefully put them on her, then he undid the buttons on her green dress and, after pushing the material aside, he kissed the skin above her heart. The undertakers had worked miracles with her appearance, and Andrew knew that Julie would've approved, but as he gazed down upon her she looked so full of life that he fully expected her eyes to open; this thought provoked another breakdown within him and he rained tears and kisses upon her face, head and hair. Before he sank to the floor overcome with grief he had enough sense left to press the button which automatically sent his love's remains to final destruction. Had he made a careful examination of her body he would've found no trace of a fresh scalpel's incision, for no pathologist had been near her.

On the afternoon of the fourth day after Julie's death Helen was seated on the settee in the upstairs room with Andrew about a foot away from her when suddenly he observed, 'You'd like to take over from Julie, wouldn't you?'

Obviously pleased by this return to apparent normality she placed her sketch pad and crayon down by her side and took one of his hands in hers. 'Yes I would,' she declared enthusiastically, 'if you'll have me.'

He said nothing for a moment, but then asked another question, 'Would you like us to make love now, like Julie and I used to?'

Helen nodded emphatically, unaware she'd stepped into a trap. She jumped to her feet and ran over to the door. 'I'll just tell Jean and John you're much better,' she exclaimed with her head round the door jamb, and then she was gone. By the time she returned, Andrew, still half crazy with grief, had got everything ready for her reception.

'Ouch,' she squealed as he brutally bound her wrists, 'that hurts, Andy.'

'I couldn't care less,' he answered savagely, muffling her mouth with the same disregard for her feelings. By the time he'd finished tying her she was lying prone on the bed, and it was in this position that he began his ravishment of her. Not once during that terrible experience did she so much as murmur or attempt to deter him and when, at last, he'd expended all his misery and frustration upon her she lay on her back with her eyes staring mildly up at him.

Self disgust compelled him to cover her face and body with the bedspread, then he quickly dressed and left the room with the sole intention of putting as much distance as he could between himself and the scene of his disgraceful actions. In the hallway Jean attempted to greet him but she promptly stepped back in alarm as he swept past heading for the front door, which he subsequently slammed behind him. Angry at himself he set off toward the town centre at as fast a pace as he could manage, scarcely aware of where he was heading and totally unaware of what he'd do when he got there.

When he finally came to his full senses he found himself seated in one of the numerous squares gazing down at the pigeons strutting about his feet; Newtown chickens, he thought, remembering what Julie had called them. Suddenly, unbidden, he heard other words she'd said, but this time just before they'd been zigzagged: 'If I die, promise you'll go to Helen; you like her and she loves you, but always remember me!' The sentence sounded so loud and clear in his skull that he looked about him, almost expecting to see her close by. On the opposite side of the square stood a telephone box; like an automaton he went across to it and, once inside he dialled a number, he wasn't even sure whose it was but when a reply came he heard himself ask for Jill.

'I'm afraid she's at the hospital,' a woman's voice answered, and she went on to supply the number.

Not really understanding why, he contacted the hospital. 'Yes?' came her voice after some five minutes wait.

'Jill, it's me, Andrew. I don't know what to do: Julie's dead.'

She recognised him immediately. 'I'm extremely sorry to hear that,' she said in a tone full of concern. Her next words were spoken slowly and deliberately. 'Andrew, love, you remember when the four of us were at the Ship Inn?'

'Yes.'

'You remember that you and I spoke about restaurants?' He did 'Well, have you got another one you might be able to go to?'

'Yes; Helen Maynard.'

Her voice betrayed her surprise. 'Charlie's daughter? Are you sure?'

'Yes, she loves me: loved me.'

'Then for goodness sake go to her as quickly as possible. If, though, her restaurant is closed phone me again and I'll come to you: I won't be able to give you a meal but there'll be plenty of tea and sympathy. Do you understand? Phone me later whatever happens. Now put the receiver down and go.'

Leaving the kiosk he set off for Julie's former home at an even faster rate than when he'd arrived in the square. On the way he mentally berated himself; Helen, in being selected by his lover to take her place, was therefore Julie's living embodiment. She'd given him all the love and devotion his own sweetheart had been capable of and in return he'd used her vilely; almost panic-stricken he increased his pace hoping he hadn't suffocated her, or destroyed her love irrevocably. This time, though, Jean was waiting for him and as he made for the stairs she blocked his way. 'But Helen......' he began.

'She's alright,' Mrs. Lucas told him, 'I've been talking to her. She's exactly as you left her, but I've removed the bedspread from her face and, at her insistence, I've replaced her gag. Now, come into the living room, I want a word with you. Don't worry,' she continued, noticing his hesitation, 'we'll be quite alone.'

'Now,' she said when they were seated side-by-side on the

sofa, 'most of us play sex games at one time or another but that wasn't a game was it?' Andrew shook his head in shame. 'Look,' she went on, placing a hand on top of his, 'I know you've been ill, and we've all had a difficult time over the last few months, but taking your troubles out on a girl who's defenceless because she loves you is really sinking to the depths of depravity. She's given you ample proof during the days since Julie's death that she worships you, so for the lord's sake have pity on the child and give her your life even if you can't give her your love. I happen to know that's exactly what my daughter wanted. You know very well John and I look upon you as our own son, and Julie's loss to us won't alter that fact; this house will always be your home if you want it, no matter what female you choose as your mate,' she patted his hand affectionately, 'but try to make it Helen.' She smiled. 'After what you've just done to her she might shy off you for a while, but she's yours believe me; so go and release her, and be kind to her.'

Jean had been preaching to the converted for it had been his intention ever since he'd left the square to somehow make amends to Helen for his brutality; he'd vowed to himself he'd never be intimate with another woman, and so if she no longer wanted him then he was determined to join Julie. To that end he fairly flew up the stairs and charged into his room; he didn't bother about trying to untie her but cut through the nylons with a knife he'd grabbed from the kitchen; as soon as she was free he pulled her to him and begged her not to hate him, showering her face, and the wheals on her wrists, with kisses.

Under the circumstances it was the wrong thing to do, such contrition after violence being a sign of weakness in many feminine eyes; but Helen, with an extra ration of the maternal instinct in her nature, regarded Andrew as a naughty boy who was being apologetic for a prank which had gone wrong. However, she also had enough womanly pride to appear not to have given in too easily; so although she didn't fight against his attentions she gave him little encouragement; even a passionate kiss in her mouth which, in view of the things he'd done to her, was quite a noble act on his part, failed to arouse any enthusiasm.

When, finally, he desisted in his attempts to prove his regard for her she firmly removed his arms from about her and then stood up; despite her semi-nakedness she managed to appear proud, 'Andrew,' she announced, 'what you did to me was unforgivable. I feel so dirty I couldn't possibly give myself to another man now, and I don't think I love you anymore.' She wiped away a tear. 'I'm going to take a shower and then I'm going home.' With true feminine guile she then handed him a verbal olive branch. 'While I'm away you can sort me out a dress and some underwear; either Julie's or mine as we're both about the same size, apart from the bra.'

As soon as she'd left the room clad in her predecessor's dressing gown Andrew rushed downstairs and obtained two cups of tea from Jean and then raced upstairs again; he quickly found out some of Julie's clothing for his new love, happy in the knowledge his old love would've fully endorsed his choice. When Helen returned she slipped off the dressing gown and, taking no notice of him, dressed herself, pausing only to take sips of the tea; she made no comment on his choice of clothes. When she was ready she tidied up the room, including the bedclothes, packed away her belongings and then offered her suitcase to Andrew. 'Wait by the gate,' she told him.

Very much later he discovered Helen had gone off to say goodbye to Julie's parents, and had subsequently been encouraged by them to forgive him and to come and live with him as a substitute for their daughter, if only for a trial period. There were at least three reasons why this offer appealed to her immensely: despite her words to the contrary she still loved and wanted Andrew desperately; she'd never stopped craving for the mother love which had so long been denied her, and she wanted to withdraw the final obstacle preventing her father from marrying the woman he'd long been courting, that hindrance being herself.

She knew that once she'd left the Maynard house Linda would obtain a flat, and the way would then be clear for Charlie's happiness. It was doubtful that a similar set of complicated factors could succeed with such gratifying results on the mainland; on Whyte Island, however, where personal faults were fewer and mutual understanding widespread, everything fell into place perfectly. But although the ideal solution to a lot of people's problems was already ordained the game still had to be played out. Helen was therefore secretly brimming over with joy as

Andrew, carrying her suitcase, accompanied her to the station; she even allowed him to hold her hand, and once, when he raised it to his lips, she looked away to hide her tears of happiness. She didn't in the least care about the bestial things he'd done to her, all that really mattered was his attitude regarding her afterward, and he was now assuring her he still loved and respected her.

Before her train departed Andrew glanced up at her as she leaned out of the open window and asked, 'If I came to visit you would you refuse to see me?'

A smile played briefly about her lips. 'I'm sure Linda would console you.'

'I don't love Linda. I never have, she was just physical with me; it was you I wanted from the first, before Linda, before Julie.' He paused, then emphasised, 'I love you.'

She looked along the length of the train in the direction of the engine, almost too overwhelmed to speak. 'Poor Julie,' she observed facing him, quickly adding. 'I owe her more than you'll ever know.' The guard's whistle blew, to be answered immediately by the distant hiss of steam emerging from the locomotive's cylinders; as the train began to move Helen played her highest card. 'Anyway,' she prompted, 'you shouldn't say you love me if you don't really mean it.'

By now almost running alongside her coach Andrew deftly trumped her card. 'If you won't have me then I'll go and find Julie.' He was disappointed when her head withdrew from the window upon receipt of these words and had failed to reappear; but she'd gone straight to the toilet, locked herself in and was at that moment crying her eyes out with joyful emotion.

As soon as the train had disappeared from view Andrew telephoned both Jean Lucas and then Gillian with an update, after which he went and made himself presentable, bought some garden flowers and a large box of chocolates, and then settled down to await the next train to Harbourtown content in the knowledge that his compassionate leave still had several days left to run.

When he awoke the following morning it took him some time to realise where he was; he was aware, now, that he'd made a complete recovery from the shock of his sweetheart's death thanks primarily to Helen, but his present environment was so alien to him that he had to make a special effort to remember the events of the previous evening.

Upon presenting himself at the Maynard's door, he began to recollect, Linda had answered his summons; as soon as she'd seen who it was she'd placed a finger against her lips and then beckoned him in; then, in hilarious exaggeration she'd tiptoed stealthily along the hall and up the stairs until they'd arrived outside her sister's room where, throwing all caution to the wind, she'd suddenly pushed the door wide open, shoved him in and, giggling hysterically, had promptly withdrawn. After Helen had recovered from her surprise at his unexpected appearance she'd played the perfect hostess, and together they'd listened to classical c.ds., chatted about inconsequential matters and consumed the splendid meal which Linda had prepared and brought up to them. Much to his disappointment, although Helen had shared her room with him that night, she hadn't offered her body or her bed; instead she'd removed the pillow, sheets and blankets from his former bed and made him up a place to sleep on the floor; neither had suggested he spend the night in his erstwhile room.

As Andrew sat up in his temporary bed, a piece of paper fell to the floor. "Dear Andy,' it read, 'You have presented me with a problem. I really do adore you, but I am a little worried about your regard for me; I know I cannot entirely replace Julie in your heart but I am not in the least jealous of her, because she made you happy and that's what I wanted for you. I told you I love you both equally for that reason, so that love for her is also love for me. No, it is a fear that perhaps you have more need of me as a temporary substitute for your love of Julie, and that in time you will take your love back and give it to someone else. But I cannot wait any longer, so if you really, genuinely believe you can be faithful to me then follow these instructions: at nine o'clock this morning go to the gate beyond the vegetable garden; there you will see a woodland path which soon crosses the bed of the stream. To your right will be seen an evergreen bush, it looks impenetrable (it's meant to) but push your way under it and follow the stream, your shoes will stay dry if you keep to the pebbles. When you find your way blocked by a rock face, wait, and you will receive, I hope, your heart's desire. H". In a footnote she'd added, "Don't bother about breakfast, or Dad and Linda. I've left a flask of coffee for you while you wait to set off. The weather forecast is good". Hardly surprisingly Helen's bed appeared as though it hadn't been slept in.

Andrew found it quite difficult forcing his way up the stream; evergreen shrubs amongst which he identified box, holly and laurel, constantly threatened to prevent his progress, and if it wasn't for the fact he knew Helen wasn't the type of person to toy with him, he'd have soon given up. But eventually he climbed over a low branch and brushed aside some leaves to be confronted by what he could only describe as a fairy dell. Directly before him the stream ran in rivulets down a sheer rock wall some thirty feet high to which adhered mosses, lichens and ferns in great number. Upon either side of the dell steep, plant covered banks were crested by more evergreen bushes which almost entirely canopied the compact area, and on one side of the stream was a slightly sloping grassy sward, still littered with leaves from the previous autumn. At the foot of the rock face the trickling water had, in the course of time, fashioned a little pool and, beyond, had also hollowed out a shallow cave.

The site was perfect for what Helen had in mind, and as he gazed at the peaceful, unspoilt scene in wonder her voice called from somewhere behind him. 'Don't look round, just go over to the grassy patch and remove your clothes; then wade across to the cave, face the wall and start counting.'

'You can turn around now,' he heard her call, after he'd followed her instructions and had reached number 97. When he looked round he saw Helen standing in the water at the point where the pond became the stream, as naked as he was. 'I'm not giving you your clothing back,' she challenged, 'until we've done all the things you and Julie did together.'

Andrew replied, 'We've already done nearly all of them, but I refuse to tie you up again.' He couldn't his eyes off her body; and although he'd seen its salient points on two previous occasions this was the first time he'd viewed it in all its unadorned glory, and he wasn't at all disappointed at its revelation.

'You won't need to,' she laughed. 'But I mean properly; not in haste or tempestuously but slowly and with loving care; then we'll both know, when we've done them, whether you can live and love with me. Meet me in the middle of the pool; we'll soon warm up.'

Up to their waists in water they embraced, Helen with her

arms about his neck, he with his arms around her midriff. Immediately their mouths touched Andrew felt her tongue slide between his lips and press urgently against his teeth in a preliminary attempt at exploration. Hardly had he got used to this sensation when her hips, which were pressing tightly against him, began to gyrate, slowly at first, then ever faster in concert with her tongue in his now open mouth as their passion increased; she stopped suddenly, panting with excitement and exertion and removed herself from his embrace. 'It's too soon,' she told him, 'too wasteful.'

She took hold of his hand and drew him from the pool then across to where the fine grass and leaves lay. There she did what Julie had done to him, notably in the reservoir lake, an act which his previous lover had undertaken many times afterward; but on this occasion, instead of a dark heaven full of stars, Andrew gazed up past evergreen foliage at a bright blue sky seemingly full of the delicate tracery of beech twigs, light green with the promise of spring; and his eyes watered with emotion at this physical proof of his new sweetheart's love. 'I wonder what bird's singing that beautiful song,' he remarked to himself.

Helen briefly supplied the answer before returning to her specific lovemaking, 'It's a wood warbler, they're associated particularly with larch and beech woodland. Pretty sound, isn't it?'

'No, we can't do that!' he exclaimed with alarm as she encouraged him onto the next stage in their mutual discovery of each other, 'I've got no protection.'

'You didn't need any yesterday,' she reminded him, 'anyway, what do you think the pool is for? If you recall, my love, you didn't give me any choice when you raped me, so you could have the decency to do what I want you to do, now!'

'Are you sure you don't mind?' he persisted.

'Yes I do mind,' she assured him, 'but only if you don't do it. I once told you I wasn't a virgin, but now I know that wasn't strictly true; so get on with it, my darling, though try to be a little more gentle this time.'

A late breakfast of sandwiches, cold chicken and wine straight from the bottle served merely as a brief interlude in their lovemaking marathon; but as they sat eating Andrew asked if they were likely to be observed. 'This was once my favourite spot,' Helen mused, holding out a chicken leg whilst he tore a piece off with his teeth, 'but I've never seen anyone else here, or signs of any human disturbance. This is an extremely difficult place to discover, as you know; but I haven't been here for a long time, it became too sad.'

'Why?' he enquired.

She took a piece of chicken into her mouth, kissed her lover and pushed the meat between his lips with her tongue. 'Because,' she sighed, 'this place was made for love, and the lover I had in mind was you.'

He frowned, suddenly puzzled. 'Didn't you bring your other lover here, and why did you wait for me while I was with Julie? You must've known it was hopeless. Why did you change your mind about waiting for me?'

She smiled wistfully. 'Please trust me, darling, when I say I'd rather not tell you. It's to do with Julie, and I promised her; but one day, for your sake, I'll break that promise. As for my previous boyfriend,' she shrugged, 'he wasn't the type to enjoy peace and quiet, the beauty and variety of natural things. I was infatuated with him, rather than really loving him; unlike you, sweetheart, he wouldn't have appreciated this spot.'

The official explanation for Julie's death was that she'd had pernicious anaemia, and that a series of brain haemorrhages had ended her life; this would, therefore, have explained away her sudden outbursts of bad temper, Andrew, though, had always had his doubts, and her death certificate would have confirmed them; but he was content to leave things as they stood because no matter what he did she could never come back to life, and so he subconsciously dismissed Helen's words; it could wait.

During the course of the remainder of the morning and the early afternoon they thoroughly explored each other's bodies and made love in a variety of ways; each of them doing their best to keep him from reaching a climax, conserving his meagre supply until the grand finale of their consummation. His attractive companion, ignoring her gender's right to choose, allowed him to decide the means by which their loving relationship could be sanctified; so he drew her back into the centre of the pool and whispered in her ear, 'Let's end our amour in the same way you began it.' At the moment of their eventual mutual climax, an occurrence which Julie and he had rarely achieved, he said, 'I love you, Helen,' and, from the way her entire body momentarily tensed, he understood it was exactly what she wanted to hear.

'Can you think of anything else we could do, sweetheart?' she asked as they washed each other down in the pool prior to dressing, for it was becoming too cold to make nudity a continuing proposition.

'There are a couple of things,' he replied, climbing from the water to sit down on the grass, 'I want to study your face and figure, just there.' He pointed to a spot where the stream raced over the pebbles in front of him. 'Move about,' he urged as she stood where he'd indicated, 'pretend you're on your own.'

After a while she looked up, laughing. 'Am I as nice as Julie, or Linda?'

'You're you,' he replied fascinated by her blatant sexuality, 'you're different from them, just as they differed from each other, but you're no less beautiful, sweetheart.' Then he asked, as an afterthought, 'I don't suppose you spent one afternoon last summer disguised as a gypsy girl, complete with a caravan and authentic accoutrements?' Her perplexed expression left him in little doubt that she didn't know what he meant, thereby making the mystery of that far off event even more enigmatic.

In comparing Helen's features with those of his two other island lovers Andrew suddenly realised what traps women's bodies became for the eternally unwary males who bought, fought, submitted and faced anything up to actual death to possess them. Linda's form with its lithe frame and smallish breasts seemed to have been fashioned for the unsuspecting, a Diana to go racing through the forests with, to lie alongside to savour her charms together with the food and drink, and to be surprised when, after some nine months, a baby appeared as if from nowhere. Julie's beautifully proportioned figure was for the connoisseur of art, her lovely breasts had been perfect for admiring and fondling, being delicately balanced by hips of exactly the right size; her gorgeous red hair, faultless face and peerless limbs completed an appearance which automatically compelled any lover to endeavour to reproduce her likeness in the shape of an equally beautiful child. Finally Helen's body; her ample breasts, each tipped with a large circle of thrusting nipple, and a great vee of dark bodily hair, had no subtlety; to which her attractive outline and almost sturdy limbs added a promise of strong children and a comfortable home environment in which to raise them.

Nature cared little for personal niceties, he decided; whether or not reproduction was caused by ignorance, admiration or selfishness was of no consequence to the natural world, all that mattered was that the species should be perpetuated. In these three women's bodies, he now realised, he'd sampled three subtly different forms of enticement; he'd enjoyed them and their varied personalities but had not yet been permanently enslaved by them; it was time he changed all that, he thought ruefully. 'Helen,' he called softly, beckoning her over. She came toward him in mystified expectation. He took both of her hands in his and then knelt before her.

'Now,' he said sometime later as she also knelt facing him, 'can you deny that I love you, and that I want you to be the mother of my child, or children, after what I've just done?' Her eyes overflowed with tears at these words, and she threw herself, weeping, into his arms.

As a continuation of their epic love session they decided to dress each other, and while Andrew was fastening his sweetheart's brassiere he remarked, 'Do you suppose Julie would've been jealous of what we did today?'

Helen promptly turned about, thereby pulling the two fasteners he was trying to join from out of his fingers. 'Oh, Andrew, love,' she cried, embracing him, 'if only you knew; if only you knew!'

Back home in her bedroom once more, his lover went across to a drawer and returned with a small green leather folder with "For Andrew" inscribed in gold letters on the front. But as he placed his fingers upon it to take it, she held it tightly. 'I don't know whether you're going to like this, darling,' she warned, adding, 'please remember, though, it isn't meant to hurt you; but you'd better sit down before you look inside.'

Scarcely able to contain his impatience, he seated himself on the edge of the bed with Helen's arm about his waist as if to support him while she sat beside him. The folder opened out into four surfaces, and when he saw the photographs which each comprised the shock was almost beyond his endurance; for it turned his brain into utter turmoil, the subjects of the pictures being so entirely unexpected. Much later he measured the photos: they were 12" high by 10"; two of them were taken from the front, and the remaining pair from behind with partial reflection from a full length mirror. He clearly remembered Julie's hinting there wouldn't be any souvenirs of her if they parted and so, when he'd sent her body off to be consumed by the flames, he'd resigned himself to never seeing her likeness again. Yet now he was staring at her beautiful face, hair and naked body in perfect colour; he recognised the photographs' venue immediately for it was one of the bathrooms at the Roman Villa.

She was obviously meant to be a patrician lady unexpectedly caught in the act of leaving her bath: the intricate decoration on the walls and ceiling, and the expensive looking gown partly draped over the side of the bath, hinted archly toward this fact. Her pose was magnificent, the expression on her face one of mild amusement aimed directly at the camera; her body was arranged so that one breast was partly in profile while the other was almost full on; one leg was raised to enable her to step out of the bath, but this action exposed the most intimate part of her anatomy to the gaze of her beholder. Such a stance could so easily have appeared crude and indelicate, but instead it made Andrew feel as though he were the intruder and his sometime love the intruded upon.

He glanced wildly and accusingly sideways at Helen, but she understood and placed a hand on the back of one of his. 'She and I took the photos when we were alone,' she explained gently, 'we also developed them; and between us we chose the four we liked best. There were many different poses, and lots of shots of each one, but we destroyed those. We did it for you, darling, and we want you to be the only man ever to see them.' Satisfied, and full of gratitude, he returned his gaze to the photograph; Julie's golden red hair had been styled in the roman fashion with a pony tail over the shoulder nearest the camera, and little ringlets above her forehead and at the sides of her head; both the hair on her head and that of her body positively shone in the artificial light.

He shifted his gaze from the old love to the new; she had been photographed in exactly the same room, striking a similar pose, and under the same lighting effect. Apart from the obvious differences between the two girls these shots varied in the colours of the gowns and the ribbons in their hair: mid green for Julie, and pink for Helen. Pointing to the other two photographs his sweetheart explained, 'We decided you might also like to have a back view of each of us so you'll have a reminder of our entire bodies; they were difficult poses, but we thought we couldn't better these.'

The photos in question were also of full length with each girl bending over slightly and with their untied hair allowed to splay out over their backs, both had their legs closed, thereby accentuating the slenderness of their forms. Apart from their buttocks and a mostly side and rearward view of their right, and therefore, only visible breasts, the photos of the girls' backs were relatively innocuous; but it was the mirror's reflection which supplied the sensual interest for the viewer. For both girls were posing at three quarter angle, thus allowing their entire bodies from the engaging smiles on their lips to their breasts and intimate hair to become startlingly evident.

As he studied all four photographs repeatedly with ever increasing pleasure and gratitude Andrew began to realise that just for his sake the pair of young women he loved above all others had, with supreme intelligence and personal sacrifice, solved the problem of his grief brilliantly. Although the set of photographs had overwhelmed him in many ways his foremost emotion was an admixture of adoration and appreciation of them both, and therefore he cherished the folder for the remainder of his life and, as far as he was aware, their three pairs of eyes were to be the only ones to observe its contents.

In the evening Helen and he had an informal discussion with Charlie and Linda regarding all their futures; Andrew was unaware of the fact, but it was a mere show put on for his benefit, for in the short period between Helen's return to her home and his subsequent arrival, the Maynard's telephone had been busily sending out messages to everyone affected by the lover's relationship; so sure was his lover, especially, that their relationship was still sound. The final arrangement was that the sweethearts would sleep in Helen's room overnight, and then they would move in permanently with Jean and John on the morrow;

most of Helen's property being sent on later.

Before retiring for the night Andrew once again looked at both his lover's pictures and failed to note Julie's photograph didn't show the outline of her ribcage, or that her face appeared extremely healthy; and he therefore missed the second clue of that, and the previous, day with regard to the fact she'd expected her own death long before she began to look ill.

Andrew roused himself from his reverie, flexed his hands and fingers held behind him and then did the same with his feet and toes. Whilst he'd been day dreaming he'd subconsciously watched the shadows of the window frames moving from right to left across the floor as the sun rose higher; by the time they'd reached the wall, he mused, Helen and he should've been long gone. Glancing down at his admirable wife, and noting she'd shifted her weight a short time previously so causing him to fear she'd been about to wake, she now lay still with her back toward him. As he surveyed her sleeping form he felt pity for her, because both her mind and body had been designed for more than the one child she'd been allowed.

Together they'd passed with flying colours the difficult and comprehensive examination necessary before a couple were permitted to procreate; he grimaced behind his gag, the nearest thing to a smile he could manage, as he thought of the lack of advice and help from their acquaintances who were already parents, including Jean and John, Susan and Trevor, upon what types of question they might be asked.

Neither Helen or he blamed any of them, for it proved how mindful Whyte Islanders could be in realising the importance of couples, demonstrating their capability of conscientious parenthood before being allowed to have children. Just as farmers wouldn't be expected to raise healthy cattle or grain from substandard stock or seed, or metalworkers to manufacture perfectly dependable steelwork from second rate metal, the authorities realised they couldn't sustain an exceptional society if any amateur parent was permitted to take on the professional, educated task of raising children.

Normally they'd have stood a reasonable chance of increasing the size of their family to the maximum of two offspring, but the island's governing body was now actively engaged in lowering the population level due to the crisis in the global economy. Even Whyte Island's internationally renowned high quality products, famed for their durability and inexpensiveness and usually much sought after, were in decline because few people could now afford to purchase them.

Even that much industrialised and rapacious country on the opposite side of the planet was experiencing economic difficulties; for, having been primarily responsible for flooding much of the world with a large variety of products through automation and high speed production, she'd eventually destroyed most of her foreign competition and thereby forced out of work the very people who'd been able to buy her products. In doing so she'd managed to undermine the economies of those nations which, through geographical, mineral, technical and altruistic considerations in addition to sheer territorial size, would've been best able to defend her against the huge and powerful neighbours which had old scores to settle with her. Now that her former allies were practically bankrupt and, or, beset by civil unrest, she was ripe for invasion by one of her old enemies. Compared to Whyte Island she'd done nothing right, but both islands now expected the same fate: imminent incursion.

For conditions on the mainland had rapidly gone from bad to worse since Andrew had revoked his citizenship; it had long been evident, as the nation's financial resources had fluctuated wildly between disaster and recovery, that the economy was failing. But the current government, instead of taking the electorate into its confidence by explaining the basic reasons for the monetary crisis had, in its frantic quests for saving on expenditure, continued to cut back on public services and had even sold some publicly owned businesses and services to private interests. They had also permitted long established industrial companies to be bought by foreign concerns.

The net result of such short sighted transactions had been catastrophic to the health and wealth of the nation. The purchasers of the public service industries had been motivated far more by profit than by social awareness and altruism and so had either withdrawn their more unprofitable undertakings, or else had invariably increased their prices beyond the reach of the poorer members of the community so, effectively, abandoning them. The foreign purchasers, on the other hand, had, in many cases, closed down their mainland interests after a few years thereby ridding themselves and their home countries of annoying competition; whilst others had recognised, in their purchases, a useful ploy for obtaining new markets under the guise of the mainland's flag. Many of the assets accruing from these misguided sales in the form of taxes on profits, and rates et cetera, however, were wasted on such prestigious projects as advanced technological weaponry and overseas aid, both first rate responsibilities undertaken by what was now a third rate power.

When Andrew had expressed concern, in Harry Larke's presence, at his erstwhile homeland's stupidity in selling off its national institutions, the factory manager had commented wryly, 'It merely indicates the mainland governments' lack of faith in their nation's future. Those cabinets would never contemplate disposing of profitable or celebrated concerns, under normal circumstances, unless those companies, whatever, had an uncertain future. There must be many on both sides of our shared channel, however, who wonder why, if the government in power doesn't seem to think they aren't worth holding onto, foreigners should think differently. So I think you'll find they're aware that the public won't be able to afford to make use of them for much longer, a fact any financial expert worth their salt ought to be aware of.'

The consequence of the mainland government's lack of aid for, and sympathy toward, its less fortunate citizenry was an inevitable rise in the incidence of all kinds of crime and vice as the latter tried to sustain a reasonable standard of living for themselves and their dependants; thoroughfares of all types became unswept and ill maintained, rubbish went uncollected and buildings became increasingly derelict both in appearance and in fact. The relevant councils, due to the poverty and numbers of those residing within their areas, were unable to collect adequate rates to pay for the cleanliness and upkeep required to keep their own particular environment decent and presentable. In a similar manner the landlords of the multitude of properties they owned weren't receiving enough rent to adequately maintain their accommodation to anything like their minimal appropriate state. Without the councils receiving regular and ample rates, entire areas of housing rapidly became slums where the residents became uncontrollable or disillusioned, and vice and crime in all its many guises flourished.

Matters were made worse as, first the regional governments, and then the national government couldn't afford to police such lawless areas sufficiently or, whenever someone was arrested, to bring them to trial and, if convicted, to imprison them adequately. Public dismay at the rising crime rate throughout the land, rather than at its causes, however, ably inflamed by the rantings of certain elements of the media, notably from that opposed to the political stance of the current government, had inevitably lead to a demand for action, and the authorities had been only too willing to oblige. Its solution to the problem was the enforcement of severe penalties against certain wrongdoers which included, as being most economical, the implementation of capital punishment for a substantial number of crimes.

Finally, after a series of bloody and destructive riots caused by unemployment and interracial rivalries, the authorities, with the full approval of the media and those members of the public still receiving a reasonable income, organised labour camps for the reception of redundant people and their families. In order to operate their scheme efficiently they invested the police and military forces with special powers; and they also began to consider future sites for their camps, one of which was to be Whyte Island; this last was particularly attractive due to its hydro electric plants with their constant supply of virtually free fuel. To this end, at about the same time as the commencement of Helen and Andrew's zigzagging, a special team of parachutists began their final, top secret briefing regarding the seizure of the island's nuclear device.

The problems besetting the mainland, and most of the other world states, had little direct effect upon Whyte Island society; apart from the decline in trade and the introduction of the maximum of one child per family, life continued quite normally. However, a prolonged coal strike on the mainland, and diminishing global stocks had brought the authorities' attention to the perils of dependency upon foreign supplies, and so a new dam containing a hydro electric plant was constructed in yet another valley and, much to the regret of many islanders, including

Andrew, the railways were electrified on the three rail system, the steam locomotives being stored upon completion of the alteration. Plans were also drawn up to breed more haulage horses, and to manufacture horse drawn vehicles and appliances against the failure of oil supplies.

Although Whyte Island, from the beginning of its later conception, had been designed to be as environmentally friendly as possible, it was virtually unique compared to other nations and, unfortunately, it therefore had to share the same global warming problems which the rest of the world was experiencing. At the end of the previous September the sun had been so hot that it was uncomfortable to stay out of the shade for too long, when the temperature ought to have been reasonably mild and pleasant and, as Helen had remarked one night as she and Andrew lay cuddling in bed listening to that month's third strong gale force wind, 'Thank goodness Newtown's sheltered by downland and all that forest.'

Her husband kissed her, then whispered, 'I pity the mainlanders, especially those living in dilapidated housing or actually homeless, for their lack of trees and hedgerow cover.'

'So do I, but many of them have brought it upon themselves for being too greedy by borrowing money they're not really entitled to just so they can experience a higher standard of living they don't deserve and, of course, due to the banks and building societies extending them too much credit. But those fools in the tropics are still cutting down their jungles, so we haven't seen the worst in the weather yet. It's a great pity the super powers haven't realised who their true enemies are.'

As a particularly vicious gust of wind spattered the window with rain drops Andrew murmured, 'And all because some people like to play at being god.'

Helen stirred again, then lay still, thereby sending Andrew into yet another reverie, though on this occasion about their life together after she'd come to live with him at the Lucas' house.

Her relationship with Julie's parents proved to be idyllic; they must've been greatly impressed by her devotion to their daughter's lover in his time of need, and their knowledge that Julie had wanted Helen to take her place had obviously set the final seal on their approval: the fact she was also Charlie

Maynard's daughter would, of course, have been irrelevant. No doubt Jean and she had already begun to come to terms with each other during Andrew's brief illness because she'd settled down to the routine of the house in a way which seemed to suggest she'd been brought up there. Mrs Lucas and she were not only like mother and daughter in their affection for each other, but also in their ways: for they were both fanatically house proud.

In a typical mainland home John and Andrew might well have trembled in anticipation at the inevitable conflict between the likeminded women; but the widespread frankness engendered by an enlightened educational system tended to defuse such a situation before it had time to fester. For, instead of both women muttering under their breaths and thinking criticisms of the other's ways and habits, everything had been brought to the surface and subsequently discussed to the benefit of all. As soon as Helen had settled in, Jean and she had conferred upon a routine they could undertake between them, and they finally decided they'd take turns in carrying out the domestic chores, a system which worked very well, as Jean, especially, was thereby able to have much more spare time to herself.

In more ways than one had Helen stepped straight into her predecessor's shoes; as she'd indicated after her rape, Andrew's former lover had been similar in shape to her apart from her larger brassiere cup size, and so Mrs. Lucas had immediately encouraged her to adopt her daughter's wardrobe which she did, though more for her sweetheart's sake than her own. This gesture provided no greater proof of the special relationship existing between Helen, Andrew and the entire Lucas family, a bond the extent of which he wasn't fully aware of at the time. Just as in the days when Julie had been alive the family, which often included Natalie and Jeremy with whom the latter had now appeared to have formed a permanent relationship, frequently went out together on various trips.

Now she was no longer a full-time housewife to her father and sister, Helen was eligible for professional work and here, again, her tasks paralleled to some degree those of Julie's; one of her secondary jobs consisting of actually taking her place in husbanding the countryside, an occupation which her lover, having previously had experience of, later took up as her companion. Julie had been an artist of the female face and figure whereas Helen was an artist of the canvas, and so it was thus hardly surprising that the painting of pictures should've been chosen for her primary employment. At that time there was a profitable market for replicas of famous oil paintings in addition to personal originals, and Helen, after a little tutorship, proved herself as capable of undertaking the former as she already was with the latter. She was also employed in reproducing copies of genuine works of art for the island's mansions due to a policy of getting rid of authentic paintings; the authorities having decided that no object, no matter how beautiful, important, unique or priceless, was worth the risk of a visitation by art thieves and thereby possible injury or even death to innocent Whyte Islanders.

Before she'd become Andrew's lover, Helen had known few real friends due to her somewhat introverted nature and her devotion to her father's comfort and their home, but now she willingly adopted the many acquaintances which Julie had bequeathed to her sweetheart, and they in their turn naturally took to her. She discovered the delights of folk singing and happily joined in the badinage, often played the piano during the interval at the Magnolia Jazz Club, and was an avid, though usually silent, fan of Carol and Jim's debating circle. However, during the course of a discussion on the popular topic of population control which took place shortly after she and Andrew became lovers, Helen unexpectedly displayed great fervour regarding a remark about prolificacy in many countries. 'People,' she exclaimed, 'who, in the well meant spirit of charity, donate aid to starving populations are either mad or stupidly short-sighted.

'Mankind for all its apparent powers of reasoning, is still only an animal and, therefore, subject to the same law of the jungle: if it overproduces itself then its food supply will eventually disappear so resulting in death for the majority, usually the less powerful, until the source of its sustenance has had time to build up again; then it can flourish once more. This law applies to virtually any creature. To keep alive large numbers of people artificially isn't only expensive, as well as detrimental, for the donors in the long term, but also merely ensures the land in question doesn't have the chance to recover meaning that the relevant starving people experience a life of misery which, if they continue to reproduce, would ultimately mean that thousands, for example, would suffer instead of hundreds. If they cannot or won't, for some reason, control or better still reduce their birth rate then it's far better nature does it for them to give the land, together with its fauna and flora, time to recuperate. Anyway, would anyone present here like to raise their hand if they'd help conceive their own child knowing it'd probably die before reaching puberty?' No one did. 'Well, then they're hardly worth bothering about.'

'I personally blame the much increased use of medicine and the advances in sanitary education in such countries for the rising birthrate,' commented a woman whom Andrew knew to be a doctor and a good friend of Jill's, 'just as scurvy can be described as a disease caused by lack of vitamin "C", so might starvation be termed a disease brought about by lack of food; therefore, as a malady in its own right, starvation is a very slow, physically and mentally painful way of dying. By comparison many of the well known diseases are relatively quick and painless up to the point of death so, in theory, by treating and presumably eliminating those recognised afflictions you're merely replacing them with a crueller form of death. Having access to medical magazines and journals I can tell you all now that members of my profession abroad are spending donations on programmes of inoculation rather than on education into the benefits of contraception or into effective use of the land for the production of locally grown food, so, therefore, donated money is just being poured down the drain as it won't secure any lasting benefits.'

At this point Carol, obviously noticing that almost everyone present needed their glasses replenishing, called for a short interlude; which compelled her partner, Jim, to light heartedly remark that it seemed as though the women were about to take over the debating club. This observation was further endorsed by Helen's recommencing the second half. 'Few people outside Whyte Island,' she stated, 'apparently realise the harmful effects overpopulation can have on their lives even though they may be thousands of miles away from the source of the problem. As a naturalist I've seen records for many of our, mostly, summer migrant bird species, and a large percentage of these show a marked decrease in numbers over the past few years despite the fact that the availability of food, habitats and nesting sites on our island have increased during the same period.

'So this can be ascribed to lack of similar requirements in those lands where they spend their winter months, due, without doubt, to loss of vegetation causing resultant droughts by global warming via chronic world overpopulation; possibly there is also additional predation by the starving populace. And so we on the island aren't only missing out aesthetically by losing many interesting creatures, but we are also being deprived of valuable allies in the fight against insect pests.

'My lover, Andrew,' she gestured, quite unnecessarily, toward her companion, 'has informed me, by way of his late sweetheart, Julie……' All those present murmured sympathetically at the mention of a much loved and missed former member of their circle, '……..that the mainland has been ravaged in the interests of blind greed, selfishness and overpopulation. As you are doubtless aware hedges, woodland and forests have been destroyed, ponds and lakes filled in, streams buried, marshy areas drained and moorlands and what was deemed as wasteland have been cultivated, and there are fewer really wild areas of countryside left over there now. Even mountainous and coastal areas haven't been ignored as they're becoming covered in blatantly visible windfarms. Some areas have been left relatively unaffected by the awful march of progress but only because they're useful as money making tourist attractions and as national "lungs" for various forms of exercise. All this is due to absolutely pointless overpopulation from which the mainland isn't exempt, and has to be undertaken simply to cater for the expansionist policy which mindless fecundity engenders.'

Ignoring an amusing groan from Jim, a girl named Penny took up Helen's theme, 'It isn't only the landscape and nature that is effected; large amounts of money which could've been used to improve and build houses for a stable population as well as to supply better medical facilities, schools and rest homes for the elderly and the otherwise infirm, and a host of other things has been lost. In other words finance meant to immensely improve society generally, has been squandered upon people who like to copulate without caring about the consequences.'

One of the males shouted out, 'Make love, not babies.' A comment which was immediately greeted with cheers, though mainly from the men.

'Anyway, of course, unless a really effective permanent solution to the problem of overpopulation was instigated immediately then the money would have been spent on: well, we all know what happens to food after it's been eaten, don't we?'

'Ladies, ladies, ladies,' Jim wearily cried out, 'all this has been discussed many times before and we've all had it drummed into our heads at school. They can't stop overpopulation in former or extant industrialised nations because it would cause widespread unemployment and ruin; they need to keep building and expanding just so they can provide work for everyone to do. Apart from Helen's dad and his colleagues, no one else of note on the planet is capable of solving the problem and even Whyte Island relies on its exports for its survival. Every time general elections come around on the mainland each of the chief parties hint that eventually everyone will have a house, a job, a crime free society and everything else will be perfect. But it's just a very stale carrot to tempt the electorate to vote for them; there can never be enough houses or jobs while the birthrate increases, they won't be able to build homes fast enough for example; every politician knows they're promising that which can't be attained.

'If senior politicians really had hearts they'd begin to educate the public, through the media, on the ultimate stupidity of having large families just like they've brainwashed them into accepting far less rational issues. When there are far few jobs available to be filled it's crass, cruel lunacy to adopt a laissez faire attitude toward the present very high birthrate and totally uneconomical. Especially as they've had the example of Whyte Island to learn from all these years.'

'Why stop at the mainland, darling?' Carol said to her partner. 'Why can't the media, especially television which, as many religious leaders globally would testify, has massive power to indoctrinate, provide an example? Now, if the T.V. department, or division, of a large consortium were to invest in and, thereby, control a network in one of those countries having a starving population, they might easily coerce the people into accepting birth control by transmitting the relevant kinds of educational films. There would then be little reason why, after a time, the country in question shouldn't prosper, in which case the consortium would be in the best position to supply the requirements of the newly affluent society. It'd certainly bring some reality into the rather hackneyed term: "Developing country".'

'You make it sound easy, Carol,' Andrew observed, 'but would they prosper if their soil, say, had deteriorated so much that it was now barren, or if the top soil had been washed away by floods?'

'It can be done,' averred a girl called Wendy who worked for the island's forestry department, 'depending upon what you've been left with. We've reclaimed some very poor downland for experimental purposes by a method entailing the use of those six foot diameter concrete sewage pipes. We lower one or, occasionally, two of them vertically into a prepared hole until the top part is at ground level, then we fill them in with reasonable loam and finally plant a tree or shrub, in the centre. Providing the soil is kept reasonably moist and nourished then the plant should thrive. As its roots begin to grow outwards they come into contact with the concrete wall and so are naturally guided downward, and the deeper they go then the less chance there is of their drying out or failing to find nourishment, or of the entire plant being blown over.

'Now, although the trees or bushes can be arranged to form sheltering screens, woods, orchards or even forests, perhaps to stabilise the soil, the prime motive for growing them is to provide a continuous source of humus from fallen leaves. Of course, it may take many years before there is enough to make cultivation a viable proposition, but at least a start will have been made. In the interim, though, human and animal waste could be utilised, and if people and other creatures are going to die of starvation and disease and lie about unburied then they might as well be used to enrich the soil too.'

Jim snorted. 'In the final analysis, it all boils down to a steady population; you can plant forests, build roads and excavate massive lakes to help third world countries, but without the cooperation of the inhabitants it'll all come to nought. They'll just go on reproducing until the trees have been destroyed, the roads neglected and the water contaminated, and then they'll all start to die off again, just as many Whyte Islanders who've been to such places could verify.'

After a long pause, as if for thought, someone suggested they all move on to a nearby modern jazz club where a popular saxophonist was expected to appear; Helen and Andrew, not being over fond of the music decided to sit on the breakwater for a while to enjoy the moonlight reflecting on the sea, and then they wandered back to their room for an early night.

Just as Julie had brought out and fashioned her lover's real character by showing him love, attention and encouragement, so Andrew did his best to do the same for Helen; under his careful tuition, so he thought, she blossomed from a rather critical, withdrawn spinster into a fun loving girl with just a hint of shyness and reserve about her. He loved her a great deal and frequently praised her beauty as well as her other attributes, and this was just the medicine she'd subconsciously always yearned for; and she repaid his interest in her with a loyalty and devotion which could scarcely be surpassed.

During their marathon lovemaking at her fairy dell he'd deliberately allowed her to take the lead; he knew she was trying to prove to him she was a lover of worthy of Julie's memory, and that she also considered no part of either of their bodies, or methods of lovemaking as unclean. This continued to be a valid consideration on her part in subsequent sexual activities, and in many ways Helen was as energetic and imaginative as her predecessor had been, but with one major difference: they never engaged in actual sex games. He still suffered remorse for what he'd done to her at the end of his illness, and the thought of ever tying her up again made him feel sick; for that reason, therefore, he'd dreaded the approach of their first zigzagging together.

Andrew's partner, on the other hand, had found herself enjoying the experience half way through, due to the very reason Julie had once outlined to their lover, and only the thought that her assailant might despise her afterward had marred the feeling of pleasure she'd felt. So, secretly, Helen wouldn't have been averse to being trussed up and ravished as long as it was accomplished less brutally and more thoughtfully. But she greatly adored Andrew, and if it made him unhappy to play sex games then she wouldn't mention her covert desire, although she certainly made up for their loss by her ardent lovemaking in their room, or any other place which took their fancy.

He enjoyed comparing his latter two island sweethearts with each other, and not merely by their photographs. Although Helen had a sense of humour she was far too staid to play the pranks Julie was so fond of which, as he was compelled to admit to himself, were simply a manifestation of a spiteful side to his late love's nature. Both girls loved horse riding, but his present sweetheart thought fishing was cruel and she didn't like sailing because she wasn't happy about having a lot of water beneath her. She wasn't a sportswoman, but self-defence and weekly exercise were considered by most Whyte Islanders as being almost as important as eating, sleeping and lovemaking, and she therefore liked both activities. Ironically, neither Helen nor Andrew had any qualms about throwing each other about and, as a consequence, they had some quite fearsome bouts, some of which the latter lost. Julie could've told them their mock fights were, in part, a substitute for sex games.

Whereas his former sweetheart had known a lot about the island's flora and fauna Helen, as her lover already knew, was an expert, and the result was they often visited the nature reserve or went on long rambles, and he soon became somewhat adept at identifying various species. He looked forward to their outings in many ways but primarily because, inevitably, they would make love wherever and whenever it took their fancy as long as privacy was assured. When, on such occasions, she did and said things to him no ordinary girl in other countries would dream of, her sweetheart was aware she was thanking him for his presence, and he realised how lonely she must once have been during her solitary strolls throughout the island's varied and attractive scenery.

Just as Andrew had taken on some of Helen's pastimes, so she repaid the complement; Julie, as she'd promised, had bought her lover the model locomotive "Grove Spring" and they'd both enjoyed seeing it running on the Harbourtown layout; and before they knew it they'd both been smitten by the urge to model. Like the majority of the island's modellers they preferred to practise their hobby at home, and to this end and with the authorities' permission they converted the spare bedroom into a workshop, and here Julie and he spent many contented hours making and painting some of the enormous variety of model railway running stock which a good layout demands.

When Julie was replaced by Helen the newcomer took to the pastime with just as much enthusiasm; it didn't take her long to improve upon the possibilities of the hobby, however, because she appropriated a corner of the workshop for photographic purposes, and so added model railway shots to her list of accomplishments. During these modelling sessions, as on other occasions, it wasn't unusual for Venus and Cupid to unexpectedly drop in, just as they'd frequently done in Julie's time.

One day while out on a walk not long after they'd begun to live in Newtown they'd accidentally come across an isolated part of the island which was perfect for practising three of their favourite pursuits: namely nature study, watching steam trains, and sensual pleasure; all private activities which they could indulge in to their heart's content at the end of a long, beautiful and interesting amble down a little used ancient farm track. Their personal picnic spot was situated at the edge of a small copse above a chalk valley; the little patch of woodland was open at one end thereby permitting a view down a grassy slope to where a section of the railway line entered a tunnel.

Here, in the height of summer, the lovers would laze the hours away, either lying on the grass covered bank or else in the shade and shelter of an open glade making idle guesses as to what locomotive might be toiling so noisily up the incline toward the tunnel entrance, or when the next train would emerge to race along the railway cutting. Occasionally they'd scan the sky or the opposite bush covered bank with binoculars for signs of birdlife, or else they'd wander about the locality searching for unusual plants, butterflies or other insects. But most of all they enjoyed lying in each other's arms and talking of their love for one another; sometimes, though not often, they'd risk uniting in the open, but usually they'd cover themselves with a blanket in the glade, or give vent to their love and passion in the shelter of the wood concealed in the depths of a shrub. It was in this, their own secret place that Andrew received his greatest shock with regard to his days with Julie since the time Helen had presented him with the nude photographs.

On a beautiful hot summer's day when the only evident clouds were like fine white paint strokes high above he lay watching his wife feeding their seven week old baby. She was seated upon a blanket laid out on the grass slope in front of the copse, and she wore a special light dress having a zip fastening at the back and a row of buttons down the front as far as the waist, both of which were, at present, partly undone. She'd shrugged the nearest side of the dress to him from her shoulder and had then removed her beautiful breast from its brassiere cup for their little daughter's sustenance. The scene was also intended for Andrew's enjoyment, for she'd deliberately drawn back the hem of her dress as far as possible just to intimidate him. Knowing full well what the glimpse of part of her bosom in addition to nylon tops was meant to convey he was patiently waiting for Helen to lay their baby in her pram and then he would lay his wife in the long grass.

At last she removed their offspring from her nipple. 'Would you like something to drink?' she enquired shyly, the provocative expression on her face signifying what the words were really supposed to mean; noticing his hesitation she added, 'I'll open up a fresh source for you.' He watched, fascinated, as she placed Clare down by her side, pulled the remaining top half of her dress from her shoulder and lifted her right breast, from her already unhooked brassiere.

'Alright,' he exclaimed, smirking, 'I'm quite willing to give it a try, but only if you'll take a drop as well.' She smiled back encouragingly, and so he knelt next to her, placed one hand on her right shoulder, the other on her bent knee and dropped his head to her breast. After a few seconds he pressed his closed mouth against hers and simultaneously gently pressed her backward, she began to giggle but opened her mouth just before he opened his.

'Oh my goodness,' she laughed, choking and spluttering as she lay on her back, 'whatever do babies see in it?'

'I'm sure I don't know,' Andrew replied as he helped her to sit up, 'but I think we'll stick to doorstep deliveries if you don't mind.'

Whilst they were in the middle of their subsequent activity in the copse he paused and gazed down at his wife. 'I think that's a sign of real adoration in a man: willingness to drink his sweetheart's milk.'

Helen tightened her arms about his neck and pulled herself up against him; after kissing him fiercely she murmured, 'It is if it tastes anything like mine, darling.'

She hadn't had an easy time when she'd presented him with Clare; he'd known all along she was made and meant for child bearing, and so it had come as no surprise to either of them when the actual physical birth was accomplished with the minimum amount of pain and discomfort. It had been the post natal depression which had given her the most trouble; she had bouts of melancholy which neither Andrew or anyone else, could do anything to ease. Her weeping fits were many and could continue for hours at a time; she was always apologetic during and after them, but he thought he understood what was bothering her and so he comforted her to the best of his ability.

Now, as they sat together once more on the blanket with the woodland behind them and their daughter chuckling and gurgling between them exercising her arms and legs, Helen told her husband about one of the principle reasons for her depressive state. 'I think I was suffering from a guilt complex,' she confessed. 'It was relatively easy to bear before because I was keeping a promise I'd made to Julie; but all those hormones must've got to work on me.' She took one of his hands and pressed it between both of hers. 'When I gave you those photos I didn't know what effect they'd have on you; but I've got two things more of Julie's to give you now. They belong to you and I just can't keep the secrets from you anymore, it wouldn't be right, sweetheart.'

She released his hand and then opened her shoulder bag; without speaking she offered him a sealed envelope. Andrew immediately recognised Julie's handwriting and hastily tore it open; in his first real island lover's perfect script he read these words:- "Dearest Andy, It seems strange that I'll be addressing you from beyond the grave. I won't deny the prospect of death is frightening to me, but one thing beside birth is certain in life and that is death and so I take comfort in the knowledge others have had to face the dark chasm, just as you will too, my darling. I hope so much that I am on the other side waiting to welcome you.

Please forgive our relations and friends, especially Helen, for not telling you the truth about me; I made them swear silence as I thought you might not understand, and that the knowledge might prejudice your future happiness. Because you must go on without me, preferably with Helen as your life's companion as she is a wonderful person and my only choice for you; she loves you dearly and will try to make you happy. I hope she will have presented you with a baby by now because we arranged for an egg to be taken from my ovary and fertilised by you and then transplanted into Helen. We hope it's a girl and has red hair like me, as I know that's what you would've wanted."

"The truth is, as you may realise by now, sweetheart, that I took my own life. I was diagnosed as having an incurable disease which, though not necessarily fatal, is debilitating; tiredness, lack of energy and ill temper are a few of its symptoms. I have always been active and the thought of becoming a helpless vegetable is anathema to me; even worse is the thought of being a burden on you."

"You remember Jill and Mike? Well, he was my specialist doctor, you can piece together the story of my illness from him if you wish; but it won't profit you, Andy. Only know, my darling, I took this desperate measure so as to preserve our love eternally. If you ever think of me in the years to come you will remember your true Julie, not a crotchety, ugly wretch. Goodbye, darling, 'till we meet again. Your own Julie".

By the time he'd reached the last words Andrew was in the midst of a variety of emotions; the writer of the letter he'd just finished was an exponent of mixed feelings, but of straightforward, by contrast, sensual emotions: not the bewilderment of which thought he needed to deal with first. Should he mourn the loss of his greatest sweetheart with added fervour after the revelation of the way she died: for his continuing happiness, rejoice that her life still existed in the form of their baby, be immensely grateful to his wife for loving him enough to allow another mother's baby to grow inside her instead of her own or ought he to be overwhelmingly pleased with lover, wife and baby for giving him a reason to carry on, to survive? For now the knowledge that the infant lying beside him was an amalgam of the three of them gave him the urge to carry on living, to see what she looked like when she was a teenager and how each parent had contributed to her features, her inherited and acquired personality.

Resolution suddenly came to him, and he leapt to his feet and helped his wife to hers for he saw her as the lynchpin of his continuing existence: Julie was now physically gone, and their baby was too young to play any real part in their continuing relationship. So it was Helen who deserved all his gratitude and love now, so he hugged and kissed her for all her kindness and thoughtfulness toward him with an ardour which astonished and pleased her until they were both emotional to the point of tears. Over the following few weeks, with the aid of the letter and with his wife's and Mike's help, Andrew pieced together the grey areas of Julie's last months.

Helen stirred again, but this time she lifted her head from her husband's lap and then, with much difficulty, managed to kneel upright; somehow she turned about to face him and, for the first time Andrew saw both halves of the rag emerging from the sides of her mouth. Her eyes conveyed pity for him as she noticed the tears staining his cheeks and so she began to shuffle the few inches separating them; having arrived at his side she stretched forward and pressed her lips against his in a kiss of sympathy. Afterward she nestled her face in the angle between his neck and shoulder and remained, almost motionless, in that position until they were released.

It was impossible for Andrew to remain unmoved whenever he thought of Julie's story, for it would've been difficult to find a greater example of such sheer courage, selflessness and devotion in one person as there had been in his first love.

When Julie had first laid eyes upon him outside the Roman Villa she had, for some reason which even she couldn't quite understand, immediately taken a liking to him and, as a consequence, she was determined to have him at any cost. At that time she felt fit and healthy, and had no reason to believe she was otherwise and so, as far as she was concerned, there wasn't any impediment to her forming an attachment with the attractive stranger. He became even more desirable when, after Linda had indicated through her somewhat lax behaviour that he was freely available, she learnt he was a mainlander; she was also taken by the way he was willing to forego the pleasure of her company because he thought they'd have no future together and so didn't wish to hurt her.

She was, however, well aware that he wouldn't be on Whyte Island if he wasn't being considered for citizenship, and therefore she decided that here was an opportunity for her to help him attain that end and, at the same time, she'd be able to derive a great deal of pleasure out of him whilst doing so. She realised, quite correctly, she'd have the chance to put her interests in psychology, philosophy and sociology to the test and, if that wasn't enough, she'd also enjoy teaching him the art of lovemaking which, she rightly assumed, he'd be particularly naïve about. Having viewed and admired his splendid equipment in the villa's bath house, this latter objective became even more of a fascinating prospect in her mind's eye. There was, thus, more than a little mercenary in her regard for him, but she genuinely wished to help him and, after becoming more acquainted with him, her mixture of love and desire quickly transformed into adoration and devotion.

Most of this detail Andrew already knew about due to what Julie had already told him and also from what he knew of her character; however, what he was unaware of was that his lover, realising her self appointed role of tutor and companion would take some time to accomplish, had decided to have a comprehensive medical check up to ensure she'd be able to see the task through. It was a mere whim on her part as there was no reason why she shouldn't be perfectly fit, but such examinations were quite common to Whyte Islanders and, as Andrew knew from experience, they were very thorough.

The results of her medical were exactly as she'd outlined in her suicide letter, and when the information was presented to her it put her in an agonising quandary with regard to her prospective lover. That was why, he now realised, it had taken them so long to meet after the episode in the Roman Villa: for Julie couldn't decide whether she ought to forget about him and so avoid that which her eventual early death might bring him, or else to risk forming a relationship to help him adjust to island society and also, hopefully, that she might be able to find someone to take her place upon her death. Of course, as Andrew and everyone else who knew her now realised, she chose the latter course, but it was only after her illness became really obvious that she shared her secret with her relatives and friends, although she excluded her sweetheart from the knowledge because she didn't want him to endanger his future by possibly wishing to join her.

For Andrew the most poignant and saddening part about their partnership was that, throughout its length, Julie was only too aware her days were numbered. Yet, although she cried occasionally when reminded of their lack of a future together and because she thought she'd never give him a child until she'd thought up her little plan, she kept her problem to herself when she might so easily have shared the loneliness and the terror she must surely have felt, with him. She must have known, too, she'd only have needed to hint to him about what she was preparing to do for him to beg to share the ordeal with her. Subsequently he was to spend many an hour pondering over their relationship, wondering whether he could have been just a little more understanding or considerate, shuddering at the passionate, almost violent, sex games they'd played, and marvelling at her cold blooded courage. Without a doubt she'd have consistently wondered when her disease was finally going to affect her, examining her mind and body for the first signs, though never allowing the strain to interfere with their loving union, or with her innate sense of humour.

With the knowledge of Julie's being aware her days were numbered came the answers to several minor incidents which had puzzled Andrew at the time, such as the phone call he'd caught her making after he'd received Helen's note thanking him for the brooch, her discomfort at seeing Mike, and her secret tryst shortly afterward. The problem of finding a replacement for herself was quickly and easily solved for Julie during their physical discovery of each other on his first day at her flat. When Helen had brought his belongings over his lover had noted how striking she was, and after he'd confessed that Helen had told him she loved him, she was in no doubt that here was the girl who'd willingly take over from her. She was therefore pleased when Helen had informed him she was going to wait exactly a year for him, but considered the girl ought to be told that, with a little patience, Andrew would eventually be hers; and this is what almost happened after the incident of the brooch. When, though, she'd read Helen's note stating it was unfair for her to interfere in his and Julie's relationship she was filled with panic, and almost immediately she phoned Helen to arrange a meeting in Harbourtown for that very night.

'When she contacted me,' Helen had explained, 'I was a bit dubious about seeing her because I assumed she was going to tell me, quite unnecessarily for I know the rules, to stop upsetting you. But Julie begged me to come down and talk, so we met in one of the little parks where she pleaded with me to wait for you. She then explained she didn't have long to live, but that it was to be a secret between her, me and that doctor.'

'Mike?' her husband prompted.

She nodded. 'Yes, Mike. But she was really distraught: she certainly loved you, darling. After she'd got me to promise we often saw each other and we soon became great friends.'

He shook his head in bewilderment. 'I didn't realise how deceitful she could be, I was entirely unaware of what was going on.'

'She may have been deceiving you, darling, but it was a deception which had your welfare at heart. When she was on her countryside job I used to go out and work alongside her; then she'd tell me in great detail about everything you liked, what you disliked and all about your personality: getting me prepared for the day I'd step into her shoes.'

She affectionately placed her arm about him as he covered his face with his hands. 'When I came to my senses,' he observed bitterly, 'after Julie's death and saw you seated there beside me I thought of you as a vulture picking at our bones. That's why I suppose I raped you. But all the time you were her appointed successor!'

After a brief pause, Helen said, 'You know when we made love for the first time? Real love, I mean.' When he nodded he continued, 'I might have been the actress, but Julie wrote the script. That was why I laughed and cried when you pondered if she'd have approved, because she organised the whole thing; always remember one thing about Julie, sweetheart: there was absolutely no jealousy in her with regard to you and I.'

As soon as he'd recovered from his surprise about their first loving union her husband asked, 'Will you describe Julie's last hour, darling?'

Hesitating, she said, 'Are you sure you really want to know?'

'Yes, I'm sure; I won't rest until I know what happened.'

'After you'd gone off to work she phoned and asked me to go over. When I got to your room she was sitting up in bed, everything had been arranged and there was even an ambulance standing by the gate. As soon as she'd received the message you were on the station platform waiting for the Newtown train she decided it was time to go. I held one hand, Jean the other and her father put the pill in her mouth. It was very quick, Andy, and I can personally vouch she didn't feel a thing.' Helen paused, obviously trying to think of something which would help soften the blow. 'It was difficult keeping the truth from you, but Julie, and all of us, knew you'd be upset; but even so we didn't realise you'd react as badly as you did.' She hugged him. 'You don't know how overjoyed I was when you finally recovered, being raped was a small price for me to pay.'

Andrew didn't know how long Helen had been leaning against him when, at last and much to his relief, he heard a key turn in the lock, and the shed door swung open. It seemed something of an anticlimax when the girl who'd told him his wife was unwell entered; she immediately came over to them, crouched behind Helen and released her hands. 'Can you manage alright now?' she asked anxiously.

His wife tore the rag from her mouth and nodded. 'I was wondering, though, whether we could be left alone for half an hour or so?'

The girl, having now stood up, smiled down at them. 'Look,' she suggested, 'I'll nip over to the pub and bring you back something to drink, on the house. I'll leave the glasses just inside the door, lock you in and push the key under the door, and I'll tell everyone to keep away. Alright? Then you can have as long as you like.'

Helen, who was now completely free, nodded and told their liberator what drinks they'd prefer. 'But do you think you could disconnect the audio equipment before you leave?'

Laughing, the girl went across to one wall whilst Helen untied her husband. 'There you are,' she exclaimed holding up the connector ends for them to see. 'I wish my bladder was as strong as yours' appear to be,' she remarked as she headed for the door.

'What on earth are you thinking of?' Andrew demanded as soon as they were alone.

His wife stopped rubbing the corners of her mouth. 'That experience has made me feel sexy,' she told him casually. 'I want you to tie my hands in front of me, push a cider soaked rag into my mouth and hold it in place with some cloth, hang my wrists above me on a convenient nail, hook or beam, bind my ankles together and then,' she paused, 'remove my clothes piece by piece, very slowly; enter me and rotate your hips. That's what I've been thinking of! Afterward we'll get changed in the pub, have a meal, if you like darling; then pick up Clare.'

'Women!' he uttered in pretended despair; he took hold of one of her hands and began to massage the wrist while they awaited their drinks.

Helen began moaning upon her first climax but continued trying to communicate with him until he'd cleared her mouth. 'Have I ever told you what a disappointing lover you are, sweetheart?'

Astounded, her husband ceased fondling her breasts. 'You could've fooled me,' he replied, 'I thought you were going crazy by the way you groaned and squealed; I've a good mind to withdraw.'

'Please don't,' she pleaded, 'this is nice and neither of us has finished yet. But Julie told me all about those sexy games you used to play together, and you don't love me enough to play them with me!'

He recommenced caressing her. 'You know that isn't true, darling. After I ravished you I didn't want you to be reminded of it ever again.'

To his astonishment she replied, 'I rather enjoyed it. I've been lying awake most of the night thinking how nice it would be if only you were free and doing the sort of thing you're doing now. Julie highly recommended this way.'

'For a start,' he gently rebuked her, 'you were meant to be thinking about how lucky we were our ordeal wasn't the genuine thing; besides you appeared to be asleep most of the time.'

Helen craned her neck forward and just managed to kiss him. 'I really was contemplating our plight, love; and I was awake, but

I had no wish to disturb you so I tried to keep still. But I want to remind, though, my wonderful darling, I'm not made of porcelain and so over the next few weeks I'm going to demand you play sex games with me.' His only answer was to stuff the cider soaked rag back into her mouth, press his pelvis tightly against hers and recommence gyrating.

They left the hut with their arms about each other and made their way toward the public house, but they never reached it. Near the centre of Whyte Island a special phone rang and was answered by a young woman; after a moment she replaced the receiver, and conferred with her two companions. Three mothers embraced briefly and then began a series of complicated but rapid manipulations at an illuminated console.

Twenty five miles to the south west, behind patio windows of toughened glass, a little three years old girl with reddish gold hair sat at the breakfast table with her grandparents. When the glass imploded she was lacerated by a million cuts and then thrown through the already disintegrating opposite wall. A number of miles away her parents were transformed, momentarily, into charcoal statues before being blown, like most other living entities in the vicinity, into tiny particles of carbon which were then dispersed by the following blast.

The enormous detonation completely devastated the island, much of the adjacent mainland, and also began to generate a great tidal wave. On the mainland, some seventy five miles from the source of the explosion, the man responsible for communicating with the nation's ballistic nuclear missile submarines at sea, already upset by his wife's declaration of the previous night that she was leaving him for another man; wasn't as calm and attentive as he ought to have been and gave the order to retaliate against a supposed aggression by a non friendly superpower. And soon salvoes of intercontinental giants, aimed at prearranged targets, began to rise into the air.

At the end of the resultant holocaust the sun was obscured by a pall of dust several miles thick, and frost eventually began to form across the equator. The following ice age subsequently destroyed all life above sea level and most of that below it; and so, once again, after many millions of years, evolution began its imperceptibly slow toil toward life in all its variety upon earth. Thus, instead of the dawn of a new era of human love and understanding, there came the dawn of a new world.